THE WEDDING PARTY

What's not to love about a wedding?
Well, except for the I'll-never-wear-this-again
bridesmaid dress, going solo to the ceremony
when your date deserts you and those awkward
encounters with bridezilla...not to mention
the silly group dances. It's almost enough
to deliver a "no, thanks" on the RSVP!

But in this 2-in-1 collection, these women
know how to get the most out of every
wedding occasion. And once they meet that
really hot guy—just right for a sexy night of
fun—the party really begins.

So sit back and enjoy the celebrations as these
stories show that the wedding is the perfect
place to get something started!

JENNIFER RAE

was raised on a farm in country Australia by salt-of-the-earth parents. There were two career options for girls like her—become a teacher or a nurse. Rather disappointingly for her dear old dad, she became neither. All she'd ever wanted to do was write, but she didn't have the confidence to share her stories with the world. So instead she forged a career in marketing and PR—after all, marketing and PR professionals are the greatest storytellers of our time! But following an early midlife crisis several years ago, Jennifer decided to retrain and become a journalist. She rediscovered the joy of writing and became a freelance writer for some of Australia's leading lifestyle magazines. When she received a commission to interview a couple of romance writers for a feature article, Jennifer met two incredible Australian authors whose compelling stories and beautiful writing touched her cold, cynical heart. Finally the characters who had been milling around Jennifer's head since her long years on the farm made sense. Jennifer realized romance was the genre she had to write. So, with little more than a guidebook borrowed from the local library and a you-can-do-this attitude, Jennifer sat down to release her characters and write her first romance novel.

When she's not ferrying her three children to their various sports, musical endeavours and birthday parties, you can find Jennifer at the boxing gym, out to dinner with her friends or at home devouring books. Jennifer has lived in New Orleans, London and Sydney, but now calls country New South Wales home.

JENNIFER RAE

AND

LUCY KING

Confessions of a Bad Bridesmaid

and

The Best Man for the Job

HARLEQUIN® THE WEDDING PARTY

Recycling programs
for this product may
not exist in your area.

ISBN-13: 978-0-373-60635-1

CONFESSIONS OF A BAD BRIDESMAID AND
THE BEST MAN FOR THE JOB

Copyright © 2014 by Harlequin Books S.A.

The publisher acknowledges the copyright holders
of the individual works as follows:

CONFESSIONS OF A BAD BRIDESMAID
Copyright © 2014 by Jennifer Rae

THE BEST MAN FOR THE JOB
Copyright © 2014 by Lucy King

This edition published by arrangement with Harlequin Books S.A.

For questions and comments about the quality of this book, please contact us at CustomerService@Harlequin.com.

® and TM are trademarks of the publisher. Trademarks indicated with ® are registered in the United States Patent and Trademark Office, the Canadian Intellectual Property Office and in other countries.

Printed in U.S.A.

HARLEQUIN®
™ www.Harlequin.com

CONTENTS

CONFESSIONS OF A BAD BRIDESMAID

Jennifer Rae

For Mick, who never gave up.

CHAPTER ONE

IT WASN'T JUST cold. It was bones-aching, tits-freezing cold. The white furry coat Olivia had purchased before she'd left home looked fabulous, but it was doing nothing to keep out the December winds that whistled along the rough country road she was now trudging down.

'Five-hundred-dollar boots,' she muttered as her cheetah print luggage got stuck in yet another muddy hole in the road. 'F...' she began, but the honk of a car horn behind her stopped the expletive coming out from between her hot-pink lips.

The road had been deserted for the last hour. Not one car or person had come along as she'd waded through the slush and ice. But this car now stopped behind her and waited. She didn't look back but moved to the side of the narrow road so it could pass. But the car didn't move and a prickle of fear spread over her shoulders and into her stomach.

'Wonderful. Now I'm to be murdered on the side of the road. What a fabulous start to my holiday,' she muttered into the wind.

Hopefully the killer would change his mind. Still, searching for an escape route seemed a sensible idea, so she anxiously swivelled her eyes to the sides of the road. The car crept up behind her again. Blood rushed to her head and burned her temples. She didn't know what she was going to do. One thing she *did* know, though, was that when she found Edward Winchester she would kick him in his forgetful shins; then slap his inconsiderate face.

If he'd picked her up from the airport *four hours ago* she'd not be here, on a deserted road, in a foreign country, freezing and wondering how long it would take the authorities to find her dead, frozen corpse in the English countryside.

The car bleated another loud honk, which made her feet slip on the icy road. What did this bloke want? For her to turn around, plonk herself in his car and ask which way she should turn her head for the knife to slit best?

The tyres of the car crunched as it crawled up behind her and the heat of the lights warmed the backs of her thighs. Blood pumped furiously through her veins and her chest heaved violently. She stopped and turned slowly, desperately trying to channel her fear into anger. She screwed up her face as fiercely as possible and balled her fists, determined she wasn't going down without a fight.

The car stopped and a figure stepped out from the driver's seat. The tall man was draped in a grey coat and on his head sat a newsboy cap. Wrapped around his neck was a red plaid scarf, tied jauntily in a knot. He looked elegant and wealthy, and his car was an expensive sports-model-type. But *not all murderers drive pick-up trucks*, she reminded herself as her nails dug into her palms.

'Get in.' His voice was loud over the sound of the wind and it was gruff—angry, even.

He sounded like a man who was used to being obeyed. Well, not this time. Olivia turned swiftly and started to walk again, as fast as she was able with her tower of bags and her stupid high-heeled boots making her ankles groan.

She heard the car door slam and the engine rev before it sidled up next to her. She kept her eyes defiantly on the road ahead. The car was keeping up with her, with the driver's side window now next to her. It came down a crack. Her heart felt as if it was about to explode in her chest.

'Olivia Matthews. Get in the car.'

She turned at the use of her name and peered at the window. It was covered with ice. It came down another two inches.

'It's cold and we're late. Get in.' The voice was deep and very English and she didn't recognise it at all. Not that she knew anyone here besides Will and Fiona.

'Who are you?'

'The Easter Bunny. Who do you think I am? I'm Edward. Get in.'

Edward. Edward Winchester. Who was supposed to have picked her up from the airport. Who had made her take the tube, then a bus, and then walk for an hour along a muddy country road looking for a house she'd never seen before.

'About time.' She let go of her bag and lifted both her arms, letting them slap down on her thighs in exasperation and relief. The boot opened with a pop and she hurried round to the back of the car. Her tired arms heaved the suitcase and two overnight bags into the boot.

She moved round to the passenger side and put her

hand on the slick silver handle, but right at that moment—to her horror—her five-hundred-dollar boots came out from underneath her and she landed with a thud right on her aching butt.

A smart bang followed by squelching footsteps meant Olivia was no longer alone. Trying to get a grip on the icy road, she put her hands down and pushed, but the pointed heels kept slipping.

'Those are the most ridiculous shoes I've ever seen.'

A strong male hand reached under her upper arm and hauled her ungracefully and immediately to her feet. She felt unbalanced, but his arm held her steady and she leaned onto his tall, thick frame, grasping at the lapels of his grey overcoat to stay upright. His grip on her arm tightened and she felt his long fingers biting into her skin through her coat.

She tried to look up, but her precarious position meant all she could do was stare into his chest. 'I didn't dress for a hike in the country. I was expecting to be picked up from the airport.'

'This is Britain…in December, those boots are inappropriate and ridiculous no matter what you're doing.'

His hand was holding her steady but his other arm suddenly snaked around her waist and she found herself pushed hard up against his coat, her nose level with his neck. His breath warmed the skin on her forehead.

Looking up, she found herself staring into chocolaty dark eyes set perfectly each side of a long, straight nose and a set of high, angular cheekbones. He looked like Will, only…*better*. Heat flew to her cheeks and neck and to other more intimate places she refused to acknowledge. She would not be turned on by another inconsiderate bastard, no matter how big or how strong or how handsome…

His eyes gazed coolly at her from a height. She couldn't move. His arm pulled her in tighter and she tried to hide the surprise on her face when she felt something long and hard press against her belly. So she wasn't the only one turned on? A small smile tugged at her mouth and an uncontrollable urge to flirt bubbled inside her.

'Perhaps I need a lesson in English dressing?' She flashed a smile and looked up at him through lowered lashes.

But his angry gaze didn't move. A muscle in his clean-shaven jaw twitched.

'Perhaps what you need…' his deep voice had lowered an octave and was now grumbling against her chest '…is a lesson in etiquette. If you're going to change your flight you should let someone know.'

He let go of her waist and she slipped and slid, grabbing for the sturdiness of his lapels again. Looking up, she realised any seductiveness on her face had evaporated in the embarrassing awkwardness of the moment. A clump of long damp blonde hair was strewn across her eyes and her gloved fingers were slipping from his coat. She felt desperately needy, and her cheeks burned indignantly, so she let go of him and steeled her leg muscles to get a grip on the icy road and move towards the car door.

'I can manage from here…thank you.' Her tone was as icy as the road, and she managed to make her way to the door even though her legs splayed inelegantly with each measured step. Her stomach clenched as his gloved hands gently pushed her rear, guiding her into the seat.

He gave her one last push before his irritating head popped in next to her. 'Would you like me to do up your seatbelt for you as well?'

She threw him her most haughty stare—the one reserved for her sister's best friend and every slimeball who approached her in a bar.

He huffed out a chuckle, flashing white teeth and a set of deep dimples, before clicking the door shut and walking to the other side to regain his position in the driver's seat.

'We're late.'

Edward realised he was being unforgivably rude, but he was in no mood to be picking up Will's friends from the airport. Well, technically it was Fiona's friend. Fiona—who was nothing to him. Yet they thought it perfectly acceptable to interrupt his day to make the two-hour round trip to the airport and on to his parents' house. And then the girl wasn't there. His normally calm demeanour was in danger of cracking.

'If you had checked with Fiona you would have known about the new flight time.'

Her voice was cool and steady and somehow it irritated him even more. She could at least have the decency to sound shaken. Or guilty. How about guilty?

'I do apologise. You're right. I should have checked with Fiona. Would that have been before or after my two o'clock meeting with the Prime Minister?'

It had been the Minister for Trade, actually, but she was annoying him. He flicked her a glance. She seemed the sort not to give a toss about anyone else. Self-centred, vain, and with an over-inflated idea of her own attractiveness if her unsuccessful attempts at flirting were anything to go by.

Although, he grudgingly admitted she had a sort of innate sexiness he couldn't put his finger on. She was wearing too much make-up, and her long, dead straight blonde hair, obscene fur jacket and tight leather pants were a little too Chelsea for his taste, but something about the curvy figure he'd held against his chest made his trousers feel a little tighter. And when she'd fallen she'd looked up at him, hair strewn across her face, her sexy light-coloured eyes looking at him so trustingly. Was it any wonder his groin had reacted so violently?

An unconscious smile lifted the corner of his mouth. Those perfect pouty pink lips had formed a little 'o' as he'd pushed her pert ass into the car and he'd felt an urge to pull her head around and kiss her. Her lips were all glossy and full and…

Great work, Winchester. All it takes is a hot body and a set of shiny lips and your mind is out of control and veering into the gutter. Nothing but a caveman.

Thankfully she appeared to have enough brains to remain silent. For exactly three minutes.

'I would suggest before you saw the Prime Minister, in case he prattled on a bit. Then you would have known you had to get out earlier and could have hurried him up.'

'Hurried him up?'

'Yes. Hurried him up.'

'The Prime Minister?'

'Yes.'

'Of Great Britain?'

'Yes.' She turned those big eyes his way finally. 'He's only a man.'

Only a man. That simple phrase summed up her stupidity. And he didn't have the patience for stupid. He decided right then that, no matter how delectable her lips, she didn't deserve another moment of his conversation and shut his mouth tight.

It took another three whole minutes for her to speak again.

'Where are we going?'

'I should have thought that was obvious.'

'The bloke at the pub told me I was almost there.'

'My parents' house is twenty minutes away. You had a long way to go in those…boots.'

'But I was going to Fiona's—I need to get changed.'

'We're going to be late as it is. There's no time for you to get changed. What you're wearing is fine.'

Edward sneaked another look at her outfit. She would certainly stand out. His sister's tedious friends would have their avaricious tongues hanging out, making complete nuisances of themselves over her. But she was stubbornly persisting.

'I have been on a plane for twenty-four hours, a bus for an hour and I have trudged up a hill…in the snow. I want to get changed.'

'I'm afraid it's too late.'

'Fine. Stop the car.'

'What?'

'I said, stop the car. I'll get changed in the back seat.'

'You don't need to change; you can freshen up when we get there.'

'I don't want to *freshen up*—I want to change. Stop the car.'

Seeing he was getting absolutely nowhere, he stopped protesting. But he let his knuckles whiten on the steering wheel as she got out and shuffled to the rear of the car.

From the boot she pulled out all her bags and hauled them into his car, dragging them across his leather seats. He winced, but remained silent and started to drive again. He was determined not to be late. Or any later than he already was, so he suppressed a frustrated sigh.

'Where is my dress? I can't find it...' She seemed to be muttering to herself, so Edward didn't bother answering.

She zipped open one brightly coloured bag and began searching through seemingly endless articles of clothing. Edward concentrated on the road.

'This weekend is nothing but a damn nuisance,' he muttered.

Picking this girl up was a damn nuisance. But it had to be done. As attending this tedious event had to be done. His mother would need him and Will would need him and it would all fall apart if he wasn't there. Fixing everything. Making sure everything ran smoothly. He squared his shoulders and sat up straighter. If he wasn't there things would not go well, and he wasn't prepared to let that happen.

'Sounds like someone is not in the party mood.'

Party mood? No, he was *not* in the 'party mood'. And now that babysitting an over-tanned party girl had been added to his ever-increasing list of things to take care of his mood was becoming increasingly blacker.

'We are not here to "party" this weekend. It's a wedding.'

Her head snapped up and he glanced at her again. Those light-coloured eyes had gone wide. Were they blue or grey? He couldn't quite make them out.

'I'm not sure what kind of weddings you've been to, Little Mr Sunshine, but the weddings I attend are always a great place to party.'

A tendon in his neck throbbed. *You're here to make sure everyone is all right*, he reminded himself, gripping the steering wheel with even more force. *You just have to get through the weekend.* Although he was sure this woman and her 'party mood' were going to make it feel like months.

He glanced in the rear-vision mirror just as she held up something sparkling and purple and sure to be vulgar.

'What is *that*?' He couldn't keep the distaste from his mouth. Why did women feel the need to cover themselves in sparkles? They looked much better in nothing more complicated than a simple dress. Granted, that body of hers wouldn't look too bad in a tight dress, but sparkles were his pet peeve.

'Don't look,' she said.

This, of course, meant that now all he wanted to do was look. But he kept his eyes on the road. He could control himself even if she was… Good Lord, was that a *breast*?

CHAPTER TWO

NOT EVEN SNEAKING a peek, thought Olivia as she slipped her tight trousers off and slid her thermal singlet up over her head. With a tug she pulled the dress down over her head. It, too, was tight but with an extra-hard tug it slipped over her.

She dared a glance in the rear-vision mirror, wondering if she'd caught his dark eyes flicking her way. But he was facing the front. Prude. He probably turned the lights out during sex. Which in her experience was almost as bad as a sleazy lout with wandering hands.

She'd known them all. The funny ones—egotistical—the stupid ones—selfish—the pretty ones—unfaithful—and the shy ones—bad in bed. Unfortunately none had lasted longer than three weeks. The brutal truth was that Olivia was convinced she was undateable. But that was all ending this weekend. False eyelashes, a week's worth of tanning on Bondi and a bag full of sparkly short dresses meant this weekend she was going to make an impression.

Olivia pulled her make-up bag with her into the front seat and Edward made a disapproving harrumph. Like an old woman.

'Haven't you got enough of that on already?' he

enquired rudely. She noticed his fists were white on the steering wheel. Angry, impatient and disapproving. Usually she charmed people when she first met them. For the first five minutes. Then, of course, they quickly lost interest. But his disinterest had taken hold a lot more quickly than normal. She wasn't sure why, but that idea made her stomach knot up tight. How ridiculous. As if a man like him would ever be interested in someone like her anyway.

'It's these finishing touches that take a girl from drab to dazzling. You'll see.'

She felt his eyes on her and ignored them. He was probably thinking that no amount of make-up could do that, and he'd be right. The truth was she was the younger, less attractive sister and the least pretty of all her friends. She'd made peace with that fact years ago, but a layer of peroxide through her naturally mousy hair and plenty of make-up made her feel much better—and this weekend she wanted to feel good. But his disapproving glances were having the opposite effect.

'What's wrong? Do I have something in my teeth? Or is one of my nipples out?' She lifted her hands to her dress and shifted the bodice, making sure the girls were where they should be. She might not have the face to compete with her friends, but she was happy with her body. Hours at the gym and pounding the pavement meant she was solid muscle. Her body she could control.

Edward's throat went thick. She was using her hands to move her breasts and the mounds of them above the line of the dress rose and fell. It was very distracting. Didn't she realise he was trying to drive? She swathed more lipstick over her already wet lips and sucked them in, spreading the gloss over them.

Olivia Matthews was the sort of woman he took pains to avoid. Vacuous women whose only purpose in life was to supply a young, attractive female body for B-list actors and middle-aged European billionaires to fondle at parties. All high heels and lip gloss. Those women were not his type. *She* was definitely not his type. Although they were terribly exciting to look at. *She* was terribly exciting to look at. And why shouldn't he look? She was making such a show of it; it would be damned bad manners not to notice.

'Your nipples are fine, as far as I can see.'

That earned him a wry side-glance. Unexpectedly, the sight of her big eyes—which he could now determine were ice-blue—swivelling his way made his gut clench a little tighter, which irritated him. The weekend was going to be bad enough without this little vixen distracting him. He turned to the road, concentrating on the ice and the precarious turns he knew were coming up.

She went back to the mirror, adding more make-up and swiping at non-existent pieces of fluff on her chin.

'So, is this a party-party tonight, or just an awkward get-together with unattractive single cousins and judgemental aunts?'

Edward snorted. 'My family's reputation obviously precedes them.'

'Does that mean they'll all be as charming as you, then?' She snapped the lid on her lipstick and looked at him.

Edward raised his eyebrows at her sarcastic tone but kept his eyes on the road. The woman seemed to say whatever came into that air-filled head of hers without worrying about consequences. Didn't she know life was all about consequences?

'My family will all be there for Will and his fiancée. I apologise if we hadn't given much thought to your need for a wild weekend of sex, drugs and rock and roll.' He wondered if he'd offended her. He hoped so—perhaps now she would behave herself.

'What? No sex or drugs? This really will be a dull weekend.'

Her tone was crisp. Now she was really annoyed. Edward's mouth twitched. He didn't want it to. But her refusal to be intimidated amused him for some reason. Who *was* this girl?

A minute's frosty silence followed her angry outburst. Edward bit his tongue. Tonight he'd have to keep an eye on his unstable mother as well as shepherding his pernicious sister away from the bride-to-be. That was going to be hard enough. His sister had taken a dislike to Fiona—labelling her coarse and insipid. And Australian. Which was reason enough to bring back transportation, according to his sister.

Three more days. Seventy-two more hours. Then he'd be back in London. Solid, uncomplicated, manageable.

'Will there at least be wine?'

Her quiet question made him turn to face her. She seemed totally unable to be quiet.

'Yes, Olivia. There will be wine. Loads of wine, if my father has anything to do with it.'

'At least your father has his priorities straight,' she said as she turned to look out of the window.

His mouth twitched again. She was inappropriate. And probably stupid. But she was amusing.

Another minute passed and she shifted in her seat. His eyes were drawn to her golden legs. They stretched out long and muscular and her thighs glowed against the light of the dash. He looked away quickly.

'Anyway, I didn't realise this weekend was all about you. I would have thought it was more important your friend was happy,' he said.

He glanced at her as she turned to face him. Her cheeks were pink and her mouth was set in a thin, grim line. She hadn't liked that comment.

'Fiona told me you were nice, but then she never was a very good judge of character.'

Her blue eyes were like icicles. Edward tried to hold back a smirk. Her little words couldn't even get close to scratching him. He said worse things to himself when he caught his finger in a drawer.

'Well, you would know her better than me—you are her best friend after all.'

She huffed. Actually huffed. Like a six-year-old. He almost laughed as he turned into the sticky S-bend that meant he was close to his parents' house.

'If the rest of your family are like you I can see I'm in for a very long night.'

'Oh, my family are not like me at all. They're much more unpleasant.' He could feel her staring at the side of his face. 'And they're not big on children, so I suggest you unfold your arms and stop pouting like that.'

She unfolded her arms and huffed again. He thought he'd made her stop talking, but if nothing else, she was determined.

'You are awful.'

This time he really did smile. A nice wide grin that made his face muscles hurt. 'You're too kind.'

Olivia turned away. What an awful man! Fiona had said he was nice. She should have suspected something then. Fiona never said a bad word about anyone. *Nice* was code for *awful*, because that was the worst word Fiona could bring herself to say about anyone. And now she was in for an evening with a bunch of stuffy old people in the middle of the sleepy English countryside with Mr Nicely Awful.

She let out a breath. She'd been so looking forward to this trip. Fiona and Olivia had been best friends since they were twenty-one. They had bonded over a couple of horrible ex-boyfriends and been soul sisters ever since. They'd partied together, they'd cried together and when Fiona had announced she was leaving to move in with Will six months ago Olivia had felt as if someone had shot a cannonball right through her. Since then she'd been lost, directionless. She hadn't realised how much she'd relied on her best friend until she wasn't there any more.

'You must be looking forward to seeing your friend again.'

His deep voice broke into her thoughts. Why did he keep talking to her? It was blatantly clear he didn't like her. Was it his English politeness? Or did he like torturing her? She suspected it was a bit of both.

'Yes, I am.'

'Fiona told me you were quite close.'

She noticed his hands had returned to their normal colour. He had long fingers and solid, thick wrists. A sprinkling of black hair peeped out from the cuff of his crisp white shirt. Olivia turned away quickly. Why the hell was she thinking about his wrist hair?

'We were…:we *are*. We're more like sisters than friends.'

She had an actual sister. One she tried not to think about too often. Her sister had asked her to come out with her and her beautiful friends a few weeks ago, when Olivia had been feeling particularly lonely. But she'd refused. Because that would have been like knitting a jumper for a penguin. Just. Plain. Stupid.

'*Are* you looking forward to seeing her again?'

Still talking to her! Olivia looked out of the window. He had a deep voice and it seemed to seep through her skin. It was grumbly and a little bit sexy, and she didn't want to think about him like that.

'I was. I mean—I am.' She'd been looking forward to seeing Fiona again. And in equal parts dreading it, if she were honest. For some reason she felt a little awkward about seeing her best friend all loved up and happy and moving on—without her. But for this moron to imply she wasn't happy for her friend and only thought of herself was horrible. And wrong. Of *course* this weekend was about Fiona.

'I'm very happy for her. Really happy for her. Really very happy.' And she was. But she couldn't help but wonder if this weekend there might just be…perhaps… someone she could meet.

'Have you convinced yourself yet?'

Olivia didn't miss the slight chuckle in his voice. Her eyes slid back to the solid block of bloke next to her as he continued.

'Or are you still suffering from a bad case of Bride Envy?'

She looked away and took a deep breath to alleviate the annoying tapping in her chest. The tapping that seemed plugged into her tear ducts. She felt it every time she thought of her prospects. She'd been trying hard to come to terms with them. She knew the deal. She was neither pretty enough nor interesting enough to hold a man's attention for very long. But there had to be *someone*. Even Ellie—her chain-smoking, beanie-wearing landlady—had recently got engaged. She had to be more desirable than Ellie!

And besides, Olivia wasn't after a husband. A boyfriend would be nice. But all she really hoped for this weekend was a nice British boy to flirt with. Perhaps they could even hold hands. She shuddered silently at the idea of physical contact. It had been so long. Over a year. She wondered suddenly if it were possible for *down there* to stop working. Like her DVD-player had when she hadn't used it in six months. Encased in dust, the green light had refused to come on. She wondered if *her* green light would come on again. Ever…

'I'm sorry. Fiona didn't mention you had a Masters in Psychology. Because that must be the only reason you assume to know who I am and what I'm thinking.'

'One would only need a Certificate in Teeth-Brushing to know you have a myriad of issues about this wedding that we can't even begin to delve into during this short car-ride.'

Incensed, Olivia could barely speak—but she managed to blurt out, 'At least I haven't come down with a bad case of My-Life-Is-So-Miserable-I-Want-to-Ruin-It-For-Everyone-Else-itis.'

He laughed out loud then and she turned to the window. He was laughing at her. Making fun of her. Humiliation burned her blood.

He obviously didn't like her at all. Not even a little bit. When she had attempted to flirt with him the bore had shot her down. He hadn't even watched her when she'd got naked. No, this annoyingly handsome man had absolutely no interest in her. Which strangely sort of made her feel a little better.

She blinked and unfolded her arms. At least she wouldn't have to worry about making a fool of herself in front of him. That thought was comforting. She unlaced her legs from the confusing contortions they were now in and let out a breath.

CHAPTER THREE

'SO WHAT DO you think of Will and Fi getting married after only eight months?' she asked tentatively, waiting for his smart remark.

He looked at her for a second, suspicion obvious on his face. 'Are you trying to get me to say something awful so you can report it back to the bride-to-be?'

'No, I'm just asking your opinion on whether you think it's true love.'

'True love?' He made a sound that sounded a lot like a snort. 'What's that?'

'It's what Will is lucky enough to have found with Fi.'

'I wouldn't associate the word "lucky" with a man in love. "Dangerous" would be a better word.'

'You think falling in love is dangerous?'

'I think falling in love is a fallacy. And any man who *thinks* he's in love is definitely in danger.'

Olivia opened her mouth to argue. But she didn't. Dangerous. That was exactly what falling in love was like. Like surfing in a bikini. Sooner or later someone would see your boobs and you'd be left humiliated, embarrassed and wishing you hadn't come. Olivia curled an arm instinctively across her chest. No one was going to see *her* boobs. This weekend was about fun. Cute boys and champagne. There would be no falling in love and no exposed anything.

'What about you?' the deep voice in the car murmured. 'What do you think about their whirlwind romance?'

What did she think? The word *devastated* popped into her mind, but that wasn't right. She wasn't devastated. Her friend was happy. She was happy for her.

She turned to face him. His face in profile was striking. A strong forehead led down to a long, straight nose and his square jaw jutted roughly. He looked manly and rugged, even with that ridiculous knotted scarf around his neck. Olivia felt herself tingle all over, particularly in those regions where the green light had stopped flashing. *No. Not this man.*

'I think it's romantic,' she said, with a defiant tilt to her chin.

He turned to look at her for just a second and the loveliness of his dark eyes hit her in the chest.

'I knew it—what you lack in intelligence you obviously make up for in foolishness,' he said with a mocking smirk.

Olivia turned her eyes away from the irritating man next to her and squared her shoulders. This was one man. There would be more. And probably more handsome men too—although she wasn't too sure about that. He was pretty damn handsome. But she wasn't attracted to him and his swoon-worthy eyes. It had just been too long.

She decided she'd refuse to talk to him any longer as her eyes adjusted to the quickly falling darkness outside and a few minutes later the car slowed to a stop.

A set of black gates opened automatically in front of them. Large, black, intricately carved iron gates. Flash, she mused absently.

As he drove Olivia focussed on the sound of the gravel crunching underneath the tyres so she didn't have to think about the silent figure beside her. The atmosphere in the car had turned awkward and Olivia shifted in her seat. A trickle of unease about the weekend ran down her spine.

She looked out of the window. A long line of bare trees either side of the driveway and a heavy layer of fog restricted her view. Edward's silence continued, as did the strange feeling that this weekend might not go to plan. Olivia felt an urge to tell him to turn around, and she almost did, but then, as they turned the corner, Olivia's breath caught.

The driveway led to a large circular courtyard and in the middle was an enormous statue of a winged man spurting water from his arrow. Behind him, rising up from the ground like something out of a Nancy Mitford novel, was an enormous stone structure. Dozens of dark windows lined the high stone walls and at either end was a peaked turret. And flying from the peak of each one were flags.

Flags. Like when the Queen was in residence. Actual flags, with something that looked like a lion with wings on them. This wasn't a house—it was a castle! What was Will? A prince?

Olivia could feel her lips had shaped into an O but she couldn't stop it. Out of the window she saw they'd passed a pristine lawn that appeared striped, and staring back at her was a peacock, its plumage spread wide in fascinating colours of teal and emerald.

'Are you joking?' she whispered to herself as perfectly trimmed topiary trees slowly passed by the car.

'We never joke,' came the quiet answer.

With a final crunch of tyres the car pulled up at the front of the house and immediately her car door was pulled open. When Olivia looked out she was faced with a grim-faced tall man dressed in black tie and tails. Complete with a top hat. He reached out a gloved hand to help her out of the car and Olivia finally broke out into uncontrollable giggles.

'Are you *serious*?' she asked him.

Edward had silently exited the car and appeared before her at the doorway of the car.

'Deadly,' he said, dismissing the Jeeves character with a nod and reaching out his own hand.

Olivia gripped it. She felt herself fall back and was grateful for the strength of his fingers as he pulled her up and out of the car. She clung to the warmth of his big palm as she stood and finally faced the monolith of a castle Fiona would soon call home.

'Livvie!'

The next thing she felt was Fiona's slender arms around her waist, and she smelled the familiar flowery scent of her best friend as she hugged her and—for just a second—made her world seem a little more normal again.

Olivia let go of the big male hand that was still holding her to hug Fiona, who was now clinging to her, her face burrowing into her shoulder. Olivia tried to pull away but Fiona held her tight for another few seconds before releasing her. Tears floated in her best friend's eyes.

'Oh, Livvie, I'm so glad you're here.'

Fiona held her hands hard and Olivia's nervousness disappeared. She was so glad to see her friend, and from the look on Fiona's face she was more needed than she'd realised.

Squeezing Fiona's hand, she smiled. 'How are you, babe?'

Fiona's big brown eyes blinked and her smile faltered. 'I… I'm… It's…'

Olivia knew that look. Something was wrong. Very wrong. A strange excitement gripped her chest. Had something happened between Fiona and Will? No. That would be bad, and Fiona didn't deserve her to be thinking like that. She gripped her friend's hand and turned to Edward. He might as well be of some use if he was just going to stand there like a giant wombat.

'Can you bring my bags in, Eddie?' she asked him, before putting her arm around Fiona's shoulders and walking with her friend up the stone steps and through the stone archway that heralded their arrival into the castle.

Could he bring her bags in? What did she think he was? Her ladies' maid? But the man his sister had hired to greet the cars had moved on and he was left out at the front alone.

Edward looked up at the cold stone wall. He hadn't lived here in over twenty years but it still made him shiver. That last day was burned into his brain. That day was all he thought about when he thought of home. He'd been relieved when he'd returned to boarding school a month after it had happened—glad to get away. But today he had to be here. His mother needed him. She was taking it hard.

'Another one gone,' she'd told him on the phone the other day. His temple throbbed again.

With a heavy sigh he heaved the multitude of bags from his car. He grumbled under his breath as the first spots of rain started to fall. A particularly cold droplet hit the back of his neck and wormed its way down his back. He shivered and moved to shake the cold feeling off. The woman was only here for four days—why would she need so much luggage?

It took a few minutes, and his body had started to heat up, but he finally managed to hoist all the bags across and over himself before heaving them into the foyer of his boyhood home. He'd dropped them with a thud when his brother barrelled towards him.

'Ed, old son. We weren't sure if you'd make it. So sorry to pull you away from London, but some things are more important than work, aren't they?'

Edward grunted and slashed a smile across his face. He wasn't sure he agreed with his brother's sentiments but he wanted things to go smoothly. For his little brother, for his mother and for everyone else. That was why he was here.

His brother shook his hand vigorously before slinging his arm around the timid little creature he was marrying in two days.

'We're so glad you're here, Edward.'

Her little voice shook. Next to her was Olivia. Dressed in her eye-burning purple sparkles, showing an extreme amount of upper thigh and with eyes that flashed like flints of steel. Her fists were clenched and that glossy, pouty mouth was pursed. For some reason his body went tight and then hard. She had a particularly sexy way of crinkling her forehead when she was cross. And it irritated him that he'd noticed.

'Your bags,' he announced, dropping the multi-coloured luggage that remained wrapped around him to the floor.

She didn't look at them, just kept those blue eyes set on him.

'I'd like a word with you.' Her voice held a warning.

He raised an eyebrow. He hadn't been ordered around like that by anyone in years. Even the Prime Minister asked him politely if he'd mind ever so much if they had a quiet chat.

He almost smiled at her audacity. She turned and walked through the door on the right that led into the drawing room and he watched her go, the ridiculous furry coat barely covering her thighs. Her calf muscles tensed as she clacked in her high heels across the two-hundred-year-old stone floors.

He turned to Will, who just shrugged.

'We'd better get back to the party, mate. Don't be long. Bunny's here with the Blenheim Blowhards. I can't survive them on my own.'

Edward grimaced. The Blenheim Blowhards were the gang of terrifyingly stupid friends his sister Bunny seemed to drag with her wherever she went. He wasn't sure why. Bunny had brains—the fools she hung around with had nothing but mash between their ears. He avoided them whenever possible.

A nervous look came over Fiona's face before Will pulled her away and into the room on the other side of the hall where the party was being held.

Edward contemplated which way to go. He didn't like being ordered anywhere, and the brash woman in his father's drawing room didn't deserve his time. But she certainly sparked his interest. What did she want— and why would she want to talk to him privately?

Intrigued, he followed the mini-skirted Mistress of Intrigue through the door.

CHAPTER FOUR

OLIVIA THREW OFF her coat and tried to form a coherent sentence in her mind as she waited for Edward. She tried to stay calm, but calm was not something she did well. Particularly not when her best friend had just burst into tears.

'To what do I owe the pleasure of your exclusive company?'

Edward's silky voice announced his arrival as he strode into the room. Olivia burned. Who the hell did these people think they were? Edward placed a hand on the floral sofa in front of him and challenged her with his eyes.

'Believe me, it's no pleasure. You need to tell your family to back the hell off.'

'Excuse me?'

Edward raised an eyebrow. Just one. Olivia's stomach jumped. Angrily she ignored it.

'Your family are being mean to Fiona and you need to make them stop.'

An irritating smirk slashed across Edward's square face. 'They're being "mean" to her? What is she—in nursery school? Fiona will need to learn to fight if she's to survive in this family.'

Olivia felt her neck go hot. Being mean to someone for no reason was her pet hate. Actually, her absolute hate. She'd been the victim of mean girls for many years and it had almost broken her. It wasn't going to happen to her best friend. Not now. Not ever.

'I don't know who you lot think you are, but if you and your toffy pals continue to be mean to my friend I will pack our things and leave.'

There. She'd said it. To his snobby face. Be mean to her friend and face the consequences.

Edward blinked. There was a fire blazing at the end of the room and fire in the eyes of the woman in front of him. He'd shed his coat and scarf but he felt uncomfortably warm.

'I beg your pardon?'

Olivia paced slowly towards him. Her long, tanned, muscular legs were moving slowly and seductively, and he had to push down the spray of moisture that had just landed in his mouth and cling to the chaise longue in front of him. Her eyes were intent on him and her chin was down. She swayed and sashayed deliberately, without smiling, until she was right in front of him—her head reaching just underneath his chin.

'I said we will leave.'

But Edward didn't hear her. All he could concentrate on was her heavy eyelashes and those golden breasts that rose and fell so heavily. He hadn't seen the full effect of that lurid purple dress before. Her tanned skin glowed against the bright colour in the soft light. She brought her hands up to her hips and he wanted to shift—to move and make himself a little more comfortable—but he didn't. He just stared down at her, his hands lightly clasped behind his back.

'You are not obliged to stay. If my family and I are so offensive to you I can call you a taxi. Or perhaps you'd prefer to walk.'

He let his gaze slide across her face and down her neck to take in the jut of her collarbones and that lovely chest of hers. Then he moved his eyes further south, roaming past the curve of her hip, her flat stomach, and down to those long, shapely legs. Strong legs that could wrap around a man's neck. His eyes lingered on her painted toenails, peeping out from that pair of very high-heeled shoes, and then he drew his eyes back up to meet hers again.

The woman had a body on her. And a sharp tongue. He wasn't used to that. The women he knew were usually softer, gentler. But there was nothing gentle about Olivia Matthews. She was hard. Fast. And made of ice. He was immediately intrigued.

'Livvie, are you coming?' The lilting voice of Fiona called from the doorway.

The *femme fatale* in front of him dropped her focus and turned to her friend.

'Come on, Livvie. Will is dying to introduce you to everyone.' Fiona sounded nervous.

Olivia—or *Livvie* as her silly friend insisted on calling her—looked back at him, her eyes hard. He smiled again, which seemed to irritate her more as she stepped closer. So close he could smell her. Cinnamon and something sweet. Peaches…

'I haven't finished with you.'

'I shall be awaiting your return with shivering anticipation.'

She huffed again. A sound he found equal parts irritating and charming. Then she turned and left, her little friend pulling on her arm and whispering in her ear.

Edward let a laugh escape. If nothing else, she was fun. Even if she did make his shoulders pull a little tighter. He strode to the fireplace and let it warm him up. The woman was trying, but at least for once he was feeling something. His usual diet of blank nothingness was becoming a little tiresome. Perhaps this weekend wouldn't be as bad as he'd initially thought. Perhaps it would allow him to feel a little before he headed back to the real world. Grey and dull and solid.

He held that thought up like a beacon, secretly hoping that the grey and dull didn't take too long to return.

'Well, this must be the best friend.'

Olivia had been whisked into a very warm room filled with bodies. A slew of faces and names had passed by her and she remembered none of them. Her blood was still burning from her encounter with the cold man in the other room. Those dark eyes of his had turned hard when she'd threatened him. She suspected he wasn't used to being stood up to.

Olivia turned to the female voice talking to her and smiled.

'That's me.' She held out her hand for the young woman in front of her to shake. 'You must be Phoebe.'

Fiona had pointed out Will's sister when they'd walked in. She wasn't very tall, but Phoebe Winchester had a presence. Her hair was streaked with blonde, as if she'd just spent two weeks in the Spanish sunshine, and it was casually tied into a knot on top of her head. But somehow it seemed impossibly elegant at the same time. She had dark eyes, like Edward, and a pretty smile revealing a set of white teeth. She looked like a girl you'd want to be friends with.

'I've heard so much about you—Olivia, isn't it?' Olivia smiled back but noticed the quick glance Phoebe made at her legs. Phoebe was dressed in a pair of white pants and a gorgeous silk embroidered top. Olivia felt underdressed and a little exposed beside her.

'You can call her Bunny, Liv. All her friends call her Bunny.' Will put his arm around Olivia and squeezed. Phoebe's—or Bunny's—smile faltered.

'Yes. Do,' she said, her eyes flickering over Olivia's hair.

Olivia was starting to feel uncomfortable. Bunny made no more attempts at conversation, just said something to Will that Olivia didn't catch and laughed loudly. Fiona had said Will's family had been making her feel uncomfortable but she hadn't mentioned Will's sister. She'd said Will's sister was the only one being nice.

'You must be excited about the wedding,' Olivia attempted.

Bunny's dark eyes swivelled again to Olivia. 'Of course. We all thought Will here was a confirmed batch. More girlfriends than a sheikh.'

Olivia's shoulders stiffened. But then Bunny smiled and let out an easy laugh.

'But he's found a great girl in Fiona. I couldn't be happier for him.'

Fiona was smiling at Bunny as if she were a block of chocolate come to life. Olivia hesitated. Bunny seemed fun, and she was very pretty and she laughed a lot, but the way she held on to Will possessively and the way she turned her back a little to leave Olivia and Fiona out of the conversation reminded her a little too much of her sister's friends.

'That's a fabulous dress, Olivia.' Her eyes met Olivia's. 'I didn't know feathers were back in.'

A cold clamp stilled in Olivia's chest. It wasn't what Bunny had said. It was the way she'd said it.

'I thought it was a bit of fun.'

Bunny smiled and then let out a muffled giggle. 'Oh, it's certainly that.' She gripped Will's arm and smiled manically at Olivia. 'Perhaps we could find you a comfy tree to roost in tonight?' The laugh that was on the tip of her lips came out as a snort.

'Bunny, be nice.'

Will's serious reprimand only made Olivia feel worse. She looked around. Everyone was dressed in pants. Or long skirts. No one else was wearing a feather and sparkle-encrusted mini-dress. No one except her. She felt as she had when she was thirteen and her sister's friends had dressed her up for the school disco. They'd teased her hair high and streaked blue eye shadow all over her eyelids. They'd assured her it was the latest 'look'. But it hadn't been and she'd been the laughing-stock of the school for the next six months.

A waiter walked past, his tray laden with glasses of champagne. Olivia swiped one and drank it down in one gulp. Defending her best friend from mean girls she could do. But when it came to defending herself...? That was proving to be much harder.

Bunny was still looking at her, waiting for her to respond. A hot rash crept up her chest. It was as if her sister's friends were in the room—pointing and laughing and making her feel inadequate.

So Olivia did what she always did when she felt inadequate. She made excuses. 'I had to get changed in the car. It was the first dress I could find.'

'Perhaps if you'd been on time you would have been able to find something more…appropriate.' Bunny laughed again and Will shushed her, but she swatted at his arm.

'It's all right, Will. Olivia's a big girl—she can take it.' Bunny sipped her own champagne before winking at Fiona and calling out to someone over the din and disappearing in the crowd.

'Liv, forget Bunny—' Will placed his hand on Olivia's arm but she shook it off.

'It's OK, Will. I'm fine. I know she was only joking.'

But the truth was Olivia felt as if she'd been slapped. First across one cheek—that pompous Edward Winchester had obviously tattled to his sister that she hadn't been at the airport when he'd gone to pick her up—and then across the other when the mean girl had called her dress inappropriate.

She'd been worrying about what to wear to this weekend party for weeks. She'd wanted to look nice, make an impression. Stand out. She'd wanted to look her best but she'd obviously got it wrong and just looked stupid.

Through the crowd she spotted the tall frame of Edward, who happened to turn her way right at that moment. A half-smile touched his lips and he nodded. Shame, embarrassment and humiliation washed over her. He was laughing at her. With his sister and probably everyone else. This was not going to be the weekend she'd envisioned. This was going to be the worst weekend of her life.

A perfectly dressed waiter walked by and she plucked another tall glass of champagne from his tray. There was only one way to survive this weekend. And that was to drink copious amounts of ridiculously expensive French champagne.

CHAPTER FIVE

OLIVIA SMILED AGAIN at one of the men in front of her. She had no idea what he was saying—or what his name was. There were two of them, and even though they were speaking English she couldn't quite follow the conversation.

'London is *so* not the thing at the mo. I mean, its totes obvs that Louise fancies me, but I just want to shop around, you know?'

'Totes, man. Louise is just too blates anyway. You need to chuck her.'

'Mmm. I'm thinking I might have to. What do you think, Livs?'

The blond man turned to her. For a second Olivia was dazzled by his bright white teeth.

'I…'

'That's a hot dress you're wearing, Livs.'

The dark-haired one had spoken. He was just about the prettiest man Olivia had ever seen. She'd spent a good five minutes just marvelling at the perfection of his skin.

'Thanks…'

'It's not endangered, is it?' The blond laughed at his own joke, then slung his arm around Olivia. 'Only jokes, sweetheart. You're the hottest girl in the room tonight. Here.' He plucked a drink from the tray of a passing waiter. 'Drink up. You're falling behind.'

Olivia took a long sip. She glanced sideways at the blond, whose name she still wasn't sure of. Chester? Hester? His arm stayed where it was. Possessively pulling her to him. Olivia shuffled a little to the left.

There was no doubt Chester/Hester was a handsome man. And he laughed a lot. He was friendly, and he included her in the conversation, but there was something about him. Something alarmingly predatory that made her body chill a little when he got too close. But she was finally being included. No one else had talked to her. The party was swirling all around her. These two had found her some champagne and asked her about Australia.

Fiona and Will were off talking to another round-vowelled relative and Olivia had avoided too many uncomfortable interactions. Except for when she'd met Will's mother, a woman who stood silently most of the time. Her large brown eyes, surrounded by wrinkles and bags, and the defeated stance of her shoulders made her difficult to talk to. She'd answered Olivia pleasantly enough, but her answers had all been one word only.

Will's father, on the other hand, was loud—and for some reason unreasonably angry. Everything Olivia said had landed her in trouble.

'You have a lovely home, Mr Winchester.'

'Are you saying I couldn't have bought this myself? Just because I inherited it doesn't mean I'm a lazy loafer.'

'Will is a charming young man. Fiona is very lucky to have him.'

'Why wouldn't he be charming? We brought him up right—he has no reason to be anything but charming. What are you implying?'

After a few more minutes of that Olivia had escaped. She'd fallen to the back of the room and sipped more champagne alone until these two well-dressed men had approached her. She'd known enough men to know what they needed. Laugh at their jokes and bat your eyelashes. No matter what language you spoke, that always worked.

She was busy laughing at something else she couldn't understand when a chill came over the group. The pretty men in front of her stopped laughing and they looked over her head. She knew what it was before she even turned. She could feel him. Looming. Watching. Judging.

'Hello, Eddie.'

'It's Edward. Hello, Olivia. Casper. Hugo.'

The air had changed. A defiant prickle spread across the group. As if Edward was the headmaster and had caught them smoking behind the bike sheds.

'Come to spoil the party, have you, Eddie? Are we being too loud?' Olivia asked, feeling a little bold from the four glasses of champagne she'd drunk.

Edward's eyes narrowed and he brought his hands up to clasp them in front of him. 'Not at all. I was coming to see if you were all right.' His eyes slipped over the two men by her side. 'I wasn't aware you two were on the invitation list this weekend.'

Chester/Hester/Casper tightened his grip around Olivia's shoulder, where his arm still lingered. She almost lost her balance.

'Wouldn't miss it. Will Winchester getting hitched? It's the talk of London.'

Edward's eyes turned glacial. 'I would put money on the fact that it's not.'

'It totes *is*, Edward,' pretty Hugo piped up. 'Party of the decade, apparently.'

'Are you all right, Olivia?'

Edward's eyes swivelled to Olivia before glancing at the large arm that was hanging over her shoulder, uncomfortably close to her right breast. Olivia didn't dare move in case the hand brushed her nipple. She had been having fun with these two, but something deep inside her knew she didn't want either of them to touch her nipple. But Edward had that look on his face. That haughty look that reminded her of Bunny. So she grabbed the hanging hand and held on to it.

'These handsome boys are making me feel right at home.'

The champagne and the jet lag had taken hold. The bubbles danced and her words came out slightly slurred. She lost her footing a little and leaned into Casper, expecting his frame to hold her, but she must have surprised him because he stumbled and so did Olivia. Great—now Edward would think she was drunk. And she wasn't. Yet.

'Perhaps you could do with some air?'

'She doesn't need air. She's perfectly all right here.' Casper's voice was an arrogant sneer. 'Haven't you got a cause to campaign for? Or some middle class nobodies to wrangle votes from, Winchester?'

She heard him snigger and wanted to throw him off. His comments irritated her and his palm had become sweaty. She loosened her hold but his fingers gripped her harder.

'Why don't you run along and get us another drink, Winchester? There's a good lad.'

More laughs.

Olivia didn't know Edward very well, but even with her limited knowledge she knew that was not the right thing to say to him. She watched his face transform. His eyes met those of the buffoon still clinging to her. His jaw twitched and he pushed his shoulders back.

'You two are here because Bunny insisted. But if you cause any trouble this weekend I'll have both of you dipped in honey and stuffed in a beehive before dragging you back to London behind my father's John Deere. Do you understand?'

Chester/Hester/Casper went stiff before he withdrew his hand.

'Someone's got their period…' Casper's voice didn't sound as confident as before.

Edward took a menacing step forward, a vein now throbbing in his neck. 'Get out of here. And I don't want to see your ugly mugs for the rest of the weekend.'

Casper and Hugo threw Edward a dark look before turning and moving away.

'What did you do that for?' Olivia turned to Edward. His face had returned to the impassive mask he usually wore.

'Seems they weren't that interested in you after all. Didn't put up much of a fight, did they?'

Olivia felt the bubbles fizz in her brain again. No, they hadn't. One look at Edward's angry face and they'd fled. But that was what men normally did, whether there was an Edward there or not. She turned to watch the crowd with a deep sigh. She had a habit of intriguing people for all of five minutes. Then—somehow—they always ran away. Even Fiona—her best friend in the whole world—had abandoned her when someone better came along.

She looked up at Edward but he was watching the crowd, his hands clasped behind his back. Looking like the pious goody-two-shoes he was.

'Couldn't wait to dob on me to your sister, could you?'

'I beg your pardon?'

His dark eyes swivelled her way and she met them.

'She had a go at me for being late. Then she insulted my dress.'

He turned to survey the crowd. 'Bunny has a habit of saying what pops into her head. You should try and ignore her.'

'This family seems awfully good at that. Ignoring people. Before you came and broke up the party those two were the only ones being friendly to me.'

'Those two were being *friendly* for one reason only.' His voice lowered an octave and became hard.

'I'm not stupid, Edward. I know exactly what type of men those two are. I've been rejected by enough men to know what they want. Or what they don't want. But sometimes it's better to have someone rather than no one.'

'You'd rather be with those thickheads, who are plying you with alcohol in the hope you'll fall over and flash your knickers at them, than be alone? You mustn't think much of yourself.'

'I'd rather laugh and talk to "those thickheads" than

stand here being insulted by the biggest thickhead of all.'

'Yet you remain.'

Olivia turned to the room full of people, not seeing any of them. Edward was annoying and frustrating and rude. But he didn't want to get in her pants. So the only reason he was standing there talking to her was because he wanted to stand there and talk to her. Somehow that put her at ease. It felt strangely comfortable, being with someone she knew she had no chance with. She didn't have to perform; she could just be... herself. The idea was freeing.

She breathed in deeply and let it out loudly.

'I know what people think of me, Edward.' She glanced at him, wondering what *he* thought of her for a second.

Edward just stood silently next to her. Solid and strong. Not touching her, not wanting anything from her.

'I'm looking for a man.' She felt Edward stiffen beside her but still he said nothing. 'Don't worry, you're not my type. Too judgy, too cold, too...'

She looked up at him and he turned to face her. She took in his wide jaw and his very dark eyes. Like pools of dark chocolate. Deep and warm and luxuriously soft. A girl could get lost in those eyes and never find her way out. His jaw twitched as he looked down at her. His face looked as if it had been carved from stone, and he was so tall and broad and...

'Too handsome.'

He coughed and looked away.

'I prefer someone less...I don't know...' She tried to find the right word. 'Intimidating.'

'A weak man who'll put up with your nonsense and bend over when you tell him to?'

'No. A sweet, sensitive man who'll love me unconditionally. A kind, gentle soul who needs me.'

'A pushover.'

Olivia gave him the hardest look she could. 'You are a cynical man, Edward Winchester. And you don't have a romantic bone in that great big—' *surprisingly lean and muscular* '—body of yours.'

A waiter walked past and she reached out to grab another glass of champagne, downing it in one long sip. All the time, Edward watched her.

'Life is not a romance novel, Olivia. It's about work and responsibility and doing what you're supposed to.'

Olivia sighed again. She knew that. She *knew* it. But she wished life *was* like a romance novel. She wished there was someone—anyone—who would be willing to love her despite her faults. But she knew that was impossible.

They stood silently, largely ignored by the milling crowd.

'I know,' she said suddenly. 'Why don't you help me?' Another waiter wandered past and Olivia grabbed another glass. 'You seem the type to think things through. Weigh up the alternatives. Make sensible decisions. Maybe you can figure out why everyone always leaves me.'

CHAPTER SIX

EDWARD LOOKED DOWN at the big blue eyes that were blinking up at him. They were smothered in black eye shadow. She looked like a raccoon. Lost, tipsy and desperate. Three attributes that should make him want to run a mile. Earlier she'd been hard and challenging. Now she seemed needy. It was an intoxicating combination and it brought out something primitive in him. Some protective gene he was sure was purely practical and had nothing to do with the fact that he found her big blue eyes increasingly irresistible.

He had been drawn to her all night, his body on alert when she moved, when she laughed, and when her eyes turned to scan the room. And to be honest he wasn't sure why. She was abrasive and unpredictable and silly, but there was a sweetness to her that, combined with her captivating sexiness, made her hard to ignore.

And now she wanted him to be honest. To find her flaws and tell them to her. Dangerous. He knew from experience that people didn't really want to know. People liked being in their little cocoons.

'Perhaps we should discuss this outside.' She was swaying on her feet and his uncle-with-the-wandering-hands seemed to be looking their way and licking his lips. The thought of that dirty old man's hands on her was making him sick.

This time she didn't fight him. She let him lead her outside and he whisked the champagne glass out of her hands on the way out—swiftly relieving a passing waiter of a glass of water at the same time.

On the terrace, it was cold. The blackness amplified by the new moon that hung grey and high in the sky. Edward closed the doors behind them to block out the noise of voices. When he turned Olivia was leaning over the balcony, looking up to the sky. Her short dress had risen up so high he could see the curve of her buttocks. He quickly averted his eyes and shrugged off his jacket. She must be freezing.

'The saucepan is upside down.'

Not for the first time Edward found himself intrigued by this woman. What was she talking about *now*? He moved closer and gently put his jacket around her shoulders, placing the glass of water on the edge of the brick terrace. He moved slowly and silently. He didn't want to spook her.

Those two great pillocks who'd been plying her with booze had been all over her. When he'd seen them with Olivia he'd known what they were doing. And he'd also known Olivia was in no state to be left alone with them.

Olivia shifted and looked at him as he placed the jacket around her shoulders, but she didn't throw it off.

'Why is the saucepan upside down?' With her strange words she pointed to the sky.

'The saucepan?'

'There. See the three stars in a row and the handle? It's upside down.'

Edward tilted his head. It did look like a saucepan. But it wasn't. It was the constellation Orion.

'That's Orion, the great warrior. The three stars make up his belt.'

'The great warrior,' she murmured. 'Like you.'

Her words were a little slurred and her limbs were loose. Jet lag and champagne were a toxic combination. Prone to make you do and say things you shouldn't. Which was why he always stopped at one drink.

'I'm no warrior.'

'Yes, you are. You saved me from those buffoons.'

'I thought you were having fun.' He moved closer. She looked cold. He wanted to warm her up.

Olivia turned to him as she laughed and he held his breath. She'd smiled before, but not like this. He found himself irresistibly smiling back at her. She moved a little closer to him but turned back to the sky. He watched her. Her long eyelashes blinked and a dimple sank into her cheek. She shifted so her chin was resting on her shoulder and turned to look at him. That smile again. He had to move. He'd hardened in an instant.

'I was. I like to have fun.'

She blinked at him and he moved even closer, letting his shoulder rest against hers. Just in case she fell. He heard her suck in a breath, and she looked down at his shoulder before lifting those big eyes to him. Her lips parted and he almost forgot where he was and, for a moment, *who* he was.

Her hair was wild around her face and her eyes were glancing at his lips. His entire body went hard and he couldn't move. He watched as she licked her full, bouncy lips. This woman was dangerous. One of those women who made you forget. But he couldn't forget. He could never forget.

He had to say something.

"'The stroke of midnight ceases,'" he recited. "'And I lie down alone. The rainy Pleiades wester, And seek beyond the sea, The head that I shall dream of, That will not dream of me.'"

Edward felt Olivia's eyes on him.

'What was that? A poem? You recite poetry?' She laughed at him and looked away. 'For someone who is not a romantic that sounded suspiciously romantic, Eddie.'

'That's not romantic. It's extremely *un*romantic. The man in that poem is dreaming of a woman who isn't dreaming of him. That's not romantic. It's foolish.'

And you're being foolish, he reminded himself as he dragged his eyes away from her plump lips. Kissing someone like Olivia would not help. Dragging a woman into his life was not something he could do. Especially not a fun-loving, free-spirited woman like Olivia. She'd hate it, and she'd resent him and they'd both end up unhappy. He moved away, put some distance between them so he could no longer feel the warmth of her skin or smell her cinnamon scent.

'The man who wrote that is not foolish. He's romantic. Wistful.' Olivia sighed and looked back to the sky.

Edward noticed she'd pulled his jacket closer.

'Probably not a man. Probably a woman. Dreaming of finding someone she can never hope to find.'

A rush of sympathy invaded his bones. She sounded so sad. So unlike the angry woman in the car or in the drawing room, threatening that she hadn't 'finished' with him.

'Then you fill your life with something else,' he said softly.

He could feel her pain. Olivia sounded confused. He suspected she didn't know what she wanted. She needed someone strong. Someone to take care of her. Edward's shoulders stiffened. Definitely not him. He caused pain; he didn't relieve it. That realisation poured a stream of cold water over him.

'You should strive for something that will give you back exactly what you put into it.'

'Like what?'

'Work. Exercise.'

'You exercise?'

'I run. Every day.'

'Me too.'

That magnetic smile lit her face again and it hit him in the chest. Then her face fell.

'I hate it, though. It gives me too much time to think. And it hurts.'

'So why do you do it?'

She faced him and ran her hand seductively from her breasts to her thigh. It sent a shiver straight through him and he stood to attention again. Her garish purple dress peeked through his jacket and the flashes of the skin on her chest and her legs were making him sweat, even as the night chill wound around him.

'This body don't come cheap. I'll let you in on a secret, Eddie. I'm not a natural beauty. Any appeal I have comes from hard work and a daily pounding of the pavement.'

Edward thought that *none* of her appeal came from pounding the pavement. She had a killer body, that was true. But she also had a set of full, pouty lips, a beautiful smile and an innate consciousness of her own femininity. The woman was sexy. *Damn* sexy. And she knew it.

'If that body is so hard to get why do you expose it in cheap stuff like that thing you call a dress? If that body were mine I'd have it covered from nose to ankle so no one could lay his perving eyes on you.'

Olivia blinked.

'You would?'

He nodded and moved closer to her. As if she were a magnet and he couldn't resist. Her small body was warm, and even though he wasn't touching her he could feel the heat emanating from her.

'If you were mine, Olivia, I'd barely let you out of the bedroom, where clothes don't matter.'

The silence that lay between them wasn't awkward. And it wasn't silent. He could see her thinking. He was sure she could see him thinking. Wanting to do something he shouldn't. Wishing it was he who'd had those glasses of champagne. Maybe then he wouldn't think so much.

Olivia swayed and grabbed the wall for support, knocking the glass of water off in the process. It smashed noisily on the paving. He moved quickly to hold her around the waist. When she fell against him her breasts were soft against his chest. Then she moved even closer, snuggling in, making his chest expand and his arms hold her even tighter. Her blue eyes swivelled up to him and he saw the question in them. The air was thick and heavy and so was her need. He answered it automatically by pulling her in even closer.

'You feel nice,' she murmured as she snuggled in, and let out a little mew.

For some reason that turned him on even more. Her soft hair tickled his chin. He leaned down a little to bury his nose in it and breathe her in. But he wasn't here for this. He hadn't come here this weekend to fondle innocent women on the terrace.

'Olivia, are you all right?'

'I am now,' she murmured, pulling herself closer.

Damn, that wasn't what he'd wanted her to do. Holding her close to him felt good. Too good. And he didn't deserve good. Not when his brother needed his support and his mother needed his explanations and his father needed help to calm down. Being out here with Olivia was a selfish indulgence. He tried to push her away but she held tight, and she was so close and so responsive she just snuggled back in. This was getting out of hand.

'Olivia, you're too…'

The word *intoxicating* embedded itself into his mind as her scent circled around his face. She *was* intoxicating. She lifted her head and her eyes darkened. He knew the look on her face. Pure desire. He was sure she could see the same look on his face.

'Too what?'

She licked her bottom lip and his mind went blank. All thoughts of guilt disappeared and something more animal took over. Slowly, he brought his hand around to trace a finger along the edge of her chin. He wanted to touch her lips. Just once. Then he'd stop. All her lipstick had come off. Her lips were bare and delicious. He moved a single finger up to trace them and she stood still. Her breath warmed his finger. With his thumb, he swept a line past her open lips and she responded by poking her pink tongue out. It caught his thumb and he'd never felt anything more erotic.

'Too much,' he whispered as she sucked her bottom lip in between her teeth.

Every thought fled his mind except that of her scent and the feel of her body and the sight of those plump lips in between her teeth. His erection was now so hard it hurt. With his hand on the small of her back he pressed her to him, wanting her to feel how much he wanted her.

'Too intoxicating,' he said as he looked into her eyes, which were now bright blue and hooded.

He squeezed his finger and thumb under her chin and pushed it up a little. Closer to him. Olivia wasn't looking for anything serious. She just wanted comfort. Comfort he could give. Comfort wouldn't last past the weekend. He was able to do that.

Thankfully, she moved her chin up higher, until finally he felt the warmth of her breath on his lips.

Intoxicating.

Intoxicated.

The sharp tang of champagne on her breath hit his nose. He felt her sway slightly. Realisation made his eyes roll back. She was drunk and he was taking advantage of her. Quickly he used his hands to push her shoulders away.

CHAPTER SEVEN

'OLIVIA, STOP...'

Surprise filled her eyes. She frowned and watched his lips as he spoke.

'We shouldn't be doing this...'

'Five minutes,' she said suddenly, and loosened herself from his grip. 'That's my limit.'

Her voice was angry and rough. He'd hurt her. He wanted to tell her he couldn't kiss her when she was drunk. Especially when *he* wasn't. He had to be the responsible one.

Olivia moved quickly and headed for a lounger.

She plonked herself in it, then angrily stood up again and removed the jacket from her shoulders, tossing it to his feet.

'Five minutes—that's all it ever takes.'

'Olivia...' He picked his jacket up and moved closer to drape it over her. She ripped it off again. He was reminded of a petulant child.

'Go away, Edward. You've made your point.'

'My point?'

'Yes.' Her eyes turned angrily towards him and flickered with distaste. 'I'm the girl who's gagging for it. The one you pash and dash with. I know that already—I don't need you to point it out.'

'I wasn't trying to make any point.'

He wasn't sure what he'd been trying to do. He'd been caught up. In the stars, in her scent. Maybe he was more damn romantic than he'd thought. That idea sobered him up.

'You want to know why people can't stand to be with you for more than five minutes? You're as inconsistent as an upstart peer trying to land a position in the Lords. A woman of so many faces I can't keep up with them all.'

'Then go away,' she said quietly, mechanically. 'Leave me alone.'

She sat up and shifted on the chair and her head moved to one side. His chest clenched for a second. She wasn't crying, was she? He didn't do tears.

Her breathing slowed and he moved closer. She snorted and shifted again, curling her legs up. She was asleep. Drunk and passed out.

Brilliant. *Now* what was he supposed to do? She'd freeze to death out here.

The noises from inside got closer and he heard a tap on the door. Someone was sure to come out and find her there. She'd never live it down. So he did the only thing he could do. He scooped her limp body into his arms and walked with her across the lawn to the other side of the house, where he could take her in unnoticed and with her dignity still intact.

Olivia was awake, but everything was so heavy. Her arms, her limbs. She tried to move but a groggy heaviness prevented any movement. Her shoulder was hitting against something hard. A rhythmic thump-thump that was giving her a headache. She tried to open her eyes and pull herself up but she kept being pulled back down into sleepiness. It wasn't until she felt the softness of a mattress beneath her that she was able to open her eyes.

Standing above her, the veins in his neck throbbing, was Edward. Handsome, sexy, cranky Edward, with his hands on his hips. He looked beautiful and angry. Which made her laugh.

'You think this is funny?'

His voice was so lovely. Deep and gravelly. She could feel it in her core. Right where she hadn't been touched in so long. *Soooo* long.

'I think you're funny.' She kicked her very high shoes off and her feet let out a sigh of relief.

He leaned down to reach behind her and she felt her body being tossed about until she was in between the sheets.

'I'm glad you find me amusing.'

He was now so close to her she could smell him. She breathed in heavily. He smelled so good. Like soap and man. Soap and man—that was funny. She giggled again. Then she wriggled. Something didn't feel right. The bed was soft, but something was cutting into her. She reached round and realised what it was. The zipper of this ridiculous, fabulous dress. She tugged and pulled, trying to get it off.

'Here, let me.'

Edward's big strong hands reached behind her and unzipped the dress. She breathed him in again. So lovely.

Awkwardly she lifted the tight dress up and over

her head. Then she reached for her bra clasp and flung the constricting garment off. Edward said nothing, but reached down to the bottom of the bed and pulled up a plump, warm duvet. Olivia snuggled down, feeling warm and comfortable. Finally. Bubbles of champagne still danced around in her head.

'Stay with me for a while.'

Edward hesitated before she felt the side of the bed sink. She wanted to reach out and touch him, but even as the champagne fogged her senses she knew she shouldn't do that. He wouldn't like that.

'Talk to me,' she insisted, closing her eyes against the bright light. 'And switch the light off.'

She felt him rise and the light went out. The blackness felt lovely, but in a second a warm light next to the bed went on and she felt the heaviness of Edward on the edge of the bed again. Even though she couldn't see him very well she could still smell him. And feel him.

'Edward?'

'Yes?'

'Are you still here?'

'Yes, Olivia. I'm still here. Which is why you can talk to me.'

'Oh.' She giggled. 'Edward?'

'Yes, Olivia.'

'Can you wash my face?'

'Can I *what*?'

'Wash my face? Get all the make-up off? I can't go to sleep with make-up on. It'll ruin my comp…my complex…my skin.'

She heard Edward sigh, and then his big body shifted. The door opened and shut quietly. He was gone. She was all alone and he'd left. Tears welled in her eyes and her stomach was heavy. She didn't want Edward to leave. Not him. Not big, strong, awful Edward.

But in a few seconds, before the tears had a chance to fall, he returned and she felt the comforting warmth of a hot cloth on her face. She sighed and pulled the duvet down so he could wipe her neck. With gentle strokes he moved across her face, removing all traces of her armour. He took a while on her eyes, gently moving the cloth back and forth.

'Ouch,' she complained.

'Sorry.' His deep voice was soft and calm and so very, very sexy. 'What's this?'

She opened her eyes and lifted her head. Edward held what looked like a caterpillar in his hand. She looked up into his confused face and laughed.

'It's my eyelashes.'

He looked back at them, and then at her eyes. Then he leaned closer and peeled the other set of false eyelashes off.

'Why on earth would you wear these?'

'To make my eyes appear larger and more bee-yoo-tiful!' she announced with a laugh.

He shook his head and moved the cloth over her eyes again.

'I will never understand women.'

'We're very simple, Edward. You just have to know the secret.'

'Which is?'

'Do everything we tell you and believe nothing we say.'

He laughed at that. Then he was finished. The cloth was cold and he moved it away.

'Will you put some cream on my face?'

This time he didn't sigh. He just asked, 'Where is it?'

'In my pink bag.'

'This one?'

He lifted up an overnight bag and Olivia nodded. She watched him rifle through her bag. His jacket was off and his white shirt strained across his shoulders and back as his hand sorted through. His long, lean legs were encased in black pants and she could see the outline of his muscular thigh as he moved. She was dying to touch him. But he wouldn't like that.

When he turned to her he was holding up four pots of cream.

'That one,' she said, and he unscrewed the lid, sitting down beside her again.

It felt so good to have him there. She felt safe and cared for. She never felt like this at the beauty salon when they rubbed cream on her face. Somehow Edward's long, strong fingers roaming her face felt different. Very different. As in *her breasts felt tight and moisture rushed to her core* different.

She opened her eyes and watched him. Concentration was etched on his face. Although his fingers seemed large against her skin he was moving very, very gently. She wondered for a moment what those fingers would feel like stroking something else. Somewhere else. Somewhere hotter and wetter. She drew her lip in and bit it. Edward's fingers stopped moving and he watched her mouth. Then his eyes slid to hers.

'Am I hurting you?'

Although she'd thought it impossible, his voice had become even lower. And even sexier. She wanted to touch him. But she couldn't. He definitely wouldn't like that.

'No, what you're doing is perfect.'

A little half-smile spread over his lips and she felt herself drowning in those dark chocolate eyes again.

'Then relax and enjoy it.'

She heard his words, let them wash over her and did as she was told. She closed her eyes and concentrated on the feel of his fingers as they spread across her forehead and over her eyelids. Down her cheek and over her chin, then lower. Along her neck to her collarbones, where he paused and withdrew his hand. She gasped, but then he was back with more cream. He spread it across her collarbones and further down. She arched into his hand and he rubbed gently on her chest. She felt as if she would burst with anticipation. Then he stopped.

Her eyes flew open. He was screwing the lid on, his eyes off her. 'There—is that better?'

She couldn't speak. His handsome profile rendered her mute. She just nodded and his eyes turned to hers. He watched her for a second and she felt herself grow warm under his gaze. She lay still, watching him watch her. Then he leaned forward and she held her breath. He was going to kiss her. The most handsome, beautiful man in the world was going to kiss her. *Her!* But his lips touched her forehead instead.

'Sleep,' he said quietly, before pulling a bottle of water from her Mary Poppins-esque make-up bag. 'Drink some water. I'll see you in the morning.'

He stood to leave. She didn't want him to go. She wanted him to stay and touch her some more.

'Eddie?'

He turned and looked at her. So beautiful. So kind.

'You're not awful. You're nice.'

He smiled widely enough that she could see his perfect white teeth.

'Sleep. We'll talk tomorrow.'

She closed her eyes and within seconds was asleep.

CHAPTER EIGHT

WHEN OLIVIA WOKE up it felt as if she'd left her brain on the pillow. She put her hand to her head. It ached so much she thought she was having one of those brain aneurysm thingys. Then her brain caught up and told her about the dead rat in her mouth. She slapped her tongue on the top of her mouth, trying to wet it.

Opening her eyes slowly, she tried to remember where she was. The sun was streaming in through the gap between a set of pale flowery curtains. She was in a very big, very soft bed. Slowly, she looked around. She was in a bedroom. Teal-blue wallpaper printed with spring flowers surrounded the walls and near the door was a dark wooden dressing table. The mirror was facing her. Her hair was sticking up everywhere and there were black circles under her eyes. And she was naked. Except for her ludicrously small G-string. And she had no idea how she'd got here, where she was, or why she was naked.

An awful thought fell into her mind and she looked beside her. A heavy sigh escaped her lips. She was alone. Thank God.

Slowly and carefully she eased herself out of the bed. In the corner were her bags—all stacked up neatly.

Next to the green lamp on the bedside table was a bottle of water and her face cream. She couldn't have been too drunk if she'd managed to find her cream and think about water. She took a long slug of the water before getting up to move closer to the dressing table. Her make-up was all off. Except for the dark kohl eyeliner around her eyes, which was impossible to get off without the proper cleansers. She felt a little better. She must have been sober enough to remove her make-up.

Turning to her bags, she moved slowly, allowing her head to catch up. She needed a shower. And a cup of tea. And probably a big, fat, greasy bacon and egg roll. Her stomach growled in agreement. She was starving.

She found her clothes and her shampoo and all the other things she needed in the morning in order to look respectable and bundled them up. But where was the bathroom? Pulling out her short satin kimono, she slipped it on before heading to the door. She hadn't had a chance to figure out how this huge house worked last night. All she'd seen was that big long room with the fireplace and the ballroom where the party had been held.

How had she managed to find her way up here?

Peeking out through the door, she saw a long, deserted hallway. There had to be a bathroom somewhere. Padding silently along the wooden floor, she counted doors so she'd know how to get back. With relief, she spotted a door that had a picture of a shower on it, with the word *Bathroom*. Thank goodness these people had had the foresight to imagine half-naked women wandering the halls looking for a bathroom and labelled their doors.

Slipping in, Olivia was greeted by an enormous

room. On one side was a wooden vanity unit with a large mirror, and at the end of the room, under the window, was an enormous copper bathtub. And that was it. No shower. Just a sink and a tub.

Sighing, she put her things on the vanity and took another look at her disgraceful state before shaking her head and heading for the bathtub. A bath was no match for a shower. Standing beneath hard rushing water and soaking your head was the only fix for a hangover as big as this one. But there *was* no shower—only this enormous tub that would probably take six days to fill.

Olivia tried to piece together the events of last night as the hot water ran loudly and the steam rose.

She remembered the uncomfortable car-ride with Edward and the sight of this enormous castle. She also remembered Fiona and how upset she was. She'd told Edward, warned him not to be mean to her friend. A little niggle of regret nipped at her. Was it really Edward's fault his family were mean? But then…Bunny. Laughing at her. Making her feel awkward and stupid.

The party had swirled around her and she remembered the champagne—how many glasses had she drunk? Then Chester/Hester/Casper and the man with the beautiful skin. She'd finally started having some fun until Edward had come and scared them away. Then…then he'd taken her outside.

The bathtub was filling quickly. She splashed some water onto her face.

The terrace. She was looking at the stars. The saucepan was upside down.

Then…then…

Oh, no.

No.

She remembered cuddling Edward. He'd said something nice. Recited poetry. Surely she hadn't fallen for poetry? But Edward didn't like her. No—he'd pushed her away. She felt the rush of heat rise up her neck. He'd pushed her away. She must have thrown herself at him.

She shed her kimono and lowered herself into the water. It felt so good and she hoped it would wash a little of her shame away. She found a facecloth and soaked it in the water, placing it over her face. Maybe she could hide up here all day. She didn't want to face Fiona. Or Will. Or Bunny. Or Edward. Definitely not Edward.

How could she be so stupid? How drunk had she been last night?

Half an hour later Olivia knew she couldn't hide any longer. Her hair was washed, her body clean and her fingers were starting to wrinkle. Quickly she climbed out and rubbed a soft towel over her skin before slipping into her clothes and wrapping the towel around her hair.

Questions about last night still lingered. Like how she'd found her way to her bedroom. And what had happened after she'd thrown herself at Edward?

Peeking out of the door, she decided to make a run for it. She counted the doors and was in the comfort of her bedroom in seconds. She had to go downstairs. She couldn't hide up here all day. Fiona had said something about wedding get-to-know-you activities, or something daggy like that. Which sounded like sensible shoes activities. She was sure she'd packed *one* pair of sensible shoes.

After blow-drying her hair till it was straight and shiny, and painting on her face, Olivia was ready.

Ready to face everyone. So, with a toss of her blonde locks, she took a deep breath and opened the door.

'Put that bloody thing away, Edward.'

Edward forced down a deep sigh. His father was irritable this morning. He'd been snapping at everyone while his mother barely spoke a word.

'I'm expecting a call.'

'Put it away, Ed. Fiona and I are going for a walk into the village—why don't you come with us?' Edward could think of dozens of reasons why he didn't want to join his lovesick brother and future sister-in-law on their walk into town. But he was here to make things easier this weekend, not harder.

'I have some work to do, but I'll meet you there later.'

'Work! You never stop, Ed. Why don't you come with us? Rosie and I are going to the pub. There's little else to do here in the wilderness.'

Bunny was helping his mother cook breakfast, which was lucky as his mother kept stopping to stare out of the window.

Bunny's friend Rosie smiled at him. She was a strange-looking girl. Her teeth were too big for her mouth and her eyes too big for her head. And she slurped when she talked. He'd barely spoken to her, but for some reason the girl had taken a liking to him.

'Oh, *do*, Ed,' she slurped. 'We only have Casper and Hugo with us, and they're being such bores.'

She batted her eyelashes and Edward almost laughed.

'Maybe later.'

He felt good this morning. He'd been up since six.

He'd been for his run, gone out to the terrace to clean up the smashed glass from last night, had a phone conference with the Defence Office and managed to work through part of a problem with the new fiscal policy. Getting work done always made him feel good. But there was something else this morning. Something that was making him feel good and at the same time making him nervous. And he knew what it was. Olivia.

He flicked the pages of the paper in front of him. He couldn't figure her out. Angry and fiery one minute, drunk and needy the next. But she was interesting. And charming when drunk. Giggly and smiling and asking for his help. She'd enjoyed it when he'd rubbed her face with cream.

A sharp pain shot through his belly and straight into his groin. He remembered the way she had bitten her lip when he was rubbing her. He'd almost done something he was sure he would have regretted. But he hadn't. He'd controlled himself and left her to sleep. Alone. Even though he'd had to physically push his shoes into the floor to stop himself from getting into bed with her. Especially after she'd whipped off that ridiculous dress and then her bra.

His hands went still. Her breasts were perfect. Even better than he'd thought they would be. Full and heavy and a handful. And her nipples… Rose-pink and standing to attention—with that sensual swirl of colour around the nipples begging to be kissed…

'Hello—we're up!'

'Oh, good Lord, the Blowhards have arrived.' Edward's father folded up his newspaper. 'I'm leaving.'

Which was exactly what Edward wanted to do at the sight of the two silliest men in England.

'Regina, the beds were *divine* last night,' gushed Hugo.

'Pity we were alone in them, though,' guffawed Casper Bolton-Smythe.

The hairs on Edward's neck stood on end.

'You were alone?' Bunny asked between bites of crunchy toast. 'You were looking pretty pally with The Peacock.'

Laughter fell all around the group.

Edward stood up. 'Bunny, that's enough…' He started to tell his sister what the rules were, but stopped when he saw her.

Peeking through the rails of the stairs.

She looked small today. Much smaller than she had yesterday. Slowly she moved down, silently stepping on each step and cautiously looking around. Then her eyes met his and they locked. She looked like a fox caught in the glare of a light. Terrified. He stood still and looked back. He wanted to go to her, but he didn't move in case he spooked her. She started to descend the stairs again and he felt himself holding his breath. For some reason.

His heart started to beat faster. Had she heard Bunny? Was she all right?

Something about Olivia made him lose focus. He should be watching his mother, or thinking about keeping Will calm before the wedding. Instead his whole brain was filled with *her*. She was wearing jeans and a tight white jumper which made her tan stand out. Her eyes were slashed with make-up and her lips were pink. Her hair was long and straight. She looked fashionable and slick but he didn't take any notice of that. He saw underneath all her armour.

She was terrified; he could see it in the way her eyes darted around the room before resting back on his. Begging him to help her. And he wanted to—but he couldn't. She couldn't rely on him. His family he could control. They knew what to do and how far they could go. This girl seemed to have no limits. When she was angry she went off. When she was upset her eyes filled with tears. And every time her emotions shifted his did too. Which was highly disconcerting and not what he was used to. Steady, grey, dull, solid. That was his world. Olivia was too emotional, too highly strung, too colourful—and it was too much for him.

CHAPTER NINE

'Morning,' Olivia mumbled.

Eight sets of eyes were staring at Olivia as she stood frozen on the stairs. Bunny's eyes were travelling up and down her length and Hugo was mumbling something low to Casper. And Edward was staring.

She must have really made a fool of herself last night. His expression was hard. Unfriendly. She wanted to die. Or go home. But she couldn't. She was here for Fiona. So instead she found herself at the bottom of the stairs, avoiding the silence and the stares and smiling at Fiona.

'No feathers this morning, Olivia?'

Bunny and her horse-faced friend laughed.

'I only wear my feathers on special occasions.' Olivia smiled, trying to make a joke.

'Oh, shut up, Bunny. The feathers were fabulous.' The cold arm of Casper Bolton-Smythe slipped around Olivia's waist. 'You're just jealous you can't pull them off as well as Liv.'

He smiled down at her and she squinted against the brightness of those white teeth. Her sister had used to use bicarbonate of soda to whiten her teeth. She wondered if Casper did the same.

'Morning, Olivia, how are you feeling today?'

Edward's deep voice held a gruff undertone. As if he was angry at her. Probably angry that she'd thrown herself at him last night.

'Fine,' she mumbled, before taking a seat next to Fiona.

Olivia shifted awkwardly, still feeling eyes on her.

'I'm starving,' she whispered.

'Don't count on anything edible,' Fiona whispered back.

Will's mother was staring out of the window, a pair of tongs in her hands. The smell of burnt bacon filled the room.

'Mum!' Bunny jumped up, but Edward reached his mother before Bunny could. He took the tongs and pulled the bacon out of the pan before rinsing it under cold water. His mother just stared at him and smiled.

Quickly and efficiently Edward got out another pan and put on more bacon and some sausages. He cut up some tomatoes and put them in the pan too.

'Go and sit down, Mum. Honestly—what's wrong with you today?' Bunny's impatient voice sounded across the din.

Edward's mother dutifully sat down at the kitchen table and continued to stare out of the window. Edward poured a cup of tea and brought it to her, then sat back down at the table.

'So, what are the plans for today, Fi?' Olivia asked, crunching into the toast Fiona offered.

'We're going for a walk into the village. Will says there are some wonderful views along the way.'

'Views? I'm going back to bed.' Hugo grabbed a piece of toast and headed up the stairs.

'Well, I *like* views. Especially this one.'

Once more, Olivia felt Casper's arm snake around her shoulders.

Olivia had had enough of being polite. This snake was just not getting the hint. She grabbed his hand and lifted it up and over her head.

'Perhaps you're due to have your eyes checked, Casper? There is certainly nothing spectacular about this view—and even if there were I'm not sure I'd want you looking at it.'

Casper's eyes went hard for a moment. Then it passed and a silly smile spread across his mouth.

'Ooh, a challenge. I do like a challenge.'

'God, Casper, you are such a sleaze,' offered Bunny as she scooped bacon out of the pan and onto Olivia's plate.

Olivia didn't hesitate; she dug in desperately as if she hadn't eaten in days.

'Slow down, Olivia, you *will* be fed again.'

Olivia didn't miss the disdain in Bunny's tone. She glanced up, her mouth full of bacon. Bunny looked impossibly cool again today, fashionable without wearing one trendy thing. The look on Bunny's face made Olivia feel even more uncouth and small-town than she was.

She swallowed hard. 'Hungry,' was all she could say.

'Let her eat, Bunny. You *are* in a mood,' said Casper, sitting down next to Olivia.

Edward went to the sink to fill the kettle. Olivia glanced at him as he walked past. Today he was dressed in jeans that hugged his butt and a knitted navy jumper. He looked warm and cosy and impossibly sexy. She couldn't help wondering what he'd look like first thing in the morning. Before he got dressed. All sleepy and sexy and reaching for her…

'Are you hung-over, Liv? I didn't realise you'd had that much to drink. Did you get to bed all right last night?' Fiona sipped her tea and considered Olivia with her large brown eyes.

'I was fine. I got into bed and washed my face and… and…and…' Realisation hit her in an instant.

She looked at Edward, who was now watching her with a strange look on his face. She hadn't found her way to her room on her own last night. Edward had *carried* her. She rubbed her neck. She'd been banging into him as he climbed the stairs. Then he'd put her in bed and…her dress… It had been sticking into her. He'd unzipped it. And…

Olivia felt the blood drain from her face. She remembered. She'd pulled her dress off. Then her bra. Her *bra*! She'd been naked and he'd been there. She quickly turned away from Edward's knowing gaze.

She remembered everything now. He'd been close. So close she'd sniffed him. Sniffed him like a dog. He'd smelt good too. Then—oh, God. He'd taken her make-up off and she had demanded he rub cream onto her face. No wonder he was looking at her like that. As if she was an idiot. Because she was. A pathetic, drunken idiot who threw herself at men.

All of a sudden her hunger dissipated. She stood up. She had to get out.

'Actually, I think I'm done. I might go for a run.'

She felt hot and suddenly couldn't bear to be in the same room as Edward. He'd seen her naked. And without make-up! Even her mother hadn't seen her without make-up. Not since she was fourteen anyway.

'I'm going for a run. I'll meet you in the village later.'

She didn't really feel like running. The thought of her brain jiggling was making her sick.

'Give me ten minutes and I'll come with you.'

No, no, *no*. Not Edward. Not him. He'd seen her drunk. Needy. Desperate. Asking him to—oh, God! She'd asked him to stay. Patted the bed so he'd sit next to her. She felt dizzy. She had to get out.

'Actually, I don't think I *will* run. I might walk. Yes, a walk. I am feeling a little sick, Fi; I might go for a walk.'

'Excellent. I'll meet you at the back door.'

Edward's eyes were fixed on hers. He wasn't letting her go. Her shoulders slumped. He obviously had something to say and she'd have to face him some time. So she said nothing more and turned to head back up the stairs.

'Edward, I can explain. I was jet lagged and I hadn't eaten in two days, and Fiona was upset, and that champagne just went to my head…'

Olivia had wrapped her fluffy coat around her but she was still cold, and they hadn't even left the house yet. They were in the mud room, pulling on wellies and fighting two Irish Wolfhounds for space.

'Here.' Edward pulled something plasticky and puffy from the closet and handed it to Olivia. A coat. A big, ugly, puffy coat.

'What's this?'

'You'll freeze to death in that pathetic thing you call a coat, and I'm in no mood to talk to the authorities today. Put this on. It's one of Bunny's.'

Bunny wore *this*? It didn't look like anything Bunny would wear, but when she slipped it on she knew there was no way she was taking it off. It was lined with wool and the warmest thing she'd ever had on her body.

Edward opened the door and between the dogs and the coat she managed to bump into him as she passed. His hot breath hit her cheek and a warm trickle of heat flooded her veins. She'd never known a man to emit as much heat as Edward did. Nor had she ever known a man to smell as good as he did.

She pushed past, ignoring the bubbles that had popped in her belly.

'Edward, I'm so sorry…' she began again once they were outside, trudging through a thin layer of frost and ice.

'Stop apologising.' Edward's hands were shoved into his pockets and the collar of his grey coat was up. 'You had a rough day. You drank too much champagne. It happens.'

'But I… I…' *Threw myself at you. Tried to kiss you.* Heat rushed up and burned Olivia's cheeks. As if someone like Edward would ever kiss *her*.

She sneaked a quick look at him. Today he was even taller and more handsome. Even more unattainable. He probably kissed tall, elegant women with names like Binky and Squidge. Women whose Daddies owned empires and who spent the weekends skiing in the Alps. Not trashy, try-hard foreign girls like her.

'You needed help. I helped you. It was nothing.'

'It wasn't nothing. What if one of the others had found me out there on the terrace? Drunk.'

She shuddered as she thought of Casper. What if he had found her instead of Edward? She couldn't see him carrying her up the stairs—it might have crumpled his jacket.

'Thank you, Edward. For listening to my drunken rant and for taking me to bed.' She gulped. 'And for ignoring my propensity to throw myself at strange men,' she added quietly.

She saw his face turn but he didn't say anything. Instead he pointed to a fork in the road up ahead that led to a muddy pathway.

'I want to show you something,' he said as he walked alongside her.

When they got to the rise, the valley was spread out below them. Although there was a slight fog Olivia could see a patchwork of fields and acres of winter wildflowers. It felt magical. As if she'd entered another world.

Edward held her elbow as they headed towards an outcrop of rocks. He helped her find a foothold and they climbed to the very top. The rock was so large they could both stand on it. Edward moved closer, his sleeve against hers. She couldn't feel it but she knew his skin was just beneath a few layers of fabric. The thought made her tingle.

Stupid, stupid, Olivia, she berated herself. Always wishing for things she couldn't have. Always falling for the wrong men. Not that she was falling for Edward. She just wanted to feel his skin. That was just lust. Hot, dirty lust. She glanced at his profile. So handsome, so strong. She'd never been with a man like that. She'd never even been able to talk to a man like that. And now here she was—stuck on a big rock with a man like that.

Edward moved to the edge and sat down.

'Come. Sit,' he ordered, holding out his hand.

She took it, still mesmerised by his jaw and the way it was twitching. Her skin buzzed beneath her glove at his touch, so she sat down and quickly pulled her hand away. She had to stop fantasising about this man. He'd seen her naked. With no make-up! There was no way he'd be fantasising about *her*.

'It's beautiful,' she murmured, looking out across the fields. And so was he. *Shut up, Olivia.*

'We spent days out here when we were young. Hunting, fishing, exploring.'

His voice held a pang of longing. Fiona had said Edward hadn't been back here in months. She'd said he hardly ever came home.

'Do you miss it?'

Edward paused. 'I do. I miss it very much.'

Looking through her hair, Olivia thought she caught his jaw working at the side of his face. She thought for a moment he was going to say something else, but he didn't. So she lifted her hand to pull her hair across one shoulder. She'd have a better view of him if she didn't have to peer through her hair.

At her movement he looked at her.

'What's that?'

A warm finger lightly pressed a spot right below her ear and Olivia went stiff. His touch was like torture. She remembered the way he'd touched her skin last night and the way she'd arched into his hand… An uncontrollable blush spread across her face. He drew his finger away and she reached up to her neck and rubbed the skin that still tingled.

'It's a tattoo. My sister has the same one.'

'Are you and your sister close?'

'Not particularly. Not now, anyway. We were when we were younger. But after she…'

For some reason she didn't want to tell Edward about Ana. She didn't want Edward to know. He was here, with her. Touching her skin and talking in that deep English voice. She didn't want her sister interfering.

'I keep my hair long so no one will see it.'

Olivia sat perfectly still as Edward's face came closer.

'What is it? An oar?'

'A tennis racket.' She shivered. He was still close. She could feel his breath on her neck. She wanted to close her eyes and push her neck into his lips, but he wouldn't want that.

He came even closer and his scent circled around her. Warmth rolled off him in waves.

'It's cute,' he said, close to her ear.

The tiny hairs on her ear stood to attention. Her nipples stood to attention. Her whole body was on alert. The green light was well and truly turned on and flashing. If he decided to throw her back on this rock, Olivia was pretty sure her long-forgotten parts would know what to do with the large, hard body of Edward hovering above them.

She had to get away from him—away from his scent and his warmth. She shifted her head, letting her hair fall back over the shoulder closest to him, but he lifted his hand and caught it.

'Wait. Let me look.'

The way he spoke—all low and gruff—was as if he was saying something completely different. Something much hotter. Olivia's bones disappeared.

She couldn't remember the last time a man had spoken to her like that. She couldn't remember the last time a man had been this close to her. No. She could. Just over a year ago. At her sister's victory party. He'd kissed her in the hallway of her sister's flat. Told her she was hot. But not as hot as her sister. She'd pushed him so hard the back of his head had hit the other side of the hallway. He'd sworn at her and left. Olivia had felt grubby and used.

But Edward didn't make her feel like that. He seemed to bring her skin alive, to make her feel something else. Something much lovelier.

His hand held her hair and he pushed it back over her shoulder. His knuckles brushed her skin and she gasped. Slowly his lips came closer, until she could feel him breathing in her ear. So warm, so safe. Then, as her eyes rolled back, his warm lips pressed to the skin on her neck. Soft, gentle, reverent. She felt the wetness of the tip of his tongue as it came out a little to touch her skin and she shivered. The combination of his scent, his warmth, his strong hands and his hot lips made something burst deep inside. Something that she wasn't sure she was quite ready to let out.

She pulled her neck away and her hair slid through his fingertips. She turned to face him.

'Edward…'

His eyes froze. The expression on his face froze; then it went hard.

'I'm sorry, Olivia,' he said quietly as his eyes turned away.

She felt the cold envelop her when his gaze left hers. He was embarrassed. Shocked that he'd done that. She could feel his mortification and it mortified her.

'Maybe we should get to the village. Meet the others.'

Edward's voice was rough, embarrassed, and Olivia's whole body burned. He'd realised who he was with. He'd remembered last night. *That* was the look in his eyes. Shock, realisation, disgrace.

Olivia needed to move—to get away from Edward and his too-honest reaction. And from the awful feeling that she was beginning to feel much more for this man than she had a right to.

CHAPTER TEN

'YOU NEVER TOLD me, Will, how did you two meet?' Edward looked at his brother. He was doing everything he could to avoid looking at Olivia.

Their walk down from the rocks had been awkward. Olivia hadn't been able to get far enough away from him. What had made him kiss her neck he'd never know. Her skin was so silky and her voice was so sexy he hadn't known what he was doing until it was too late. Until she'd pulled away and he'd realised he'd stepped over the line. He'd lost control. Which was not like him. She was bringing out the worst in him.

'Actually, Olivia was going out with him first.' Fiona's little voice twittered.

Edward stilled. What the hell…?

'What?'

'No. That's not—not right.'

Olivia was stuttering. What was she nervous about? He turned to look at her. He'd be able to tell what she was thinking if he looked at her eyes. But he couldn't. She wasn't looking at him.

'I wasn't "going out" with Will. I mean we went out. Once. But it wasn't like he was mine. I mean, you only did it out of politeness—didn't you, Will?'

'You went out with Will?'

Fire throbbed in his neck. The idea of his brother's hands on her was making him sick. He reached for his beer and sipped it, trying to look casual. Inside he was anything but casual. That silky skin, those beautiful breasts… Had his brother touched them? Edward's shoulders ached. He was going to have to hit something. Very soon. Or, better yet, someone.

'Yes. Once. That was how Will and Fiona met.'

Olivia's eyes finally met his and her chin tilted up. Defiant Olivia was back.

'You were going out with Will and he chucked you for Fiona?'

'No. *No.*'

'You bastard.' Edward directed a hard look at William.

'Settle down, mate, it wasn't like that.' Will held his hands up.

Edward turned back to Olivia and his knuckles whitened where his hands were clasped together. 'Were you two together? Were you intimate?'

'Edward—what a question! Intimate? Who talks like that?' Will shifted in his seat. 'No. *God*, no.'

Edward didn't watch Will. He watched Olivia and the way her shoulders slumped when Will said, '*God*, no.' Had she wanted to be intimate with Will? Did she still want him? Was that why she was dressing in short dresses and laughing so much? Was she trying to attract Will's attention away from Fiona?

'No! No… It was nothing, Edward! Will and I just went out for dinner. That's all.' Olivia looked up at him, her blue eyes glassy.

'When was this?' Edward asked quietly.

'It was the night Will and Fi met. Eight months ago.'

'Did you like him?'

Olivia coughed and glanced at Fiona, then at Will. Edward didn't take his eyes off her. A slow, pink blush crept up her cheeks.

'Of course I did. Will's great.'

'I see.'

He couldn't look any longer; he had to turn away. Olivia wanted Will. *His* Olivia. Wait—what? Olivia wasn't his. She didn't belong to him. He'd just met her, and put her into bed, and kissed her neck that tasted like honey. Sweet and thick. His body went hard again. Damn thing. He wished it would settle down and do as it was told.

Edward heard Will slurp his beer. 'What happened to you and that dolly bird you were getting about with, Ed?'

Edward glared at him.

'You know—that woman with the hair. The perfect hair. You should have seen her, Liv. Her hair *was* perfect. Every day. Even when she'd just got out of bed. I tried to mess it up once, but it wouldn't mess. It just fell back perfectly.'

'Idiot,' said Edward.

'What happened to her? What was her name?'

'Penelope.'

'Penelope. Of course. Perfect Penelope. What happened?'

'Nothing.'

'You mean you're still with her? Is she still perfect?'

'Can we change the subject?'

'OK. Sure. Let's talk about me. Did I tell you they're

looking for a senior manager? Guess who's in line for the job?'

Olivia couldn't guess, and nor did she want to. She was still reeling over Perfect Penelope. Of *course* Edward had a perfect Penelope. All handsome, lovely, financially secure and mentally balanced men did. And when they had a perfect Penelope they didn't want a Loopy Livvie. At least not for long.

The memory of Edward's lips on her neck made her blush again. She caught him looking at her and self-consciously searched in her pocket for her lip gloss but it wasn't there. *Damn it.*

Why was he looking at her like that? His eyes were watching her as if he was trying to figure something out.

The fire they were next to was getting hot, so Olivia slipped the white jumper she had on up and over her neck. Her white T-shirt underneath came up, and when she untangled herself from the arms of the jumper she spotted Edward looking at her naked torso. Then his eyes bounced back to hers. She had to turn away. She couldn't look at him. Not when the shame of that kiss flooded through her every time she looked at his lips or glanced at his long fingers on the tabletop.

He'd been angry at her all the way back, perhaps because he thought she was throwing herself at him. He probably liked women who waited, women who were more subtle. But Olivia's mother had always told her she was as subtle as a fox in a chook pen. She'd never been good at hiding her emotions. It was probably why she had such bad luck with men. Maybe she should try holding back a bit more, teasing them. Ana was an expert at it and she had men flocking to her.

But then Ana was six foot tall and looked like a Brazilian supermodel.

The lunch came and everyone ate silently. Olivia was glad Bunny and the others had already left. She knew Bunny would sense the tension. Then she'd tease her and Olivia would probably end up in tears. Or in a bar fight. And Olivia didn't want to let her emotions show any more than they already had.

Edward didn't look at her again. He was casually sipping his beer between bites—as if the kiss he'd planted on her neck earlier had meant nothing. As if he did that kind of thing all the time. He probably did. Or maybe he'd been thinking of Perfect Penelope when he'd kissed her.

Olivia stood abruptly. 'I think I might head back.'

'You all right, Liv?' Fi looked up from her steak and chips. 'You look a bit pale.'

'I think the jet lag's caught up.'

'Do you want me to come with you?'

'No, no. You stay. I'll see you at the house.'

Before anyone else could protest she picked up her coat and left. Once outside she pulled the coat around herself, shocked for a second at the freezing wind, and put her head down to walk along the winding lane to the edge of the village.

Edward could have his Perfect Penelope. He deserved her and her perfect hair. They deserved each other. He was probably bad in bed anyway.

'Olivia.'

Edward's commanding voice made her stand stock still. He walked up behind her but she didn't turn.

'I'll walk with you.'

Olivia didn't say anything. She didn't know what to

say. She just waited for him to catch up, then kept walking. Edward said nothing more either. They walked in silence for a long time and the awkwardness grew. They rounded the corner and the village retreated behind them. Still they said nothing. Olivia pulled her collar up higher. The wind was getting stronger. Edward was silent next to her until she felt his hand on her arm.

'This way.'

'I thought the house was this way.'

'Shortcut.'

His eyes were glowing, as if he had a secret. A smile lurked on his lips. She couldn't help but follow him. They walked in silence for another ten minutes until they came to a very high black iron gate. The wind was blowing even more heavily and Olivia was grateful for the big puffy coat that made her look like a marshmallow man.

'What is it? Where are we?'

'I want to show you something.'

Edward's voice had gone quiet. Olivia remembered what had happened the last time Edward had wanted to show her something. What was he doing? Trying to kill her?

She hesitated, shifting her eyes back to the road.

'Olivia.'

Even through her gloves she could feel the cold of Edward's fingers as he picked up her hand.

'I'm sorry about before. I was just... I shouldn't have... It won't happen again.'

His eyes burned with sincerity. It wouldn't happen again. A ball of disappointment dropped in her gut. Of course it wouldn't happen again. He'd made a mistake, kissing her. She wanted to leave, go back to the house and pull the duvet over her head. But he was pulling on her fingers.

'C'mon,' he said, and locked his fingers together, crouching down.

'C'mon, what?'

'Jump.'

Olivia looked up at the locked black iron gates.

'Are you scared?'

He had a challenging glint in his eye and sexy half-smirk on his lips. Olivia gritted her teeth against the flutterings in her stomach. She could resist him and his sexy smirk. She put one foot on his hands and jumped, clearing the gates and landing clumsily on the other side.

'Are you all right?' he called through the gates.

'Yes. How are you going to get over?'

Edward found a foothold in the iron gates and started to climb. Then he jumped and fell lightly to his feet next to her.

'Now what?'

When his fingers looped through hers the breath caught in her throat. He leaned in closer, right next to her ear, and said, 'This way.'

They walked through what seemed like a very dense forest until they arrived at a wall of shrubs. Before them was an opening, and on either side was a tall, pale statue.

'That one is Aesop and that's Cupid,' he explained. Climbing tendrils of ivy curled around their bases. 'See here?' He pulled her over to the statue of a cherub figure with wings, eyes closed and holding a ball of string. 'Cupid says, "Yes, I can now close my eyes and laugh: with this thread I'll find my way.'" He moved her over to the other statue. It was an old man in a long cloak, holding a book. 'But Aesop says, "Love, that slender thread, might get you lost: the slightest shock could break it."'

'I don't understand.'

'Aesop represents Wisdom. Cupid thinks you can get through the maze guided by Love, but Aesop's saying that you need Wisdom—or Love won't last.'

'Sounds deep.'

Edward chuckled. 'I suppose it is a little. But when we were young we saw it as a challenge. Inside this maze are forty-nine statues. Each one represents one of Aesop's fables. We'd bring a ball of string each and go through them all. We'd tie it to this statue and walk through. You had to figure out the meaning of each one before you could go on.'

Slowly Edward led her by the hand into the maze. The structure was still there but it had become overgrown. The hedges were growing low on the ground and some of them were growing into each other. Edward hacked at them with his hands and feet so they could get through.

The maze was beautiful. It felt as if they'd been swallowed up by it. Olivia couldn't see out or any further ahead than the next hedge. She was glad Edward had hold of her hand or she was sure she'd get lost.

'My string always broke. I'd lose my temper and pull it too tight.'

'What about Will?'

'Will would get distracted. He'd drop his string or lose it. Bunny would always run off chasing rabbits—

which is how she ended up with the name Bunny. But James always made it through. Every time.'

'James?'

'There—look! The Cock and the Pearl.'

'Excuse me?'

Edward smiled before pulling her up to a statue of a rooster with something round in its beak. 'The Cock and the Pearl. It's a fable about a rooster who was strutting up and down the farmyard among the hens when he saw something shiny in the straw. When he dug it out, it was a pearl. But he just threw it away.'

'Why?'

'What does a rooster want with a pearl? He'd rather have a single piece of corn than an entire string of pearls.'

Olivia looked up at him. She was sure he was trying to make a point, but she felt a little as she had when she'd been with Casper and Hugo. Confused and behind the conversation.

'He would?'

Edward laughed and pulled on her hand again, leading her further and further into the maze. 'Think of it this way: you could have six hundred pairs of those ridiculous boots you were wearing when I met you, but if you gave them to me I'd just throw them away.'

'Those boots cost me five hundred dollars!'

'But what good are they to *me*? They won't fit, they'd be uncomfortable and I'd not have a thing to wear with them.'

She pushed his shoulder when he grinned.

'But give me a good sturdy pair of runners and to me they'd be worth more than all your boots.'

'So what you're saying is one man's trash is another man's treasure?'

'Sort of. I rather think it means that if someone doesn't like you it's a reflection on them—not you.'

He squeezed her hand and flashed a wide smile and her knees gave an involuntary wobble. Did he have to be so gorgeous?

'What's this one?' she asked, trying to shake off the nervous stutter in her chest.

Edward let go of her hand and circled around the statue. 'Ah…this one was tricky. Took us a long while to figure this one out.'

Olivia watched as he walked, his hands jammed in his pockets. He was looking up and she could see the shadow of his stubble on his face. He looked older, harder. He stood still for a moment. The muscle at his jaw worked and he seemed lost in thought. Olivia looked at the statue of a snake with its tongue out and its head up in attack. At his feet was a small boy who lay dead. She knew this one. Something about a farmer and a snake.

'The snake bit the farmer's son, didn't he?'

'Yes,' said Edward quietly.

'And then he bit his cattle.'

'He bit his cattle because the farmer cut off part of his tail. In revenge for killing his son. But after his cattle were killed the farmer brought food and honey to the serpent's lair. Told him he wanted to forgive and forget.'

'But the serpent refused. He said that what they'd done to each other could be forgiven, but never forgotten,' Olivia remembered.

Edward was silent. His jaw worked frantically.

Olivia moved closer and wrapped her arm around his biceps, somehow knowing that he needed comfort. He looked down at her and Olivia saw sadness in his eyes.

'What is it?' she asked softly.

Slowly, carefully, Edward pulled his hand out of his pocket and reached for her face. Olivia stood still, waiting for his touch, anticipating the gentle feel of his fingers on her skin. Gently his cold fingers stroked her cheek as his gaze trailed over her face, down the curve of her neck and back again. His hand looped around her ear and his eyes locked with hers. Hard.

'Edward, what is it?' she whispered.

His gaze broke and he took his hand away and looked at the statue. Olivia felt as if he'd torn something from her.

'Nothing.' His voice was raw. He shuffled before taking her hand and leading her further into the maze.

CHAPTER ELEVEN

It took them more than an hour to get through the maze. They figured out all the fables, laughed at the stupid ones and tried to find the hidden meaning of the tricky ones. Edward held her hand the entire time, and when they reached the other side the first spots of rain fell.

They started to run until Olivia spotted the flags of the castle and the large stone building looming ahead of them. She was stumbling in her big gumboots and her feet slipped, but Edward grabbed her around the waist to stop her from falling. She was laughing as he scooped her off the ground and barely felt the rain as it turned into freezing sleet against her skin.

Edward was so close and his body was so warm. He'd lifted her high enough so that her mouth was level with his. She could feel his breath warm against her lips, and when she lifted her eyes she saw something that shocked her.

He wanted her.

He wanted to kiss her.

She didn't think.

She wrapped her arms around his neck, pressed her lips to his and forgot to think or breathe. All she did was feel. His lips pressed hard against hers. Her lips tingled and her body heated until she forgot the wind and the ice and the cold and felt a blast of fire flood her veins. Then he opened his mouth and a rush of emotion made her whimper. He was kissing her back. Really kissing her back.

He tilted his head to get better access and she pushed closer to him, winding her fingers through the curls at the nape of his neck. He tasted like beer and smelled like soap and she couldn't think of anything but him. The muscles in his shoulders were hard as she moved her arms around them. The roughness of his stubble against her top lip and the deep groan he made when she nipped at his bottom lip made her body shiver.

But then, as he had last night, he pushed her away. Let her drop and pushed at her shoulders. His eyes blazed and his lips were swollen.

'What? What is it?'

'Olivia. I'm sorry. I can't.'

'Can't what?'

But he didn't answer her. He just let go and stepped back.

He didn't want her. He'd been caught up in the rain and the romance of the maze and he didn't want her after all. After all the mistakes she'd made she'd thought she'd be used to rejection by now. But his rejection seemed to bite hard.

'Can't what? Can't kiss me? Or don't want anyone to see you kiss a girl like me.'

'Olivia. You're behaving like a child. We can't just… do this.' His eyes flashed.

'A child! Me? I'm not the one who sees the shiny toy

and wants to play with it but doesn't want to buy. I'm not the one who breaks the string, Edward. That's you.'

'You don't understand. It's Will's wedding and I…'

'And you *what*? What difference does it make where we are? Stop making excuses. You don't want to kiss me because you don't think I'm good enough for you. Isn't that right?'

'No, that's not right.'

'Then what is it?'

She watched his face. Pieces of ice were getting caught in his eyelashes. His lips were turning blue. She felt her hair damp across her face. She probably looked a mess. Nothing like Perfect Penelope. How could she compete with perfection? She'd been a fool to think someone who looked like him, who was as interesting as he was, would be interested in her. Loopy Livvie.

She didn't wait for his answer. She dodged around him and ran all the way up the lawn and into the warmth of the house.

Things had become way out of hand. For the first time in a long time Edward felt out of control and he didn't know what to do. He tipped the glass in his hand and the ice clinked. What was always going to be a difficult weekend was now more complicated than ever.

Why the hell had he kissed her? He knew the answer to that. She was beautiful. And funny and sweet and charming and sexy as hell. But he still shouldn't have kissed her. She was Fiona's best friend—the Maid of Honour. Could he be any more obvious? And Will had been her first choice. It might have been her here, marrying his brother, if Fiona hadn't turned up. He took another sip of his Glenfiddich and enjoyed the burn as it snaked down his throat. He had enough to contend with in his mother and his father and Bunny and the Blenheim Blowhards without throwing Olivia into the mix.

Anyway, he should have been working—not traipsing the countryside indulging in the attentions of a pretty girl. But when they'd walked near the maze he hadn't been able to help himself. James had been on his mind since he'd arrived. Especially since his mother seemed so lost this weekend. He'd wanted to go there—but somehow he couldn't. Until Olivia was with him.

When he'd kissed her neck earlier he'd felt her shock. She'd trembled beneath his lips as if afraid that their tentative friendship had been ruined. He'd thought taking her to the maze might repair the damage he'd done. He didn't want to fight with her—quite the opposite. He wanted to be closer to her.

'Which is exactly why I need to stay away from her,' he mumbled to himself as he took another slug of whisky.

He wondered where she was. Probably downstairs with Bolton-Smythe and his wandering hands. Laughing and flirting and wearing one of those short dresses of hers.

He heard laughter in the library as he got closer. Bunny could be heard hooting at something and the dull tones of Hugo—or was it Casper?—rang out across the hall. He knew she'd be in there.

He shouldn't go in. He should try and get some work done, check on his mother. Find his father. But he didn't. He went into the library. They were all sitting around his father's prized Egyptian alabaster offering table.

Bunny saw him first. 'Ed—there you are! Come on—deal him in, Casper. Poker, darling.'

'Not Ed. I've fallen into that trap before. He'll rob us all,' grumbled Casper unsociably.

'No, don't deal me in. I'm not playing. I'll just watch.' Edward saw Olivia at the table but he avoided her eyes. She didn't say anything and didn't look up at him either.

He found a seat at the other end of the room and picked up a book that was sitting nearby and pretended to read.

A hoot came from the table. 'You've lost again, Fiona. Terrible luck.' Bunny laughed and dealt the cards again. 'Are you playing this time, Olivia, or are the rules still too confusing for you, dear?'

Edward resisted the urge to stand. He wanted to see what Olivia would say to Bunny's obvious provocation. He almost hoped she'd cry and leave the room. Deep down, though, he knew that even if she did it was almost certain he wouldn't like her any less.

Olivia's face reddened. 'I think I've figured it out, Bunny.'

'Excellent. How about we make this more interesting, then?'

Casper's high-pitched voice chimed in and the muscles in Edward's neck tensed.

'What do you have in mind, Casp?'

'Strip poker, obvs.'

Bunny's horsey friend sucked in a gasp. 'Casp, no. Strip poker is for sad weirdos and women who wear kitten heels.'

'Then it's perfect for you, Rosie.'

Rosie laughed a very loud and annoying bray before turning her gaze onto Edward.

'How about you, Ed? Do you want to play strip poker?'

She tossed her hair off her shoulder and gazed at him in a way he was sure she thought was seductive.

'No, thanks.'

'They don't play strip poker in the provincials, Casper.' Hugo stood and lit his cigarette. 'They'd scare the wildlife.'

Edward didn't miss Hugo's pointed look towards Olivia and Fiona. Or the muffled laugh from Bunny. Apparently neither did Olivia.

'Strip poker sounds fun. Deal me in.'

Her chin was up. That bravado she brought out whenever she was nervous was back. He wanted to tell her not to play their game. But he didn't. He glanced at Olivia. Tonight she had on a tight black dress and not much else, and her hair was pulled up on to the top of her head.

Sitting to Olivia's right was Will, and Edward wondered if his brother had ever touched her. Or kissed her. His blood burned at the thought. Edward's leg started to jiggle, so he stood and paced to the other end of the room.

'What have you got, Olivia?' asked horsey Rosie sweetly.

Olivia blanched. Edward suspected she didn't play much poker.

'Ahhh…'

'C'mon, love. Throw down your cards. We haven't got all night.' Hugo was irritable. He was probably losing and worried everyone would laugh at his third nipple.

'Well, I fold,' announced Bunny with a flourish of cards.

'Good—we've already seen everything you have, Bunny. Time to see some new blood.' Casper's eyes were set on Olivia as everyone hooted at his not-very-hilarious comment.

Edward pushed his teeth together. Hadn't he told that idiot he didn't want to see his face for the rest of the weekend?

Olivia laid out her cards. A pair. Not good. Fiona threw in two pairs. A roar went up and they all beat the table and called for Olivia to 'take it off'. She smiled nervously and Edward was sure she could see his heart beating through his chest. There wasn't much to take off. She only had on the dress and a pair of shoes. *Please choose the shoes*, he begged.

She made a show of standing up and his mouth went dry. The dress fitted her curves perfectly. She turned around and Edward started to panic—but his eyes didn't leave Olivia. If she took her dress off he'd stop her. He couldn't let anyone else see… Wait. What was he saying? She didn't belong to him, he reminded himself. She could show anyone. He had no rights to her.

His shoulders tightened again as she turned and smiled at them all.

She reached up and unhooked her great big dangly earrings, smiled, and put them in the centre of the table.

Casper grumbled and the others laughed and Edward felt the tension leave his body. But it jacked up again when they dealt out another round. This time it was Bunny's turn to take something off and she quickly whipped off her top. No one blinked.

Will lost and removed his tie. Fiona lost and her shoes went into the centre. Olivia lost again and her shoes were placed on his father's antique table.

Then they played another round after Casper had filled Olivia's wine glass right to the top. There were only two players left. Casper and Olivia. What the hell would she take off this time? There was nothing left but that dress. He could hear the grandfather clock tick loudly as he waited.

She lost.

He saw the look in Casper's eyes. He'd been watching her closely all night, laughing at her jokes and putting his greasy hand on her leg from time to time. Edward felt like punching him.

'Oh, come on, nobody's looking. Just take your dress off. I'm sure it wouldn't be the first time.'

Bunny's friend Rosie laughed hysterically at Bunny's terrible joke.

'Enough. You don't have to do it, Olivia.' Edward's gruff voice echoed through the large room. Everyone turned to face him. Finally he felt Olivia's eyes on him and he stared at her. That familiar defiant tilt lifted her chin. Her pretty mouth became a tight white line.

'I'm perfectly able to pay my debts,' she ground out.

Casper licked his lips and it took every ounce of control in Edward's body not to hit him.

Olivia snaked a hand down the back of her dress and wriggled. What was she doing? She put another hand in her sleeve and wriggled again. Then, in seconds, she pulled her black lacy bra off and threw it on the table. Her breasts sank a little lower in her dress and he could clearly see the outline of her nipples. Standing to attention. Begging to be kissed and licked and—God help him—sucked.

He had to walk away. This woman was trying to kill him.

'Deal me in.'

Everybody stopped talking to look at him.

She didn't look at him, but picked up her cards.

'Call.' Her voice was soft and seductive but still she didn't look at him.

Edward looked at his cards. Four of a Kind. He couldn't lose. Unless someone had a Straight Flush. But that was unlikely.

There were only three of them left. Olivia, Will and himself.

Olivia looked him square in the eye and he felt as if he'd been hit. His eyes shifted to those heavy breasts that bounced when she moved. He wasn't going to last much longer.

He spread his cards out on the table.

Will tossed his useless cards into the middle of the table. Olivia stood solid, but she was bluffing. He could tell by the tightness of her lips—she had nothing. Slowly she fanned her cards out.

Straight. She'd lost.

CHAPTER TWELVE

WITH HER EYES locked on his, Olivia stood. Edward stopped breathing. Her eyes weren't covered in that black stuff, like last night, but they were blazing blue. Bluer than he'd ever seen them. With her eyes still on him she moved her sensual body until she was standing up with her hands on her hips.

'You win,' she said. 'I've got nothing else. You'll have to have my dress.'

She turned and her fingers reached for her zipper. Everyone was silent. Edward's gaze zeroed in on her back. He felt as if there was only the two of them in the room. She slowly pulled the zipper down, exposing her smooth tanned skin inch by excruciating inch. Further down it went, until the dress fell off one shoulder. She held it up but kept pushing the zip down.

All he could hear was his own breathing. His trousers pulled across the front and he had to push his legs wider apart to allow for the extra length that was now there. He felt harder than he ever had in his life. Rockhard. When he saw a telltale dimple in the small of her back he jumped up, almost knocking the damn table over in the process.

'Stop.'

She turned her head.

'What for?'

'I have a deal for you.'

'What kind of deal?'

'Double or nothing. If you win you get to make me do anything you want until midnight.'

She lifted an eyebrow. 'Like what?'

'Anything.' He wanted her to lift that zipper. He could hear Casper's heavy breathing beside him. 'Want me to strip naked and go in to dinner? I'll do it.'

'Oh. My. God. That's brilliant!' howled Bunny. 'Yes, do it. Make him bark like a dog every time Dad tells someone off.'

'What if I lose?'

'Then *you* have to do what *I* say.'

She considered him, her eyebrow cocked and those blue eyes on fire. Then she zipped up her dress and sat down.

'Deal.'

Never had a game of poker been so serious in the Winchester house. The cards were dealt, drinks poured. Everyone sat in coiled anticipation. Edward's palms were damp. He could win this.

Olivia's eyes were unreadable. She smiled and set her cards down.

'Call.'

He flipped his cards over. A Full House. She could beat it. But she wouldn't. Her eyes flickered with confusion. Then she flipped her cards over and his brain froze.

Four of a Kind.

She'd won.

The room went up in hoots of laughter.

But Olivia wasn't smiling. She stood slowly—a seductive movement that heated his blood.

'Well, what do you want?' he asked.

'Follow me.'

Olivia had spotted the conservatory on her way back that afternoon. It was located at the rear of the house and was filled with leafy plants and colourful flowers. She wanted to be alone. With Edward.

Inside the conservatory it was warm. The heaters overhead glowed, trying desperately to warm the foreign flowers. At one end sat two chairs that could be laid right back and Olivia headed for them. Edward followed. She wasn't sure what she was going to say to him—and she definitely didn't know what she was going to make him do tonight.

Relaxing into a chair, she realised that she could see straight through the roof. But there were no stars out tonight. Edward silently sat next to her and she sneaked a look at him. The long column of his neck was tilted and the lump in his throat stuck out. She longed to touch him. To run her fingers along his neck and over his hard shoulders, down the mounds of his chest and to his stomach. But he wouldn't want that. She looked up at the ceiling again.

'So—what's my punishment to be?'

'I haven't decided yet. Something embarrassing. And humiliating.'

'Sounds fair.'

They were silent for a while as the tension surrounding them started to crackle. Olivia needed to defuse the situation. If Edward suspected what she was feeling right now she was sure he'd leave. And she didn't want him to do that. Not again. Not now they were alone.

'What do you do, Edward—for a living—exactly?'

Olivia felt his deep brown eyes warm her skin.

'I work for the Treasury. I look after Fiscal Policy and Statistics.'

'Wow. That sounds exciting,' she teased.

He looked up, craning his neck back. The angles of his cheekbones stood out against the warm light of the heaters. 'What do you do? Besides going to parties and having a good time?'

Olivia flinched. Was that how he saw her?

'I work in insurance. Well, I do now. Before that I sold real estate, and before that I was in marketing.'

'The Artful Dodger?'

He was teasing her. She did feel a bit as if she was dodging. She laughed. 'Something like that.'

They fell into silence again.

'What's going on here this weekend?' she asked quietly after a time.

'It's called a wedding. When two people meet and fall in love...'

'No.' She threw him a wry look. 'With you. What's going on with you...and me?'

Edward's eyes met hers. 'What do you mean?'

'You seem so angry at me. Then you're all lovely and nice. Then you're angry again. Is there something in particular I've done to annoy you, or is this your usual personality?'

She wondered if he'd tell her the truth. She wondered if he'd say that he was annoyed because she was trashy and throwing herself at him and that he actu-

ally couldn't stand her. Or would he be his usual polite self and lie?

He turned back to the ceiling. 'I don't know, Olivia.
I'm not myself this weekend. You should probably just
ignore me.'

She felt the anger rise in her. Edward had ridiculed
her, lectured her, put her to bed, kissed her neck and
held her hand while walking through a love maze. And
now he'd lost to her in a poker game. She was going to
get the truth out of him one way or another.

'You should try being more honest.'

His head snapped around to look at her. 'Honest?
Says the girl who smothers herself in slap and dresses
like a hooker when she's nothing like that at all?'

Olivia blinked. 'I do not *smother* myself in slap.'

'You wear too much make-up.'

She thought about that for a second. Make-up did a
lot to hide her imperfections—and what was she supposed to do? Expose her ugliness to everyone? If he
knew what lay underneath that make-up he might not
be so keen for her to take it off. But then…he'd seen
underneath, hadn't he? When he'd taken her make-up
off. Maybe that was why he kept pushing her away.
He knew what he would have to face in the morning.

She turned to the sky and her stomach felt heavy.
Her heart felt heavy and her arms were heavy at her
sides. 'Everybody has something to hide,' she said.

'What are you hiding, Olivia? Why are you the perpetual party girl? Why do you feel the need to throw
yourself at dropkicks like Bolton-Smythe?'

Olivia sat up. 'Throw myself? I have not thrown
myself at anyone.'

Edward sat up too, and faced her. 'But you don't tell them to leave. You tolerate them. Why?'

He was angry. She could see it in the lines in his forehead and the way his hands gripped the side of the lounger. Angry? Why would he be angry? Unless he was… No. He couldn't be jealous. He didn't want her. He couldn't. But maybe Edward was one of those men who didn't like to lose. Perhaps he just wanted to be the one to score with the easy Aussie chick first.

She stood up and moved slowly until she was right in front of him, her breasts level with his lips. She only had to push a little closer and he'd be able to place his lips around her nipple and suck. The idea made her shiver. She needed to stay in control. She was going to teach him that she wasn't as easy as he thought.

Slowly Olivia dragged her hands up past her hips and over the curve of her breasts until she reached her hair. Then she pulled out the pins and let her hair fall down in a long curtain that surrounded her shoulders. His lips parted and his eyes locked with hers. Hard.

'What game are you playing, Olivia?'

'No game.' She smiled, moving closer, so his lips were mere inches from her breasts. 'I'm just trying to get you to be honest with me.'

Honest? The woman wanted *honest*? What he honestly wanted to do was drag her over to the wall, lift her barely-there dress up and take her. Like a wild animal.

He loosened his grip. This was getting out of control. She knew how he felt and she was teasing him— taunting him. She had no intention of giving herself to him. Once this weekend was over she'd move on to the next party. He and his broken family would be forgotten. Time to take back control.

Carefully he lifted his hands, letting them slide over her hips and dip into her waist. Then he pushed harder to feel the sides of her breasts, before cupping them and flicking his thumb over her now-hard nipples. She gasped and her arms fell to her sides. That was better. He was in charge now.

'Tell me about your life in Australia, Olivia. Tell me about your family. Tell me why you're here and why you play so many silly games.'

He heard the shake in her voice when she spoke but he still didn't let go, flicking her nipple again when she hesitated.

'I have a sister. A very beautiful, very talented sister.' She stopped talking so he flicked again. Then she went on in a rush, 'Ahh… She plays tennis for Australia. She's tall and beautiful.'

He didn't say anything. Just waited for her to continue. His hands stayed where they were even though he longed to massage her soft breasts.

'And then there's my mother. And that's it. Just the three of us.'

'What about your father?' he demanded.

'He died when I was twelve. He had a heart attack on the front lawn, mowing the grass.'

Edward let his hands drop to her waist and held her there. He hadn't been expecting that. 'Olivia. I'm so sorry.'

He knew exactly what she was going through. And he knew how something like that could change a person for ever.

CHAPTER THIRTEEN

SHE LOOKED DOWN and met his eyes, then pushed his hands away and sat down. The moment was gone. 'You don't have to feel sorry for me. My dad and I didn't really get on. Anastasia was always his favourite. She cried for weeks afterwards, but I...' She turned to the roof. 'I didn't really feel anything.'

'Olivia.'

He held out a hand. Her words didn't match the shake in her voice and they didn't match the grief that spread across her face. He wanted to hold her, but she wouldn't let him. Her wall had gone back up.

'I don't miss him. Really.' She really didn't. She'd barely known him—he'd spent every weekend away with Ana, coaching her for tennis. So why did the tears well in her eyes? 'My mum took over coaching Ana. That became our life. Tennis. Every day. Summer and winter. Until I left home.'

'Did you play?'

'Couldn't hit a bowling ball.' Olivia laughed, but she didn't look at him. If she saw those big brown eyes looking at her she'd cry. She preferred his cruel teasing to this. Preferred his hands on her body, as he showed her what she could never have, to this.

'So what were you good at?'

Olivia thought about it. Nothing. She couldn't think of anything. She let out a sigh. She'd lost control. Her nipples were still hard from where he'd flicked them. He'd challenged her earlier when she'd tried to show him she could resist him and she'd lost. The feel of his hands on her breasts and the warmth of his breath on her stomach only proved what she already knew. When Edward was around resistance was impossible. He brought her out of herself and made her feel something she wasn't. He made her want something she could never have. Especially not with him.

'We're supposed to be talking about your punishment.'

She sat up to face him. He looked gorgeous tonight. Dressed in a tuxedo. She'd almost fallen off her chair when he'd walked in the library. His black hair was slicked back and his jaw was freshly shaved. She could smell his cologne. He was still watching her, his forearms resting on his wide thighs. She felt the urge to touch him bubble up inside her again. So badly that she had to stand up.

'What should I make you do?' She caught a whiff of his scent and moved quickly because it was filling her head and making her knees weak. As was the way he was looking at her. Focussed and steady.

'I could make you be my slave. Fetch my drinks; feed me my dinner... No.' She paced the room, taking in the orange and pink of the tropical flowers that were reaching for the heaters—avoiding the chilly windows that looked out over the frosty lawns.

'I know.' She came to sit opposite him again, realising in that second what his ultimate punishment would be. 'I want you to kiss me.'

He didn't move, simply raised his eyebrow.

'I've already done that.'

His deep voice vibrated through her and she felt the oxygen all around her start to thin.

'Not like that. Properly. I want you to kiss me like you can't live without me. Like you'll die if you can't kiss me.'

That'll teach him. He thought she threw herself at men. He thought she was gagging for it. He thought she'd fall at his feet when their lips locked. But she wouldn't. Not this time. She was going to show him that she was in charge of her emotions and that he didn't affect her. Not now. Not now she knew he was playing with her. Teasing her.

He shifted and his lips parted. Her heart beat up a hard, steady beat. She shifted forward and pursed her lips, tightly shutting her eyes. Just a kiss. Just lips on lips. Nothing more. She had to get Edward out of her system because she'd never be in his.

'Stand up.'

His voice growled and her eyes flew open.

'What?'

'Stand up,' he ordered as he stood above her, looking down. 'Move over there. If I'm going to do this, I'm going to do it properly.'

She stood up. Perhaps this wasn't such a great idea. His commanding voice was making her shake, and the heat of him behind her was making her legs a little unsteady. Why did she always think she was tough? She wasn't so tough.

'Stand there,' he told her, and she stood in front of

the window, next to a line of hot-pink orchids. She could feel the chill from the window behind her back and the heat on her forehead from the heater above. He watched her before moving, prowling around her.

'You are beautiful, Olivia…'

'No, you don't have to say that…' she protested, but he stopped her. He put his thumb against her bottom lip and his eyes went hard. They were dark and somehow…dangerous. Her heart stopped beating.

'Quiet.'

He prowled again, not touching her with his hands but touching her everywhere with his eyes. She felt naked, exposed…and more beautiful than she had ever felt in her life.

'You are funny and charming and the most frustratingly annoying woman I've ever met…'

She started breathing again, ragged and uneven. A fiery heat spread over her body and her nipples hardened. She couldn't help but push her breasts out, trying to touch him as he prowled past again. Everything stopped except the throbbing that had begun deep, deep down in her centre.

'Do you know what I want to do to you?'

His voice had lowered and Olivia had to close her eyes against him. She felt the hotness of his breath as he came closer and leaned down to brush her neck with his lips.

'I want to rip that silly dress off and hold you up against the wall…'

Her breathing became more erratic as his lips reached the spot underneath her ear where her tattoo lay.

'Poi voglio fare sesso con te.'

The words were rough and raw, and Olivia had no idea what he'd said but his voice was deep and sexy and his manly scent was assaulting her nostrils and she wanted him to kiss her. To lift her up and drive himself into her.

She gasped and opened her eyes, and all of a sudden his mouth pushed hard onto hers. She felt him, forceful and needy. He held her shoulders, then his hands slipped down her arms until his fingers laced with hers. His knee pushed up against her centre, parting her legs, and she fell open for him, pushing forward to give him more. She wanted him closer, wanted his hot lips all over her skin. He tilted his head and she opened her mouth, letting him in, getting lost in the feel of his hot, lush mouth sliding against hers. He made her feel so alive, so desirable that she just wanted more and more of him. His mouth moved down her neck, planting open-mouthed kisses on her skin and making the air around them feel thin and hard to suck in.

He kissed lower and lower, tugging at her dress until her bare breast was exposed to him. He stopped and moved his head back, looked at it for a second, before letting out a groan and taking her nipple into his mouth. Hard. He sucked and kissed and nipped and soothed and Olivia slipped her fingers into his hair and pulled. Then she pushed him closer, wanting to feel the relief of his rough tongue against her.

Something was happening. Something Olivia didn't understand. It was wild and manic and she never wanted it to stop. He pushed her dress further down, exposing the other breast, and moved to give it his attention. Giving her his attention, as if she deserved it. As if she was worth it.

'Edward...' she whispered, barely able to breathe let alone talk.

He groaned in response and she felt the vibration move all the way through her breast and rush down to her throbbing centre.

'Touch me,' she begged, and his hands moved slowly over her hip to the hem of her dress.

His long fingers trailed their way up her thigh until they hit the lace of her underwear. Then he was inside them, stroking her slickness and sending her mad with want. She pushed against him, felt his mouth still on her nipple, and he pushed his fingers in deeper. She tried not to scream out but she couldn't help it. He moved his mouth up to hers and kissed away the noise.

'La mia bella,' he said, in a way that made her weak. 'You drive me crazy, Olivia.'

He was driving *her* crazy. She threw her head back at the pleasure his fingers were sending through her body and could feel his eyes on her, watching her.

'So beautiful,' he said gruffly as he nuzzled at her neck, breathing heavily.

She did feel beautiful. With this gorgeous man worshipping her body with his tongue and stroking his long fingers inside her she felt like the most beautiful girl in the world. But she wasn't. She was plain old Olivia. So with all the energy she could muster, she pushed him away, tried to slow her breathing. In front of her, Edward's breaths were coming shallow and fast. His lips were swollen and his eyes still dark. The heat between them was making her dizzy. She pushed at his chest again, making him step further back.

'If that's how you kiss, I'd like to see how you make love.'

He stepped closer and she felt his large frame push her against the window.

'How about I show you?'

'No.' Her eyes widened. *'No.'* She pushed him again, more firmly this time. 'I'm good.'

But she wasn't good. She was bad. So, so bad. She should never have asked for that kiss. She'd thought it would be good—she'd had a sample outside this afternoon in the freezing rain. But his voice and his smell and that Italian! Where had that come from?

Her body still buzzed and her skin still tingled. A cool breeze blew across her chest and she realised she was still exposed to him. She lifted her dress and righted it on her shoulders.

Edward took one more look at her before he moved away, running a hand through his mussed-up hair and putting one hand in his pocket. She watched him walk away as she shifted the hem of her dress down.

He shook his head and ran his hand through his hair again. He walked over to the window on the other side of the room and rested a hand on the glass, staring out.

'Edward,' she started, unsure what to do or what to say. Her heart was still thumping in her chest. She shouldn't have done that. She'd forced him to kiss her. She'd shown him what she wanted deep inside and made him do something he didn't want to do. And now he regretted it. She could see it in the way his shoulders slumped. 'I…I'm sorry.'

'Apologising again?'

He turned to face her and she could see the fury in his eyes. A ball knotted in her stomach. She'd done exactly what she'd sworn she wouldn't. She'd thrown herself at him and now he thought even less of her than before.

'I lost control, Edward. But you can't be angry at me for that. You did too. I could feel it.' Her heart still beat heavily and she crossed her arms over her chest, trying to calm the beat and the disappointment that was creeping over her skin. Disappointment in herself and disappointment in him. She'd hoped he would see beneath her faults but he didn't. He was just like all the others.

He shook his head and turned back to the window.

'I should be the one apologising. I should have stopped. I should have known better.'

'You had to kiss me. We had a deal.'

He turned and the fury was back. He was in front of her in three long strides and the sudden sight of him up close made Olivia breathe in too deeply. Lights danced in her head. She felt faint. And then his big hands gripped the tops of her arms.

'You think I kissed you because of some stupid deal?' His deep chocolate eyes didn't look warm now. They looked hard and angry. 'I kissed you because I wanted to. I needed to.'

CHAPTER FOURTEEN

OLIVIA WATCHED EDWARD'S eyes explore her face. As if he was drinking her in. It made her feel different. He'd wanted her. He'd needed her. Maybe for just a moment, but it was a moment she'd remember for ever.

'You needed to?' Her voice shook a little as she spoke. 'Why?'

His eyes softened and Olivia felt herself drowning in them. Everything about him made her feel something. His anger, his warmth, the way he pushed her away and pulled her back. It all made her emotions scatter and it made her feel out of control, but safe all at once. A lump formed in her throat. She'd never felt this much for anyone. As if she wanted him so much it actually physically hurt. And as if the idea she couldn't have him was going to cause long-lasting scars.

'You make me do things I shouldn't, Olivia.' His deep voice vibrated right where his chest almost touched hers. 'You make me want things I can't have.'

He was angry at her. He didn't want this. He didn't want her.

'I got carried away, Edward.' She didn't normally do that… It was him and the way he looked and the way he smelled and the way he tasted… Her eyes rested on his mouth and she shuddered at the memory of his tongue. 'I shouldn't have done that. I only asked you to kiss me because I wanted to punish you. I wasn't… I didn't expect that to happen.' His eyes stopped the exploration of her face and looked right into hers.

'You did that to punish me?'

Yes, she had. She'd wanted him to feel the way she had felt when he'd pushed her away this afternoon, but it had backfired. Now she felt even worse than she had then.

'It was just a kiss. Nothing more.' What was it about him that made her braver, bolder? Around him she seemed more willing to take chances. But she shouldn't. She knew what would happen if she took a chance. What she should have done is kept away from Edward. She knew he had a way of scaling her walls which made her act differently. Normally she would wait for someone to notice her. Hope that someone would kiss her the way Edward just had. But they never did. They always chose her sister or one of her pretty friends. One of her confident friends. Never her.

For some reason, though, she didn't feel the same way around Edward. She felt more assertive, more comfortable in her skin. As if showing her true self was what he wanted. But he didn't. And he would never want her the way she wanted him. And now she'd gone and stuffed everything up by making him kiss her… and then making him touch her. Shame flooded her veins. She had thrown herself at him. Shamelessly. And he didn't want her. She'd made a fool of herself. Again. No wonder he couldn't get away fast enough.

They stayed like that for too many minutes. The air

grew uncomfortable and Olivia regretted every minute of it.

'Here you two are.' The ringing tones of Bunny made her jump. 'We've been looking all over for you.'

Olivia stepped away, tugging at the hem of her dress.

'Ed. Dinner's about to start. Are you coming?'

'In a minute,' he barked at Bunny. Angry again.

Bunny left and Olivia didn't dare move. Edward's eyes turned to her and they flashed. She took in his mussed-up hair and his slightly off-centre bow tie. She'd never seen him look sexier and all she wanted to do was throw herself at him again. But she didn't. And she never would again.

Edward turned to Olivia. She looked as he felt. Battle-shocked. He'd been trying to push her. He knew that now. He'd wanted her to admit she had feelings for him. The way he had feelings for her. He'd wanted to know how she felt. And now he knew. Olivia loved fun and adventure. She moved around and partied with the likes of Bunny and her friends. She'd only asked him to kiss hcr to tease him. Underneath all her beauty she was just as insincere as all the others.

'You have till midnight to tell me what you want me to do. Then this deal is over.' He wanted to get away from her. He felt tricked and stupid. He thought he'd seen an honesty in her that didn't exist and he now felt like a fool.

Olivia crossed her arms across her chest. 'The deal's off. It was stupid anyway.'

'No, it's not.' Edward could hear the harshness in his voice but he couldn't keep it out. He was angry. At Olivia for provoking him and at himself for allowing her to. That kiss had been too much. He'd wanted her more than he'd ever wanted anyone. He would have made love to her right here in his mother's conservatory if she hadn't pushed him away. He was out of control and he didn't like it. Control was all he had left. 'When I make a deal I stick to it. You get to tell me what to do, so figure something out.'

'All right. I have a deal for you. From now until midnight you have to tell the truth.' She uncrossed her arms and waved them as she talked. Her cheeks burned red and her eyes flashed with anger. 'You need to be honest, Edward, with me and with yourself. I know how you feel, I know what you want, and it's time you admitted it to yourself.'

She wanted him to admit how he felt. She wanted him to say that he wanted her more than he'd ever wanted anyone. But then she'd just pull away and tease him again. She wanted the power and he wasn't about to hand it to her.

'I'm always honest, Olivia. And if it's honesty you want, I'll give it to you. You should stay away from me. I'm going to hurt you. That's what I do. I neglect people. I'm selfish and irresponsible. Even if you get under my skin you need to know that I'm not the man you think I am.'

Edward heard the words pour from his mouth. He wanted to keep her away. He didn't want her tempting him again. He'd felt her respond to his kiss. Sweet and deep and loving. As if she wanted him as much as he wanted her. But that would never happen. Olivia didn't want him. She was just teasing him. She needed someone strong and brave and trustworthy. He could barely take care of his family—there was no way he'd be able to take care of her too.

For once her face was blank. Normally he could read what she was feeling, but this time he couldn't tell.

'What do you mean, I get under your skin?' she asked quietly, her arms still crossed.

'You know exactly what I mean.' She was pure temptation in that dress, with her blue eyes big and innocently looking up at him and those lips begging to be kissed again. 'You make me lose control, Olivia. I'm not myself around you.'

She stepped closer and the air thinned. She unfolded her arms and took yet another step. Slowly she raised her hands and rested them on his chest. Her hands were cool and he had to tell himself to breathe. She was too close and his heart was beating too fast. The memory of her breasts, the feel of her slick beneath his fingers... It was too much. As if he was a werewolf and she was the moon—he felt like howling.

'Don't, Olivia.'

'Why not? What's so bad about losing control?'

Her voice was low and seductive and it soothed him.

'I never lose control.' He ground the words out, keeping his body very still. If she moved those hands he'd be gone again. He'd lose control and he *never* lost control. Not any more. Not since... 'You need to stay away from me.'

The spark of hurt in her eyes was unmissable. She stepped back and he shifted his head from side to side, running his fingers through his hair where Olivia had messed it up. He closed his eyes and turned away, trying to get the image of her out of his mind. Hot, out of control and exactly what his body ached for.

She wanted the truth.

He'd show Olivia what it meant to tell the truth.

'I don't do relationships, Olivia. If anything were to happen between us this weekend it would just last the weekend. A fling. Nothing more.'

He wanted to know what her reaction would be. Would she agree? His body throbbed when he thought of her. Sex. That was all this was. An animal need for her beautiful body and those pouty lips.

'You want to…to have a fling with me?'

He turned around and saw her standing with her arms still crossed across her chest. Her face was pale and he immediately regretted what he'd said. She acted like a woman of the world but right here, with a myriad of flowers surrounding her, she looked like an innocent in the Garden of Eden. And he was tempting her—like the snake he was.

'No. I don't know. Damn it, Olivia, I don't know what to think. You need to leave me alone.' And before he could say anything else he regretted he turned and strode from the room.

Dinner was served and Olivia sneaked in and sat at the end of the table. The only light came from the tall silver candelabra. This was a special occasion. The eve of the wedding.

Edward's vision of Olivia was obstructed by a candelabrum. Which was a relief—because when he looked at her she made him think about things he shouldn't. Like quitting his job and taking her off on a plane to the Caribbean and living like hippies. Making love all day and only stopping to eat mangos and drink wine. He switched his mind back to the food in front of him.

Congealed duck fat and vegetables. It was terrible.

'How's the terrine, Ed?' Bunny asked sweetly from across the table.

He'd revealed to her the result of his deal with Olivia and his sister was milking it. She'd already asked him what he thought of Rosie's outfit and how he thought England's chances were in the Rugby World Cup. *'Non-existent,'* he'd said—which had made his rugby-loving patriotic father go off like a rocket. He'd only just settled down.

'It's interesting, Bunny.'

'In what way?' she asked innocently, taking a bite of hers.

'In the way that it tastes like the jellied insides of a rabid squirrel.'

'Edward. Please. We're trying to eat,' his father scolded.

Bunny giggled and almost spat out the sip of wine she'd taken.

'What's got in to you this evening? Honestly—in my day there was only polite conversation around the dinner table,' grumbled his father loudly as he topped up his wine.

'Just trying to be honest, Dad.' He avoided Olivia's eye.

'There is a place for honesty, Edward, and it's not at the dinner table,' his father retorted.

Thankfully the Blowhards had decided dinner with the Winchesters wouldn't be much fun and had chosen to dine in the village. That left only immediate family. And Olivia. And Bunny's horsey friend Rosie.

'Who has a wedding in December, Will? The weather's terrible. You could have waited until Summer. We would have had a much better selection of bridesmaid dresses then.'

'I'm sorry, Bunny, that was my fault. If I'd known you were so against a winter wedding I would have moved it.' Fiona's meek voice came from the other end of the table.

'What are you going on about?' Edward's father roared from the head of the table. 'Are you complaining again, Bunny? It's not your wedding; let them do what they want! Perhaps if you stopped hanging around with those deadbeat friends of yours someone would think about marrying *you*.'

'I'm not interested in getting married, Daddy.'

She might not be, but she sounded a little edgy.

'Well, you should be. What else have you got? A ridiculous job in PR—as if that's a real job—and let's face it: you're not getting any younger. The clock's ticking, girl, and it's time you got moving.'

'Righto, Dad—I think that's enough.' Edward could tell Bunny was getting upset. He didn't want any trouble tonight. He needed to take back control.

Bunny sat silent. Her face was impassive but Edward could see her jaw clench.

'Marriage is not for everybody, Daddy. There are plenty of people who don't want to get married and there are plenty of people who will never get married. I mean, look at Olivia. She's happy to be the party girl at every event. Do you see her complaining? No. She just puts on another ridiculous dress and wraps her arms around another faceless idiot. Not everyone is cut out for love, Daddy.'

The room was silent. Bunny's face was bright red. Edward wondered if she was happy with herself. She looked him directly in the eye, lifted her wine glass and took a long, deep sip.

The only sound was the clinking of cutlery on plates.

Edward flicked his eyes to Olivia. He wondered how she was feeling. If it was anything like him, she was feeling pretty raw.

'That is enough, Bunny. Apologise to Olivia.' Edward's voice was hard, uncompromising. He'd been trying to keep everyone happy all weekend. But Bunny had pushed it. She always pushed it. And normally he ignored it, but not tonight. Tonight Olivia wanted him to be honest. And he was going to be honest.

He could admit it now. Olivia drove him wild and he liked her. She was sexy and funny and sweet and passionate and he wanted her. Even if it was just for one weekend. He needed to tell her that he wanted her. He was sick of lying. He was sick of his family picking at each other. He was sick of no one knowing how anyone felt.

The table was still silent, waiting for Bunny's retort. Tension crackled along with the fire.

'How's work, Eddie?' Edward's mother's weak voice made him look up. It made everyone else look up too.

'How do you *think* it is, Regina?' Edward's father roared from the other end of the table. 'The country's in a mess. That Prime Minister is an idiot—taxes everything that moves and won't pay attention to the real problems.'

Edward looked at his mother. She bowed her head. He looked at his father. Heat surged through him. It was enough. Olivia wanted the truth? He'd give her the truth.

CHAPTER FIFTEEN

WITH AN ANGRY scrape, Edward moved his chair back.

'I'd like to say a few words…'

Everyone stopped and looked up at him.

'This weekend we've all come home to celebrate something special. A wedding. Between Will and Fiona. Two people who love each other so much they can't stand the thought of not being together. They're going to spend a lot of money giving you a good party so you can celebrate their love for each other with them. What they *don't* want is a bunch of whingeing, whining ungrateful sods telling them where they should have their wedding and making them bend over backwards to make you lot happy.'

He went around the table and looked each of them in the eye. Even Olivia. Until he reached his mother.

'But there's someone missing tonight.'

His mother looked up and he saw the tears well in her big sad eyes. He almost stopped, but he didn't. Olivia wanted the truth and he was going to give it to her.

'James. My little brother. He should have been here tonight. He always loved a party. And even though we fought sometimes the four of us did everything together. And I miss him. I miss his laugh and I miss the way he thought he was invincible. And on the day James died something broke. This family. James would never have wanted that. He would have wanted us to remember him at times like this. Not be sniping and swiping and acting like a bunch of caged tigers in a circus.'

There were no sounds of cutlery this time. Just complete and utter silence.

Edward reached for his glass and lifted it high. 'These are the times we remember the people who can't be with us. To James.'

A long silence followed his speech, until Will cleared his throat.

'To James.'

'To James,' said Fiona.

Then Olivia spoke up. 'To James.'

Then Bunny. 'To James,' she said quietly.

He looked at his father, who lifted his glass and said gruffly, 'To my boy James.'

Then Edward looked at his mother. Her hand didn't move. She stared straight ahead, a strange, strangled smile on her face. Then she put her head in her hands and let out an ear-piercing wail.

Olivia jumped up and Bunny rushed to her mother's side. Then Fiona joined them and together the women lifted her from the table and took her out. Will stood up too. Edward met his brother's stare, then turned from them all and fled.

Honest? What the hell had he been thinking? No one ever wanted to hear the truth. He knew that. But Olivia… She'd insisted. Olivia, who knew nothing about honesty. Who had to get drunk to be honest. Yet she'd forced him to be honest and he'd sent his mother into hysterics.

'Ed. Mate…'

'Go away, Will.'

'You did the right thing…'

He wanted to throw something, or hit someone, but Will was too far away and the only thing on his father's desk worth throwing was the inkwell. James had brought it home from a naff market stall a month before he died. He glowered at it. Then turned his hard look onto Will.

'I don't want to talk about it.'

Will ignored him and sat in the leather armchair in front of the desk. He stretched his long legs out and put one foot on his knee. But that was Will. All ease and comfort. No worries, no responsibility. Like when he'd pushed Olivia aside for Fiona. Will felt no guilt about anything.

'I appreciated your words out there, mate…'

'I didn't do it for you.'

Will raised an eyebrow. 'Who *did* you do it for, then?'

He wasn't sure. Himself? Olivia? He didn't know. He swivelled around in the leather armchair and stared out of the window. The night was black—the clouds were out. It would probably snow tonight.

Will was silent and Edward was grateful for it. He needed to think.

'Want a drink?'

Will rose and went to his father's secret Scotch stash in the bookshelf. Edward heard the clunk of ice and the glug of the whisky. He took the glass when Will handed it to him and heard the creak of leather as Will sat.

'So, what's going on with you and Liv?'

That made Edward turn. 'What are you talking about?'

'It's pretty obvious you're keen. You have your tongue hanging out every time she walks past. I don't blame you, mate—she is pretty fit.'

Edward's eyes went hard. Was he being that obvious? He'd thought he'd kept himself pretty tame. Or was Will noticing because he was worried about what he'd given up?

'You're not supposed to be noticing.'

Will's brows furrowed. 'I'm getting married, not having my eyes plucked out.'

'If you wanted to look at her you should have kept her to yourself instead of throwing her over for Fiona.'

'I didn't throw her over. I'd only just met her.' Will stood and paced to the window.

'You never think about who gets in your way, Will. You never worry about who you might hurt. Did you ever think that maybe you hurt Olivia that night? No, of course not.'

Will swung around and stared at him hard. 'What's the matter, Ed—are you losing your touch? Have you found a woman who won't fall at your feet?'

'Don't be an idiot, Will. Olivia and I hardly know each other.'

'When I saw Fi I knew in a second that I would marry her. You don't need long to realise that you love someone.'

'I don't *love* her! This wedding has turned you into a blithering idiot.'

Will sauntered back to the chair and sat again, before taking a long sip and shooting his brother a sly look. Edward watched him, seething. In love? Only fools fell in love.

'How do you feel when she's not around? What are you thinking about most of the time? What are you going to do when she leaves?'

Edward balled his fists. If it wasn't his wedding tomorrow his brother would be sporting a very black eye. He wanted to open his mouth and deny it. Roar at Will for daring to suggest that he could let his emotions take over. But he didn't. He felt sick when she wasn't around. He thought about her all the damn time. And when she left…? He couldn't even think about that.

'That's not love. It's lust.'

'So you're in lust with her?'

Edward didn't answer. It was none of Will's business how he felt about Olivia. And besides, she didn't feel the same way.

Will took another slug of whisky. 'Well, you've stayed true to type anyway—I'll give you that.'

'I don't have a type.'

'Yes, you do. You always go for the women who will never get serious.'

Edward blinked. No, he didn't.

'You love the chase but you always make sure there's not enough to make it last.'

'That's not true.'

'Yes, it is. What about Perfect Penelope?'

'What about her?'

'Penelope was beautiful. Untouchable. Wasn't she some European princess or something? She used to complain all the time. No one would ever be good enough for Perfect Penelope.'

Penelope had been beautiful. But also boring. It had taken about three months for him to figure that out… and leave.

'And that other one—the French one—what was her name?'

'Giselle.'

'Giselle. She was a mad flirt.'

Giselle had been a disaster. Fun, friendly—too friendly. With every bloke she met. That hadn't lasted long either.

'And now Olivia.'

'Olivia's nothing like…the others.'

'Of course she is. She's hot and fun and not looking for anything serious. Perfect for you. You can have your weekend and then move on. No need to get serious; just the way you like it.'

Edward shifted in his chair. What did Will know? He didn't deliberately choose women he could never end up in a relationship with. Did he? Perhaps it was time he thought about settling down, with a steady, responsible woman he could rely on. Not a sexy, crazy woman he couldn't keep his hands off of. No, Olivia wasn't the type of girl one married. She liked a good time too much. Liked to do things her own way. And she didn't feel anything special for him anyway.

Except for that kiss. In the conservatory. She'd been holding on to him as if he was an oxygen mask and she needed him to breathe. And he'd liked it. He liked that she'd clung to him and wanted more. And he liked that he'd wanted more from her. Much more.

And therein lay the rub.

He wanted more than she was willing to give.

The woman was an expert at pulling him in and pushing him away. She couldn't stick at anything. All those jobs, no steady relationship… Something clenched in his chest. He'd finally found someone he could talk to and laugh with and relax around and she would be gone in two days. She'd fly away with her too-blonde hair and never look back. He wasn't sure he'd be able to let her go when the time came. Better not to even go there.

'Olivia might be all right for a bit of fun, but I can assure you I'm not interested in having fun with her.'

Will looked up and stared at something behind him. Edward swivelled in his chair and saw her. Standing in the doorway. Her face pale and her short black dress clinging desperately to her body. She still hadn't put her bra back on. Her breasts looked full and her nipples hard and his body heated at the memory of them bare in the conservatory.

The look of shock on her face was palpable. How much had she heard?

'Oh. I see.' That was all she said before turning and fleeing.

CHAPTER SIXTEEN

THE TEARS HIT Olivia's cheeks before she'd even left the doorway. She'd come to see if Edward was all right. She'd come to tell him his mother had settled down and was drinking tea in the drawing room. She'd come to tell him he'd been brave and strong and that she thought he was the nicest man she'd ever met.

'Olivia might be all right for a bit of fun, but I can assure you I'm not interested in having fun with her.'

His words ran over and over in her head. She'd been right. That was all she was good for. Fun. No one ever took her seriously. *He* didn't take her seriously. All she wanted to do was get into bed, wash her stupid make-up off, get this stupid dress off and cry herself to sleep.

How could she ever have thought he'd want her? Her, with her inappropriate dresses and her snub nose and her freckled skin? He'd told her to stay away. He'd warned her. But she was too stupid to listen. She thought that maybe he felt something for her too. He'd said she'd got under his skin. But that was just another lie. He felt nothing for her. He was just laughing about her to his brother. *Not interested*. That was what he'd said. Even after their walk to the rocks, their afternoon at the maze…that kiss. Even after all that—he still didn't want her. She was still unlovable.

She felt something inside her break and she hoped it wasn't her heart. Because if he broke her heart she wasn't sure if it would ever mend.

Slowly and deliberately she walked down the hall, counting the doors until she came to number seven. Her door. She put her hand on the handle.

'Olivia.'

Edward's deep voice behind her made her still.

'Wait.'

She turned slowly, her brain taking a while to catch up with her body.

'You misheard in there. Will and I were talking about something else. I can explain…'

He stepped closer and Olivia stepped back. She was up against the door. He was too big and too close and she was still feeling sick.

'Olivia…you have to listen to me.'

Real concern flashed across his features and it made her feel even sicker. She'd been humiliated. By a man she realised she cared for more than she'd cared for anyone in a long time. A man who had made her feel beautiful and desirable. But it was all lies. He hadn't been honest with her at all. Bunny was right. Some people weren't cut out for love. *She* wasn't cut out for love. No one could ever love her.

'Olivia…'

Edward lifted a finger to her face and touched her cheek. She flinched and let her head fall to the side.

'I wasn't saying what you thought I was…'

'I don't care what you were saying.'

'Olivia, please, we need to talk. I have to tell you… how I feel. What I want.'

She felt the anger that was simmering inside her pop and spit and start to boil over. 'I don't care what you want, Edward. I don't care what any one of you wants. You all see me as someone easy. Fun. In for a good time. Well, let me tell you something, Lord Winchester.' She stood up straight and took a step forward, poking her finger into his hard chest. He moved back, surprise evident on his face. 'I *like* being single. I *like* being alone.'

'Olivia…'

He didn't move. His eyes searched hers, then her face, as if he were desperately seeking something— perhaps a different answer. She wanted to give it to him, to tell him how she really felt. *Want me! Need me!* But the words wouldn't pass through her lips. She held them in her brain, in her eyes, and she met his gaze.

'Can't we talk about this?'

'No. You're exactly like all the others.'

She felt his heavy body move closer and saw his eyes narrow. His lips formed a thin line and she felt his anger push against her.

'Don't compare me with anyone else. I am me, and you are you. This is about us and no one else.'

His voice was low and quiet but it rumbled with a threatening growl. The pale hairs on the back of her neck stood to attention and she tried to back away, but behind her was the thick timber door.

She couldn't get enough air; it felt as if it was coming into her by short bursts only. His black gaze sent a prickle of heat across her skin and a bead of perspiration formed between her breasts.

'There is no you and me, Edward. You made that clear when you told Will you weren't interested in me.'

'I told Will I wasn't interested in having fun with you because I want more than that. More than one weekend.'

Liar. He was a liar. He thought she was worthless. Useless. Talentless. The spare. A body of organs in case her perfect sister needed a liver or a kidney or a couple of extra fingers. Pointless, ugly Olivia. The one no one wanted. The one no one even knew existed.

She pushed on his chest but he didn't move. She balled her fists and hit him but he still didn't move. So she punched and pushed and cried. *Want me, need me.* Her mind kept repeating the mantra over and over. *Want me, need me.* The voice screamed and her fists pounded into him until his strong arms came around her.

The hard edge of his shoulder pushed into hers. It forced her back further against the heavy door. His thigh pushed against her legs and she gasped as she involuntarily sucked in an Edward-laced breath.

'Olivia.'

His voice was soft and deep and calm and soothing but she struggled on. Wanting to hurt him, wanting to push him away.

'Olivia.'

He held her arms and squeezed her tighter. He held her until she stilled and the only sound was her quiet sobbing. Then she slipped her arms around his waist and he pulled her in tighter, his nose in her neck.

'My beautiful Olivia.'

His whispered words were making her shake and cry but he held her still, stroking her hair and kissing the tears on her cheeks. She looked up and met his soft brown eyes. He kept her close and looked right back at her, making her feel beautiful all over again.

'It's all right. I'm right here.'

Something hard caught in her chest. She slipped her hand behind her back, turned the handle and opened the door. With her other hand she slipped her palm into his, and when she felt the door open behind her she didn't think—just pulled him in.

Olivia pulled on Edward's hand, leading him further in. When she turned the tears were gone from her eyes, to be replaced with something different. Something much more seductive. Almost predatory.

'Stay with me.'

Her voice was urgent, desperate. She slipped her small hand into his other palm and pulled him towards her as she walked backwards. Her hair had come loose from the knot on top of her head she'd hastily rearranged before dinner and strands were hanging around her face. One side of her dress slipped from her shoulder, revealing her smooth skin beneath.

'Come on, Edward. I dare you. Just come with me.' Her eyes burned with challenge. Her voice was soft and melodic. Like a siren or a faerie. She looked wild and determined and he'd never wanted her more.

But he couldn't.

She was sad and angry and upset.

He couldn't take advantage of her when she was like that.

He had to think. For both of them. He held her hands tightly and brought his body up still.

'Olivia, it's been a rough night…for everyone.'

The sweet challenge in her eyes changed to something harder. She stopped moving and squeezed his hands.

'I need you, Edward.'

'You need a rest. It's a big day tomorrow. You need to sleep.'

Anger flicked over her features. 'What? Are you going to put me to bed again? Pull my blankets up and tell me to go to sleep like a good little girl?'

Her cheeks pinkened and more hair fell around her face. She shook her head to get it out of her eyes. Out of those ridiculously long eyelashes.

'But I'm not a good girl, Eddie. I'm a bad girl. A very bad girl.'

She let go of his hands and before he knew what she was doing she'd slipped her zipper down and let her dress fall to the ground. Edward's mouth dried up completely. His body grew even harder than it already was. She stood before him naked except for an absurdly undersized black pair of panties. Ludicrously undersized. One flick and they'd be gone.

His eyes took in her muscled stomach and her breasts. Perfect and heavy and her nipples were pointing to attention. He remembered the taste of them. The way they'd gone rock-hard as he swirled his tongue. He wanted to reach out, pull her into his arms, throw her on the bed and lose himself in her body. In every bump and curve and moan and shiver and sweet, soft taste. But when he reached her eyes he knew he couldn't. She wasn't turned on. She was angry. Furious.

'Olivia. What are you doing?'

'What does it look like?' She lifted her arms and he noticed the cording of muscles in her shoulders. She really worked out. 'I'm throwing myself at you. Giving myself to you on a platter.'

Her voice was hard, her face etched with fury—but her eyes. They were open wide and they looked far more innocent than her body. Far younger and far more vulnerable. Something was broken inside Olivia and he wasn't sure if he'd be able to fix it.

Slowly, he moved forward. He didn't touch her, just kept his eyes on hers and his voice low.

'If you throw yourself at me I'll catch you. What are you going to do then?'

Confusion flickered over her eyes and she seemed suddenly to realise he was close. She stepped back, a little unsure. He lifted his shoulders, slipped his jacket off and moved slowly closer, cautiously—keeping his eyes on hers. Her body twitched so he stood still—watching her; waiting until she stilled. Then he slipped his jacket around her shoulders.

'There,' he said quietly, his eyes still on hers.

She watched him for a second, her eyes open wide, and then she pulled his jacket off and shoved it at him.

'Fine. Forget it. If you don't want me I'll find someone who does. One of those London twits should be willing.'

She went to walk past him and he grabbed her arm, pulling her back to his body. He could feel her cold skin through his shirt. 'You're not going anywhere.'

CHAPTER SEVENTEEN

'LET ME GO.' Olivia's voice had changed. It was thick with dislike.

He held her steady. His blood was running hot now. There was no way in hell she was going outside of this room. Not like this. All fired up for revenge. And definitely not dressed in those outrageously small panties.

'I am here, Olivia. If you want to yell at someone, or punch someone, or…' He let his eyes slide over her face, taking in the curve of her jaw and the smooth skin of her neck. 'It'll be me. You're not going to be with anyone else tonight.'

Right at that moment he felt it. He was sure of what he was saying and the resolution felt so secure he didn't even question himself. She was his. No one else's. Whatever she wanted to do it would be to him.

The fire bounced off her eyes and he felt it on his. Hot. Greedy.

Still holding on to her arm, he picked his jacket up off the floor where it had fallen. 'Put this on.'

For a moment he thought she was going to yell at him or punch him, but she didn't say anything. She flicked her arm from his grasp and pulled the jacket from his hands, slipping her arms through it before heading to the bed and perching on the edge, her face turned away and her arms crossed in front of her.

She looked defiant and angry. But she wasn't getting away that easily. 'Now, talk to me.'

Olivia's heart was pumping. She could hear it in her ears. She could hear Edward's voice in her ears. *'Olivia might be all right for a bit of fun, but I can assure you I'm not interested in having fun with her.'*

She'd thought she had hardened up. She'd thought that no one's careless words could ever hurt her again. She'd thought she'd made peace with who she was and what she was. But obviously—the searing heat that ran through her body told her—she wasn't.

She was still the little girl lying awake, wondering why her parents didn't like her. Still that pimply teenager who was too shy to talk to the boys because she knew they wouldn't ever go for her. Still that silly party girl who drank too much and dodged responsibility. Dodged life.

Edward was right—the Artful Dodger. She'd made avoiding hurt an art form. But now instead of dodging her feelings she was smack-bang in the middle of them. She wanted to get away from them. She wanted to get out and find a stupid drunk London toff and have him throw insincere compliments at her and avoid dealing with the hurt. But Edward wouldn't let her.

She sneaked a sideways glance at him. He was sitting by the door in a flower-covered armchair. His long legs looked even longer as he leaned over on them, his forearms resting on his knees, his once perfect hair all messy and lying in waves across his forehead. He was looking at her. He was always looking at her. She felt like a fly caught in a web. As if she couldn't get away from him. And, like a spider, he was insisting she spill her guts.

She turned away again, shifting on the bed. She was naked and acting like a child. She knew it but she couldn't stop. She breathed in deeply, hoping it would calm her, but a waft of Edward's strong male scent surrounded her. The jacket was laced with his sexy smell and it was making her head spin.

'Olivia, look at me. We need to talk and I'm not going anywhere until we do.'

'You want to talk? Then tell me about James.'

Edward's face paled. She'd struck a nerve, exposed his weak spot, just as he had exposed hers. If he wanted her to spill then he would have to do the same. Edward could be lovely and kind, but there was a part of him that was all locked up. A part she couldn't get to and she needed to know.

'That's what I want to talk about.'

Edward stood up and paced. He strode to one side of the room and inspected the landscape picture that was hanging there.

'What do you want to know?' he asked quietly.

'Why doesn't anyone talk about him? I didn't even know you had another brother.'

Edward paced to the other side of the room. His muscular thighs strained against his black trousers and Olivia watched his legs until he stopped and spoke.

'It's hard for us. James was so young and it was a terrible time.'

His words hung in the air. His tone had changed. She could hear the pain and she didn't know why, so she didn't know what to say.

'What happened?'

'We were all at the lake. I got distracted and James paid the price.'

Olivia heard the raw pain in his voice and wanted to go to him, but she was sure he wouldn't want that. And she didn't want to torture him any more.

'I'm not the man you want me to be, Olivia. You need someone who can take care of you. Someone who can focus on you. And I can't. I have too many other things to focus on.'

Edward turned to face her. Even though she was wearing nothing but a tiny G-string—and she was alone in a strange room with a man who was almost a stranger—she felt safer than she had in a long time. He was telling her not to trust him but she had never trusted anyone more. Ever.

He stopped pacing and came to sit next to her on the bed. She could feel the warmth from his big body and hear him breathing. His face colour went back to normal and calm descended over him again.

Olivia stayed still.

He had followed her. He was still with her and right then she realised she didn't want him to leave. She didn't want him to give up on her.

'Did you mean it when you told Will you didn't want me?' Her throat was thick, but now was the time to be honest. There was only the two of them here and Olivia had to know. She had to hear from him that there was nothing between them.

'That's not what I said. I said I didn't want to have fun with you. I don't want to use you,' he said gruffly.

The look on his face was one she'd not seen on a man in a long time. Concern. Interest. He sat silent, his hands clasped in between his knees. He was waiting. For her to speak. As if what she had to say was important. It made her shift again and she pulled the jacket closer around her, suddenly aware of how exposed she was.

'Why not? We both know what this is. One weekend. You'd only have to focus on me for one weekend. Then I go home and you can go back to your life… your responsibilities.'

She watched his reaction with a pounding chest. She was offering him comfort. She wanted comfort from him. That was all. One weekend. She knew she couldn't keep his interest for longer than that—but one weekend. She could do that.

But he didn't move. He didn't want that. He didn't want one weekend. He didn't want to focus on her. Disappointment made her sick. She wanted to walk out, away from his dark eyes that seemed set on hers. But the pull of him was so strong. The sight of him watching her. The air around them seemed to hum with a throbbing chant. *Do it, do it, do it.*

'I'm sorry I kissed you again, Edward.'

Edward's eyes slid to her lips. He was so close and so handsome and so incredibly out of her reach that she was feeling a little sick. That she'd even considered *thinking* he might sleep with her was ridiculous. Her mouth turned up in a wry smile. As if. But then she remembered his words. *'My beautiful Olivia,'* he'd whispered into her hair. *'I'm right here.'* Her smile disappeared as longing beat a message on her heart. Deep, long, sad longing.

'I'm sorry I threw myself at you and got naked in front of you and cried and hit you and…'

Edward's lips were soft but firm against hers. She felt his big, leathery palm against her cheek and she couldn't breathe. She pulled away and looked at his eyes, which were dark and intense.

'Edward…'

Then he kissed her again, and this time he wouldn't let her pull away. He slipped his hand around the back of her neck and pulled her in closer, opening his mouth and moving against her to draw her in. For a moment she was confused, but once the taste of him landed on her tongue and his deep, dark scent wound around her face she let herself fall.

'Stop talking, Olivia. Stop apologising,' he murmured into her hair, before letting his chin drop so he could plant a row of wet kisses down her neck.

'But you…and I…'

His head popped back up.

'Olivia,' he said in a stop-arguing tone. 'Stop talking.'

She stopped talking. Her heart beat hard in her chest.

'And kiss me,' he added darkly.

This time she didn't hesitate. She slipped her arms around his neck and pulled him close. He responded with a force that surprised her. His breathing was ragged and his hands roamed inside the jacket, finding her hips and her stomach and her breasts. His lips kissed her mouth and her cheeks and her jawline and his mouth moved lower and lower.

'You have the most beautiful body I've ever seen.'

His words vibrated on her skin as he took her nipple in his mouth and kissed it with a long, deep, wet kiss. She felt her body spasm in pure pleasure. Then he moved to the other nipple and flicked his thumb over the hard nub before taking it greedily in his mouth.

Olivia felt as if she was flying. All she could see was the top of his dark head and all she could hear were the groans of his pleasure that filled the silence. She let a moan escape and he looked up.

'Lie back,' he ordered. 'Let me see you. Let me touch you.'

Olivia shivered at his words and the way he'd said them. As if he was begging her.

He slid one large hand down her thigh, past her knee and over the muscles in her calf, before taking the heel of her shoe and slipping it off. Then, his eyes on her body, he moved to the other foot and slipped her shoe off before moving his hands over the base of her foot, up her calf and over her thigh, stopping at the top of her preposterously small panties.

'These are very silly things,' he said, and smiled.

Olivia's heart flipped. The man was handsome, but when he smiled…? He was almost too gorgeous to look at. She kept looking regardless.

'Why don't you take them off me, then?'

His smile disappeared and his eyes turned dark.

'But if I take them off you'll be wearing nothing. You'll have nothing left to hide behind.'

There was a seriousness to his voice that she couldn't miss. She knew he was out of her league. He was too handsome and too smart and too together. But she felt it was right that she should be here with him. As if she was good enough for him just the way she was.

'I don't want to hide. I want you to see me.'

He leaned down until his face was close to hers.

Softly he brushed his lips against hers and she let her head fall back. He kissed her eyes and her cheeks and her lips again, before moving to a spot underneath her ear that made her body hum when he kissed her there.

'I see you, Olivia.'

Her eyes closed and she couldn't see what he was doing. But she could feel it. Feel his hands as they spread over her belly. His fingers as they clasped the top of her underwear and pulled it down. Then his hands moved firmly up her legs and behind her buttocks, until she could feel his hot breath against her, heating her right where she needed to be touched.

She pushed herself up further and sighed, but he didn't touch her. His hands came up behind her back and he lifted her. Up off the bed. Her eyes flew open and she saw the predatory glint in his eyes. Opening her legs, she wrapped them around his waist and he lifted her until her lips were level with his. His breathing was hot and heavy, and one hand had moved up to her hair while his other held her strong in the small of her back.

His hot lips slid against hers and pushed with a violence that surprised her. He wanted her. Couldn't get enough of her. With a smile she pulled away and burrowed her face into his neck.

'One weekend,' she murmured.

The deep lust in his eyes was evident and his lips were swollen where he'd been kissing her.

'One weekend,' he said gruffly.

She looked at his eyes. All serious. She wanted more. So much more. But all she could have was one weekend. And she was going to take it.

* * *

Edward's eyes slid to her lips and he stilled. His breathing was heavy. Olivia shifted, as if she were searching for the tip of his erection and trying to press it against her. Did she know how much she drove him wild? Did she realise how out of control she made him? But he couldn't lose it. Not this time. One weekend, she'd said. That was all this was.

'One amazing weekend.'

She came closer and pressed her lips against his. He responded by opening his mouth. She pushed her hot mouth against him and he felt his brain spiral. Her fingers gripped his hair, holding on to him, and he had to pull back. He had to stay in charge. It was the only way he could do this.

She pushed herself down on him again but he held her up. When her eyes looked at him, holding a question, he leaned forward and nipped at her bottom lip. It was full and soft and bounced back out from between his teeth again. A soft whisper escaped and that fuzzy feeling came back.

He held her against the wall, felt her soft skin squirming beneath him. He ran his lips down her neck to the hollow in between her collarbones. He wanted to taste her. He wanted to touch her all over. But he couldn't. He had to restrain himself. But it was hard as she bucked against him.

His jacket slipped from around her shoulders and he could see all of her, naked and glorious. He pushed his hand down and found the slick opening he'd dreamt about last night. Her sweet cinnamon scent wafted around him and she went silent, before quietly groaning. He moved up and down smoothly, watching her to see what she liked. He found the hard nub and used his finger to flick against it. He wanted to see her buck. But he wasn't expecting it to be so violent. She looked at him, her eyes wild.

He flicked again and watched in wonder as she came undone beneath him. Her fingers dug into his shoulders and the sound of her coming in the back of her throat had him transfixed. She was so responsive and so turned on and his control almost slipped again. *Almost.* She stilled. Then her eyes opened and she looked at him.

'What the hell was that?'

A look of pure lustful pleasure spread across her face and he felt his chest expand with the idea that he'd put it there.

'A taste,' he said.

She'd been beautiful before—but post-orgasm she was practically goddess-like. Her cheeks were flushed, her eyes blazing. Her skin glowed.

He moved his hand and she shivered. He was rock-hard and ready. He wanted to push her down on the bed. He wanted to kiss her all over. He wanted to drive himself into her. But he couldn't. He mustn't. He had to stay in control. So he let her go, kissed her swollen lips and left.

CHAPTER EIGHTEEN

'YOU LOOK BEAUTIFUL, Livvie.' Fiona was fussing and needed calming down, but Olivia's stomach was churning and she couldn't think straight this morning. She felt as if she'd been dragged backwards through a thorny bush. Dishevelled, exhausted and confused.

But the mirror she was standing in front of said something different. The long white dress she was wearing was beautiful. It swept across her collarbones and covered her arms and fitted snugly around her waist until falling in elegant waves to her toes. A hint of silver sparkle from her feet peeped out. She'd never seen herself look so good. Almost as if she really was beautiful.

Turning her head and shifting her body, she breathed out heavily.

Olivia helped Fi into her dress. She fixed her hair. She did all the bridesmaid duties she could think of but the hammering in her stomach was still there. And she knew why.

Edward. With his dark eyes and his magic fingers. 'A taste,' he'd said mysteriously before he'd left. A taste? What the hell did *that* mean? Did he want more? Was he coming back?

She'd waited, but luckily the orgasm he'd left her with had knocked her out pretty soon after he'd gone so she hadn't waited long.

But this morning confusion and nerves in her stomach were making her sick. Before, she'd thought she cared about Edward. But now, after the way he'd kissed her, the way he'd touched every magic button she had as if he knew exactly what to do…as if he knew her.

But he didn't. And she didn't know him. And that wall he had was still up. She knew he wouldn't let her in. He wouldn't talk about anything important to her. She knew that she was just a fling.

'Do you know anything about James, Fi?'

Fi turned so Olivia could clasp her pearls around her neck. 'Not really. Will doesn't talk about him much. Last night he told me about the lake and how he died, but he seems to clam up whenever I ask.'

Family trait.

'How did he die?'

'He drowned. Edward, Will and Bunny were all at the lake and James wandered off. He couldn't swim.'

Olivia's heart lurched. They had all been there. 'How old was he?'

'Eight. Will was ten and Ed was twelve. It must have been awful.'

Olivia had been twelve when her father died. She tried not to think about that day but flashes now flew through her mind. She saw her dad fall. He was lying on the grass and she didn't know what was wrong. She thought he was joking. Her mother flew past and Olivia remembered the screaming. The crying. The car ride to the hospital.

Her grandmother had come to pick her up and she

hadn't seen her mother or Ana until the funeral. But she hadn't sat with them; she'd sat with her grandmother. As if she wasn't part of the family. As if she wasn't allowed to grieve.

She wondered if Eddie had grieved? She wondered if he'd cried for his little brother or if he'd been as stoic as a little boy as he was now. Her heart was heavy. She wanted to see him. She wanted to wrap her arms around him and tell him everything would be OK. That was what she'd wanted to hear when her father had died. But she couldn't do that.

Last night Edward had left. She shouldn't have been surprised. They'd agreed this was a one-weekend thing. But she'd wanted him to stay. So much her stomach still ached.

'You look beautiful, Fi, and I'm so happy for you.'

A shot of something painful went through Olivia's chest. Fiona was a bride. A real-life bride. Something she would probably never be. But she wasn't jealous. She was happy for Fi. Her and Will made a beautiful couple. But Olivia couldn't help wishing… But she couldn't think like that. Not today.

'Liv.' Fiona's arm rested on Olivia's and her big brown eyes fell on her. 'Thank you for being here. I can't wait until it's my turn to be here for you.'

Olivia sniffed out a laugh. 'You'll be waiting a while, I'm afraid…'

'I'm not so sure about that.'

'You know me, Fi. I'll be chasing men till I'm in my eighties. Waiting outside funeral parlours to pick up the widowers.'

Fiona didn't laugh, didn't smile. 'You don't need to

chase anyone,' she said quietly. 'From what I've seen it's Ed who's doing the chasing.'

Something caught in Olivia's stomach at Fi's words.

Fi had noticed what was going on. Of course she had. They'd been best friends for six years. 'I'm not silly, Fi. I know I'm not Edward's type. I know I make mistakes when it comes to men. It's hard, you know… with Ana.'

'Ana has nothing to do with it. Yes, she's gorgeous. But she's not smart and funny and sexy and an awesome dancer. You are so much more than Ana will ever be.'

Fi's words warmed Olivia.

'Don't give up on him, Liv. He's one of the good ones.'

Olivia knew that. He was one of the best ones. But this would only last one weekend. She had to hold his attention for one weekend. Then she'd be gone and he'd forget about her and it would be over. Except for the way her skin tingled when she thought of his kisses and the way her heart hammered when she thought of the way he smiled at her. She wondered if it would ever be over for her.

Edward tugged at his tie. Next to him, Will was shifting, but the smile was wide across his face. It had been there since he'd seen him at breakfast this morning. Even when the priest had come to say the bride was running late he'd remained smiling. But it was becoming a little manic, he noticed. Like a clown.

Despite the cold, Edward was hot. He was dressed in full wedding garb—from waistcoat to tails—and everything was too tight and scratchy. The crowd in the pews were shifting and whispering.

Last night snow had fallen and the ground was covered, which had made it hard for their father's vintage Bentley to navigate the twists and turns of the road into the village and on to the small church. But they'd made it in one piece. He hoped the girls would too.

Will leaned towards him; 'What if she's changed her mind?'

The manic smile was still painted onto his face and Edward noticed tiny beads of sweat on his forehead.

He put his hand on his brother's shoulder. 'She'll be here. It'll be the snow holding them up.'

He wished he felt as confident as he sounded. He knew Fiona would be here. Fiona was deeply and stupidly in love with his unworthy brother. But he was still anxious. About seeing Olivia.

Last night, when he'd left her, he'd been about to lose control. One weekend, she'd said. But she was so gorgeous and so damn responsive. She'd come undone with just a few flicks of his fingers. As if she'd been as turned on as he had. He'd managed to keep it together last night, but he wasn't sure if he'd be able to if it happened again.

Which was why he had to let her go. Women like Olivia couldn't be held down. They liked to move on. They couldn't stay still and he wasn't sure he'd be able to let her walk out through the door when the weekend ended.

The atmosphere in the church changed and Edward tapped Will on the elbow.

The bride had arrived.

And the bridesmaids.

Edward adjusted his tie again and stood with his hands clasped in front of him, waiting for the door at the end of the long aisle to open.

Finally it did and Fiona floated forward. A long, lacy veil hung from her head to the floor. But he wasn't watching for Fiona. It took a half-dozen more heartbeats before he saw *her*.

Dressed from head to toe in white, with a bunch of flowers in front of her. She looked like a bride. She looked beautiful. As usual.

He shifted and turned to the front of the church with Will. He could feel her moving up the aisle.

Will threw him a look, the smile gone from his face. Edward knew he should smile reassuringly back but he couldn't.

Not yet. He had to breathe out first.

The solemn words of the priest began the ceremony. He could sense Will's nervousness so he pushed him in the arm. Will pushed him back. Edward found himself grinning. It felt a little strange to have his brother acting so differently, but it made him feel better too. He didn't feel like himself either. He'd felt ripped apart after dinner last night. Hearing his mother's wails had brought back the memory of the day James had died.

Edward shivered and finally looked down past Will, past Fiona, to the profile of Olivia.

Last night he'd wanted Olivia. Wanted to forget who he was and where he was and who she was and bury himself inside her. Be with her. Stay with her. Take comfort in her scent and her feminine curves.

The pretty pout of her lips and the snub of her nose seemed so familiar it put him at ease. Her long eyelashes blinked, then she turned and her eyes met his.

He let a half-smile creep across his lips. Cautiously. He didn't want to spook her. But she wasn't spooked. She tossed her head and kept her eyes on his. Then, to his surprise, she let her blue eyes slide to his lips—then down his body to his toes and slowly back again. The woman was punishing him. He could feel it in the way she looked at him, as if she'd touched him. He could see it in the way she bit her lip and stared at him.

His groin shifted. Brilliant. He was getting a hard-on in the church at his brother's wedding. He should look away—think about vasectomies or something. But he didn't. He kept looking at her and she kept looking at him. That full red lip still between her teeth. He wanted to leap over the pulpit and kiss that look off her face. Then rip that dress from her lithe little body and make her scream his name as the minister looked on.

He turned away. *Really not helping.*

The service took another excruciating half an hour. His feet were falling asleep. But finally the minister declared them husband and wife and Will managed to whip the long veil up and over to plant a very non-churchy kiss on Fiona's surprised lips.

The normally reserved group of family and friends broke out in laughter and cheers and Will lifted Fiona off her feet to carry her down the aisle in typical Will style.

Edward sneaked another glance at Olivia. She was smiling at the newlyweds, distracted, so he slipped her arm under his to make their way down the aisle.

'You look beautiful.' She looked up at him as if surprised to see him. Her eyes were brighter and her eyelashes sooty, but she didn't have the caterpillars on, he noticed.

'Thank you.'

'I think we should talk.'

'I think you should be quiet.'

Olivia stopped to hold his mother's outstretched hands and he watched as she kissed her. Calmly and quietly. It made something ache in his chest. That she'd stop and acknowledge his mother, knowing how hard this day was for her. He leaned in to do the same and his mother clung to his arm. She wouldn't let go and her eyes welled with tears, so he pulled her up and took her with him as well.

The three of them made their way down the aisle, and as Olivia's hand held firm to his forearm he realised that he hadn't felt this good in a long time. Years. He realised he was tired of being lonely. He wanted someone to be in this with him. Someone serious. Not just someone for a weekend.

CHAPTER NINETEEN

OLIVIA LET GO of Edward's arm. Fiona's veil was trailing in the snow so she picked it up and stood silently as the bride and groom greeted the guests now pouring out of the church. Her back was freezing as it was bared to the weather, but somehow a hot rash had broken out across her skin. Every now and again, in between greeting relatives and family friends, Edward would glance at her. She couldn't read his look. She was just aware of him watching and it was making her incredibly self-conscious.

Her arm still tingled where it had been resting on his sleeve. He was warm, and it was as if an invisible magnet drew him to her, but she had to resist. He'd said nothing about last night. He didn't smile or whisper anything else in her ear. Just glanced at her, which was making her even more nervous.

Once the crowd started to thin Olivia helped Fiona into the waiting car before slipping into a seat in the car behind them. She was expecting Bunny to get in with her, but it was Edward's large frame that moved smoothly into the car. Her heart stopped. The air grew thin and she became very hot. The fabric of the dress started to itch around her neck.

Edward didn't speak; he sat silent, looking out of the window, so Olivia turned to look out of hers. This was even worse than she'd thought it would be. He regretted it. He'd changed his mind. One weekend had turned into one night. And not even a whole night.

She shut her eyes tightly. She'd come so quickly. One flick and she'd shattered. She couldn't explain why—in truth it almost always took her much longer than that. But Edward was so handsome and he made her feel so beautiful and his hands were so confident. And he knew just where to touch. She squeezed her legs together. *Mustn't think of his fingers*, she chanted in her head. *Mustn't think of his hands*. But out of the corner of her eye she spotted them, spread across his knee, and she had to suck in a breath to stop the rush of moisture that headed south.

Edward's head snapped around. 'Are you all right?'

'Yes. Fine.' He didn't want anything more and she wasn't going to beg.

'Olivia. About last night…'

'Forget it. It was nothing. It's over. I was emotional—you were upset. It happens. We don't have to talk about it.'

He didn't speak, just kept looking at her, so she turned back to the window.

The car ride seemed to last for hours but finally the house came into view. The wedding party was having photos taken before the reception started in the ballroom.

When the car stopped Edward got out. As if he couldn't get out fast enough. Olivia pushed back the tears she feared were lingering behind her eyes and gathered her skirt. Someone opened her car door and she stepped out into the cold—and found herself staring straight into the dark, fathomless eyes of Edward.

'Olivia. We need to talk.'

'C'mon, Ed. Let's get these photos over and done with—I need a drink.' Bunny's small frame whirled past and grabbed Edward by the arm.

Edward threw Olivia an apologetic look and she tried to slow the beating of her heart. His attention had been diverted so what did they need to talk about?

The hairs on her neck rose every time she got close to him. She shivered every time the bossy photographer told her to take his arm or get closer to him. Thank God Fiona needed her attention and Regina needed endless cups of tea and Bunny was doing most of the talking so she never had to be alone with him.

Finally the bridal party headed indoors to the reception. Olivia spotted Casper waving at her from a distance. She headed his way, preferring to talk to him about his latest business venture than to be ignored by Edward.

'Hello, darling, you're looking beautiful today.'

Casper's smooth words washed over her. She didn't want to be here with Casper. She could only think of one person. But she couldn't see Edward anywhere. Someone started tinkling on a glass until the whole room joined in. The bride and groom had arrived. They swept into the room like a royal couple, waving and smiling, and Olivia's breath caught when she spotted Edward following them. His grim face was back. He swept one look over her before taking his seat at the table.

Olivia found her seat at the wedding table in between Fiona and Bunny and the MC began to introduce the speeches. Everyone dutifully raised their glasses and Olivia took a long sip. Edward still wasn't looking at her. She shouldn't have pushed him. She shouldn't have made him talk about James last night. It was obviously too painful. And she shouldn't have exposed herself to him the way she had. Now she'd pushed him away for good. Which was what she always did.

The speeches were long and terribly funny and by the end of them, Olivia found herself having much more fun than she'd intended. But she was getting a little tipsy from the toasts, so when the entrée was cleared she took the opportunity to leave the room and get some air. She wanted to be fully in control, so she wouldn't make a fool of herself as she had the first night here, when she'd passed out on the terrace. Edward had come to her rescue that night but she didn't want him to any more.

'I hope you're not going to pass out. I'm not sure I have the energy to lift you up all those stairs again.'

Edward's deep voice made her spin. Which made her head swim. She smiled uncontrollably. His face made her do that. It was so handsome and square and his smile made her stomach flip.

'I think I can manage tonight.'

'That's a shame.'

He stepped closer and Olivia sucked in a breath.

'Why?'

'Because lifting you up is a great opportunity to feel your bum.'

She could see the hot lust in his face. The way his

eyes half closed when he spoke to her. The way his lips parted as if waiting to taste her.

'You shouldn't say things you don't mean,' she said, secretly pleased.

'I never say things I don't mean.'

He was right in front of her now, and Olivia's heart was beating so hard she thought he'd be able to see the pulses. Nerves made her heart race and her palms feel damp. He wasn't touching her, just standing there, his dark eyes intent on her.

'You look beautiful today. That dress…it's…'

His hot breath was on her shoulder. His body moved closer and she breathed in heavily when his fingers stroked slowly along her collarbone.

'Bellissima.'

Olivia shivered. What was he doing now—why was he playing games with her? She didn't want to hear him talking like that, all gruff and deep and foreign. It was making her nervous. She took a step back but his large palm reached out and clasped hers. It took a moment for Olivia to adjust to the feeling of him being there so close and in control.

'Wait, Olivia. Don't walk away from me.'

He moved closer again—so close she could feel his hard chest against her breasts. *Five minutes. Then he'd be gone.* His attention would move on. She knew it, but even so she couldn't help wanting to make the most of their five minutes. His free hand reached around her back and his fingers trailed along her spine as she sucked in another breath. She stood still, unable to move, not wanting to react.

She wasn't sure she could deal with his rejection again.

Then his hot lips landed on her bare shoulder, caressing it with gentle kisses, and she moved backwards quickly, as if she'd been shocked by an electric current, and pulled away from his grasp. His square jaw tilted down and he looked at her through hooded lids. He wasn't smiling. He looked dark and dangerous, which made her heart still.

'Stop it. Stop touching me.'

He stepped forward until she had to tip her head back to look at his eyes. His manly soap scent swirled around her and his dark eyes flashed.

'I thought you wanted one weekend.'

'I did. I do.'

'Then what's wrong?' His dark eyes were filled with concern and confusion.

What *was* wrong? Here he was, still wanting her. Why was she hesitating?

'Nothing,' she lied, because she didn't know how to tell him. *I want more. I want you all the time, not just this weekend. I want you to want more.*

'I can't let you go, Olivia.'

She stepped back, but he reached out and wrapped a long arm around her waist, pulling her closer.

He leaned down as if to kiss her and Olivia felt as if she had fallen so far that it was dark and there was no way out.

'Why did you leave me? Last night?' Her voice cracked and she ignored it. 'What's wrong with me? Why doesn't anyone stay?'

Edward stopped and his eyes moved to hers. He pulled her closer and his fingers curled around hers. The warmth of them travelled up her arm.

'There's nothing wrong with you. I had to leave. Not because of you but because of…me.'

'What do you mean? I don't understand. I don't understand why you push and pull and tease and torment me!'

'Me? You're the one who torments, Olivia. With your gorgeous body and your beautiful eyes and your smile and the way you make me feel like you care about me.'

'I do care about you.'

The words were out before she thought about them. She wished she could suck them back in. She'd revealed too much. He would surely run now.

His breathing had become heavy but he didn't let her go. He just held her closer.

'Then let's do this. One weekend.'

CHAPTER TWENTY

SHE WAS TRYING not to touch him, but every time she breathed in, her breasts came perilously close to touching his hard chest.

'We can't run from this.' His voice dipped dangerously low.

'I don't want to run.'

'What do you want to do, then?'

He pulled her into his chest and she watched his eyes go darker.

'I want you,' she whispered.

'Come with me,' he commanded, before pulling her towards the stairs.

She thought he was going to lead her up them, but he took her to the side, past a tall plinth and a marble bust, to the narrow space between the wall and the stairs. It was dark and smelled of furniture polish. The noise of the ballroom faded a little and a violent wave of heat warmed her from her skin to her bones. In this confined space there was nowhere to move, nowhere to go.

His body moved closer and his hand reached up to brush a stray lock of hair out of her eyes.

'One more night,' he said quietly.

Olivia's body was tense. She wanted him. She

needed him. When he woke up tomorrow she knew he'd only change his mind again anyway. But she had tonight.

Olivia couldn't wait any longer. She brought her hands to his chest to feel the hard muscles underneath his shirt. Slowly she undid the buttons on his waistcoat and he watched her fingers work. Then she stood on her toes and pressed her lips to his. He responded, pushing forward, but then he pulled back.

'Olivia. Are you sure this is what you want?'

Lust darkened his eyes. Yes, this was what she wanted. One night. Even though she wanted more. But that was impossible. At least this way she could save herself the heartache of watching him leave. One weekend. Then it would be over. She nodded at him, and before she could even suck in a breath he'd moved.

His big body pushed into hers, pressing her against the timber panelling behind her. His mouth was on her lips, her eyes, her hair and then her throat. His fingers looped around her ear and then moved down her neck until his thumb rested in the hollow of her collarbone and his kisses became deeper and more desperate. His thigh muscled in between her legs and she let out a moan as she pressed herself into him.

'You're a hard woman to resist, Olivia.'

'I am?' That surprised her.

He kissed her again. Hard. On the mouth. She opened her lips and let his hot, lush tongue explore. His hands were moving around to her back and pressing against her bare skin. This was real. He was here, kissing her—almost desperately. She needed him closer; she wanted to feel his skin. She moved her hands from his chest to his shoulders and slipped them underneath his jacket until he shrugged it to the floor. Now she had access to those hard, powerful shoulders and his wide back.

His muscles moved as she explored them and his hands came up to her shoulders and tugged. Her beautiful white dress fell down easily, as if it wanted to let him in. Beneath she was wearing nothing except tiny white satin underwear. He stopped to look at her.

Olivia felt the last of her sanity fade. Her body slumped against his and she pushed her breasts into his chest. Soft against hard. Her mouth met his so violently it left them both breathless and heaving. With one easy movement, he lifted her.

'I can't wait, Olivia. I need you now.'

His sincere tone, his raw voice, made her insides fire with pure lust. She could feel the cold wall against her back, hear the tinkle of his buckle as he undid his trousers and the crinkle of foil as he sheathed himself. She couldn't wait either. She wanted him. She needed him.

She undid the buttons of his shirt frantically, leaving the top one as it was too complicated and would take too long to get his damn tie off. When her hands hit his skin underneath she groaned in pleasure. Under her fingers his hard muscles tensed and she ran her hands across the rough hairs on his chest. He lifted her again and she gasped at the feel of him—hard and erect and pushing on the satin of her underwear.

His eyes met hers and locked. One hand held her head steady at the back.

'Look at me,' he growled.

He sounded fierce, almost angry. Her heart was beating against his chest. She felt it too. The angry lust.

The blood pumped through her veins. Why couldn't she have him? Why couldn't this last longer?

'I need you, Edward. Now.'

Their eyes held and with one hand he pulled aside the satin of her underwear. In one long stroke he plunged inside her. Olivia tensed and went still. She had to remember to breathe. So long, so thick, so hard. A bubble formed in her chest. Anger coupled with complete satisfaction. Then he moved and she couldn't think at all.

He used his arm around her waist to lift her slightly and bring her back down onto him. He was hot inside her and she tensed around him, trying to capture everything before he lifted her again. He groaned and let his head fall to her shoulder, and she gripped frantically onto the curls at the nape of his neck.

'Edward, please.' She was begging, but she didn't know what for.

He didn't speak, but moaned again and drove himself upwards. The sheer size of him and the pleasure rocking through her body became too much to hold on to.

'I'm coming,' she whispered in his ear.

He moaned.

'Please…' she begged as the wave of something violent passed through her core and into her belly.

She held fast to him, digging one hand into the hard muscles of his back and the other against the wall to brace herself. The orgasm seemed to last for ever. It shuddered from her core and racked right through her body.

Once the cut of pleasure dulled she became aware of him throbbing inside her, waiting patiently for her to come back down. Then with a rough tug he pulled the back of her hair until her face was on his.

'Now it's my turn,' he said gruffly, before pushing himself into her again. Over and over. Until she swelled and built again and with a final moan came with him.

It took a few seconds for Edward to come back down. He held a shivering Olivia against him but he couldn't move in case he dropped her. With an effort he met her eyes, bright blue and blazing. She looked shocked. Which was what he felt. Shocked at what he'd done and the way he now felt. Completely spent, bodily exhausted and still shaking with anger.

Anger? He wasn't sure why he was angry but he was. Angry at himself, angry at her. Angry at every damn person here tonight. With a hiss, she shifted and tugged on his shoulder. He let her down as gently as he could before righting himself.

She stood in front of him, shivering with cold, and something clamped over a vein in his chest. She was so small and so vulnerable and he'd taken her behind the stairs with a room full of people waiting.

What kind of a man was he? This was Will's wedding day. His mother could barely speak from grief and his father was out there picking a fight with everyone who walked past. He should be in there. Solving their problems. Fixing his family. Not here, satisfying his urges with an innocent woman. She didn't even want him. She'd let him know this was a one-off. She didn't want it repeated.

'Edward…'

Her voice shook and with horror he noticed her eyes welled with tears. He felt like the world's biggest ass.

He bent down to retrieve her dress and she took it from him, stepping into it and covering herself up.

'Olivia.' He didn't know what to say. *Sorry? Sorry I took you like an animal possessed? Sorry I could barely wait? Sorry for treating you exactly the way you didn't want to be treated?*

She folded her arms across her chest and blinked at him.

She looked so beautiful. So shocked still. So different from a moment ago, when she'd been encouraging him and pushing down on to him—wanting him as much as he wanted her. But now it was over a strange feeling of being let down crept over his shoulders.

He picked his jacket up off the floor and shrugged it over his shoulders. The delicate scent of the perfume she was wearing tonight as well as the faint cinnamon scent that was just *her* was now mixed with the scent of sex. It reminded him where he was. Behind the stairs. Like a couple of randy teenagers. Shame made his tongue go heavy. She deserved better.

'Say something, Eddie.'

She was looking at him with watery eyes. He still couldn't speak, so he leaned down and gripped the sides of her small face with his palms. Then he kissed her forehead.

'I'm sorry, Olivia.'

He couldn't think of anything else to say. He wanted her to see how sorry he was. He tried to convey it with his eyes and the warmth of his hands, but she still looked shocked. Her eyes were asking him something. They wanted an explanation. But he didn't have one. One hand absently rubbed her other arm. Anything they had—or could have had—he'd now destroyed.

But that was what he did. He was careless and selfish. She didn't deserve that.

So with one last look at her face he turned and fled.

Olivia's face dropped into her hands and she slapped her forehead repeatedly. 'Stupid, stupid, stupid,' she berated herself with a whisper.

She'd ruined everything. He'd seen her tears. Seen how overcome she was by her feelings for him and he had been frightened off. He'd never want more now. As if he ever had. They never wanted more from her.

Olivia pushed her way out of the narrow space she was in, past the plinth and the marble bust. The eyes of the bearded statue were looking at her. Accusingly.

'Oh, shut up,' she told it, before hearing a roar of applause from inside. Something was happening and soon someone would notice the Maid of Honour wasn't there. She wondered if anyone would guess she'd been with the Best Man.

Quickly she slipped down the hall and back into the double doors.

'…and then he said: "It wasn't a horse, Uncle Rob, that was my girlfriend!"'

The crowd roared with laughter and Olivia took the opportunity to sneak back to the table, lifting her eyes to Fiona on the way. She didn't dare look up at the other end of the table. But when the crowd let out an audible gasp and whispers became tittering laughter Olivia stopped. What? What had she done? She turned to look at them before Fiona's small frame moved quickly behind her.

'Your dress, Liv, everyone can see your undies.'

Fiona fumbled with the back of her dress and

Olivia put her hand around to find that in her haste to get dressed she'd not pulled her dress down properly.

Quickly Fiona hustled her into her seat. Olivia couldn't look up. A hot rash crept up her neck and across her shoulders. She couldn't look at Edward. She couldn't look at Will. She could barely look at Fiona. Instead she put a hand on her forehead and mumbled a string of expletives.

Fiona coughed and Olivia looked at her. Fiona motioned in front of her, then leaned into her ear. 'Those black things on the table are microphones.'

Great.

CHAPTER TWENTY-ONE

HUMILIATED, EMBARRASSED, MORTIFIED and disgraced, Olivia put her head down into her hands and closed her eyes.

A chair scraped against the polished floorboards and a heavy electronic thump meant the microphone was being moved. She couldn't remember feeling any worse about herself ever. *Ever.* Not when her mother had left her at a service station once when they were coming back from a tennis tournament. Not when she'd heard her sister's best friend talking about how horrible it must be to have such an ugly sister. Not even when Fiona had left.

Her mind shuffled through the painful memories and she screwed her eyes up even tighter. Until she heard the deep, low tones of Edward's gentle voice.

'There comes a time in everyone's life when they meet someone who changes their life. Someone who cannot be surpassed in intelligence, beauty and talent. It's a pivotal moment.' He turned to look at Will. 'And that moment came for Will twenty-eight years ago, when he met me—his big brother.'

Edward's opening line made the room erupt in laughter and Olivia could feel the attention shift off her and onto Edward, who stood tall and authoritative at the end of the table.

Edward's speech was filled with bouts of raucous laughter and a few 'ahhhs' at the soppy bits. Finally, at the end, he raised his glass and asked everyone to do the same.

'I'd like to thank Fiona for her choice in brides-maids. Bunny and Olivia are both beautiful and charming, and Fiona is lucky to have them both in her life.'

He turned to look at her then and their eyes locked. Dark against light. He didn't smile but Olivia felt the power of his look. She didn't understand what it meant but she was grateful for it anyway.

He sipped his champagne and continued. 'Tonight we're here to celebrate family, friends and love. So congratulations, Will and Fiona. To the Bride and Groom.'

He lifted his glass and a cheer went up while drinks were clinked before the MC took the microphone back and announced dessert.

Olivia realised she'd missed the main course. Her stomach growled in protest. After the action behind the stairs she was hungry, and a little tired, but the buzz of Edward being in the room was keeping her awake. And keeping her body tense.

Besides that one long look, Edward had avoided her eye, and she, gratefully, had avoided his. She wanted to leave. To go up to her room and hide and then sneak out tomorrow and never have to see any of these people again. But Fiona was smiling at her, and then she was next to her, whispering something about the first dance.

Fiona clasped her hand and led her to the dance floor before leaving her for Will. Olivia stood still. Alone and wondering what to do next. She still felt silly and embarrassed. Sure everyone would put two and two together and know what she'd been doing and who she'd been doing it with. She couldn't do this. She had to leave.

But a big, warm hand in hers stopped her escape.

'Dance with me.'

Edward's dark look was back. Olivia's heart was beating. Hard and fast and out of control. A prickle of heat ran through her as she looked at his hand, big and dark over hers. A smile spread across his lips as his other hand grasped her bare back. His large hand lay warm and sensual across her skin. He pulled her close and the breath left her body.

'I don't think that's a good idea.' Olivia lowered her voice and used two hands to push against his chest. 'Everyone here knows what we did.'

He smiled down at her and stood still, as if her push did nothing. 'They have no idea. But they'll get suspicious if the Maid of Honour won't dance with the Best Man.'

She didn't want to dance with him. He was too hot and too close and the memory of what they had done behind the stairs was still burning through her with his touch. Deep down she throbbed, annoyed she wanted him again. But he was right. It would look worse if she refused to dance with him. So she let him take her hand while she slipped her other hand around his tense shoulder.

The music started. A sappy love song full of '*I love you*s' and '*You complete me*s'. Olivia's stomach turned.

'So you finally came to your senses, did you?' she asked, her voice harder than she'd meant it to be.

His feet moved and his arms pulled her along with

him in a slow circle around the room. He was a strong partner and she felt safe in his arms.

'What are you talking about?' His eyes flashed.

Olivia smiled at a passing couple.

'You know exactly what I mean.'

She gasped at the feel of his thigh in between her legs as he turned her around to face the other way.

'I said I was sorry. What do you want me to do, Olivia? Get on the microphone and make a public announcement?'

He spun her again—a little wildly, she thought. But his hand was strong on her back and held her firm. He pulled her a little closer and she could feel him hard against her. The feel of it made her a little weak. She had to resist the pull of him. She had to stop throwing herself at him. She'd already made a fool of herself so many times around him she'd lost count.

With a shove, she pulled herself back. 'I don't need your apologies. I need to understand why you did that.' She couldn't help but feel disappointed. She didn't want to think he regretted what they did, but the way he'd said 'sorry'. So sincerely. She didn't want him to be sorry. She wanted him to feel as much as she did.

Colour stained his cheeks. He gripped her hand a little tighter and flung her around another corner.

'What do you want me to say? "I'm an animal"? "I can't control myself"?' His dark eyes went even darker as he pulled her in firmly again. 'Well, it's true. When I'm around you I seem to forget who I am and where I am. All I can think of is you.'

'Is that why you took me up against the wall behind the stairs like a two-dollar hooker?'

He stopped. Someone crashed into them and apol-

ogised in the English way of apologising even when
they weren't at fault.

'You wanted it as much as I did, Olivia.'

Olivia pulled her hands away from his. She moved
so he wasn't near her, so her brain couldn't cloud over
with his scent and the way he looked and how he made
her feel.

She turned to go, furious that she'd been stupid
enough to really believe that when they were together
he thought she was more. Something else. Something
more beautiful, more wonderful than she really was.
But he was like all the rest. She was just the girl you
grabbed at the end of the night, when all the pretty ones
had been snapped up.

His long fingers around her forearm stopped her.
'We're not done here.'

Her heart pumped. The blood rushed in her ears.

'*I'm* done. I'm done with people thinking they can
take what they want from me. I'm done with allowing
everyone to make me feel stupid and inappropriate,
and I'm done with accepting lies from men who don't
really want me.'

He breathed heavily. Another couple bumped into
them and apologised but Olivia didn't feel it. All that
existed was him and her, and a bubble formed around
them as he considered her words. She could see his
brain thinking behind those dark eyes. His hand held
her tight and she couldn't move. She was trapped.

'I do want you. Very much.'

'Don't tease me, Edward.'

'I'm not teasing you.' He pulled her back in and his
feet started to move. His eyes didn't leave hers. 'I want

you. Even if you make me lose control. Even if I can't think of anything else when you're around.'

He spun her again with that move that she loved. The one where his knee pressed right up against her hot, wet centre.

'I want you.'

'You want me for a one-night stand.'

He spun her again, angrily this time, and she had to let her feet leave the ground so she wouldn't fall. He had hold of her around the small of her back and he pressed her even closer.

'You want to know why I'm angry all the time? I'm angry because all you want is a one-night stand. I'm angry that I can't stop thinking about you—all the damn time. You're smart and funny and sweet, Olivia, and you have the most beautiful smile I've ever seen.'

He thought she had a beautiful smile? What a lovely thing to say. No, she was mad at him. *Mad*.

His head dipped and his lips came closer to hers. She watched the outline of them. He had a small freckle right below his lip. She stared at it hungrily. Wanted to kiss it. No. She couldn't trust him.

'I'm sorry I lost control behind the stairs, Olivia. I should have waited,' he murmured as his hot breath passed over her eyes, closing them briefly. 'But I couldn't wait. You're so gorgeous—I couldn't wait.'

He was serious. He thought she was gorgeous. And for the first time in her life she felt gorgeous. And strong. She dragged her eyes from his lips and pushed her shoulders back.

'I want the truth, Edward.' Her voice was a whisper; she heard the crack in it.

He moved even closer. So close she could feel the steady thumping of her heart against his.

'The truth is you captivate me, Olivia. I want you. I want to be with you.'

Olivia felt it. Felt his heart against hers and knew he was telling the truth. He wanted her as much as she wanted him.

He was telling the truth; Olivia could see it. She could feel it and as she watched him, the barbed wire surrounding her began to fall. Her mother's lack of attention, her sister's unbeatable achievements, her best friend's abandonment. None of it mattered. She was gorgeous to him. She was…what had he said? She captivated him. To him she was captivating.

With all the energy she had left, she lifted her arms around his neck and he pulled her off the dance floor. Edward found a dark corner and gently pushed his lips against hers. They were smooth and soft, and when they parted Olivia sighed and let him in. She held him close and breathed him in. She shifted so she could be closer to him and his tongue moved inside her mouth, searching for hers. He occupied her mind and her mouth and her body and she wanted him there. She wanted him to know her—all of her—and she wanted to know him.

'I want to be with you too.'

He smiled and her heart pounded. 'Good, because I'm not letting you go. I'm not giving you another chance to change your mind…or find someone else.'

Olivia soared. He really did want her. As much as she wanted him.

'We'd better get back to the dance floor. Fiona might

be looking for me. We're supposed to be out there having fun.'

'We could be here having fun,' he said, kissing her deeply again.

She smiled and her heart swelled as if it actually believed. As if it really thought this was real. With a final check that her dress was where it should be Olivia followed Edward back onto the dance floor.

There was a little whispering behind hands and a couple of sidelong glances—mostly from Bunny and Rosie—but Olivia didn't care. Edward danced with her all night. And when he wasn't dancing with her he was smiling at her. And when he wasn't looking at her she was looking at him. Amazed that this was real. He wanted her. He wasn't going to leave. At least not tonight. And maybe not tomorrow either.

That kiss hadn't felt as if it was a one-night kiss. It felt like something more, and for the first time in a long time she felt that maybe she'd like to see more of a man and perhaps he felt the same way about her. Captivated.

By midnight her feet were aching and her hair had all but come down over her shoulders. It had an annoying natural curl to it that she usually straightened to within an inch of burning it off, but today Fiona had wanted her hair natural. Now it hung down her back in kinks and curls, but she didn't care. Edward had run his fingers through it when they danced. He'd buried his nose in it when he'd sat next to her and told her how good she smelled. And he'd looked at her as if she was the most beautiful girl in the room.

Olivia had never felt better. She'd never felt this happy and this relaxed and this comfortable in her own skin. She'd spent weeks worrying about this weekend. But she'd had no idea how much it would transform the way she thought.

CHAPTER TWENTY-TWO

'WE'RE LEAVING, DARLING. Thank you so much for being here for me.'

Fiona reached up to kiss Olivia's cheek and Olivia hugged her back with a smile. She was happy for her friend. Happy she'd found love and her life was about to begin.

'Come and catch the bouquet.'

Olivia stopped.

'No, no. That's not for me.' A cold trickle passed through her. A weekend of romance she could do, but marriage made her nervous. She definitely didn't want to catch that bouquet. She didn't want to do anything that might break the tenuous string that bound her and Edward tonight. What if he thought she was one of those girls who were dying to get hitched and ran from her again? No, she was staying right out of this one.

But Fiona pulled her to the front of the reluctant crowd of participants anyway. With a squeal, Fiona hoisted the bouquet and the older women on the side-lines called out.

'Catch it! Grab it!'

Olivia looked up. It was heading straight for her. Nope. Not *this* black cat. Olivia stepped sideways and apparently so did everyone else, because the bouquet landed with a thud on the floor. The dozen or so girls dressed in varying shades of silk and satin all stared at it as if it were a bird fallen dead from the sky.

'Oh, for goodness' sake, you bunch of cissies!' Bunny stepped forward and hoisted the bouquet in the air with a fist-pump. A loud cry went up and the crowd clapped before she ran and threw her arms around a surprised Casper.

When the time for the garter toss came it seemed the men were as reluctant as the women. Marriage had become like a reality TV show. Great fun to watch, but no one actually wanted to be on it. Finally Will managed to drag a few men forward, including a reluctant Ed, who looked at Olivia and winked.

That wink ran straight through her body, touching every sexual organ she had. And some parts she was sure weren't meant to be sexual but now felt as if they were. She knew what that wink meant and it had nothing to do with the garter. It had everything to do with the fact that this toss meant the night was nearly over and they could be alone. Be together. Olivia's heart raced and her palms went damp. *Relax. You've done this already. He won't be disappointed. He won't leave.*

She calmed herself as the men jostled each other. She could practically feel the rising testosterone levels in the room. None of these men might want to get married, but none could resist the primal call of a gladiator-esque battle. Even if it *was* for a frilly little piece of lace.

A loud manly cry meant the garter had been tossed. The men scrabbled for it. There were punches thrown, choice words used, and finally the victor stood tall, the garter aloft.

Edward.

Smiling wide, as if he were eight years old and had won the hundred-metre sprint at the school athletics carnival.

The crowd cheered and he received many pats on the back before the crowd dispersed and he moved to Olivia's side, murmuring in her ear, 'I know of a good use for this.' He reached over her shoulder and placed the white garter in her outstretched palm.

She didn't move, just enjoyed the heat of his mouth at her ear and the burn of his fingers against hers. 'Really?'

'Yes. Want to come and see?'

'Come where?'

He stopped for a moment and then breathed into her ear. 'To my room.'

She closed her eyes. His room. They were really going to do this. Start something.

She was suddenly nervous. 'I'm not sure if…'

He leaned down to her ear again and rested his hands on her shoulders. 'I have an *en suite* shower in my room.'

A shower! She'd kill for a shower. An honest-to-God shower-head she could put her face under and let the water run over her shoulders. Sex with a handsome man and a shower. How could a girl resist?

She put her hand behind her, brushed the bulge in his trousers and found his hand. 'Take me to your lair.'

With a deep, dark chuckle he gripped her hand and finally pulled her away from the maddening crowd.

* * *

He did have a shower. An awfully big shower. A shower built for two. The nerves in Olivia's stomach were jumping so much she felt sick. And dizzy. His hand held hers as he led her past the doorway to the *en suite* and over to the enormous four-poster bed in the middle of the room.

'This room is enormous.' She didn't know what to say. She just wanted to keep talking.

His fingers slipped through hers and lifted to trail across the neckline of her dress.

'It is,' he said, his eyes direct and his mouth unsmiling.

'Is this the room you slept in when you were growing up?' She wanted to turn away, move away as he stepped even closer, but she couldn't. His eyes held her steady.

'Yes.'

'It's nice.'

He stayed silent, his eyes flicking to her lips and then back again to meet hers. He held them for a second before he bit his bottom lip. Olivia watched it. Memorised it. His mouth. His lips. Then his tongue as it darted out to lick the place he'd bitten. Torture. She couldn't breathe. She needed space. This was all happening so fast. She wasn't ready. A one-night stand she could do—but more? Could she really do more?

'I…I'd kill for a shower.'

His eyes lifted again and finally he smiled.

'There are towels in the vanity. Help yourself.'

She had to look away from him. She had to get away from him. She was scared and had no idea why. She wanted this. She wanted him. She'd asked for this so why was she hesitating? Why was she stalling?

The bathroom door clicked behind her and she let out a breath. This was insane. A beautiful man was here, wanting her. Wanting more of her. She should be jumping into his arms, not hiding in the bathroom. But here she was. Hiding.

Olivia shrugged out of her dress and turned on the water. The shower-head was one of those non-environmentally friendly ones that shot out buckets of water. Olivia was glad of it as she stepped in, letting the hard beads rain down over her shoulders and her back. Instinctively she put her head under, then froze. When she emerged she'd be wet. Her make-up would be washed off and her hair would be frizzy. He'd see her as she really was.

A shudder ran through her naked body and she turned the heat up even more. She wasn't ready for this. She'd never shown a man the real her. Not once. But here—in Edward's room—there was nothing to hide behind. If she stepped out of that bathroom he'd see everything. What would he do? Run?

'Olivia? Are you all right? Do you need anything?'

Yes. She needed to get out of here. Escape. Find some man who only wanted her for five minutes. She knew what to do with those men. Get angry at them, laugh with her girlfriends over them and move on. She didn't know what to do with one who wanted to stick around.

'I'm fine. Don't come in.'

A pause. 'I wasn't going to. Are you sure everything's all right? You sound…unsure.'

The concerned inflection in Edward's voice hit her

in the stomach. Disregarding their first meeting, Edward had shown nothing but kindness to her. Kindness and some kind of strange, haunting desire for her. She could feel it every time they were in a room together. She could see it when he looked at her or when he held her hand to keep her steady.

She'd accused Edward of not being honest. But she was wrong. Edward was being honest with her right now. He wanted her and he wanted her to be all right. This was the type of man she deserved. This was the type of man she'd been waiting for.

She stood taller in the shower and pushed her shoulders back. The water ran down her face, washing off every last bit of make-up, leaving her exposed. She wanted him to see her like this. She needed him to want her when she was like this.

Edward stared at the naked and dripping wet woman standing in the doorway. Her hair was pulled back off her face and her athletic body was before him—curving in at all the right places, her breasts full and her nipples standing out. The sight of her made every thought in his head immediately disappear. He slapped his tongue on the top of his mouth, trying to make his eyes move to hers.

She thrust out a wet arm and pulled him. He almost stumbled. Almost. Once inside the steamy bathroom his senses returned. The heavy rush of the shower beckoned to him. His shoulders tensed and with painful clarity he realised he'd gone rock-hard.

He knew Olivia had been nervous earlier, but from the way she was looking at him and the way she was pressing her body along his he knew she wasn't nervous any more. The wild animal in him roared again.

He had to keep a steady head. This time he had to slow down. Let her catch up.

Slowly and gently he ran his hands up the sides of her body. Along her hips and into the curve of her waist. His hands were getting wetter and his shirt was soaking but he kept going. His eyes connected with hers and they were darker. Blue rimmed with black and greedy. For this. For him. He couldn't wait. She moved, shifting against him, and he had to suck in a steam-laced breath.

Not yet.

'Do I look…all right?' She smiled nervously.

An inarticulate grunt escaped from his chest. Did she look all right? Was she serious?

'You look unbelievable.' She was killing him. Carefully he put his arms on her shoulders, hoping the action would calm her. Hoping it would calm him too. 'You're beautiful.'

The smile on her face froze.

'I know I'm not beautiful, Edward. You don't have to say that.'

'I told you once I never say anything I don't mean and it's the truth. Your eyes, your mouth…' He let his eyes linger on her big, bouncy bottom lip. He wanted to put it between his teeth. 'Your breasts, your stomach…' He ran his hand down her body until he reached the slick opening he knew she liked him to touch. 'You're beautiful everywhere. Especially here…'

She sucked in a hiss and her head fell onto his shoulder. *Control*, he reminded himself. *Stay in control.*

'Wait till you meet my sister—then you'll know what beautiful is.'

He removed his hand and gripped her shoulders. 'I don't want to meet your sister. Don't you understand. Olivia? It's you I want. You.'

The eyes looking up at him were wide and he suddenly realised the truth. She really didn't know she was beautiful. Somehow she had the idea in her head that she wasn't. But right here, right now, she was bare to him. She'd let him in. She'd let him see the real her. He lifted his hands to place her head between them.

'You are the most beautiful woman I've ever seen, Olivia.' They weren't just words. He meant it. He'd only known her for a few days but she'd shown kindness and compassion and understanding and comfort. Yes, this woman was beautiful. And he had to show her. He had to make her feel the way he felt.

He lifted a hand and pushed his thumb roughly over her lips before dipping his head and tasting them. Sweet and full. He kissed her bottom lip and she swayed towards him. He kissed her top lip and she moaned.

Her eyes were closed; she was feeling it now.

Now he had to touch her. A droplet of water slid from her chin down her neck. He chased it with his tongue. Closing his eyes and tasting her skin before finding another drop and chasing it down her chest to the valley between her beautiful breasts. He wanted to taste this woman. Feel her skin and remember it.

She let out a hiss and arched her back. Now she was really feeling it. And he had to feel those gorgeous breasts. He cupped one, all the while watching for her reaction. A small smile spread across her lips, so he flicked the hard pink bud with his thumb. Her body vibrated. He could feel it again—that uncontrollable white-hot urge to push her against the wall—but he stilled it. Calmed it and let it coil in his gut. He wasn't sure how much longer he'd be able to hold on.

Olivia smiled at him and his brain spun in his head. Deep dimples sank into her cheeks and she looked so happy. He loved making her smile and he loved making those small whimpering noises come from the back of her throat as he was doing now. She was still wet and dripping, so he leaned down and took one of those tempting buds in his mouth. He licked, then he kissed. Long and deep and hard. He knew he had to go slowly with Olivia, that she was cautious. But he also knew once he gained her trust she would respond.

That thought made him press himself against her. He wanted her. Needed to be inside her. He flicked her nipple against his tongue. He had to touch her all over. Now.

CHAPTER TWENTY-THREE

'EDWARD…' OLIVIA WAS sure Edward was trying to kill her. Slowly. Kiss by torturous kiss. She wanted him. With a hot desire she'd never felt before. As if she had to have him or she'd hit someone. But he was teasing her. Kissing her skin, playing with her nipple.

His hands dropped to her backside and pulled her in to him and she gasped. She was pressed against him and he was hard and ready and his eyes were almost black. She recognised that look. The look of no return. A shiver vibrated through her body and she lifted her hands and pushed them against his chest.

'I want you in the shower.' Her voice came out all low and raspy and she liked it. She liked the way he made her feel. *'Beautiful,'* he'd said. She had never felt more aware of her curves and her body than she did now. His eyes slid over her hungrily and his hands wandered, skimming over her skin with the lightest of touches.

She stepped into the shower and tried to slow her breathing. She was losing control again, just as she had behind the stairs. He did that to her. The knowledge that he wanted her was like a drug and it was making her feel invincible. Behind her, she knew he'd be undressing. She wanted to see his body, take him all in, but she couldn't turn yet. She had to take one step at a time.

In less than a minute the door creaked open and she closed her eyes, her heart still racing out of control.

'Are you ready?' he asked with a wicked growl.

She was more than ready. She was about to scream if she didn't feel him against her soon. Then his skin hit hers and fireworks went off in her head. The tickle of the hairs on his chest, the feel of his hard stomach and the long, silky rock-hard feel of him pressed against her. All doubts evaporated. She was his and he was hers. Tonight she trusted him.

She wanted to turn and look at him but his hands ran down her arms and came over hers.

'Not yet. Don't turn around.'

Her heart was beating frantically now. He was in control and she had to keep trusting him. He put her hands against the tiles in front of her, then ran his fingers down her arms and over her waist before pressing his hands around her backside.

His hands stroked almost lovingly, and she held her breath in anticipation as his hand came around her hip and dipped lower to gently explore underneath her. His fingers moved slowly and she tensed every muscle in her body until he found her slick opening and stroked. Olivia couldn't move. She couldn't think. All she could do was feel. His head was near hers; his lips were against her ear and his other hand held hers fast against the wall.

'Fottutamente bello,' he growled, and Olivia cried out as his fingers found the small nub that made her body shiver. He stilled, then stroked her again, kissing the back of her neck and nipping at her shoulder with his teeth.

It was too much. The torture of the wait…the lingering doubt pressing against her ribs. She had to trust him. She wanted to trust him. She pushed herself against him, wanting to feel him against her skin. To make sure he was still hard and still wanted her because she wanted him. Badly.

'Edward, I need you.'

His mouth came to her cheek and his voice had turned deep—very deep. 'I need you too. Turn around.'

Olivia spun eagerly around, but she wasn't prepared for what she saw. He was perfect. From his broad shoulders to the wide chest smattered with black hair and his torso, which tapered down to show off his hard earned abs. A lone scar ran from his hip into the hair that formed at the bottom of his abs. She wondered how he'd got that.

She wanted to touch him. His skin was glistening from the water and he wasn't moving. Instead he was watching her watch him. So she reached out and ran her fingers from his chest down to his stomach, until her fingers found the silky tip of his penis, long and hard like satin-covered steel. She shivered and her blood rushed to her core. He hissed at her touch and she felt stronger. Braver. He was enjoying her touch, enjoying *her*, and he could see her now. Every bit of her. He wasn't running. He was pressing himself closer, whispering into her ear. Carefully she wrapped her hand around his length and closed her eyes.

'I wasn't sure if you would want to go through with this,' she said quietly.

'Why wouldn't I?'

His voice was gruff and raw. He throbbed in her hand but she didn't move.

'I wasn't sure if you were serious.'

He lifted his head off the shoulder he was kissing to look at her. 'You want serious?' he asked, a wicked glint in his eye.

He moved, slipping himself out of her palm, and Olivia's heart jumped in her chest when she realised where he was going. His legs were long, so even on his knees his head came to her stomach.

She placed her hands on his head. 'Edward, you don't have to…'

'How many times do I have to tell you to stop talking?' He leaned on his haunches and looked at her. Assessed her. Then his hands came around her backside and he violently pulled her forward, onto his waiting mouth.

Olivia wanted to scream. She wanted to call out—but she was too shocked to do anything. His tongue was inside her and he was sucking and kissing and then using his fingers to stroke and something flicked a switch in her brain. All rational thought left. All she could feel was the hard beads of water on her back, the joy of Edward's tongue inside her and his fingers as they pressed her to him.

She shifted a little and moved, allowing him better access, and he groaned. The vibration of his deep voice ran through her body and caused her to stumble, but he held her strong, lifting her until she was thoughtless and senseless and couldn't move. Couldn't move until the pressure built and everything went black… and then her body shook and she exploded.

Her body spasmed and her hips rocked and she cried

out, gripping the walls and wondering if she had ever felt this good.

No. Definitely not. Not ever. Not once.

Slowly Edward stood and pressed himself along her body.

'Was that serious enough for you?'

She let out a laugh, her boneless body barely able to stay up. But he held her still and shivering until she came to and realised he was still there, holding her body against his so she wouldn't fall. She wondered if she'd ever get enough of him. The way he looked at her as if she was beautiful. The way he spoke to her in Italian—she had no idea what he said when he talked to her like that, but she knew it was dirty and she liked it.

Aftershocks rocked her body but he stayed where he was, holding her and waiting. She couldn't move—didn't want to. She wanted him there for ever. But a blast of cold water made them both jump.

'Leave it,' she said as he turned to face her. 'I need to cool down.'

His eyes fired again as they swept across her body and she laughed.

'What are you thinking, Edward?'

He shifted in closer, his big body covering hers, and dipped his mouth to lick the water from her shoulder. She did the same to him and tasted the saltiness of his skin.

'What am I thinking?' he asked, his voice low and deep and raw. 'I'm thinking that it's my turn.'

He pulled her in close against the hard planes of his body and she melted into him. Let him hold her up.

'I want you to come like that again,' he growled in her ear, before turning the water off completely and pulling her dripping body out of the shower, out of the bathroom and over to the big, waiting bed.

It was late. Olivia wasn't sure how late, but the house had gone quiet and a heavy blackness had settled outside. She'd slept a while, wrapped in Edward's arms, and then slept a while with her body scrooched right to the side of the bed. Then the bed had shifted and Edward had got out, returning with a drink of water. Olivia was pretending to be asleep still, but she wasn't. She was lying and waiting to hear his breathing change. But all she heard was a large intake of breath, and then a sigh, so she decided to turn and face him.

'Edward?'

He was lying on his back and his hands were tucked under his head. His large biceps bulged and Olivia felt a strange urge to bite them. She muffled a laugh and he turned his head.

'What are you laughing at?'

'Nothing. You.'

She moved closer, comfortable now he was talking to her. As she snuggled against him her heart let out a sigh as one of his big arms came down around her body and pulled her in closer. He kissed her lips and shifted a little, so he was looking into her face.

'What do you find so amusing about me?' he asked. He smiled and Olivia snuggled even closer.

'It's not you I find funny. It's me. And the things I think when I'm with you.'

'What are you thinking right now?'

'Actually, I was thinking about how I wanted to bite your biceps.'

His forehead furrowed. 'Please don't tell me you're actually clinically insane?'

'Well, not clinically. But I do have moments of insanity.'

'Like tonight?'

'No, tonight I am the most rational I've ever been. Tonight I made love to a man who makes me feel like someone else.'

Edward shifted, his brow still furrowed. He propped himself up on one arm and used his other hand to trace a line from Olivia's eyebrow to her chin. Her skin tingled at his touch and she shivered.

'I don't want you to be someone else. I like you. I like your beautiful eyes and your gorgeous smile and I like the way you bite your tongue when you come.'

A hard, heavy ball of desire dropped to Olivia's stomach. They'd been at this all night. Was he ready to go again? Because she sure as hell was. She sucked in her bottom lip and bit down. Hard. Trying to still the red-hot stab his look was generating in her.

'Admit it. You hated me when we first met.'

'I didn't hate you. I thought you were ridiculous. And stupid. But I didn't hate you.'

Olivia shot him a fierce look. 'You thought I was stupid?'

'You told me the Prime Minister was "just a man".'

'He is.'

'Just a man whose entire life revolves around running this country.'

'Just a man who goes home to his wife and kids every night. Just a man who is probably lying in bed with a hard-on, like you are right now.'

A look crossed Edward's face that told her he'd

never thought about the Prime Minister's hard-on before and nor did he ever want to again. She laughed at him again.

'Just like *you're* just a man, Eddie. A man who saw a girl he wanted and couldn't wait to jump in bed with her.' She raised an eyebrow, expecting him to laugh, but he didn't.

'This isn't something I do often. I'm not… I don't…'

'You don't what? Have sex with women you find attractive?'

'Find myself attracted to a woman so much I can't keep my hands off her. I'm usually better at controlling myself.'

Heat rushed to her face. He couldn't control himself around her? That made her sit a little higher.

'Earlier, behind the stairs, you lost control then, didn't you?'

The darkness made her bolder. She could see the shadows of his face in the moonlight but his face seemed softer, and it felt as if there were only the two of them in the entire universe.

'I'm sorry about that, Olivia.'

'Sorry? Are you crazy? That was the best time of my life. I mean—one of them. The time in the shower was pretty hot, and then earlier—when you swung me around—that was…' She rolled her eyes, remembering the way he'd seemed even bigger and throbbed even harder from that position.

She had to shift. Beneath the sheets she was completely naked; it would take no time for him to be inside her again.

'But you were upset.'

Olivia stopped. Upset? Yes, she had been. But not because he couldn't control himself.

'I was a bit emotional. Because it was so good. And you… I never thought you… I mean that you and me…' She met his eyes and they were watching her. Waiting for an answer. She saw something vulnerable in them and realised he felt bad about before because he thought he'd hurt her. 'I wasn't upset. I was happy. Happy you wanted me as much as I wanted you.'

'Of course I wanted you. Didn't I make that clear?'

'No. Yes.' She realised she'd second-guessed him. She spent too much time imagining what he thought instead of listening to what he said. 'I didn't get it. But I do now. I know what you want now.'

'Good. Because I want more of it.'

His eyes were dark and his face moved closer. His scent was everywhere. On the sheets, in the air, on her skin. He enveloped her.

'But only one night.' Olivia was guarding her heart. She needed to hear from him now if this wasn't going anywhere.

His forehead furrowed. 'There's something between us, Olivia. A chemistry that doesn't happen often. I was trying to resist it.'

'Why?'

He looked surprised.

'Because you're…vulnerable. And you're easily spooked. And you need someone who's going to treat you right.'

'You make me sound like someone who can't take care of herself.'

'Everyone needs a little bit of help. There's no shame in admitting that.'

'What about you? Do *you* need help?'
'No. I am a freak of nature and need no one else.'
'What about James? Did he need help?'

CHAPTER TWENTY-FOUR

EDWARD WENT STIFF. Even against the moonlight she could see him go pale. She wasn't sure why she'd brought up James but she wanted to know. She wanted them to be honest with each other and she wanted to know.

'James is gone. No one can help him now. All I can do is help everyone else.'

'What happened to James was not your fault.'

'How would you know? You weren't there.'

'Then tell me.'

He didn't speak for a while, so Olivia waited. She wanted him to talk to her. She wanted him to let her in. Even though he'd made love to her—over and over—she still felt he was holding back. As if he didn't trust her. And that made her nervous. She wanted all of him. And that made her nervous too.

'We were at the lake, playing in the maze. James wandered off…'

Edward's voice was quiet, barely a murmur. Olivia had to stay perfectly still to hear it.

'Will had been teasing him about the fact that he'd never win because he couldn't ever get the last riddle. The one in the lake—'

Edward's voice cracked and so did Olivia's heart. Edward wasn't himself right now—he was a twelve-year-old boy who'd lost his brother.

'It wasn't your fault, Edward. You didn't tell him to go into the lake.'

'But I didn't stop Will from saying those things. I laughed along with him. I may as well have pushed James in.'

'Why do you take all the guilt on yourself?'

'Because… Because… I don't know. I was the eldest. I should have been watching. I should have known better.'

'You were twelve. And you were mucking about somewhere you'd been hundreds of times before, saying things you probably said to both your brothers all the time. That's what brothers do. You had no idea he would do that.'

'I should have saved him.'

His voice cracked again and he stopped talking. Olivia waited until his jaw stopped flickering.

'Ed. What happened to James was an awful accident. He could have gone into that lake without you and Will saying anything. He was a little boy who was curious and unaware of the consequences. It wasn't your fault.'

Edward stayed stiff and still in the moonlight. Olivia drew closer to him and reached over to kiss the edge of his cheekbone.

'It wasn't your fault,' she whispered, and he turned to her. She kissed his forehead, then his eyes. Then she gently kissed his lips. 'You are a good, kind man, Edward. A beautiful, strong, nice man. A man I want to make love to.'

He watched her lips as she spoke, then leaned towards her and kissed her lips as gently as she had done to him.

'You make me feel different, Olivia. You make me feel like there are only the two of us and nothing else matters.'

'Nothing else matters,' she repeated, pressing herself closer to the hard muscles of his strong body. She wanted to be close to him. She wanted to offer comfort and support and strength and to give him everything he'd given her.

Her lips met his and his mouth opened, letting her in. Their kiss was deep and laced with something very different. Something intense that meant something. Olivia curled her arms around his neck, pressing his head closer, and his hands came around her hips, bringing them right into him.

They moved and shifted but stayed close. When he slipped himself inside her she moved closer, keeping her hips moving with his. He moaned and she shivered. There were no fancy tricks this time. No crazy positions. Just two bodies moving in time, staying as close as they possibly could, and Olivia had never felt more loved in her entire life.

When the sun woke her the next morning Olivia didn't move. She was still wrapped up in Edward. In his legs, in his arms and in his scent. And she wanted to stay there. But the buzz of his phone made him grunt sleepily and shift.

He smiled at her and then the phone buzzed again. His brow furrowed and he swung his arm away, knocking his glass of water off the side table as he found it.

'What?' he grumbled into it.

Olivia moved away as his conversation continued. She didn't want to. But his conversation sounded like work and it sounded urgent. He swung his legs over the side of the bed and sat up. Olivia watched the muscles in his naked back move as he stretched them out.

She couldn't resist. She moved closer and sat behind him to massage his shoulders. She needed to touch him. He responded by moving his head around and pressing his lips against hers. When his eyes met hers they were greedy. He smiled and she smiled back. They didn't need words. But then he looked angry and turned away, barking something into the phone.

He was busy and she was naked. And in his room. With no clothes except the ones she had on last night.

'I'll have a shower,' she mouthed, and he nodded before she moved off, trying to think of her next move. How was she going to get out of his room without being seen?

As she twisted the hot water handle she smiled. Easy solution. Don't leave. Except she had to. Her flight home was today. Damn.

'How are you feeling this morning?'

The bathroom door opened and Edward stood with absolutely no shame, naked and aroused in front of her. She wasn't sure if she'd ever be able to completely satisfy this man. But the idea of trying filled her with a bubble of something delightful.

'Tired. And wondering how I'm going to get out of your room without anyone seeing.'

He moved closer, wrapped his long arms around her waist and kissed her deeply. 'So don't leave. I have to do some work, but after that we could stay in bed all day.'

'Oh, OK. That would be great. With everyone wondering where we were. Fiona would send out a search party and pretty soon they'd find us here. Naked and enjoying each other.'

'So?'

'So then I'd be embarrassed.' She pushed on his chest. 'I'm going to have a shower. Alone. You do your work and think of how to get me out of here without anyone seeing.'

The angry look returned to his face. But it wasn't the 'real' angry look. It was the 'I want to have sex with you' angry look. That angry look she couldn't resist.

'First of all, there's nothing embarrassing about spending the day with me. That is the stuff of girlhood dreams.'

Olivia snorted, ready to tell him what she thought of that comment, but he kissed her words away.

'Secondly, this is my shower, and if I want to get in it with you I will.'

And he did. And he made it worth her while to let him in.

She got out of the shower shivering, and it had nothing to do with the cold water she'd blasted over herself before she stepped out.

Wrapped in a towel, and drying her hair with another, Olivia found Edward sitting on his bed, papers and laptop around him, dressed in boxer shorts. His golden torso was lean and muscled and it made Olivia's mouth water.

He looked up. 'I've got to get this finished. Then we can spend the morning together before you leave.'

'No, I have another idea.'

He raised an eyebrow.

'What if I stayed?'

Edward's fingers paused above his laptop.

'Stayed? For the day?'

Olivia adjusted her towel, pulled it a little higher.

'No. Stayed. Indefinitely.'

Edward's heart thudded. She wanted to stay? That wasn't the plan. He felt his control slip slightly. He licked his lips.

'Don't you have to go home? What about your job?'

She paced towards him and he got distracted when her towel slipped. He had to focus. She wanted to stay. She wanted more than one weekend.

'Don't you want me to stay?'

Yes. He wanted her to stay. He wanted to see her naked. He wanted to kiss her. He wanted to be with her.

But she couldn't stay.

She was right in front of him now, and looking down at him with those big blue eyes of hers. Cinnamon and soap whirled around her. It made his head spin and his groin shift.

'I thought you only wanted one weekend.'

He saw the moment she started thinking again. Her eyes changed; her forehead furrowed. She shifted and pulled the towel off her head, letting her wet hair tumble over her shoulders. He felt his control perilously close to the edge.

'I did. But now…I want more.'

Edward's throat was so dry he couldn't speak. She wanted more. She wanted to stay.

Olivia blinked before tossing the towel over her arm. Gently she placed a hand on his shoulder and his skin burned with the contact. He wanted her. Again. Just one touch and he wanted her again. His attraction to her was dangerous and out of control.

Edward pushed his laptop onto the bed. She wanted to stay. With him. This wasn't supposed to happen. She couldn't stay. Not with him. Will was right. He didn't do relationships. Those others—he'd known they would never go anywhere. But Olivia? She was like a drug. When he wasn't with her he thought about her, and when he was with her he thought about nothing else. He couldn't let her into his life because then nothing else would matter. Work, his family—she'd be too distracting and then what?

'Olivia, you said this was one weekend. One more night, you said—remember?'

'I know what I said.' Her voice had an edge to it. She pulled her towel up higher and flicked her hair over her shoulder. 'But I've changed my mind.'

'Just like that?'

'No.' Her eyes flashed now. He could see her getting frustrated, and he wanted to stand up and hold her as he had the night before the wedding. 'Not just like that. I thought that last night...we shared something special.'

'We did. But now it's over.'

Her face changed. Slight irritation turned to full-blown anger. He'd said the wrong thing and her angry face was back. He'd seen that look before. When she'd threatened him in the drawing room. And she'd looked just as sexy then as she did now. More now—because she was almost naked and he knew what she felt like, what she tasted like. But he had to control himself and his feelings. This couldn't happen. Sure—it would be nice. For a while. Then she'd get bored and leave.

'So that's it, is it? One night and it's over?'

He stood up. That wasn't fair. 'You made the rules, Olivia.'

He watched as she sucked in a deep breath, as if readying herself for something. 'I like you, Edward. A lot. I think this could become something…more. I don't know what. And I know you feel the same way I do. I *know* you do.'

His stomach clenched. Her words stabbed at him. Her cheeks pinkened. He wanted to kiss her. But he couldn't. This would never work. He couldn't concentrate when she was around.

'Olivia, this weekend was nice…'

'Nice? *Nice!* This weekend was more than nice. This weekend was…life-changing.'

The phrase hung in the air between them.

'Olivia, I have loved being with you.' He stepped forward to hold her hand. 'But this can never go anywhere. I have a busy job and a life in London, and you… Well, you wouldn't fit in.'

She pulled from his grasp as if burned. Her eyes opened wide, and although he could see the fire spitting in them there were tears as well. He'd hurt her.

'Olivia, please. You have to understand. I lead a very boring life. I've worked in the same place for years. There's no wild parties or good times in my life. You would hate it.'

CHAPTER TWENTY-FIVE

OLIVIA FORCED BACK the tears. He was pushing her away. After everything they'd shared he was trying to get rid of her. As if she meant nothing. He was telling her she didn't fit in. She wasn't good enough.

'I thought you liked me...'

'I do...'

'No, you don't.' She snapped her arm out of his reach again and stepped back. 'You see me as the perpetual party girl. A woman you can't take seriously. I'm a joke to you—this weekend has been a joke to you.'

'No, Olivia.' This time he didn't hesitate. He grabbed her hand and held it hard. 'That's not it.' Anger flashed in his eyes. 'I take you very seriously. But you would get bored. I know what you need. Excitement and fun and adventure. I just don't *do* that—and besides...I can't take care of you. You distract me.'

'I distract you?'

'Yes. And I can't be distracted. I have to stay focussed. You deserve someone who treats you as if you're the most important woman in the world.'

But you do! She wanted to scream at him. She wanted to tell him how he made her feel. Important. Desired. Beautiful. Loved. She blinked as the thumping in her chest turned into heaving. His focus had lasted exactly as long as he'd said it would. One weekend. And now he didn't want her any more.

'But I thought I "captivated" you.'

'You did. You do. But you don't want this—you don't want me.'

His eyes never left hers. They burned into her and she could see what he was saying behind them. *Don't make this harder than it is. Accept this for what it was—one weekend. And leave me alone.*

This weekend had changed Olivia. She felt as if she'd fallen into a screaming heap but then Edward had picked her up and tended her wounds and made her feel whole again. He'd made her realise she was beautiful. But now he was putting her on her feet and sending her on her way and she had to be strong. Move on.

She breathed in deeply and pushed her face into a smile. 'You're right, Eddie. I mean, this was fun, but it's time to move on to the next party.'

He smiled back. She'd thought the pain would relieve itself when she saw him smile, but it didn't. It just got worse.

'I won't forget you, Olivia.'

His words cut right down deep. She almost doubled over with the pain of them. 'I'd better go and get dressed.' She turned to leave and through her blurry vision found the handle of the door.

'Olivia, wait...'

She looked back, searching his face desperately for some sign that he'd changed his mind. She wanted to see in his eyes that he'd got it wrong and he wanted her to stay, and for a moment she thought she saw it.

Something flickered in his eyes and his jaw twitched. She hesitated, holding her breath.

'I have some work to do, but I'll see you downstairs at breakfast…before you leave.'

She wanted to smile and flick her hair nonchalantly, but she didn't. She just turned and fled before he saw the first tear fall.

The phone rang as Olivia walked out through the door and Edward answered it mechanically. It was the Prime Minister. He tried to concentrate but it was difficult.

She'd trusted him and he'd hurt her. It wasn't that he didn't want her to stay, but they would never work. He didn't want to hold her back or make her hate him.

It was good that she'd left. If he saw her again he wasn't sure he'd be as strong next time. His control always seemed to vanish when Olivia was near. He'd catch her scent and he'd forget everything he was going to say.

She was leaving.

But he'd meet someone else. Someone who didn't send his heart racing and make his brain vanish. Someone who wore sensible dresses and didn't get drunk and pass out on the terrace.

Except he didn't want anyone else.

'I want more,' she'd said.

More.

She'd wanted to stay. She'd wanted him. And he wanted her. More than anything. More than he wanted to keep his job. More than he wanted to do the right thing. He wanted her. He needed her. Olivia wasn't a distraction. She was his salvation. And he'd be damned if he couldn't take care of her.

No. He couldn't let her go. He *wouldn't* let her go. This was real.

'I'm sorry, Prime Minister, I'll have to call you back.'

The voice on the other end of the phone stilled.

'I have to speak to someone about something very important. I'll call you back when I'm done, sir.'

The Prime Minister didn't answer, so Edward just hung up. On the Prime Minister. Who was, after all, just a man. Just as he was. Just a man trying to figure out how the hell he had made the monumental mistake of letting Olivia walk out through the door thinking he didn't want her.

CHAPTER TWENTY-SIX

THERE WAS SOMETHING wrong with the plane. Something about wing damage and incorrect airflow from South America. Whatever it was it sounded serious. And stupid. So very stupid. Just as she felt. So incredibly stupid.

It would take a long time to get over Edward. But she had to get over him. She had to pick herself up and move on. But all she wanted to do right now was get the hell out of this place. This weekend had become a car crash. She'd been humiliated, ridiculed and tortured.

And she'd fallen in love.

She stepped backwards, away from the counter, and bumped into the man standing behind her. He apologised and she stared at him blankly. He stepped back and averted his eyes awkwardly.

She was going mad. Stark, raving bonkers.

Love? She wasn't in love.

But then she remembered the way he'd made her feel. And the way he'd looked at her, as if she was beautiful. And she remembered the way she'd wanted to be there for him when he'd mentioned James at dinner. The way she'd wanted to hold him and tell him everything would be all right.

'There has to be a flight going to Australia somehow. Maybe I could get something to Asia and change there?'

The very large woman in a tight pink dress shook her bouncy curls at her. 'Sorry, luv. It's too late now. But we'll have something in the morning for you.'

One more night. One more night before she could be out of here and away from this nightmare.

With a sigh, she checked her phone and found a B&B about half an hour's drive south of Heathrow, then went out to the front to hail a taxi. She hadn't worn her ridiculous boots this time, but her tower of bags was still heavy as she dragged it across the shiny tiles of the airport. Once outside, she wrapped her fluffy coat tight and stood impatiently in the cold queue to wait for a taxi.

'Olivia.'

Olivia didn't turn around. She just froze. Solid. That voice. That deep English voice laced with gravel. The voice that had turned her to mush last night when it had told her she was beautiful. Now that voice made her feel weak and anxious and a little bit sick. Slowly, she turned.

'What are you doing here, Edward?'

'Looking for you.'

He was here.

'Why?' Her heart hammered. He didn't move but stood watching her. He had on his dark grey coat and his red scarf. His ebony hair flopped over his forehead and his deep, dark eyes transfixed her.

'You said you wanted to stay.'

Olivia had to remind herself to breathe.

Edward was here.

Tears stung her eyes and something sad pierced her heart. Edward. The man who had seen beneath her make-up to what was underneath. And still wanted her anyway. Desperate longing tugged at her, but she stood still, rooted to the spot. He was here. He'd come. But he didn't want her to stay.

'I made a mistake. It was just one night.'

'Next up, luv, move along!'

The taxi queue shuffled and Olivia awkwardly lifted her bags to move along with it. In seconds Edward was by her side—lifting her bags and setting them down ten inches from where they were.

'Olivia, we need to talk. I need to explain.'

Olivia wondered why he'd come down here to go through all this again. It was over and he was done. But if he was done, why was he here? Perhaps he was worried about how she felt. She wanted to hate him. But she couldn't. Because he was nice. And kind. And thoughtful and sweet and the sexiest damn man she'd ever seen.

A layer of stubble had spread across his jaw. Olivia wanted to touch it. She wanted to feel it rubbing across her skin. *Stop!* She couldn't think like that. It was over. It couldn't go anywhere. It was just one weekend.

'You didn't have to come down here, Edward. I get it. I'm not upset, really. I just thought that…' She shook her head. She hadn't blow-dried her hair this morning, and it was a bit frizzy and crazy, but it didn't matter. He wasn't looking anyway. 'It doesn't matter. I just want to get home.'

She turned away from him, because she wasn't sure she could look into those beautiful dark eyes any longer without crying. And she didn't want to cry in front of him.

The cold wind that was whipping past her suddenly ceased. She felt the warmth of his big body at her back and then his hot breath on her ear. She breathed him in. Soap and man. A scent that was now so familiar to her it was as if it had always been there.

'Don't go.'

She was convinced she hadn't heard him right.

'What did you say?' she asked as she spun around. He was close, mere inches from her face, but he didn't touch her. His dark gaze grew darker and his eyes held her still.

'I said don't go. Stay.'

'Stay?'

'Stay.'

Olivia drew in a ragged breath. Her brain was shifting inside her head.

'Stay, Olivia. Stay here. Stay with me.'

Olivia stepped back, away from his scent and his overpowering physical presence. It was too much. *He* was too much. He didn't want her to stay. He'd find out she wasn't interesting and she wasn't funny and she wasn't as beautiful as he'd thought she was. Then he'd leave. They always left.

'I'm not staying.'

'Why not?'

He stepped closer again and all the oxygen in the air evaporated. He was too big and too close and too potent. She couldn't breathe.

'I don't want to stay.'

'I can't give up on you that easily, Olivia. I can't give up on us.'

His words were like a balm, but she hardened her heart. This wouldn't last. 'I wasn't thinking straight this morning, Edward. I was tired and hungry. It isn't anything to do with you. I don't do…relationships. I just get too…too…'

'Scared. I know. I know you're scared. I know that's why you're running. I'll let you in on a secret.'

A half-smile tipped his mouth and Olivia's heart fell to the floor. Her hands hung loosely down at her sides but she longed to touch him. She wanted to feel his hard chest and his soft lips on hers. She wanted to feel the rough abrasion of his stubble against her top lip. She wanted to kiss the damn freckle just underneath his mouth which drove her wild. But she didn't move.

'I'm scared too. Scared of you. Of this. Of what I feel for you. I've never been like this before. Out of control and desperate. Desperate to see you.'

Olivia's breaths were short and sharp. He was desperate to see her?

She studied his face. His cheeks were slashed with pink, his hair was falling across his lined forehead and his dark eyes were almost black. He looked down at her, still not touching her. A steady beat pounded through the veins in her neck.

He felt the same way she did and fear clutched at her heart. This wasn't some one-night stand. This wasn't a casual fling. This was real. He was really here, wanting her as much as she wanted him.

'The truth is, Olivia,' he said quietly, 'I know we've only just met but—it feels like I've known you for ever. And if you leave me it'll hurt…right here.' He laid his palm on his chest.

If there was ever a time Olivia had needed a paper bag—this was it.

'You said I won't fit in to your life.'

'I don't want you to get bored. I don't want you to lose interest.'

'Me? Lose interest?' Was he mad? 'It's you who will lose interest. In me.'

He moved closer so her breasts now brushed his hard chest. He lifted a hand and moved a piece of hair from her face.

'Olivia, I love your hair and I love your short dresses and your sparkles and your gorgeous lips…' He paused to breathe, looking directly at her mouth. 'I love the way you say out loud what you're thinking. I love the way you get it wrong and you fall over and then get back up again. I love the way you touch me and the way you kiss me. And I love the way you smile. You have a beautiful smile.'

Olivia's heart whispered, and something buried inside her struggled to get out. The feeling took over her entire body and she couldn't think. His words washed over her, flooding her veins with their intensity.

'How could I ever lose interest in you?'

His lips were so close. His hot breath warmed her mouth and she swayed towards him.

'You will.' Her heart pounded and her head swam. 'I'm not beautiful and talented and perfect. I'm not the right girl for you, Edward. You need someone more… steady. Someone who can be in a relationship for more than one weekend.'

'*You* are what I need.'

His voice rose and it made Olivia step back. His eyes flashed and she saw something she hadn't ever seen in him. Raw emotion. She watched as he breathed in and out and something simmered in him.

'You were right. This weekend was life-changing.

This weekend meant something to me and I thought it meant something to you too.'

It had meant everything to her. It had changed her life.

'Edward. You…you made me feel something I'd never felt before. You made me feel like I was everything to someone. You made me feel like I was beautiful. I'll never forget you. I'll never forget how you made me feel.'

Olivia's heart hurt as if it had been slashed with a knife. He didn't understand. Love… Love was something she'd never have. He'd grow tired and she'd be heartbroken. She had to protect herself.

'But don't you understand? When I'm with you I want something I know I can't have.' Olivia couldn't look at him any more. She blinked and breathed in deeply. 'You take on all the responsibility, you take on all the blame, but you never let anyone in. Not really. You hover and help and worry, but you never let yourself fall. And the problem is I wanted you to fall. Deeply, ridiculously in love…with *me*. But we have to be honest. Some people are not cut out for love.'

Edward's eyes were shining. His big body moved slightly closer and Olivia couldn't breathe for a second. She couldn't take it all in. His eyes, his stubbled jaw, that freckle. His heat, his scent—it was everything she wanted. And it was out of her reach.

His eyes travelled across her face and paused at her lips, then his eyes locked on hers.

'You're wrong.'

Olivia pushed her forehead into a frown. 'When I

told you I wanted to stay you pushed me away. You broke my heart, Edward. I can't let you do that again.'

Hearing the words come out of her mouth made Olivia's heart ache. Tears threatened her eyes. She wanted him. More than anything or anyone. She desperately wanted to throw herself into his arms. But she was so tired and so broken she just didn't know if she'd be able to recover if he let her down.

His eyes grew sad again and his mouth turned down into a frown.

'Olivia, I'm sorry. I was…confused and frustrated. I've never felt like this before.'

He stepped away and Olivia felt the chill of the air again.

'You're right. You should go. If that's what you want. If you need time to think, or if you don't want this. It's up to you. It's your decision.'

Her decision? Her life had always depended on others. Her sister, her friends… She'd never been able to make a choice that was just for her. Until now. Until Edward had stood in front of her making her feel wanted and desired and everything to someone. Just as he was everything to her.

The bubble returned. The one in which there was only him and her and the rest of the world fell away.

'I just need you to know that I love you, Olivia, and I will for ever.'

'Edward…'

'I love you.'

His words were rough and raw and sincere. He was trying to make her understand. And she stopped and finally listened.

'You…you love me?'

'Desperately. Ridiculously.'

A shaft of light shot through Olivia's brain. This wasn't just talk any more. This was serious. He was close and he smelled divine and he'd just said he loved her.

'I want more than a one-night stand, Eddie. I want more than a weekend. Can you really give me more?'

His lips parted. His eyes turned dark and his breathing changed.

'I can give you much more.'

The wind blew Eddie's hair and he looked wild. Out of control. His eyes hungry. He wanted her and he couldn't control it. No one had ever felt that way about her. But he did.

Her heart seized when his lips fell gently onto hers. He moved slowly, his lips gentle, and she could feel him holding back. As if he was afraid to show her how he really felt.

She pulled back a little and he stopped and looked into her eyes.

'I'm serious, Edward. If I stay—I stay. Do you really want that?'

His lips moved closer and she stopped him with a hand on his chest. His lovely, muscled, hard, hot chest.

'I know I haven't done this the right way. I should have taken it slower. I should have let you know how I felt before I took you to bed. But…'

He moved closer and his lips met her neck, but his hands still didn't touch her. His restraint was driving her crazy.

'I couldn't wait. I've never wanted anyone the way I want you,' he said roughly.

Olivia sucked in a ragged breath and lifted her head away from the feel of his rough jaw on her sensitive skin. She had to think. She had to tell him what she wanted before she lost every thought in her head.

'Then you have to fix it. You have to call me and send me flowers and take me out to dinner and woo me.'

'*Woo* you?'

His sexy smile was turning lethal. Olivia's bones melted a little but she held strong.

'Yes. Woo me. Woo the *hell* out of me.'

He sucked in a deep breath, then lifted his hand to trace her cheekbone. 'Olivia, I want nothing more than to woo the hell out of you. You are going to be so sick of my wooing you'll beg me to stop. But I won't. I'll woo you and woo you until you scream my name.'

Olivia had a sneaking suspicion his idea of wooing was a little different from hers.

His hand moved to the back of her head and pulled it in to meet his lips. His kiss was long and hard and deep and it left Olivia feeling faint. She didn't care who saw. She wanted to rip her ridiculous coat off and have him on top of her right at the Heathrow Departures gate.

'You deserve to be wooed, Olivia. Often. By someone who knows what they're doing,' he murmured gruffly into her hair before kissing her cheekbone softly.

Olivia sucked in a breath and pulled away from him. The sounds of the airport vanished. She couldn't hear anything else but his voice, nor feel anything else but his touch.

'I want you, Olivia. I want to be with you and I want you to stay.'

'But what if I distract you?'

His eyes met hers and they burned with truth. 'I want to be distracted by you. I can't keep living in the past. I can't keep trying to make up for my mistakes. I have to move on, and I want to move on with the only girl who drives me wild.'

Olivia's eyes fell to his mouth, where a wicked smile had appeared. Her body throbbed. He loved her and she loved him. He needed her as much as she needed him. He wasn't going to break her heart. He was going to mend it. This was the man she'd been waiting for. The man to send her mad with want and to make her feel as beautiful as she knew deep down that she was. *This* man.

She pushed herself up onto her toes until her lips sat tantalisingly close to his ear and then she whispered into it, 'I want you, Edward. I need you. I love you.' She tried to convey with her eyes what her heart was bursting to say. 'And I want to stay.'

She was his. For real. A woman worth loving. A woman worth staying with.

'And, Edward?' She pulled away so she could see his eyes. His dark, beautiful eyes which captivated her. She knew it now. She wasn't incapable of love. She'd just never met anyone worth fighting for before. She'd never met anyone who deserved her love. Until now.

'Voglio avere sesso con voi.'

A slow smile spread across his face. 'Do you have any idea what you just said?'

'I get the general idea of it,' she said with a wide smile.

'That's my bad girl.'

Her arms circled his neck as their lips met in a deep, wild, uncontrollable kiss and finally, Olivia let herself fall desperately, ridiculously in love.

* * * * *

LUCY KING

spent her formative years lost in the world of
Harlequin romance novels when she really
ought to have been paying attention to her
teachers. Up against sparkling heroines,
gorgeous heroes and the magic of falling
in love, trigonometry and ablative absolutes
didn't stand a chance. But as she couldn't
live in a dream world forever, she eventually
acquired a degree in languages and an eclectic
collection of jobs. A stroll to the River Thames
one Saturday morning led her to her very own
hero. The minute she laid eyes on the hunky
rower getting out of a boat, clad only in Lycra
and carrying a three-meter oar as if it were a
toothpick, she knew she'd met the man she was
going to marry. Luckily the rower thought the
same. She will always be grateful to whatever it
was that made her stop dithering and actually
sit down to type *Chapter One,* because dreaming
up her own sparkling heroines and gorgeous
heroes is pretty much her idea of the perfect
job. Originally a Londoner, Lucy now lives in
Spain, where she spends much of the time
reading, failing to finish cryptic crosswords
and trying to convince herself that lying on the
beach really *is* the best way to work.

THE BEST MAN
FOR THE JOB

Lucy King

For my editor, Megan.
Thank you for your always invaluable insight
and advice!

CHAPTER ONE

TEN MINUTES AFTER the vicar had pronounced her brother and his fiancée man and wife and the register had been signed, Celia Forrester stood on the steps of the altar of the pretty Shropshire church and braced herself for the moment she'd been dreading all day.

In terms of things she'd rather not do, on a scale of one to ten, going to the gym hovered at the two mark. Pulling an all-nighter at work ranked around a four. Dinner *à deux* with her father, an eight.

Having to take Marcus Black's arm and walk down the aisle beside him, however, hit a ten.

Up until about a couple of hours ago she'd thought she'd escaped. As Dan's best friend—and consequently, best man—Marcus had been expected some time yesterday afternoon, but to the consternation of everyone apart from her he hadn't shown up. Her brother had muttered something about a missed flight and a possible arrival in time for the reception but, in all honesty, Celia had been too relieved to pay much attention.

All she'd been able to think was that she had a stay of execution and that, with any luck, by the time Marcus got there—if he got there at all—she'd have indulged in the gallon of champagne she needed to handle the horribly edgy and deeply uncomfortable effect he had on her, should she be unable to implement her customary plan A and avoid him.

She'd had no problem with following Lily—the other bridesmaid and Zoe's sister—and her brand-new fiancé, Kit, down the aisle alone. She was good at doing things alone, and she'd been more than happy about the delay in having to talk to too-gorgeous-for-his-own-good, serial womaniser and general thorn in her side Marcus Black. Quite apart from the unsettling way he made her feel, he loathed her as much as she loathed him and no doubt he would be expressing it at the first available opportunity, namely the church, so who could blame her for savouring any delay to the moment?

But then a couple of hours ago, when the three of them had been sitting in the spare room of Zoe's parents' farmhouse with rollers in their hair and tacky nails, news had reached them that Marcus had made it after all, and just like that the Get-Out-of-Jail-Free-card feeling she'd been holding onto had blown up in her face.

The degree of shock and disappointment that had rocked through her had surprised her. Then her skin had started prickling, a rush of heat had swept through her and she'd instantly felt as though she were sitting on knives.

She'd managed to hide it, of course, because firstly she was used to hiding the way he made her feel, and secondly today was a happy one that was all about Dan and Zoe and not in the slightest bit about the trouble she had with Marcus, but it had been hard. Even harder when she and Lily had entered the church behind Zoe and she'd seen him standing next to Dan at the altar, looking tall, dark and smboulderingly gorgeous in his morning suit.

But she'd done it, and she'd continue to do so because fifty pairs of eyes were trained on the proceedings and so right now she didn't have the option of giving him a cool nod and then blanking him. She was simply going to have to suck it up and accompany him down the aisle.

In approximately thirty seconds.

The organist began belting out Widor's Toccata and as Dan and Zoe turned and stepped away from the altar, their smiles wide and unstoppable, Celia pulled her shoulders back and plastered a smile of her own to her face.

She wouldn't let him get to her, she told herself, adopting the unusual strategy of channelling serenity and inner calm. She wouldn't think about the struggle she'd had throughout the ceremony resisting the constant temptation to keep looking in his direction, especially when she could feel his eyes on her. Nor would she dwell on the way that, despite her deep disapproval of him and his clear loathing of her whenever they met, he somehow managed to turn her into someone she didn't recognise, addling her brain, making a mockery of her intellect and rendering her body all soft and warm and fluttery.

No, she'd simply rise above the inconvenient and highly irritating attraction and get on with the job. She could ignore the heat of him, the mouth-watering scent of him and the invisible thread of attraction that seemed to constantly pull her towards him. She could bury the desire to drag him off somewhere quiet, press herself against him and let chemistry do its thing. Of course she could. She had done so for years, ever since the night, in fact, he'd tried to get her into bed. For a bet.

Besides, it was, what, thirty metres between the altar and the heavy oak door, so all she had to do was keep a smile on her face and her mouth shut and not let him get to her. After that, during the inevitable photo session and then the reception, which was to be mercifully short, she'd do what she always tried to do and avoid him. Simple.

Taking a deep breath and steeling herself, she glanced up at him to find him looking down at her with those wickedly glinting blue eyes that had seduced legions of women over the years.

'Shall we?' he said, a faint smile playing at the mouth that had given her an annoying number of sleepless nights over the years, as he held out his arm.

'Why not?' she said coolly, taking it.

See? This was fine. She barely noticed the hard muscles of his forearm beneath her fingers. And so what if his elbow was now pressed up against her breast and the feel of him, the heat of him, would be making her heart beat hard and fast and her body tingle if she let it? All that was relevant right now were the five stone steps she had to negotiate in heels three inches higher than she normally wore, and she needed to concentrate.

'Ready?' he asked, his deep, lazy voice tightening her stomach muscles and making her cling onto his arm a little tighter for a second. Just in case she stumbled, of course.

'Couldn't be readier.'

Reassuring herself that in five minutes or so this

would all be over and she'd be free of him, Celia glanced down and lifted the longer back of her dress so it didn't catch on a heel.

'Those shoes look lethal,' he murmured as they descended the first step.

'They are.'

'And spiky.'

'That too.'

'Appropriate.'

And just like that, despite all that serenity and inner calm she'd been striving for, her intention to keep her mouth shut evaporated. 'Good of you to make it, by the way,' she said a touch acidly.

'I nearly didn't.'

'So what held you up?' she asked, once she'd safely navigated the remaining steps and could relax her grip on Marcus' arm. 'Unable to prise yourself away from an overly clingy lover? Or a pair of them perhaps? Surely it couldn't have been a trio?'

She felt him tense and wondered fleetingly if her barb had stung. Then decided it couldn't have because for one thing his many and varied bedroom exploits were no secret, and for another they'd traded mild insults like this for years and it had never seemed to bother him before. Nevertheless she kind of wished it had because it would be satisfying to know she got to him the way he got to her.

'You know something?' he said, shooting her a slow stomach-melting smile. 'I rustled up that ash cloud especially because I knew it would wind you up.'

'My word, you literally do have a God complex,' she said, annoyed beyond measure that he of all people should still be the only man ever to melt any of her internal organs. 'Why am I not surprised?'

'Lucky you're always there to smack me down.'

'It's my sole purpose in life.'

'Really?' he murmured. 'I thought your sole purpose in life was work.'

'I excel at multitasking.'

'Of course you do. Heaven forbid you should fail at anything.'

'I try not to.'

They began proceeding down the aisle at a pace that would have had a snail overtaking them. In crackling silence, until Marcus said conversationally, 'You know, I'm rather amazed you're here.'

Celia kept her smile firmly in place. 'Oh? Why?'

'I wouldn't have thought that you'd have been able to drag yourself away from your desk.'

'It's my brother's wedding.'

'Nice to know there are some things that take priority. I kept expecting your phone to go off during the service.'

She bristled and her jaw began to ache with the effort of maintaining the smile. So she worked hard. Big deal. 'I'm not a *complete* workaholic.' Well, not to such an extent she'd forgo something as important as this.

'No?'

'No,' she said firmly, choosing to ignore the fact that she *had* spent much of the morning on her phone, dealing with calls to and from the office and a string of emails that couldn't wait.

'I read about that pharmaceutical merger of yours going through. Congratulations.'

Despite the indignation Celia couldn't help feeling a stab of pride because the six months she'd spent pushing that deal through had been the toughest of her working life so far, yet she and her team had done it, and now the partnership she'd been working towards for what felt like for ever was that tiny bit closer.

'Thank you,' she said demurely, ignoring the way his body kept brushing against hers and sent thrills scurrying through her. 'And I heard you'd sold your business.' For millions, according to the gossip magazine she'd picked up and flicked through at the hairdresser's a fortnight ago, which had been light on detail about the sale and heavy on speculation about what one of London's most eligible bachelors was going to do with all his money and free time.

'I did.'

'So what are your plans now?'

'Do you really want to know?'

Not really, because she'd willingly bet her lovely two-bedroomed minimalist flat in Clerkenwell that she knew what he'd be doing for the foreseeable future. What he did best, but even better. 'I'm guessing it'll involve partying till dawn with scantily clad women.'

'Am I really that much of a cliché?'

'You tell me.'

'And spoil the fun you have baiting me?'

'You think I find it fun?'

He raised an eyebrow as he glanced down at her. 'Don't you?'

Celia thought about it for a second and decided that, as she didn't know exactly what to attribute the thrill she always got from winding him up to, 'fun' would do. 'OK, perhaps,' she conceded. 'Just a little. But no more than you do.'

'Well, I'm all for equality.'

'Yes, so the tabloids say,' she said witheringly as the interview with one of his conquests that she'd read in that magazine popped into her head. Apparently he was intense, smouldering and passionately demanding in the bedroom, and sought the same from whoever he was sharing it with. Which was something she could really have done without knowing because now she did it was alarmingly hard to put from her mind.

'You know, Celia, darling, you have such low expectations of me I find I can't help wanting to live down to them.'

Before she could work out what he meant by that he turned away and directed that devastating smile of his at a couple of women at the end of a pew on Dan's side, and as she watched them blush she mentally rolled her eyes. How very typical. That was Marcus all over. Lover of women. Literally. Lots of women.

But not her. Never her. Not that she thought about that night fifteen years ago when she'd been so desperate to lose her virginity to him. Much.

'What's with the death grip?'

Celia blinked and snapped her train of thought away from the treacherous path it would career down if she let it. 'Huh?'

'On the flowers. What did they do? What did they say? Because I know from personal experience that it doesn't take much.'

Celia glanced down at the beautiful bouquet of pink roses and baby's breath that matched her dress and saw that her knuckles were indeed white, and she mentally swore at herself for letting him get to her.

She really had to relax because if she didn't she'd

never make it to the door with her nerves intact. This walk down the aisle was taking for ever. What with the way Dan and Zoe kept stopping to talk to people in the pews, they were progressing at about a metre an hour and she wasn't sure how much longer she could resist the temptation to push past the bride and groom and make a run for it.

'The flowers haven't done anything,' she said, taking a couple of deep calming breaths and surreptitiously rolling her shoulders in an effort to release some of her tension.

'Am I to take it, then, that you don't really approve of Dan and Zoe?'

Celia stilled mid-roll and stared at him for a moment, unable to work out where that had come from because Zoe was the best thing that had ever happened to Dan, as she'd told him after supper last night just before giving him a big hug and wishing him luck. 'Why on earth would you think that?'

'Because you spent the entire ceremony looking like you wished you were somewhere else.'

Oh. She hadn't wanted to be anywhere else. She'd wanted Marcus to be somewhere else, preferably on another planet, but she'd thought she'd managed to hide that. Clearly she'd been wrong. 'I'm surprised you noticed.'

'Oh, I noticed,' he murmured, his gaze drifting over her and making her skin feel all hot and tingly and tight. 'You look beautiful, by the way.'

That was the trouble with him, she thought irritably as she stamped out the heat with every ounce of self-control she had. Just when she felt like slapping him, he went and said something charming. 'Thank you.'

'You're welcome.'

'And you look very handsome,' she said, because he did and it would be churlish to ignore the fact. More handsome than usual if that were possible.

'My, my, a compliment,' he said softly. 'That's a first.'

'Yes, well, don't get too used to it.'

'I won't.'

They advanced another agonisingly slow couple of paces, then stopped, and he said, 'So you do approve?'

'Of Dan and Zoe?'

'Well, I know you don't approve of me.'

'I approve wholeheartedly,' said Celia with a serene smile. 'Of them.'

'They're good for each other.'

She nodded. 'They are.'

'And are your parents behaving?'

She narrowed her eyes at her parents, who were accompanying each other down the aisle in stony silence and about as far apart as it was possible to get given the width restriction of the aisle, which was pretty much par for the course. 'Just about.'

'And how's work?'

Insane. 'Work's fine.'

'Then what is there to be so tense about?'

'Tense?' she asked, blowing out a slow breath. 'Who's tense?'

'You are. If it isn't the wedding, it isn't your parents and it isn't work, I might be inclined to think it's me.'

'Hah. As if.'

Off they set again, and this time, thank heavens, it looked as though the end was in sight because Dan and Zoe had run out of guests to chat to and the great oak door was being opened and Celia could practically taste freedom.

'Admit it,' he said softly, his voice so warm and teasing that it did strange things to her stomach, 'I make you feel tense.'

'You don't make me feel anything,' she said, her pulse drumming with the need to get out of here and away from him.

'Oh, Celia, you break my heart.'

'I didn't know you had one. I thought it was another part of your anatomy entirely that kept you alive.'

'So cruel.'

'I dare say you'll survive.'

'I dare say I shall.'

And then, thank God, they stepped out into the July sunshine and she felt as if she could suddenly breathe again. She dragged in some air and blinked as her eyes became accustomed to the brightness after an hour in the church, then she took her hand from Marcus' arm and stepped away.

She didn't miss the strength of it. Or the heat of him. It was blessed relief that was sweeping through her. Of course it was, because what else could it be when the whole past ten minutes had been a nightmare she never wanted to repeat?

'Right,' she said, looking up at him with a bright smile and shading her eyes from the sun. 'Well. Thank you for that.'

'Any time.'

'So I'm going to congratulate the happy couple and mingle.' And then she was going to find the champagne and down as much of it as she could manage.

'Good idea.'

'I guess I'll see you later.'

'I guess you will.'

And with the thought that despite the conventional conversational closer hell would probably freeze before either of them sought the other out, Celia gave him a jaunty wave and off she went.

Marcus watched Celia kiss and hug her brother and new sister-in-law in turn, then laugh at something Dan said, and his eyes narrowed. Ten minutes in her company and already he was wound up like a spring. He wanted to punch something. Wrestle someone. Anything to relieve the tension that she never failed to whip up inside him.

Standing there in the warm summer sunshine while people streamed out of the church, he shoved his hands in his pockets and resisted the urge to grind his teeth because this was supposed to be a happy day and the last thing anyone wanted to see was a grim-faced best man.

But it was hard to relax when all he could think was, how the hell did Celia do it? And why?

Generally he had no trouble getting on with the opposite sex. Generally women fell over themselves for his attention and once they'd got it went out of their way to be charming. But she, well, for some reason she'd had it in for him for years and he'd never really been able to work it out.

On the odd occasion he'd pondered the anomaly, usually after one of their thankfully rare yet surprisingly irritating encounters, he'd figured that it seemed to boil down to the number and frequency of women that flitted in and out of his life, but he didn't see why that should bother her. The last time he checked it was the twenty-first century, and where he came from men and women could sleep with whomever they liked without censorship.

And so what if he enjoyed the company of women? he thought darkly, watching her peel away to take a phone call. He worked hard and he played hard. He was single and in his prime and he liked sex. He never promised more than he was willing to give and when relationships, flings, one-night stands ended there were never any hard feelings. The women he dated didn't appear to object, so who could blame him for taking advantage of the opportunities on offer?

Well, Celia could, it seemed, but why did she disapprove of him so much? Why did she care? What he got up to was none of her business. As far as he was aware he'd never hooked up with any of her friends so she couldn't have a grudge about that. And it certainly wasn't as if she were jealous. She'd made it very clear she didn't want to have anything to do with him the night he'd made a pass at her years ago and had been very firmly rebuffed.

So what was her problem? And more to the point, what was his? What was it about her that got under his skin? Why couldn't he just ignore her the way he ignored everything he didn't need to be bothered with? Why, with her, did he always feel the urge to respond and retaliate?

Marcus sighed and pinched the bridge of his nose as the questions rattled round his head, and thought that he could really do with a glass of champagne if he stood any chance of making it through the reception.

'Is there any particular reason you're scowling at my sister?'

At the dry voice of the groom and his best friend, who'd evidently managed to drag himself away from his new wife and had stealthily materialised beside him, Marcus pulled himself together.

'Nope,' he said, snapping his gaze away from Celia and switching the scowl for his customary couldn't-give-a-toss-about-anything smile.

'Sure?'

He nodded and widened his smile because there was no way on earth he was going to let Dan in on the trouble he had with Celia. 'Quite sure. Congratulations, by the way.'

Dan grinned. 'Thanks.'

'Great ceremony.'

'The best. And thanks for being my best man.'

'No problem. I'm glad I made it in time.' He'd bust a gut over the past couple of days to get here—and whatever Celia thought it had had nothing to do with over-clingy lovers—and he might be knackered, but he wouldn't have had it any other way because he and Dan had been good friends for nearly twenty years.

'So am I,' said Dan, and then he asked, 'So why the thunderous expression? What's up?'

Marcus shrugged. 'Just trying to remember my speech.'

Dan shot him a knowing look that held more than a hint of amusement. 'Sure you aren't ruminating about the lack of single women here?'

Oddly enough—when it was generally the first thing he ascertained at any kind of social gathering—searching for likely conquests this afternoon hadn't crossed his mind. 'Maybe a bit,' he said, largely because Dan seemed to be expecting it.

'Sorry about that, but we wanted to keep the wedding small.'

'No problem.'

'Has it been a while, then?'

'Six months.'

Dan's eyebrows shot up. 'Wow. Because of...what was her name again?'

'Noelle.' As the memory of his last girlfriend, who'd turned into a complete psycho stalker, flashed into his head he shuddered. 'And yes.'

Dan grunted in sympathy. 'I can see how after everything she did you'd be a bit wary, but, come on, six months? That must be a record.'

'Not one I'll be boasting about.'

'No,' agreed Dan. 'Why would you?'

'Quite.'

'And not one you'll be breaking today, I should think,' Dan mused.

'What makes you say that?'

'Celia's the only single woman here.'

'Is she?'

'And judging by the way you were looking at her just now I'm guessing she's not a likely target.'

Marcus inwardly recoiled. Celia? A target? As if. He couldn't stand her. And as she could stand him even less, even if he were insane/deluded/drunk enough to make a pass at her again, which he most certainly was not, in all likelihood he'd get a knee to the groin.

'Didn't we just clear that up?' he muttered, really not wanting to dwell on that particular outcome.

'Not very satisfactorily.' Dan rubbed a hand along

his jaw and frowned, as if in contemplation. 'You know, Zoe mentioned she thinks you do it a lot.'

'Do what?'

'Scowl at Celia.'

'Do I?'

Dan nodded. 'Pretty much every time you come into contact, apparently.'

'Oh.'

'So what's with the two of you? Why the friction? What did she do to you?'

Interesting that Dan thought it would be that way round when everyone else would have automatically assumed he'd be the one to blame. 'She didn't do anything to me,' he said with a casual shrug. Apart from reject him. Resist him. Ignore him. Avoid him. And drive him bonkers by getting to him when he'd never had any trouble not letting her get to him before. 'We just don't get along. That's all. Sorry.'

'No. Well, she is something of an acquired taste, I'll grant you.'

One that he'd briefly acquired when he'd been an angry and out-of-control teenager but wouldn't be acquiring again, so he hmmed non-committally and sought to change the subject. 'Zoe looks radiant,' he said, watching the bride smiling and chatting, happiness shimmering all around her like some kind of corona.

'She does,' said Dan with the kind of pride in his voice Marcus couldn't ever imagine feeling, which was just as well because marriage was not for him. 'She also has a different take on it.'

'A different take on what?'

'You and Celia.'

Marcus frowned. So much for changing the subject. And what was Dan doing, making it sound as if he and Celia were a thing when they were anything but? 'Does she?'

'Yes.'

'Right.'

'Want to know what she sees between the two of you?'

Not particularly. 'Knock yourself out.'

'Chemistry. Tension. Denial.'

Huh? Marcus reeled for a moment, then rallied because Zoe was wrong. Totally wrong. 'She sees a lot,' he said, keeping his expression poker.

'She does.'

'Too much.'

'Perhaps.'

'What makes her such an expert anyway?'

'She's made an art out of reading people. She's generally right.'

'Not this time.'

Dan shot him a shrewd look. 'She reckons it's like that kid analogy,' he said.

'What kid analogy?' asked Marcus, although he wasn't sure he wanted to know.

'The one about pulling the pigtails of the girl in class you fancy.'

At the odd spike in his pulse Marcus shifted uncomfortably. 'It's nothing like that,' he said, wondering what the hell the brief leap in his heart rate was all about.

'If you say so.'

'Celia deeply disapproves of me, and I—' He stopped because how could he tell his best friend that he thought his sister was an uptight, judgemental, work-aholic pain in the arse? 'Anyway, wouldn't it bother you?' he said instead, although now he thought about it perhaps the question came fifteen years too late.

'You two together?'

Marcus nodded. 'Hypothetically speaking, of course. I mean, she's your sister and I'm not exactly a paragon of virtue.'

'It wouldn't bother me in the slightest,' said Dan eas-ily. 'Celia's perfectly capable of looking after herself and, actually, if I was going to issue a big-brother kind of warning I'd probably be issuing it to her.'

'Why?'

'She's a tough nut to crack.'

'One of the toughest,' Marcus agreed, because she was, and not only because she was the only nut he'd wanted but had never managed to crack. Not that he thought about that night much because, after all, it had been *years*.

'She'd drive you to drink trying.'

'Undoubtedly.'

'And that would be a shame.'

'Just as well you don't have to worry about me, then, isn't it? Although I do think you ought to be worry-ing about Zoe,' he added, now just wanting this oddly uncomfortable conversation to be over. 'She's been cornered by your mother and a couple of your aunts.'

'So she has,' said Dan, that smile on his face wid-ening as his gaze landed on his wife. 'I'd better res-cue her.'

'Off you go, then.'

Dan must have caught the trace of mockery in his

voice because he stopped and shot him a look. 'One of these days it's going to happen to you, you know.'

'What is?'

'Love and marriage.'

Marcus shook his head and laughed. 'Not a chance.' He valued his freedom far too much, and anyway, he'd seen what love could do. The pain it could bring. The tragedy it could result in. He'd been part of the fallout.

Dan arched an eyebrow. 'Too many women, too little time?'

'You said it.'

'If you really believe that then you're going to end up like my father, heading for sixty and still chasing anything in a skirt.'

'That's a risk I'm prepared to take.'

Dan laughed and clapped him on the back. 'One day, my friend, one day,' he said, then set off for Zoe, leaving Marcus standing there frowning at Celia and thinking, Chemistry, tension and denial? What a load of crap.

CHAPTER TWO

THREE HOURS LATER, Celia had worked her way through one cup of tea, two glasses of champagne, a dozen of the most scrumptious mini sandwiches and petit fours she'd ever eaten and a hefty piece of wedding cake. She'd survived the photo session, listened to the short yet witty speeches, and had had conversations with everyone except Marcus and her father.

The reception so far had been beautiful. The weather was behaving, the sky a cloudless blue, the sun beating down gently, a perfect example of one of those heavenly yet rare English summer days. Zoe's parents' garden, with its immaculate lawn, colourful and fragrant borders and sharply clipped hedges was an idyllic setting for a small, tasteful, traditional wedding celebration. The music coming from the string quartet sitting beneath the gazebo drifted languidly through the warm air and mingled with the happy hum of chatter, so enchanting and irresistible that every now and then couples came together and swayed along.

She had to admit that, even to an unsentimental person such as herself, the romance of the afternoon was undeniable. She could feel it winding through her, softening the hard-boiled parts of her a little and making her feel uncharacteristically dreamy. Even her parents seemed to have been caught up in it, appearing to have reached a sort of unspoken truce and, although not talking, no longer shooting daggers at each other from opposite ends of the garden. Her brother looked happier than she'd ever seen him and his bride sparkled like the champagne that had been flowing so wonderfully freely.

Yet as mellow as she was feeling and as much as she liked her brand-new sister-in-law, Celia couldn't help wishing Zoe were more of a people person. If she were, there'd have been several hundred guests at the reception instead of the fifty or so that were milling around the garden.

And OK, so as bridesmaid and sister of the groom she wouldn't have been able to wriggle out of the photo session either way and she'd still have had to steel herself against the weight and strength of Marcus' arm around her waist and the heat of his hand on her hip as they posed, but at least she'd have been able to ignore him after that.

As it was, though, guests were thin on the ground and she couldn't be more aware of him. Everywhere she looked there he was in her peripheral vision, smiling and chatting and generally making a mockery of her efforts to blank him from her head.

Despite the fact that she'd positioned herself about as far from him as possible, for some reason, he was utterly impossible to ignore. Not that she hadn't tried, because she had. A lot. In fact, she'd used up practically all of her mental and emotional energy trying, and as a result she hadn't really been able to concentrate on anything. She kept losing track of conversations. Kept finding herself gravitating towards him. Every time she told herself to get a grip and hauled herself back on track his laugh would punctuate the air and she'd have to battle the urge to whip her head round to see what was amusing him.

All afternoon the people she'd been talking to had looked at her closely and asked if she was all right before edging off presumably in search of less ditzy company, and she really couldn't blame them.

It was driving her nuts. She abhorred ditz. And she hated the way she was being so easily distracted now when she'd always prided herself on her single-mindedness and her ability to focus.

Why was she having such trouble with the effect Marcus had on her today when she generally managed to keep it under control? Why couldn't she blank him out as she usually did? Why did she keep trying to get a glimpse of him whenever she heard the sound of his voice, and then sighing wistfully when she did?

What was wrong with her? What was this weird sort of ache in her chest? And more importantly right now, she thought, her attention switching abruptly from Marcus and the strange effect he was having on her equilibrium, how was she going to deflect her father, who'd clearly clocked the fact that she was on her own and was bearing down on her, no doubt intending to launch into his usual spiel about her career, her lack of a husband and the direct correlation between the two?

As the pathetic—and pointless—need for his approval surged up inside her the way it always did and briefly smothered her confusion at the way her emotions were running riot this afternoon, Celia cast around for a conversation to join, a guest to corner, anything to avoid him and his own particular brand of paternalism, but she was on her own. The nearest little group contained Marcus, who unbeknownst to her had circulated into her vicinity and from the sounds of it was entertaining for Britain, and that made it a no-no.

Or did it?

As her brain raced through the very limited options open to her Celia made a snap decision. Oh, what the hell? He might not be her greatest fan but Marcus was within grabbing distance, and nothing could be worse than having to suffer her father's prehistoric ideas and deep disappointment when it came to his one and only daughter.

Aware that her father was fast approaching and there was no time to lose, Celia reached out and clamped her hand on Marcus' arm. He went still, then turned, surprise flickering across his face. Ignoring the sizzle that shot through her from the contact, Celia looked up at him in what she hoped was a beseeching fashion and said softly, 'Help me? Please?'

Well, well, well, thought Marcus, glancing down to where she was clutching his arm and then shifting his gaze to her face, which bore a sort of pleading expression he'd never have associated with her. Who'd have thought? Celia Forrester, a control freak extraordinaire, staunchly independent and so uptight she was in danger of shattering, a damsel in distress. Actually asking for help. *His* help. She must be desperate.

Resisting the temptation to shake his head in astonishment, he excused himself from the people he'd been talking to, intrigued despite himself by the urgency in her voice and the despair in her expression. 'Why? What's up?' he asked.

'My father.'

He flicked a glance over her shoulder and saw that Jim Forrester was indeed making a beeline for her. And it was making her jumpy. Which wasn't entirely surprising. 'I see,' he murmured with a nod. 'What help do you want?

'I need small talk.'

'What's it worth?'

She stared at him for a second. 'What do you mean, what's it worth?'

He grinned because had she really expected him not to take full advantage of having the upper hand? 'Exactly that.'

She narrowed her eyes at him. 'What do you suggest?'

'How about asking me nicely? Then again. And again.'

She gaped. Then snapped her mouth shut and frowned. 'You want me to beg?'

His smile deepened at her discomfort and he had to admit that there was something rather appealing about having Celia in his debt with this brief and strictly one-off foray into chivalry, should he agree to it. 'The idea has merit, don't you think?'

She glared at him, her eyes flashing with indignation, but a second later the attitude had gone and she shrugged. 'Fine,' she said flatly as she started to turn away. 'Forget it. You go back to doing whatever you were doing. I can handle Dad.'

And for some reason Marcus found himself inwardly cursing while now feeling like the biggest jerk on the planet. She might be a pain in the neck, but he knew how difficult she found her father and he knew how much she loathed *him,* which meant that she *was* desperate.

And maybe a little vulnerable.

'Look, sorry,' he muttered, frowning slightly at the flare of a weird and deeply unwelcome kind of protective streak, because Celia was the last person who needed protecting and the last person he'd ever consider vulnerable. 'I can do small talk.'

She stopped mid-turn and looked up at him. 'Really?'

'Of course.'

'What do you want in return?'

'Nothing.'

She arched an eyebrow sceptically, switching back to the Celia he knew and could handle. 'Seriously?' she said.

'Seriously.'

'Then thank you,' she said a bit grudgingly, which he supposed was only fair.

'You're welcome.'

'Celia,' boomed her father behind her and he saw her jump. Wince. Brace herself.

But she recovered remarkably well and after taking a deep breath turned and lifted her cheek for her father's kiss. 'Dad, you remember Marcus Black, don't you?' she said, stepping back to include him in the conversation.

'Of course,' said Jim Forrester, flashing him a smile that was probably calculated to be charming but in a couple of years could easily stray into sleazy, and holding out his hand. 'How are you?'

'Good, thanks,' said Marcus, shaking it and then letting it go. 'You?'

'Excellent. Great speech.'

'Thank you.'

'So how's business?'

'Quiet.'

Jim's eyebrows shot up. 'I heard it was doing well. So what happened? Hard times?'

He smiled as he thought of the relief he'd felt when he'd signed those papers and released himself from the company that he'd devoted so much of his time and energy to. 'Couldn't be better.'

'Marcus sold his business, Dad,' said Celia.

'Oh, did you? Why?'

'The thrill of beating the markets had worn off,' he said, remembering the strange day when he'd sat down in his office, stared at the trading screen flickering with ever-changing figures and, for the first time since he'd set up the business, just couldn't be bothered. 'It was time to move on.'

'You burnt out,' said Celia, looking at him in dawning astonishment, as if she couldn't believe he was capable of working hard enough to reach that stage.

'Nope,' he said. 'I decided to get out before I did.'

'So what are your plans now?' asked Jim.

'I have a few things in the pipeline. Some angel investing. Some business mentoring. I'd also like to set up a kind of scooping-up scheme for able kids who slip through the system and are heading off the rails, which gives them opportunities other people might not.'

He caught the flash of surprise that flickered across Celia's face and a stab of satisfaction shot through him. That's right, darling, he thought dryly. Not partying till dawn with scantily clad women. At least, not only that. And perhaps not every night.

'Philanthropic,' said Jim with a nod of approval. 'Admirable.'

It wasn't particularly. It was just that he'd been given a chance when he'd badly needed it and he simply wanted to pay it forward. 'I've done well,' he said with an easy shrug, 'and I'd like to give something back.'

'Let me know if I can help in any way.'

Jim had a divorce law practice so it was doubtful, but one never knew. 'I will, thanks.'

'I'm up for partnership, Dad,' said Celia, and Marcus thought her voice held a note of challenge as well as pride.

'Are you?' said her father, sounding as if he couldn't be less interested.

'I'll know in a few months.'

'That's all very well and good,' Jim said even more dismissively, 'but shouldn't you be thinking about settling down?'

Marcus felt Celia stiffen at his side, and guessed that this was a well-trodden and not particularly welcome conversation. 'I enjoy my job, Dad,' she said with a sigh.

Her father let out a derisive snort. 'Job? Hah. What nonsense. Corporate lawyer indeed. There are enough lawyers already, and I should know. You should be married. Homemaking or whatever it is that women do. Giving me grandchildren.'

Dimly aware that this was in danger of veering away from small talk and into conversational territory into which he did not want to venture, moment of chivalry or no moment of chivalry, Marcus inwardly winced because, while he hadn't seen Celia's father for a good few years, now it was coming back to him that as far as unreconstructed males went one would be pushed to find one as unreconstructed as Jim.

Going on what Dan had said over the years their father had never had much time for Celia's considerable intellect or any belief in her education, as had been proven when Dan had been sent to the excellent private school Marcus had met him at while she'd been sent to the local, failing comprehensive.

Now it was clear that Jim had no respect for the choices she'd made or the work she did either, but then over the years Marcus had got the impression that the man didn't have much respect for women in general, least of all his wife and daughter. He certainly didn't listen to either.

'And one day I'd like to be doing exactly that,' she said, pulling her shoulders back and lifting her chin, 'but there's still plenty of time.'

'Not that much time,' said Jim brutally. 'You're thirty-one and you haven't had a boyfriend for years.'

Celia flinched but didn't back down. 'Ouch. Thanks for that, Dad.'

'How are you ever going to meet anyone if all you do is work? I blame that ambition of yours.'

'If my ambition is to blame then it's your fault,' she muttered cryptically, but before Marcus could ask what she meant Jim suddenly swung round and fixed him with a flinty look that he didn't like one little bit.

'You married?' he asked.

Marcus instinctively tensed because for some reason he got the impression that this wasn't merely a polite enquiry into his marital status. 'No.'

'Girlfriend?'

'Not at the moment.'

'Then couldn't you sort her out?' said Jim, with a jerk of his head in his daughter's direction.

Celia gasped, her jaw practically hitting the ground. 'Dad!'

Marcus nearly swallowed his tongue. 'What?' he managed, barely able to believe that this man had basically just pimped out his daughter. In front of her.

'Take her in hand and sort her out,' Jim said again with the tact and sensitivity of a charging bull. 'Soften her up a bit. You have a reputation for being good at that and with the business gone and your future projects not yet up and running you must have time on your hands.'

'Stop it,' breathed Celia, red in the face and clearly—and understandably—mortified.

Not that Marcus was focusing much on her outraged mortification at the moment. He was too busy feeling as if he'd been hit over the head with a lead pipe. He was reeling. Stunned. Although not with dismay at Jim's suggestion. No. He was reeling because an image of taking Celia into his arms and softening her up in the best way he knew had slammed into his head, making his pulse race, his mouth go dry and his temperature rocket.

Suddenly all he could think about was hauling her into his arms and kissing her until she was melting and panting and begging him to take her to bed, and where the hell that had come from he had no idea because she didn't need sorting out. By anyone. Least of all him. And even if he tried he'd probably get a slap to the face.

God.

Running his finger along the inside of his collar, which now felt strangely tight, Marcus tried to get a grip on his imagination and keep his focus on the conversation instead of the woman standing next to him. The woman who couldn't stand him.

'I don't think that's a very good idea,' he muttered hoarsely and cleared his throat.

'Of course it isn't a good idea,' said Celia hotly.

'Why not?' said Jim with an accusatory scowl, as if he, Marcus, was being deliberately uncooperative. 'She might be a bit of a ball-breaker but she's not bad-looking.'

'Hello?' said Celia, waving a hand in front of her father's face. 'I am here, you know.'

Marcus knew. Oh, he knew. And not just that she was only a foot away. It was as if Jim had unlocked a cupboard in his head and everything he'd stuffed in there was suddenly spilling out in one great chaotic mess.

To begin with, not bad-looking? *Not bad-looking?* That was the understatement of the century. She was gorgeous. All long wavy blond hair, eyes the colour of the Mediterranean, full pink lips and creamy skin. A tall hourglass figure that made his hands itch with the need to touch her. A soft, gorgeous, curvy exterior behind which lay a mind like a steel trap, a drive that rivalled his own and a take-no-prisoners attitude that was frighteningly awesome.

Today, in a pink strapless dress and those gold high-heeled sandals with her hair all big and tousled and her make-up dark and sultry, she looked absolutely incredible. Sexy. Smouldering. And uncharacteristically sex kittenish.

It was kind of astonishing he hadn't noticed before. Or maybe subconsciously he had. The minute she'd walked into the church and he'd laid eyes on her, hadn't everyone else pretty much disappeared? Hadn't it taken every drop of his self-control to keep his jaw up, his feet from moving and his mind on the job?

With hindsight it was a miracle he'd managed to get down that aisle without dragging her off into the vestry. He'd felt her touch right through the thick barathea of his sleeve and it had singed his skin and tightened every muscle in his body. The scent of her had scrambled his brain and the proximity of her had heated his blood. As for the pressure of her breast against his elbow, well, the lust that that had aroused in him had nearly brought him to his knees.

If he hadn't been so deeply in denial he'd have had bad, *bad* thoughts about her. In a church, for heaven's sake.

He'd told himself that it was exhaustion messing with his head, which, come to think of it, was the excuse he always made when it came to the irrational and inappropriate thoughts of her that occasionally flitted through his mind.

But it wasn't exhaustion. It was denial, pure and simple. Because how could he be so in thrall to someone who clearly didn't feel the same way about him? How could he be so weak?

So was *that* what bothered him so much about her, then? The one-sided attraction and the back-seat position it put him in? Was the fact that he'd never stopped wanting her the reason why the way she constantly judged him and always found him lacking pissed him off so much?

Despite what she thought of him he fancied the pants off her, which meant that, despite his protests to the contrary earlier, Zoe had been right. On his side at least, there was chemistry, tension and, up until about a minute ago, a whole heap of denial.

And as denial was now apparently not an option he might as well admit that her rejection of him still stung despite the fact that it had happened years ago. She was the one who had got away, and that was why she got to him, why he always retaliated when she launched an attack on him.

'So what do you think?' said Jim, interrupting the jumble of thoughts tangling in his head. 'Would you be up for the challenge?'

'He thinks you're insane, Dad,' said Celia fiercely. 'And so do I. I know I'm a disappointment to you but, for goodness' sake, this has to stop. Now.'

Actually, with the realisation that he wanted her, what Marcus thought was that he was suddenly bone-deep tired of the animosity that she treated him with. It had been going on for years, and he was sick of not knowing what it was about or where it came from.

After spending so long in denial it was surprising just how clearly he could see now. His vision was crystal, and he wanted answers. So whether she liked it or not he was going to get them before the afternoon was through.

'Want to go and get a drink?' he muttered, figuring that there was no time like the present and that with any luck she'd consider him the lesser of the two evils in her vicinity right now.

'I thought you'd never ask.'

CHAPTER THREE

OH, GOD, THOUGHT CELIA, lifting her hands to her cheeks and feeling them burn as she abandoned her horror of a father and trailed in Marcus' wake. How on earth was she going to recover from this? Would she *ever* get over the mortification and the humiliation? Not to mention the mileage that Marcus would get out of that disaster of a conversation. Her father might not know it but he'd given him ammunition to last him *years*.

How *could* he have suggested she needed sorting out? She'd always known he didn't have much time for her career and that he thought she ought to be stuck in a kitchen, barefoot and pregnant, but he'd never expressed it so publicly before.

And in front of Marcus of all people.

What must he be thinking?

Well, no doubt she'd be finding out soon enough because given their history what were the chances he'd let such a scoop slide? Practically zero, she thought darkly as a fresh wave of mortification swept through her. He probably couldn't wait to get started.

But that was fine. She'd survive whatever taunts he threw her way. She always did. And this time she didn't really have any choice, as she'd known the minute she'd elected to go with him instead of staying with her father. She'd made the split-second decision on the basis that by actually living in the twenty-first century Marcus was the marginally more acceptable of the two, but with hindsight maybe she should have just fled to the bathroom instead and to hell with the weakness that that would have displayed.

As they reached the bar Celia pulled herself together because she had the feeling that she'd need every drop of self-possession that she had for the impending fall-out of what had just happened.

'What would you like?' he asked.

'Something strong,' she said, not caring one little bit that it was only five in the afternoon. She needed the fortification. 'Brandy, please.'

'Ice?'

Diluted? Hah. 'No, thanks.'

Marcus gave the order to the barman and the minute she had the glass in her fingers she tossed the lot of it down her throat. And winced and shook her head as the alcohol burned through her system. 'God.'

He watched her, his eyes dark and inscrutable, and Celia set her glass on the bar and kind of wished he'd just get on with it because her stomach was churning and she was feeling a bit giddy.

Although now she thought about it his eyes lacked the glint of sardonic amusement he usually treated her to and his face was devoid of the couldn't-care-less expression it normally wore when they met. In fact she got the odd impression that he wasn't thinking about her father or that conversation at all, which made her think that perhaps he wasn't planning to launch a mocking attack on the pathetic state of her love life just yet.

So what *was* he going to do? And more to the point, what was *she* going to do, because she could hardly stand here looking at him for ever, could she? Even though deep down she wouldn't mind doing just that because he was, after all, extremely easy on the eye.

A rogue flame of heat licked through her and she wondered not for the first time what things would be like between them if the antagonism didn't exist. Kind of secretly wished it didn't because he was still looking at her as if trying to imprint every detail of her face onto his memory, and every cell of her body was now straining to get up close and personal to him and the effort of resisting was just about wiping out what was left of her strength.

'Want to take a seat for a bit?' he murmured, and she snapped out of it because, honestly, what was *wrong* with her today?

Deeply irritated by her inability to control either her thoughts or her body, Celia pulled herself together and focused. Yes, she'd just had a pretty uncomfortable experience, but what was she, eighty? Besides, she was on edge and restless, as if a million bees were swarming inside her, and she needed to lose the feeling. 'I'm going to take a walk,' she said, gripping the edge of the bar and bending down to undo her shoes.

'I'll join you.'

No way. 'I'd rather be alone.'

'I'd like to talk to you.'

She glanced up. 'What about?'

'You'll see.'

'No, I won't.'

He tilted his head and smiled faintly. 'Don't you think you owe me for helping you out back there?'

Had he helped her out? She didn't think so, although that wasn't his fault. 'I thought you said you didn't want anything in return for your help.'

'Humour me.'

Straightening and dangling her shoes from the fingers of one hand, Celia didn't see why she should humour him in the slightest, but maybe it wasn't such a bad idea because on reflection she'd made some pretty inaccurate assumptions about him today. Therefore she owed him at least one apology, and it would probably be less humiliating to do that on the move when she'd have an excuse to keep her eyes on the ground on the lookout for random tree roots waiting to trip her up.

'OK, then,' she said coolly. 'Let's walk.'

'This way?' he said, gesturing in the direction of the walled kitchen garden that would at least afford them privacy for the talk he wanted to have and the apology she had to give.

'Fine.'

They set off across the lawn and as the chatter of the guests and the music faded Celia felt her coolness ebb and her awareness of him increase. He was so tall, so broad and so solid and every time his arm accidentally brushed hers it threw up a rash of goosebumps over her skin and sent shivers down her spine.

She sorely regretted taking off her shoes. They might be tricky to walk in, particularly over grass, but they'd added inches. Without them she felt strangely small despite the fact that she was well above average height, and a bit vulnerable, which, as she was the least vulnerable person she knew, was as ridiculous as it was disconcerting.

She tried to distract herself by mentally formulating an apology that would let her keep at least a smidgeon of dignity, but it was no use. She couldn't concentrate on anything except the man walking beside her. There was something so different about him at the moment. He seemed unusually tense. Controlled. Restrained. Maybe even a bit dangerous...

Which was utterly absurd, she told herself firmly, shaking her head free of the notion. Not to mention idiotically fanciful. Marcus wasn't dangerous. No. The only danger here was her because with every step she took away from the safety of the crowd she could feel the pressure inside her building and her self-control slipping.

'You can relax, you know,' he murmured, shooting her a quick smile that flipped her stomach and unsettled her even more.

Suddenly totally unable to figure out how to handle the situation, she fell back on the way she'd always dealt with him and shot him a scathing look. 'No, I can't.'

'Why not?'

'You have to ask?'

'Clearly.'

She stopped. Planted a hand on her hip and glared at him, all the tension and confusion whipping around inside her suddenly spilling over. 'Oh, for goodness' sake, just get on with it, Marcus.'

'Get on with what?' he asked, drawing to a halt himself, a picture of bewildered innocence.

'The "talk" you wanted to have. Come on, you must

be dying to gloat about the sorry state of my love life, not to mention all the other things my father said.'

He thrust his hands in his pockets and looked at her steadily. 'I'm not going to do that.'

She rolled her eyes. 'Yeah, right. Why change the habit of a lifetime?'

Marcus pulled his hands from his pockets and shoved them through his hair while sighing deeply. 'Look, Celia,' he said, folding his arms across his chest and pinning her to the spot with his dark gaze. 'How about we try a ceasefire on the hostilities front?'

For a moment she just stared at him because where on earth had that come from? 'A ceasefire?' she echoed, as taken aback as if he'd grabbed her and kissed her. 'Why?'

'Because I'm sick of it.'

She blinked, now blindsided by the weariness in his voice as well. 'You're sick of it?'

'Aren't you?'

She opened her mouth to tell him she wasn't. But then she closed it because hadn't she been wishing the animosity between them didn't exist only minutes ago? 'Maybe,' she conceded. 'A bit.'

'I suggest a truce.'

'And how long do you think that would last? Five minutes?'

'Let's try and give it at least ten.'

'For the duration of the "talk"?'

'If you like.' He tilted his head and arched a quizzical eyebrow. 'Think you could do that?'

Celia didn't really know what to think. A ceasefire? A truce? Really? Was it even possible after fifteen years of animosity?

Maybe it was. If Marcus was willing. She could be civil, couldn't she? She generally was. So with a bit of effort she could manage it now. Particularly since, despite herself, she was kind of intrigued to know what he wanted to talk to her about. And besides, she didn't like the way he was making her sound like the unreasonable one here. She wasn't unreasonable at all, and she'd prove it.

'Why not?' she said, tossing him a cool smile from over her shoulder and continuing towards the kitchen garden.

Well, that had gone a lot more easily than he'd expected, thought Marcus, going after her. He'd anticipated much more of a battle, much more withering sarcasm and scathing retort, but then perhaps that conversation with her father had knocked her confidence a bit. Not that she'd ever dream of showing it, of course.

Nevertheless a mortified, confidence-knocked Celia was novel. Intriguing. More alluring than it probably should have been. As was a chat without all the acrimony, he reminded himself swiftly, which was the main point of this little exercise.

'So I'm imagining that wasn't quite the way you were intending the conversation with your father to go when you asked for my help,' he said once he'd caught up with her.

Celia snapped her gaze to his and shot him a look of absolute horror. 'Not exactly.'

'So much for small talk.'

She shook her head as if remembering the conversation in all its awful glory, and winced. 'I still can't believe he said all that stuff about, well, you know, sorting me out and things.'

'Nor can I.' Although, to be honest, he was now so aware of her, it was pretty much all he could think about. That and getting to the bottom of why she detested him so much.

'I'm so sorry.'

'Why? It's not your fault.'

'I guess not, but, still, he put you in an awkward position.'

'I doubt mine was as awkward as yours.'

'Probably not.'

'Nor is it your fault your father's stuck in the Dark Ages.'

'No, but that doesn't make it any easier to bear.'

They reached the kitchen garden and he held open the gate. Celia brushed past him, making all the nerve endings in his body fizz and his pulse race as her scent slammed into him.

'Where does it come from?' he asked, just about resisting the urge to take advantage of her proximity and pulling her into his arms because that was not what this was about.

'His attitude?'

He nodded and followed her down the path that bisected the garden, watching the sway of her body that was exaggerated by the flimsy fabric of her dress and ignoring the punch of lust that hit him square in the stomach.

Celia shrugged and sighed, then bent to look at the label stuck in the earth in front of a row of something leafy and green. Her hair tumbled down in long golden waves and Marcus found himself scanning the garden for a soft piece of ground he could pull her down to.

'Who knows?' she said, and he dragged his attention back to what she was saying. 'The fact that he was a doted-on only child? That he had a stereotypical fifties mother? Or was he simply born a chauvinist?'

'Why do you put up with it?' he said, clearing his throat and determinedly shoving aside the images of Celia writhing and panting beneath him, her dress ruched up around her hips and her body arching against him.

She straightened, swept her hair back with a twist and looked at him. 'I don't have any choice. He's still my father even though I'm never going to be what he thinks I should be.'

'Which is no bad thing,' he said, briefly trying to imagine Celia as a housewife and failing.

'I agree. I can't cook. I don't have a clue where my iron is and I haven't used a Hoover since my last day at university.'

'Yet you still want his approval?'

She nodded. 'Stupidly. I always have. Although I really don't know why I still bother. I mean, he barely knows you yet he admires you in a way he's never admired me even though he's known me for thirty-one years. We work in similar fields, for goodness' sake, yet he's never offered *me* help. Whatever I achieve he'll never think it amounts to as much as marriage and a family would. Which is ironic, really, when you think about how badly he screwed his up.'

'Is his attitude to women why your parents divorced?'

She shook her head. 'I think that was mainly because of his many, *many* affairs. But the attitude couldn't have helped.'

'So what did you mean when you said your ambition was his fault?'

'Exactly that. The divorce hit me hard. Despite what he'd done I adored him. When he moved out I spent quite a lot of my time at school pathetically crying in the bathrooms. As a result I was bullied.'

That odd protective streak surged up inside him again and he frowned. 'Badly?' he asked, pushing it back.

'Not really. Small-scale stuff. But one day I'd had enough and decided to channel my energies into studying instead of blubbing my eyes out.'

'Is it a coincidence you're a lawyer?'

She arched an eyebrow and shot him a quick smile. 'What do you think?'

'I think Freud would have a field day.'

'Very probably.'

'But why corporate law? Why not divorce law?'

'Experiencing it once—even though sort of vicariously—was quite enough,' she said with a shudder.

Marcus watched her as she began to walk further along the path and thought that, while he did think she had a problem with her work-life balance, her drive and focus when it came to her career were admirable. She'd worked hard and deserved everything she had. 'What you've achieved is impressive,' he said, reaching her with a couple of long, quick strides. 'Especially with so little encouragement.'

She glanced over at him, surprised. 'Thanks.'

'You deserve everything you have.'

'Wow,' she said slowly. 'I never thought I'd hear you say that.'

'Neither did I.'

They continued in silence for a moment. Celia brushed her hand over a planter full of lavender and a faint smile curved her lips, presumably at the scent released.

'Anyway, you haven't always had it easy, have you?' she said.

'No,' he said, although he'd got over the death of his parents and the trouble he'd subsequently had years ago.

'So you've done pretty impressively too.'

Funny how the compliment warmed him. The novelty of a sign of approval after so many years of the opposite. Or maybe it was just the sun beating down on the thick fabric of his coat. 'Thanks,' he muttered.

She turned to look at him and her expression was questioning. 'Why am I telling you all this anyway?'

'I have no idea.'

'Must be the brandy.'

'Must be.'

'I don't need sorting out, you know.'

'Of course you don't.'

'I don't need rescuing.'

'I know.'

She shot him a quick smile. 'I definitely don't need to see my father for at least a decade.'

'A century, I should think.'

At the fountain that sat in the middle of the garden they turned left and carried on strolling down the path, passing raspberry nets and then runner-bean vines that wound up tall, narrow bamboo teepees before stopping at a bench that sat at the end of the path amidst the runner beans.

'I'm sorry, Marcus,' she said eventually.

He frowned, not needing her continued apology and not really liking it because, honestly, he preferred her fighting. 'So you said.'

'No, not about that,' she said with a wave of her hand. 'I mean about the things I implied you were going to do with your time now you'd sold your business. It was totally childish of me to suggest that you'd be partying with floozies. Your plans sound great. Different. Interesting.'

'I hope they will be.'

'I was wrong about that and I was probably wrong about why you were late getting here too, wasn't I?'

'Yup.'

'No trio of clingy lovers?'

'Not even one.'

'Shame.'

'It was.'

'So what happened?'

'I was in Switzerland tying up a few last details surrounding the sale of my company but was due to fly back yesterday morning. I should have had plenty of time, but because of the ash cloud my flight was cancelled, as were hundreds of others. By the time I got round to checking, all the trains were fully booked and there wasn't a car left to rent for all the cash in Switzerland.'

'What did you do?'

'Found a taxi driver who drove me to Calais. From there I got on the train to cross the Channel, rented a car in Dover and drove straight here.'

'Oh.' Celia frowned. 'When did you sleep?'

'I didn't.'

'You must be tired.'

Oddly enough he wasn't in the least bit tired. Right now he was about as awake and alert as he'd ever been. 'It's not the first time I've gone twenty-four hours and I doubt it'll be the last.'

'You're very loyal.'

'Dan's my best friend. Why wouldn't I be?'

She shrugged and carried on looking at a point in the distance so that, he assumed, she didn't have to look at him. 'Well, you know...'

Something that felt a bit like hurt stabbed him in the chest but he dismissed it because he didn't do hurt. 'Maybe I'm not everything you think I am,' he said quietly.

She swivelled her gaze back to his and sighed. 'Maybe you aren't.'

'Just what did I do, Celia?'

'What do you mean?'

'Why the hatred?'

'I don't hate you.'

He lifted an eyebrow. 'No? Seems that way to me. You never pass up an opportunity to have a go at me. You judge me and find me lacking. Every time we meet. Every single time. So what I want to know is, what did I ever do to earn your disdain?'

She frowned, then smiled faintly. 'I've just told you about my father's relentless philandering and the misery it caused,' she said with a mildness that he didn't believe for a second. 'Can't you work it out?'

Ah, so it boiled down to the women he went out with. As he'd always suspected. But he wasn't going to accept it. It simply wasn't a good enough reason to justify her attitude towards him.

'Yes, I date a lot of women,' he said, keeping his voice steady and devoid of any of the annoyance he felt. 'But so what? All of them are over the age of consent. I don't break up marriages and I don't hurt anyone. So is that really what it's all been about? Because if it is, to be honest I find it pretty pathetic.' He stopped. Frowned. 'And frankly why do you even care what I do?'

Celia stared at him, her mouth opening then closing. She ran a hand through her hair. Took a breath and blew it out slowly. Then she nodded, lifted her chin a little and said, 'OK, you know what, you're right,' she said. 'It's not just that.'

'Then what's the problem?'

'Do you really want to know?'

'I wouldn't have asked if I didn't.'

'Well, how about you trying to get me into bed for a bet?' she said flatly. 'Is that a reasonable enough excuse for you?'

Marcus stared at her, the distant sounds of chatter and music over the wall fading further as all his focus zoomed in on the woman standing in front of him, looking at him in challenge, cross, all fired up and maybe a bit hurt.

'What?' he managed. What bet? What the hell was she talking about?

'The bet, Marcus,' she said witheringly, folding her arms beneath her breasts and drawing his attention to her chest for a second. 'You set about seducing me for a bet.'

As he dragged his gaze up to the flush on her face

her words filtered through the haze of desire that filled
his head and he began to reel. '*That's* what's been both-
ering you all these years?' he said, barely able to believe it. '*That's* what's been behind the insults, the
sarcastic comments and the endless judgement?'

She nodded. Shrugged. 'I know it sounds pathetic
but that kind of thing can make an impression on a
sixteen-year-old girl.'

An impression that lasted quite a bit longer than adolescence by the looks of it, he thought, rubbing a hand
along his jaw as he gave himself a quick mental shake
to clear his head. 'You should have told me.'

'When exactly?'

'Any point in the last fifteen years would have been
good.'

She let out a sharp laugh. 'Right. Because that
wouldn't have been embarrassing.' She tilted her head,
her chin still up and her expression still challenging.
'In any case, why should I have told you?'

'Because I'd have told you that there wasn't a bet.'

She frowned. 'What?'

'There wasn't a bet.'

'Yeah, right.'

'Really. I swear.'

She stared at him and the seconds ticked by as she
absorbed the truth of it. 'Then why did you say there
was?'

Marcus inwardly winced at the memory of his arrogant, reckless, out-of-control and hurting teenage
self. 'Bravado.'

'Bravado?'

'I was eighteen. Thought I knew it all. When you

pushed me away it stung. Battered my pride. It hadn't happened before.'

'I can imagine,' she said dryly.

'Your knock-back hit me hard.'

'I find that difficult to believe.'

'Believe it.'

'You called me a prick-tease.'

Marcus flinched. Had he? Not his finest moment, but then there hadn't been many fine moments at that point in his life. 'I'm sorry. I wanted you badly. You seemed to want me equally badly. And then you didn't. One minute you were all over me, the next you basically told me to get off you and then shot out through the door.'

'It wasn't entirely like that.'

'No? Then what was it like? Why did you stop me that night?'

'I was a virgin. I got carried away. And then I suddenly realised I didn't want to lose my virginity to someone who'd probably be in bed with someone else the following night.'

'I might not have been.'

Celia rolled her eyes. 'Yeah, sure.'

And actually, there was no point denying it, she might well be right. At eighteen, with the death of his father six months before and his mother's all-consuming grief that had left no room for a son who'd been equally devastated, and ultimately no room for life, he'd been off the rails for a while. The night of Dan's eighteenth birthday party, which had fallen on the anniversary of the date his father had been diagnosed with pancreatic cancer, he'd been on a mission to self-destruct, and he hadn't cared who'd got caught up in the process. In retrospect Celia had had a lucky escape. 'Well, I guess we'll never know.'

'I guess we won't.'

'I was pretty keen on you, though,' he said reflectively.

'Were you?'

'Yup. Even though you were Dan's sister and therefore strictly off-limits.'

'Not that off-limits,' she said tartly. 'If I hadn't put a stop to things we'd have ended up in bed.'

'No, well, I didn't have many scruples back then.' As evinced by the fact that following Celia's rejection he hadn't wasted any time in finding someone else to keep him company that night.

'And you do now?'

'A few. And you know something else?' he said, taking the fact that she was still standing there, listening, as an encouraging sign.

'What?'

'Despite everything that's happened between us over the years it turns out I still am pretty keen on you.'

CHAPTER FOUR

JUST WHEN CELIA didn't think she could take any more shocks to the system, bam, there was another one.

She was still trying to get her head around the fact that Marcus thought that what she'd achieved with her career was impressive. That she'd got quite a large part of him badly, *badly* wrong. That there'd never been a bet and the enormity of what that meant. That ever since that night her attitude towards him—and men in general—had been fuelled by one tiny misunderstanding and could have been so very different if teenage angst hadn't got in the way.

So, on top of all that, the news that he wanted her was too much for her poor overloaded brain to take.

'What?' she said, rubbing her temple with her free hand as if that might somehow remove the ache that was now hammering at her skull.

'I want you,' he said, taking a step towards her and battering her senses with his proximity. 'A lot. I think I always have.'

'You have an odd way of showing it,' she said, edging back a little and feeling the pressure inside her ease a fraction.

The look in his eyes, dark and glittering and entirely

focused on her, made her stomach flip. 'I don't take rejection well,' he said softly.

'No, you don't.'

'And you haven't exactly been encouraging.'

'Why would I be?'

'You wouldn't. Yet despite that you're the sexiest woman I've ever met.'

Celia swallowed hard and tried to keep things rational because this was Marcus and he had the patter nailed, but it was hard to think straight when she wanted to be anything but rational. 'Has it occurred to you that I might simply be the one that got away?'

'Yes.'

'And?'

'Does it matter?'

Did it? She didn't have a clue about anything right now except for the desire sweeping through her. 'I guess that depends on what happens next.'

'What do you want to happen next?'

'I don't know.'

But she did. Because if she was honest it was what she'd wanted for years now, even though she'd done her best to bury it. Hadn't she been wishing that the animosity between them would abate? Hadn't she been wondering what would remain if it did? Hadn't she had hot, steamy dreams about it?

And now it seemed as if the ill will had gone, and she didn't have to wonder what would remain any more because she could feel it. Right down to her marrow. Electricity. Excitement and want. Unfettered by the past. Unleashed by the present.

He took a step towards her, then reached out and ran

his hand from her shoulder slowly, so slowly down her arm, watching as he did so.

'You really don't know?' he murmured and she shivered.

'Still working on it,' she said, because what with the speed this was going, what with the whiplash one-eighty their relationship had undergone, some kind of caution here seemed prudent.

'Did you know your sister-in-law thinks we have chemistry?' he said softly, his fingers circling her wrist and resting over her thundering pulse.

'I didn't.' But it didn't surprise her because Zoe was perceptive like that.

'She thinks there's tension.'

'There's certainly been that.'

'Apparently she also thinks we're in denial.'

'Right,' she said weakly because she could barely breathe with the lust slamming through her, let alone speak.

'Although I'm not any more.'

Celia swallowed and thought that, seeing as how Marcus was being brutally honest at the moment, what else could she do but return the courtesy? 'I never have been,' she murmured.

'No?'

'I've always been attracted to you. I haven't wanted to be. It's been driving me insane.'

His jaw tightened. His eyes darkened. He twined his fingers through hers and tugged her closer and her heart began to thump wildly.

'So what do you suggest we do about it?' he said softly, so close that he dazzled her. Scrambled her thoughts. Melted her brain. Rendered her all soft and mushy inside.

Nothing was one option. The sensible one probably and definitely the one that would cause her the least emotional upheaval.

But Celia had been sensible all her life and look where it had got her. She had a great career and pots of cash in the bank, but while her friends were tripping over themselves to rush up the aisle, as her father had so thoughtfully pointed out, she hadn't had a boyfriend in years.

Which generally suited her fine. She didn't want a serious relationship right now. With the prospect of partnership on the horizon she didn't have the time or the energy needed to devote to one. Yet, this afternoon, for the first time in months, she'd been aware of how alone she was.

A medley of images now spun through the fog in her head: Dan and Zoe smiling adoringly at each other as they cut the cake; the look she'd caught Lily and Kit exchange during the speeches, a look that held love, acceptance, hope and such heat; all those couples swaying to the music.

And her. Standing alone moments before her father had sought her out, her chest squeezing with loneliness and envy.

The irony was that if it hadn't been for Marcus' stupid bravado her relationship history for the past fifteen years could have been very different. She might not have been so wary of men. She might not have been so suspicious of their motives. She might not have scared off anyone who showed more than a passing interest in her. She might even have eased up a bit on her career in order to have a relationship. A marriage. A family.

But what was the point of dwelling on that now? She couldn't change the past. And she was happy with her life. Today's stab of loneliness was nothing more than a blip. Tomorrow she'd be back in London, back at work, and she'd be fine.

She was glad she and Marcus had the opportunity to clear the air. It gave her some sort of closure. Maybe once the deal she was working on was out of the way she might be able to start a whole new chapter of her life romance-wise. Maybe she'd stop pushing men away. Maybe she'd find someone who was as driven as she was, who held the same values she did. Someone as sensible and level-headed as she was.

The problem was, right now, she wasn't feeling in the slightest bit sensible or level-headed. She was feeling reckless. Wild. Weirdly out of control. Her body was behaving way beyond its remit. Emotions were churning through her and playing havoc with her common sense.

All because of Marcus, because she wanted him. God, she wanted him. Had for years, but had always thought it one-sided. Now, though, she knew it wasn't, and she could feel the attraction burning between them, fierce, mutual and utterly irresistible.

It had been so long since she'd had sex. Even longer since she'd had good sex. And with the amount of practice he'd had he'd be very good at it, she was sure.

She was under no illusions about what he was. She might have been wrong about some things, but she knew he enjoyed playing the field. She knew he didn't do commitment, didn't do long-term, which suited her fine because she didn't want either from him. She just wanted to explore this sizzling chemistry because for one thing it would undoubtedly give her proper closure and for another who was she to fight with such a force of nature?

Mind made up, Celia ignored the little voice inside her head telling her she was mad and dragged her gaze up from the expanse of his chest. She saw a muscle in his jaw begin to pound and his eyes darken, and desire flooded through her.

'Well?' he said, the tension radiating off him suggesting that he was finding it as hard to cling onto his self-control as she was.

'You know those scruples of yours?' she said, her voice weirdly low and husky.

'What about them?'

'Do they include anything concerning friends' younger sisters now?'

'Nope.'

'Good,' she said as fire licked through the blood in her veins and her heart thundered wildly. 'Then how about we finish what we started?'

One quick tug was all it took and then Celia was flush against him, her eyes widening and her lips parting on a gasp, although what she thought she was surprised about Marcus had no idea.

What did she think would happen when she'd basically just told him she wanted to have sex with him? He might not have acknowledged it before but he'd been waiting for this for fifteen years. He wasn't going to wait one more second. Couldn't anyway, because the heat and want now flaring in the depths of her eyes, so different from the disdain and disapproval he was used to, were seducing him so completely that everything faded but her.

What did he care about the wisdom of this? The implications? The potential fallout? He couldn't even think about any of that. Not when the soft, pliant feel of her against him and the thready sound of her breathing, altogether such a contrast to her usual smart-talking, insult-delivering toughness, were obliterating what remained of his self-control.

All he cared about right now was the fact that her dislike of him had been largely based on a misunderstanding, and despite all the odds against such a thing happening she was in his arms. Gazing up at him. Waiting for him to kiss her.

So he did. As anticipation thundered through him he lowered his head and covered her mouth with his. Tongues touched and at the bolt of electricity that shot the length of his body he nearly lost his mind.

As instinct took over and wiped his brain he disentangled his fingers from hers and slipped his hand to the small of her back. He slid his other hand up her arm to the nape of her neck and then buried it in her hair, holding her head steady as he increased the pressure, deepened the kiss.

Celia moaned and pressed herself closer, sort of sinking into him. He heard the thud of her shoes and her bag hitting the path, and then her arms were round his neck, threading through his hair, and her soft breasts pushed harder against his chest, as if she needed the pressure, was desperate for the friction.

When he drew back after what felt like hours but could only have been a minute or two, she looked dazed, her eyes all unfocused, her face flushed and her breathing ragged. Which pretty much mirrored the way he was feeling.

'You pack quite a punch,' he murmured, thinking with the one brain cell that was working that if he'd known they'd generate this much heat he'd have ignored the sarcasm and put her mouth to better use long ago.

'So do you,' she said shakily. 'But if someone had told me this morning that I'd be kissing you now I'd have had them sectioned.'

'It's not exactly the outcome to the afternoon I'd have predicted either,' he said, his heart racing and the blood pounding through his veins.

'You mean this wasn't what you meant by a cease-fire in hostilities?'

'Not exactly.'

'An interesting turn of events, then.'

And about to get even more interesting, if things went his way, which he intended them to because this kind of combustible compatibility shouldn't be allowed to go to waste.

'Very,' he said, pulling her tighter and leaving her in no doubt of how much he desired her.

He felt her tremble and it sent a reciprocal tremble shuddering through him. 'What exactly do you want, Marcus?' she breathed.

'You. Here.'

'Now?' She shivered in his arms, the idea clearly appealing if the way her pupils were dilating was anything to go by.

'Now.' There'd be time for finesse later. They had

all night for long and slow. He just wanted her and he wasn't sure how much longer he could last.

'Flattering,' she breathed with a faint smile.

'At this point, desperate.'

'Same here.'

'So?'

The flush on her cheeks deepened, her breath caught in her throat and her eyes darkened. 'Be careful of the dress,' she murmured and he felt like punching the air in victory.

'I will,' he said instead and brought his mouth down on hers once again.

This time they didn't stop to talk. Hands roamed everywhere, their bodies pressed together tightly; they only broke apart to take in great gulps of air before kissing again.

So hard and tightly wound he wasn't sure he could stand it much longer, Marcus slid his hands over her hips, down, and then round, delving beneath her dress and finding warm, smooth skin. He swept his hand up her thigh, felt her tremble against him, and then he was cupping the hot centre of her through fine, silky lace.

Celia tore her mouth from his and dropped her head back, letting out a soft moan when he tilted her pelvis up and slid first one finger into her and then another. So hot and wet, so tight, instantly clamping around him as if she intended to never let him go.

He moved his fingers inside her. He stroked. Slid in and out. Found her clitoris with his thumb and teased. And all the while trailing his mouth along her jaw, down her neck and over her collarbone.

She clutched his shoulders and arched against him, whimpering and panting. Her hips jerked and he could feel her tightening around him. And then she moved her hands to his head, yanking it up and pulling it forwards, planting her mouth on his to smother her moan as she came, shaking in his arms, convulsing around his fingers and making him burn with the need to be inside her.

Shudders racked her body and she kissed him wildly as she rode it out, and then she was tearing her mouth away, breathing hard as she grappled with the button of his trousers and unzipped his fly, slipping her hand inside.

The minute she touched him, Marcus lost it, the desperation to bury himself in her as deep as he could overwhelming all logical thought and reason. He reached behind him, searching for the tiny hidden pocket in the lining of one of the tails, in which he'd stashed a condom months ago, which took longer than usual because his hands were shaking so much.

Not least because Celia was thrusting her hands beneath the waistband of his shorts and pushing them and his trousers down. She wrapped her fingers around him and moaned faintly, and he gripped her wrist and yanked her hand away before he exploded. He tore open the packet with his teeth, shook away the foil and, dimly remembering her concern about her dress, whipped her round.

He swiftly rolled the condom on, grimacing with the effort to control himself, then he bent her forwards and positioned her hands wide apart on the back of the bench. He lifted the back of her dress, rolling it up to her waist in the vague, distant hope that that would stop it creasing. He put his hands on her waist, slid them down over her hips. Tore at one side of her knickers, then the other, and the fabric floated to the ground. He pushed one knee between her legs, parting them. And then, holding her steady, he drove into her.

She was hot and wet and tight and felt like velvet, and he felt his self-control unravel.

With a soft groan she arched her back and threw her head back. She pushed back, and ground against him, and Marcus lost his battle to keep this clean. Leaning over her and wrapping a hand in her hair, he brought her head up and lowered his so that his mouth was close to her ear, and he started telling her what he wanted to do to her, how she felt.

She moaned again and mumbled something that sounded a lot like 'hurry' and he began thrusting in and out of her, harder and faster, all animal instinct and primitive need, until he could hear her breathing turn ragged, could see her knuckles go white as she clung onto the bench, could feel her tightening around him, squeezing him and wiping his mind of everything but her and the yearning for release clawing at his insides.

The pressure within him built. The heat surged like wildfire. She spread her legs wider, rotated her hips faster and ground against him harder. Then he felt her tense, heard her take a breath, and somehow, despite the haze of desire in his head and the hammering of his heart and the roaring in his ears, he untangled his hand from her hair, whipped it round and clamped it over her mouth a second before she came.

Her harsh, muffled cry and the feel of her unravelling around him shot him over the edge, and, pulling her back, he drove into her hard and fierce, and with a scorching rush of heat and a surge of blinding white pleasure he lodged deep and emptied himself into her.

His heart was thundering so frantically and his head was spinning so fast he didn't hear the ringing of a phone at first. But he did feel her jolt. Squirm. Shake her head free of his hand.

And it snapped him to. Enough, at least, to figure out the noise was coming from the tiny bag she'd dropped to the ground.

'Leave it,' he said gruffly, not wanting to let her go just yet and so strengthening his hold on her.

'I can't,' she said, her voice hoarse as she tried to wriggle out of his grip. 'It might be important.'

'So's this.' Because for some reason he had the feeling he ought to apologise. Ask if he'd hurt her with his roughness.

'*This* is finished,' she muttered, pushing him back with her bottom and then jerking forwards and freeing herself from him.

Still reeling from the intensity of the experience and oddly weak-limbed, Marcus felt the loss of her heat immediately. But even though he'd like nothing more than to drag her to the ground and do that all over again, although this time face to face and to hell with her dress, what could he do but take his hands off her? Wherever it had been a minute or two ago, her mind was now clearly on the call coming in, and he swore softly because there went the opportunity to apologise.

While Celia hastily shoved her dress down in a way that undid all the care he'd taken with it earlier and then dived for her bag and delved inside for her phone, Marcus dealt with the condom, his mind blitzed. As she turned away and walked off, talking into her phone and clearly not happy about something, he had nothing left to do but think.

For the first time in his life he had no idea what he was going to say once she finished the call. He didn't have a line. Didn't have a protocol because he'd never had scorching sex with someone who only about an hour ago had loathed him.

So what happened now? he wondered, watching her frown then throw her hand in the air, frustrated by the conversation. Where did they go from here? Back to the insults? Back to the hostility? A new kind of awkwardness? Or was this the beginning of something different, something faintly intriguing?

Marcus frowned and stalked back, taking a moment to pick up Celia's knickers, balling them up and shoving them in his pocket because the sight of those in the bin might give the gardener a bit of a fright come Monday morning.

Did he want something different? Something intriguing? He shouldn't, but did he? Did she? Right now, with his heart still beating fast, his body still thrumming with the lingering effects of his climax and his head a mess, he didn't have a clue. The only thing he did know was that, whatever Celia might think, this wasn't finished. Not by a long shot.

CHAPTER FIVE

'CELIA! THERE YOU ARE! Thank God.'

At the voice that rang out behind her Celia nearly jumped a mile in the air and spun round to see Lily, her fellow bridesmaid, striding towards her, although what she was needed for she had no idea because as far as she was aware her bridesmaid's duties had ended a while ago.

But then, right now she had no idea about anything. Five minutes after what had just happened, what she and Marcus had just done, and she was still totally adrift. Her heart was still thundering, her body still buzzing and, having had less than a minute to think about it, her brain a mess trying to process it all.

How on earth had it happened?

One minute they'd been kissing, the next she'd been shattering first in his embrace, then over the bench, and loving all of it. Aware of her femininity and feeling powerful in a way she never had before, she'd revelled in the intensity, the desperation she could sense in him and the feel of being enveloped and then possessed by him.

And what the hell was that all about anyway? Since when had she wanted to be possessed? Since never was the answer to that because in her opinion being possessed by a man smacked of submission, and submissive was something she'd never been.

But then this afternoon had been full of new experiences. She'd never gone from a kiss to sex and then to it all being over so fast. The whole thing had lasted, what, maybe five, ten minutes? And as for the foreplay and the sweet-talking that she usually enjoyed, well, that had been practically non-existent.

Mind you, perhaps it hadn't been all that fast. Perhaps there'd been fifteen years of foreplay. And perhaps she wasn't as into sweet-talking as she'd always thought, because she certainly hadn't minded the filthy things he'd muttered in her ear as he leaned over her.

But who knew why she'd lost all self-control like that? She certainly didn't. After two of the most mind-blowing orgasms she'd ever had she could barely think straight, and Lord only knew what nonsense she'd spluttered to Annie, her secretary, who'd been calling about a document that was urgently needed by her boss but was missing.

Anyway, with Lily fast approaching, why what had just happened had happened wasn't something she had time to consider. Which was actually quite a relief because she had the feeling that it was probably a bigger deal than she was able to cope with right now.

All she could think of doing was wiping the past ten minutes from her mind and applying one hundred per cent of her focus on Lily. So she snapped her phone shut, fixed a smile to her face and tried not to think about the fact that she wasn't wearing any knickers.

'Lily,' she said, sounding mercifully normal even though inside she was chaos. 'What's up?'

'I've been looking for you all over the place,' said Lily with the breathlessness of someone who'd been running. 'And then your phone rang and I thought I recognised the ringtone.'

'How lucky,' she said, although what was really lucky was that Lily hadn't found her ten minutes ago.

'What are you doing here all by yourself?'

'She's not here all by herself.'

Celia's mouth went dry and her heart lurched at the realisation that Marcus was behind her. Again. Although this time hopefully fully dressed and not bending over her. Not that she was going to think about him thrusting inside her, how deep he'd been, how good it had felt...

As heat rushed through her and a wave of desire nearly wiped out her knees Celia felt her cheeks burn, silently swore and gave herself a quick mental shake.

'Oh,' said Lily slowly, swinging her gaze from Celia to Marcus and then grinning knowingly. 'I see.'

'We've been chatting,' said Celia, blushing even more hotly and obviously sounding as guilty as sin.

Slowly returning her attention to Celia, Lily gave her a quick once-over, her gaze lingering on her burning face, her hair that was no doubt all over the place, her crumpled dress and her lack of shoes. 'If you say so.'

'I do,' she said, rallying her strength and shooting her co-bridesmaid a look that had quelled many an argumentative client, but merely made Lily grin.

'Well, whatever you were planning on doing next,' she said breezily, 'you're going to have to put it on hold because Dan and Zoe are about to leave and there's a bouquet that needs to be thrown.'

At the thought of that, all heat vanished and Celia stiffened, then groaned, closed her eyes and pinched the bridge of her nose. 'Oh, God,' she muttered as the implication of the bouquet-throwing part of the day suddenly struck her. 'Like I need any more humiliation today.'

'What's humiliating about a bunch of flowers flying through the air?' asked Marcus dryly, sounding so laid-back and unaffected by having just had her over a bench it made her nerves jangle.

'You wouldn't understand,' she said, turning and looking at him and then wishing she hadn't because her gaze locked on his mouth and all she could think about was those deep drugging kisses and the not-so-sweet nothings he'd growled into her ear.

'Try me.'

She dragged her gaze up and that was even worse because traces of heat and desire lingered in his eyes, reminding her of what she really was trying to forget. 'You can't. You will never have to experience the mortification I'm about to suffer,' she said, knowing she was going to sound pathetic and wishing she'd just nodded and gone with Lily without saying anything. 'I'm the only single girl here. Everyone else is married. I'll have to stand there alone and everyone will be watching. Wait until you see the looks being cast my way—which will range from smug to pitying—and then you'll see.'

Marcus tilted his head and looked at her intently, as if spotting a crack in her armour and trying to see through it. Not that he'd find anything even if he could, apart maybe from a horseshoe magnet with both its ends quivering in his direction.

'You're not the only single girl here,' he said, rubbing his fingers along his jaw, and she couldn't help watching, remembering how they'd felt inside her. 'There's Lily.'

'She's engaged,' she said, wondering where the hell her inner strength and self-control were when she needed them. 'Doesn't count.'

'Sadly, this is true,' said Lily thoughtfully.

'Then I'll join you,' he said.

Celia stared at him. What? No. She didn't need him being all nice on top of the fabulous sex. That really would screw with her head. 'Sorry?'

'I'll join you. Hustle you for the bouquet.'

'You?'

'Why not? I'm single. And, actually, technically so are you, Lily, despite being engaged. And while we're at it why don't we recruit Kit? That might make it a bit more of a battle.'

'A novel idea,' said Lily with a grin. 'I'll go and get him. So, are you coming?'

This she said to Celia, who thought that she already had. Deliciously. Twice. In the space of about five minutes. 'Absolutely,' she said, wishing she could give herself a good kick. 'Give me a moment to put on my shoes.' And find her underwear, regain her composure and exert some sort of control over her brain.

'Great.'

Celia watched Lily lift her dress and rush off, and muttered, 'You're mad,' in Marcus' general direction.

'Probably,' he said, thrusting his hands in his pockets, at which point his jaw tightened and his dark eyes glittered. 'You can thank me later if you like.'

Celia hmmed non-committally because she wasn't sure if his plan was going to make things better or worse, stalked over to the bench and scoured the ground. 'Where the hell are my knickers?'

'In my pocket.'

'Can I have them back, please?'

'Not really much point.'

'Why not?'

Colour slashed along his cheekbones as he gave her the kind of smile that suggested he was enjoying a memory. 'There's not much left of them.'

'Oh.'

He tilted his head and his smile widened, becoming wicked. 'Don't you remember me ripping them off you?'

Celia bit her lip and felt her blush deepen. She'd been so lost in desire and desperation she hadn't felt anything except the deep hammering urge to have him inside her. 'I forget the details,' she said a little huskily.

'I don't think I'll ever forget any of the details. I think they'll for ever be burned into my memory. That was hotter than I'd ever have imagined. You're hotter than I'd ever have imagined.'

Celia really didn't know what to say to that. 'Thank you. And thank you for suggesting the bouquet thing,' she added, deeming it wise to get off the subject of hotness and the circumstances surrounding it.

'You're welcome. But you should know my motives aren't entirely altruistic.'

'No?'

Marcus shook his head and looked down at her, his eyes burning right through her. 'It occurred to me that the sooner Dan and Zoe leave, the sooner we can.'

* * *

He might not yet know it but Celia wasn't going anywhere with Marcus.

Now that the heat and the recklessness of her behaviour in the kitchen garden had faded, reality had struck with the force of a mile-high pile of legal documents hitting her desk.

What the hell had she done back there? What had she been *thinking?*

Well, she hadn't been thinking at all, that much was clear. Because if she had, she'd have considered the fact that they'd effectively been in public. That fifty or so people had been within spitting—*hearing*—distance. That a dozen security people—thanks to Dan's high profile and his deep dislike of the press—had been monitoring the perimeters of the garden, on the lookout for gatecrashers and long lenses and possibly even couples having wild sex amongst the vegetables.

If someone had discovered them…

Dear God. It didn't bear thinking about. Quite apart from eternal humiliation and probably being the subject of rumours for years to come, she could have been fired. Her partnership prospects would have been history. She could have been struck off for bringing her profession into disrepute. Her father would have been beside himself with the knowledge that Marcus had followed up on the suggestion that he sort her out.

And OK, so none of that had happened, but the fact still remained that at some point shortly after walking into that garden with him she'd *completely lost her mind.* A couple of hot and heavy kisses and she'd abandoned the self-control she valued so highly. For the first time in her life she'd given in to the needs of her body. Without a single moment's consideration. He'd given her an out, given her a chance to put a stop to things, and all she'd said was, 'Be careful of the dress.'

Be careful of the flipping *dress*.

As if he could do anything he wanted with her and all that mattered was that she looked presentable afterwards.

Not that she'd even managed that. Her hair was a mess and her face was still burning—although hopefully if anyone noticed they'd assume it had something to do with the hideousness of standing in the drive with Lily, Kit and Marcus while Zoe smiled widely, turned and, to the cheer of the guests, tossed the bouquet high into the air.

And as for her lack of underwear... Well, even though technically it wasn't her fault, who went commando at a wedding where there was the possibility of a breeze or an ignominious fall to the ground courtesy of four-inch heels?

It was as if she'd been taken over by someone else today. Someone who wasn't cool and collected and totally unflappable, but tense and jumpy and chaotic. Someone who was ruled by emotion instead of reason. Someone who did things like have sex in the open air with a thoroughly unsuitable man.

And now all those things that had seemed so exciting half an hour ago—the recklessness, the loss of control, the overwhelming desire to slake the clawing lust—now just seemed wrong. Shameful somehow.

Even though physically she'd adored what she and Marcus had done—who was she to deny the fabulousness of two earth-shattering orgasms in quick succession?—she was beginning to realise that she'd just become one of his conquests. One in a very long line of women he'd taken to bed and then forgotten about. Not that there'd been a bed involved, but still.

It shouldn't really have mattered, but, annoyingly enough, it did. Because while she was under no illusion about him, maybe by assuming a quickie with Marcus would deal with the attraction she felt for him, she'd been under an illusion about herself. She'd had a better time with him than she'd expected to. Hadn't thought that kind of pleasure actually existed. Was kind of knocked sideways by the fact that it did, and that she'd experienced it. And while she'd never fall for the mistake of thinking she could be the one to reform him, even if she wanted to, which she didn't, if she hung around she could well find herself wanting more instead of closure.

Given everything she'd endured today and the way her emotions had got the better of her it wasn't entirely surprising. Her confidence and her self-belief had been bashed. Things she'd always thought she'd known had been proved false. And as for her emotions, well, those were all over the place.

But however justifiable her behaviour today had been she still didn't like it. She didn't know what it meant. Didn't have the energy to work it out.

Nor did she have the energy for the night of heaven Marcus was no doubt planning, tempting though her body clearly thought it was. She needed space, time and distance to figure out that today was nothing more than a blip, that the sex, even though spectacular, had been just that and that she'd be back to normal in a jiffy.

So, all in all, she thought, watching the bouquet

sail through the air and land in Marcus' hands, it was lucky she'd booked herself on the seven-o'clock train back to London.

God only knew where the suggestion he join Celia in the drive for the throwing of the bouquet had come from. All Marcus knew was that he'd caught that flash of vulnerability again and he'd found himself wondering how the hell he could have ever thought her up-tight and judgemental when she clearly had a core of marshmallow. A deeply hidden core of marshmallow, admittedly, but there nevertheless.

And as a result of the glimpse he'd got of it, he was now waving goodbye to Dan and Zoe, who were heading off on a two-month honeymoon in South America in a vintage convertible, while clutching a bunch of pale pink roses and feeling a bit of a berk. But he reckoned he could live with that. Especially if it meant that Celia felt obliged to express her gratitude for his chivalry in bed later.

As his pulse began to race at the thought of the long, hot, steamy night ahead, during which he'd make sure she expressed her gratitude over and over again, Marcus wondered if she'd be up for meeting up once back in London.

Now that they'd lost the hostility he wouldn't mind getting to know her a bit better. He might have been acquainted with her for close on the twenty years he'd known Dan, but he didn't really have a clue how she worked. As an adolescent he hadn't been interested, at eighteen he'd just wanted to get into her pants and as an adult the animosity had acted as a barrier to thinking of her as anything but a thorn in his side. Now, though, he was thinking he'd quite like to find out.

Which was odd because up to this point he'd never really wanted to explore the minds of the women he'd dated. It wasn't that he didn't think they'd be all that interesting. In fact, he was sure they would be, because he didn't date bimbos. The women he went out with were bright and entertaining, yet despite that he'd just never been sufficiently engaged to want to try to dig all that far beneath the surface, even with those who lasted weeks instead of only one night. He didn't really know why this was, it was just the way it had always been.

Celia, however, intrigued him. Her mind, her work ethic, her ambition and her drive as much as the spectacular body beneath the dress. With hindsight she always had fascinated him, even when she'd been needling him. Maybe *particularly* when she'd been needling him. And he didn't really know the reason for that either.

What he *did* know, however, was that he'd like to see more of her. Literally, of course, because he still hadn't seen her naked, but also because this thing between them deserved a lot more exploration.

And while anything long-term clearly wasn't an option when they had polar-opposite views on marriage and family, that didn't mean that if she was up for it they couldn't have some fun in the meantime, did it?

In fact, why wait till later? he thought, lowering his hand and vaguely wondering if it would be all right to just dump the flowers on the ground as his heart began to thump. Why not whisk her away now as he'd implied earlier he wanted to? She was right there, standing beside him and waving as the car headed down the drive.

What could be quicker than sending her up to get her stuff and then dragging her off to his hotel? Or hers. He wasn't fussy.

'So another couple bites the dust,' he murmured, deciding as he watched the red brake lights disappear round the corner that etiquette probably took as dim a view of abandoning the bouquet as Celia would of him throwing her over his shoulder and carting her off.

'In a cloud of dust,' she said, screwing her face up in disgust and now flapping her hand in front of her face to wave it away. 'Do you mind?'

'What about?'

'Your best friend's just got married,' she said. 'Your relationship will change.'

Contemplating the idea, Marcus figured that Celia was probably right about that, although he wasn't unduly worried. It wasn't as if he and Dan saw each other all the time. They met up once, maybe twice a month at the most, and he couldn't see why that should change. 'Zoe doesn't strike me as the sort of woman who'd ban her husband from seeing his friends,' he said.

'No. She's lovely. And I think they're going to be very happy.'

This she said with what he would have thought was a trace of wistfulness if it had been anyone other than Celia, but, because it *was* Celia, she was probably not considering her own happiness but the way *her* relationship with her brother would change.

But then to his faint alarm she sighed deeply, and he shot her a quick glance only to find a kind of dreamy expression on her face that he'd never have expected.

'Are you all right?' he asked, not sure quite what to make of it.

'Fine,' she said, giving herself a quick shake and smiling at him brightly—too brightly, perhaps. 'You?'

'Never felt better.' Oddly enough, it was true. He might not have slept in the past twenty-four hours but he felt great. Amazing the effect some seriously wild, uninhibited, unexpected sex could have on a man…

'Congratulations, by the way,' she said, her smile still fixed in place, her eyes oddly unreadable.

'What for?'

'That,' she said, glancing down at the bunch of flowers he was still, for some unfathomable reason, holding. 'It means you're next.'

Marcus gave a theatrical shudder to mask the less theatrical one he felt deep inside. 'Hell will freeze over first,' he muttered.

'Then you really shouldn't have caught it.'

'I like to win.' And he had, even though Kit and Lily had put up an excellent good-natured battle. Celia, come to think of it, hadn't put up any kind of a fight. She'd just stood there looking as if she'd been miles away.

'And what will you do when word gets out? You'll be swamped.'

'I'll use you as my shield.'

She tilted her head and looked at him sceptically. 'Meaning what exactly?'

Who knew? All he knew was that as long as they had mileage, and they clearly did what with the electricity that was bouncing back and forth between them, he'd be pursuing it. 'Meaning go and get your things, Celia, and say your goodbyes.'

'I'm just about to.'

'Good.'

She took a deep breath and pulled her shoulders back, her smile fading a little. 'About us leaving together, Marcus…'

'What about it?'

'We won't be.'

That was fair enough. Her parents were here and he could understand her desire for discretion. He was perfectly happy for them to leave separately and meet up later. 'Fine,' he said easily. 'Where were you planning on staying tonight?'

'At home.'

He went still at that. Frowned. 'What?'

'I'm heading home,' she said, drawing out the syllables as if he were a bit slow on the uptake, which he was because he was having trouble processing what she was saying. 'So if you'll excuse me I'd better get a move on.'

Leaving him standing there like a tongue-tied brainless idiot, she turned and set off for the house at such a cracking pace she was practically through the front door by the time his brain had kicked in and he realised that she really was intending to leave and that if he wanted to stop her he was going to have to be quick.

Setting his jaw, he strode after her, dumped the roses on the table just inside the door, which was groaning with presents, and when he saw her halfway up the stairs swiftly crossed the hall. 'You're leaving now?' he said, wondering why she'd changed her mind.

'I have a train to catch,' she said without breaking stride. 'In just under an hour.'

'You weren't planning to stay?'

'No.'

'Why not?'

'Because I knew this wouldn't be the kind of wedding that goes on till dawn and I have to be at work early tomorrow.'

'Tomorrow's Sunday.'

'So?'

Taking the stairs two at a time, he caught up with her in a matter of seconds. Long enough for it to get into his thick skull that she had no intention of changing her plans despite what had happened earlier. Which disappointed him more than it ought to, although he didn't have time to wonder about that right now.

At the top of the stairs he gripped her wrist and she stilled, but he could feel her pulse racing beneath his fingers, which he didn't think was hammering just from the exertion of climbing the stairs. 'What's going on, Celia?'

'Nothing's going on,' she said flatly, tugging her hand away and rubbing her wrist. 'I just have to get back, that's all. I really do.'

He believed her because her dedication to her work was something only an hour or so ago he'd been admiring. Now, though, it just pissed him off because basically she was letting him know in no uncertain terms that, regardless of the attraction that still existed between them, continuing where they'd left off was at the bottom of her list of priorities. While it was at the top of his.

'You know, you really need to address that work-life balance of yours,' he drawled, oddly hurt by the idea she attached so little importance to it.

'To make it more like yours, you mean?' she said, marching across the landing towards a bedroom.

He followed her through the door and leaned back

against a wall as he watched her pick up a suitcase, drop it on the bed and fling the top back. 'Working on a Sunday isn't normal.'

'It is if you have a tricky deal that needs to be pushed through in record time. Not to mention a document that's gone missing and of which I have the only copy.' She scooped up a handful of clothes, dumped them beside the suitcase and began folding and packing, folding and packing, still looking everywhere but at him. 'I wouldn't expect you to understand, what with you now being a man of leisure.'

The mocking judgemental tone that he'd assumed had gone was back, and it annoyed him even more. 'I've put in my fair share of weekends at work.'

'At the moment I work *every* weekend,' she said pointedly, and he found himself frowning and wondering, what the hell was this? Some kind of competition? 'Taking today off was a luxury,' she added, 'and I need to make it up.'

'What about what happened this afternoon?'

'What about it?' She paused in the folding/packing thing she had going on and stared at him as if she didn't have a clue what he was getting at. Which wasn't entirely surprising since he wasn't sure *he* had a clue what he was getting at. So she didn't want to spend the night with him. What was the big deal? Why was he pursuing it? And, actually, wasn't he beginning to sound a bit pathetic? A bit needy? A bit desperate?

He was, so he bit back the urge to ask her if the afternoon had meant anything to her, because it clearly hadn't, and stamped out the disappointment swirling around inside him.

'Forget it,' he said, fixing a cool smile to his face

and reminding himself that it hadn't meant anything to him either. It had been good sex, nothing more, and it wasn't as if he'd never had good sex before.

She sighed and stopped folding. 'Look, Marcus, this afternoon was fun but we both know it wouldn't have gone anywhere.'

Did they? He'd thought that they'd been about to go back to his hotel room, and had hoped that things might carry on when they got back to London, but clearly he'd been picking up the wrong signals. No matter. 'I know it wouldn't have gone anywhere,' he said, and she was right. Ultimately it wouldn't.

'Yet you're sounding like you thought this was more than it was.'

He had. Maybe. A bit. For a moment. 'Evidently my mistake.'

'It's unlike you to make a mistake about something like this.'

It was. Which was undoubtedly why he was feeling so wrong-footed. The thing making his stomach churn was confusion at the unexpected turn of events, that was all. 'I blame the champagne.'

'Did I ever agree to leave with you?'

No, dammit, she hadn't, he realised belatedly. He'd jumped to that conclusion all by himself and he'd been an idiot to do so. 'No.'

'So that's it, then,' she said as if there was nothing more to be said. 'Just think of me as another of your conquests.'

'I'll do that.'

'But it was fun.'

'It was.'

'And *so* what I needed,' she said with a smile, look-ing at him *finally,* 'so thank you for letting me use you.'

Her words sank in and for a moment Marcus didn't know what to say. For the first time in years, he was speechless, because of all the things that he'd thought about since they'd had sex it had never once occurred to him that she'd used him.

If he'd contemplated her motives he'd have come up with something pretty much along the same lines as his. Overwhelming desire. Years of pent-up build-up. Irresistibility. An interest in seeing where things might go. He'd never have guessed that all she was after was a one-night stand. And didn't that make him a fool be-cause he'd told her that he and the women he slept with were always on the same page, yet here he was, not just on another page but in a different book entirely.

So much for the idea that Celia was vulnerable, he thought, feeling something inside him that had momen-tarily thawed ice over again. So much for the thought she needed protecting. She was made of steel. She had no soft centre. And he'd been a complete and utter idiot to imagine otherwise, because he might be many things but he didn't use people, whereas she had absolutely no qualms about doing such a thing.

'No problem at all,' he said, pushing himself off the wall and making for the door, wiping Celia and the af-ternoon from his head with the kind of ruthless deter-mination that had got him back on track and made him a millionaire at twenty-five. 'Happy to have helped. Have a good journey home and I'll see you around.'

CHAPTER SIX

OVER THE NEXT month Celia was so flat out at work that Marcus barely crossed her mind. She had a deal to think about. Contracts. Documents. Emails and calls and meetings and an ever overflowing in tray. She didn't have the mental space or the time to think about that afternoon. Except in the early hours of the morning when she did make it to bed and couldn't sleep, of course. Then, dizzy with exhaustion, she let herself remember and indulge, knowing that come daybreak the memory would be buried beneath work, work and more work.

Despite his parting shot, she hadn't seen him around. She hadn't expected to. For one thing, Dan—their only real reason for coming across each other—was still on honeymoon, and for another, why on earth would Marcus choose to put himself in her path after she'd deliberately told him that she'd used him?

She pushed open the door of the bar and cringed as the memory of the scene that had taken place in Zoe's parents' spare room flashed into her head.

It hadn't been her finest moment, she had to admit. In fact it had been one of her lowest, but she hadn't known what else to do. She'd had to get him out of

that room before she'd run out of clothes to fold and
pack and no longer had anything to distract her from
the knowledge that they were in far too close proximity to a bed and she wanted him badly, despite being
well aware that he was the last person she should want.

What had happened in the kitchen garden was meant
to have been a blip. The release of fifteen years' worth
of build-up, and closure. But as she'd stood in that
driveway waving Dan and Zoe off, a sudden wave of
longing for what they had had rushed over her and had
thrown her even more off balance.

Totally bewildered by what was going on inside her
head, she'd just wanted to escape. So she'd headed into
the house, fleeing the romance and sentimentality of
the afternoon, the happy, mildly boozed-up guests, the
sinking sun, the sky streaked with red and the length-
ening shadows, ready to pack up and leave and figure
things out in the cool peace of her flat.

Marcus had followed her, of course he had. Naturally enough, given that she hadn't given him cause to
think otherwise, he'd assumed that she was intending
to leave with him. And for a split second she'd been so
very tempted to do just that. Logically she knew that
he'd never be the man for her, but that hadn't stopped
her for one crazy moment desperately wanting him to
be. And it had scared the living daylights out of her,
which was why she'd pushed him away.

Not that she generally thought about it much. She'd
analysed it to death on the train home, staring blankly
out of the window as the countryside rushed by, her
laptop remaining closed on the table in front of her.
Once she'd got home, satisfied she'd done the right

thing by putting a stop to anything more, she'd cast it from her mind.

But as she was about to have a quick drink with Lily—who hadn't taken no for an answer—Marcus and what they'd got up to the afternoon of the wedding had snuck into her head quite a bit today. And every time she did find herself losing herself in the memory she went all soft and warm inside. It was infuriating, not least because she had plenty of other more important things to think about and really didn't need the distraction.

Spying Lily sitting at a table in the corner of the busy City wine bar and fiddling with her phone, Celia weaved through the tightly packed clientele and wondered if it was overly hot in here or if it was just her.

'Hi,' she said, eventually making it over, then shrugging out of her jacket, draping it over the back of the chair and sitting down.

'Hello,' said Lily, putting her phone on the table and glancing up with a broad beam. That faded as swiftly as her eyes widened. 'God, you look dreadful.'

Celia bristled even though Lily was right. She was looking awful at the moment, which was why she tried to avoid the mirror as much as she could because she knew her skin was pasty, her eyes were puffy and her body several pounds lighter than it should be, and who needed visual proof of that? 'Thanks.'

'Well, sorry, but you do.' Lily filled a glass with wine and pushed it towards her. 'Here. You look like you could do with this.'

'Thanks,' she said again.

'So what is it?'

Celia shrugged and took a sip. 'Just work,' she said,

her stomach shrivelling a little at the acidity. 'Things are pretty hectic at the moment,' she added, although in reality 'pretty hectic' didn't come close to describing her workload at the moment.

Lily frowned. 'Are you all right?'

'Oh, I'm fine,' she said, pasting a smile to her face and making an effort to relax. 'It's just a phase. This stage is always like this. And it's not like I'm the only one putting in the hours. We all are.'

Lily sat back and twiddled the stem of her glass between her fingers as she looked at her thoughtfully. 'Don't you ever worry about burning out?'

'All the time,' she said with a smile that was wry because in reality there was no way in hell she was burning out. She couldn't afford the time.

Still, she could definitely do with maybe a bit more sleep because she was exhausted, these headaches were a pain, and the heart palpitations that had started last week were beginning to get a bit more frequent and a bit longer in duration.

If she was being honest she hadn't been feeling all that great for a while. Maybe she'd make an appointment with her GP, although she knew he'd simply tell her that it was stress and she should ease up on work. As if it were that simple.

Or maybe tonight she'd try and get home early, although given it was already nine and the bottle of wine on the table was full that seemed unlikely. In fact, seeing as she was going to be here for a while she might as well head back to the office once she was done here, do a bit more work and then spend the night there.

But it was fine. She'd survive. She always had in the past. Anyway, the deal was nearly done and then she'd catch up. On sleep. With friends. On everything else that had been put on hold.

'So what's news?' she said, taking another sip of wine and assuring herself that she and her manic schedule could easily stick it out for another week or so.

'Nothing in particular. Busy at work.'

'Missing Zoe?' she asked, thinking that as Zoe was responsible for half of the sisters' business her absence must be making things tough.

'Heaps. But it's fine. I'm managing. Are you missing Dan?'

'A bit.'

Her brother had never been away for two months before and she regularly found herself picking up the phone to call him, putting it down a second later and feeling rather empty and alone. It didn't help that her parents had been in regular touch to have a moan about each other. Usually she shared the brunt of their non-relationship with Dan, and the fact that she couldn't only added to her current stress levels.

'Kit and I have set a date for the wedding,' said Lily, dragging her out of one pity party and tossing her into another.

A wedding, Celia thought, her heart squeezing for a moment. Another one… Then she pulled herself together and remembered that once the deal was through, rectifying her love life was something else she was going to tackle. The minute she had the time she'd embark on a dating mission to end all dating missions. And because this was Lily and she was aware of the ups and downs of her and Kit's relationship, she was genuinely pleased they'd set a date. 'When?'

'December.'

'Congratulations.'

'Thanks.'

'How are things going with you two?'

'Remarkably well,' said Lily, looking a bit surprised at the thought. 'But let's not forget that there's every possibility I'll muck it up.'

Celia smiled. 'I'd be surprised if Kit let you.'

'He keeps telling me he won't.'

'There you go, then.'

'And speaking of gorgeous men,' Lily continued. 'I ran into Marcus last week.'

At the casual mention of his name Celia felt her heart lurch and her hand shake, and she put her glass on the table. 'Really?' she said, her throat dry and scratchy as she thought that, damn, stress had a lot to answer for.

Lily nodded. 'At a party.'

'Where else?'

'Want to know how he is?'

A surge of curiosity rose up inside her but she stamped it down hard because she couldn't care less. 'Why would I want to know how he is?'

'Well, you know, after what happened at Dan and Zoe's wedding.'

Celia felt her entire body flush and this time she knew it had nothing to do with an overheated bar. 'Nothing happened.'

'Not what it looked like when I interrupted you.'

'We'd been chatting, that's all.'

'So you said. And I believe you as much now as I did then.' Lily drained her glass. 'You know, I don't blame you in the slightest. Marcus is seriously hot.'

So was she. Boiling. 'Aren't you supposed to be getting married in December?' she said a bit tetchily.

Lily grinned. 'Doesn't stop me from appreciating a fine specimen of manhood when I see one.'

Marcus wasn't a fine specimen of manhood. Yes, he was gorgeous, and he'd helped her out when she'd asked for it, but he was still as promiscuous as he'd ever been.

On the *extremely* rare occasion he'd crossed her mind in the week that followed the wedding when, despite her best efforts, the freshness of it all had meant that it refused to scuttle to the back of her mind where she wanted it, she'd found herself wondering if she hadn't made a mistake in pushing him away. Something about the look in his eye when she'd finally plucked up the guts to look at him back there in that bedroom made her wonder if maybe he'd been disappointed that she hadn't wanted to stay. If maybe he'd hoped for something more. If maybe she'd misjudged him yet again.

But she hadn't and he clearly hadn't wanted anything more because, why, only last week he'd been snapped outside some theatre or other with not just one, but two blondes hanging off his arms. The week before that he'd escorted a ravishing brunette to some charity gala in aid of cancer research. And the week before that he'd been on a beach in the Mediterranean cavorting in the waves with a bevy of Sardinian beauties.

Not that she'd been checking up on him or anything, but what was he doing about those projects he'd told her about while all this partying was going on? No mention of *them* in any of the papers.

'Well, whatever,' she said with a nonchalant shrug. 'I have no idea where Marcus is or what he's doing and I really don't care.'

'OK, you win,' said Lily with a smile and a dismissive wave of her hand that had she been firing on all cylinders Celia would have found suspicious. 'Want to come for supper next Saturday?'

As she wasn't firing on all cylinders Celia relaxed and thought that yes, she did. Very much. And not just because she was thankful for the change of subject. The deadline for the deal was next Friday so Saturday would be her first day off in weeks. She had no plans other than to sleep, so supper at Lily's after a twenty-four-hour nap sounded like a fine way to celebrate. There'd be good food, plenty of fabulous wine and possibly even a gorgeous single man or two for her to set her sights on.

'That would be lovely,' she said, with genuine gratitude. 'Thank you.'

Lily beamed and refilled their glasses. 'Great. Now let me tell you all about my wedding plans so far.'

What the hell he was doing standing on Kit and Lily's doorstep and ringing the bell Marcus had no idea.

By now he ought to have picked Melissa up and taken her to the opening night of an exhibition one of his artist friends was putting on. He ought to be sipping champagne, discussing perspective and admiring his date. Yet he'd ditched both Mel and the exhibition in order to be here.

Why he'd changed the habit of a lifetime and wilfully cancelled one plan for another he didn't want to consider too closely. He had the horrible suspicion that if he did he'd find it had quite a lot to do with Lily's mention in passing that Celia was also on the guest list, and frankly that didn't make any sense at all because Celia had made it perfectly clear that she didn't want to have anything to do with him any more and he'd taken that on board. He was totally fine with it. Hadn't thought about it for a second more, once he'd got back to London that Sunday morning.

It wasn't as if he'd been sitting at home burning with disappointment that she'd rebuffed him again, moping around like a wet weekend and feeling sorry for himself. He'd had a great time in the past month. He'd hit the social scene with a fervour bordering on vengeance. He'd dated a string of intelligent, entertaining, beautiful women, although irritatingly enough none of them had made him want to go further than a friendly goodnight kiss, let alone scratch beneath the surface. He'd taken a week's holiday just because he hadn't had one in years and now he could. And in amongst the fun he'd slowly been making plans about what he wanted to do next work-wise.

All in all he'd barely had a moment to himself, and he'd congratulated himself on not having thought about Celia once.

Yet when Lily had rung him up a week or so ago inviting him to dinner and mentioning Celia was coming, for some unfathomable reason his pulse had started thumping in a way it hadn't since that afternoon in the walled garden and he'd found himself mentally ditching his plans and saying yes, even though he didn't know either Lily or Kit all that well.

So there was little point in pretending that Celia didn't have anything to do with the reason he was here and even less point in continuing to tell himself that because he thought about her at night instead of during the day it didn't count.

In all honesty it was unsettling just how much she

did invade his thoughts during the hours of darkness. The minute he crashed into bed she was right there with him, messing with his sleep by filling his dreams and doing the kinds of things to him that had him frequently jerking awake, hot and hard and shuddering with desire.

Which meant he probably shouldn't be here, he thought, a film of sweat breaking out all over his body, because what was he expecting? That she'd be as happy to see him as he suspected he would be to see her? What was he? A masochist?

Celia wouldn't be pleased to see him any more now than she'd been to have him following her into Zoe's parents' house that sunny Saturday afternoon. No doubt she'd be making her displeasure known the instant he walked in and be reverting to acerbity at the earliest available opportunity.

Frankly he didn't think he had the stomach for it any more, not now he knew how it could be between them.

But it was too late to back out now because even as his head churned with the desire to leave he heard the sounds of a catch being turned. The door swung open and there was Lily smiling broadly and waving him in, and he had no option but to grit his teeth and brace himself to get through the next couple of hours the best he could.

'Marcus,' she said warmly, 'I'm so glad you could make it. Come in.'

'Thanks.' He stepped over the threshold and handed over the bottle and the box, and smiled as she let out a little whoop. 'Champagne and truffles,' she said, grinning even more widely. 'A perfect combination. Thank you. Come and meet everyone.'

He followed her down the hall, listening for one voice, one laugh, every cell of his body on high alert. More tense than he'd been at any point over the past month, he walked into the sitting room, the smile on his face still firmly in place. He shook hands with Kit and accepted a gin and tonic. Then he nodded and chatted as he was introduced to their friends, all the while scouring the room for Celia.

Who wasn't there.

Late? he wondered, or—

'She couldn't make it,' murmured Lily, who'd clearly been watching him scan the guests.

'Who couldn't?' he said, annoyed at both wanting to see her and at being so transparent.

She rolled her eyes. 'Celia.'

'Shame,' he said coolly, and knocked back a slug of his drink.

'Yes. A headache apparently.'

Perhaps brought on by the discovery that he'd also been invited? He didn't know whether to be thrilled, cheated or devastated that she wasn't going to be there. 'So nothing serious, then.'

'Only for my table plan,' said Lily with a grin, before sobering. 'Actually, she didn't sound too good at all.'

'Oh?'

'In fact, she sounded dreadful.'

Marcus kept his face expressionless, and ignored the stab of concern that struck him squarely in the gut. Celia would be fine. A headache was nothing to someone like her. She had the constitution of an ox, a backbone of steel and ice running through her veins. 'I'm sorry to hear that,' he said evenly.

'I saw her ten days ago, you know.'

'Did you?'

'She wasn't looking well then.'

'What's the matter with her?' he asked, purely for the sake of conversation and not out of any interest whatsoever.

'I'm not sure. It sounds like she's working hard.'

'She does that.'

'Too hard maybe.'

'She does that too.' Especially on Sundays.

'Maybe you should go and check on her.'

He went still, his hand tightening around his glass. 'Why would I want to go and check on her?' he said, the need to do just that now suddenly—and perversely—thundering through him.

'You're itching to,' said Lily, and he stamped it down because he wasn't interested in how she was, and in any case he was pretty sure that the last thing she'd want was him pitching up on her doorstep, even if she hadn't been unwell.

'No, I'm not,' he said coolly. 'How hard Celia works is entirely up to her. I couldn't care less how she is or what she's up to.'

Lily looked at him shrewdly. 'Funny, she said that about you too.'

'Did she?'

'Strikes me that there's a lot of protesting going on here.' She pretended to consider for a moment then said, 'Maybe a bit too much.'

Just about resisting the temptation to grind his teeth, Marcus had had enough of beating around this particular bush. If it went on any longer she'd crush him to dust. 'If you have a point, Lily,' he said tightly, 'would you mind getting to it?'

'My point is that you get to each other.'

'And?'

'You should do something about it.'

He'd tried. He'd failed. He wouldn't be going there again. Or even thinking about it. 'She knows where I am.'

Lily let out a huff of exasperation. 'Oh, for heaven's sake, will you just go and see if she's all right? As a favour to me? Please.'

At the genuine worry now filling Lily's eyes, Marcus felt his resolve begin to waver and silently cursed. Oh, bloody hell. What choice did he have? He might not be keen to see her but if Celia was in real trouble, as Lily clearly thought she was, would he ever be able to forgive himself if he'd had the chance to help her and had done nothing, simply out of dented pride? Would Dan? And if she wasn't in trouble, well, surely he could deal with the tongue-lashing he'd undoubtedly get.

Sighing deeply, he ran a hand across the back of his neck. 'OK, fine,' he said, and then, because he'd never be able to sit through supper, chatting and laughing while the visit to Celia's loomed, added, 'Want me to go now?'

Lily beamed. 'I think it would be best, don't you? And actually, as it would even up my table plan you'd be doing me a favour. Another one,' she added, ushering him back down the hall and opening the door he'd stepped through only ten minutes before.

'Text me her address and apologise to Kit for me.'

She nodded. 'I will. Give her my love and tell her I said to get well soon. And thank you, Marcus.'

'No problem,' he said, and with the vague suspicion that, for all his reputation, when it came to powers of persuasion he had nothing on Lily, he left.

CHAPTER SEVEN

HALF AN HOUR later Marcus had crossed London and was at the top of the steps that led up to Celia's building, thinking that here he was unexpectedly standing on yet another doorstep he'd had no intention of gracing a week ago.

As the taxi had pulled up at her address he'd noticed that her lights were off and for a split second he'd contemplated leaving her be. But then Lily and Dan had shot into his thoughts, and his conscience—which had never given him much trouble before—had sprung into life, propelling him out of the taxi and up the steps.

So he'd do what he was here to do. He'd check on her, and then go, and with any luck he wouldn't have any reason to see her ever again, bar the odd Dan/Zoe occasion that might require both their presence.

Marginally reassured by that, he pressed the buzzer and waited. He shoved his hands in his pockets and rocked on his heels for a couple of minutes. Was just about to give up when the intercom crackled to life.

'Yes?' came the muffled voice.

'Celia,' he said, leaning forwards. 'It's Marcus.'

There was silence. And then a grumpy, 'What the hell are you doing here?'

Yup, as he'd thought. No more pleased to have him visit than he was. 'To see if you're all right.'

'Why wouldn't I be?'

'You tell me. I heard you had a headache.'

'I do. I was asleep.'

'Then I apologise for waking you up.'

'Not accepted,' she said crossly. There was a rustle, and then, 'Wait. How did you hear about my headache?'

'Dinner. Kit and Lily's. You were meant to be there.'

A pause while she presumably processed this fact. 'That's right,' she said slowly, as if realisation had only just dawned. 'I was. Have I missed it?'

'Half of it at least.'

'How rude of me.'

'Not *that* rude. You cancelled.'

'Did I?'

OK, so this was getting a little odd, thought Marcus with a frown as a flicker of concern edged through his frustration. Celia sounded confused, disorientated. Which was possibly a consequence of being abruptly woken up. Or possibly not. 'Apparently so.'

'Oh,' she said vaguely. 'So why aren't you still there?'

'Lily was worried.'

'She has no need to be. I'm fine.'

At the ensuing silence he sighed and ran a hand through his hair and wished to God that her brother were here. Even either of her parents—who both unfortunately lived a couple of hundred miles away—would do because he was *not* the man for this job. However, something was telling him she wasn't all that fine, and right now there was no one else. 'Can I come up? Just for a second.'

'I'm not a child, Marcus,' she said, frustration clear in her voice. 'I don't need checking up on or looking after.'

'Then prove it and let me in. Five minutes. That's all I ask.'

There was a pause. A sigh. 'Then will you leave me alone?'

'Yes.' If she really was as all right as she claimed.

'OK, fine.'

The door buzzed and Marcus pushed it open. He leapt up the four flights of stairs to Celia's top-floor flat, and at the sight of her he stopped dead, the breath knocked from his lungs.

She was standing in the doorway, her arms crossed and her chin up, and she might be channelling defiance and trying to appear all right, but she looked absolutely horrendous. Her skin was grey, her eyes dull and her hair was all over the place. She was wearing a pair of faded pink pyjamas that had seen better days, and even though she was covered from head to toe he was willing to bet that she'd lost weight. Her cheeks were hollower than they'd been the last time he'd seen her and her collarbones sharper.

Apart from that ten minutes with him in the garden, she always looked immaculate. Magnificent. Totally together and composed. Now, though, she looked like a dishevelled ghost, the energy and drive all sucked out of her, and it shocked the life out of him.

Frustration gone and concern sweeping in to take its place, he strode towards her, then, as she stepped back to let him in, past her into her flat and spun round as she closed the door behind him.

'What on earth is the matter with you?' he said, worry making his voice sharper than he'd intended.

Celia winced and put a hand to her temple. 'Don't shout at me.'

Guilt slashed through him and he swore softly. 'Sorry.'

'I have a headache.'

'So you said,' he said, gritting his teeth in an effort to moderate his tone, 'but this looks like more than just a headache to me.'

'I guess it might be a migraine but I've never had one so I wouldn't know.'

'Have you taken anything for it?'

'Aspirin, but it hasn't made any difference.' She walked past him into the kitchen and picked up a bottle of water, holding it to her chest as if she needed the defence. 'You really didn't need to come over,' she grumbled. 'I'm sure I'll be fine in the morning.'

'Possibly.'

'I'm just tired, that's all.'

He glanced at the dark circles beneath her eyes and thought that exhausted was more like it. And she was way too thin. 'When did you last eat?'

She frowned then shrugged. 'Yesterday evening. The deal went through and we went out to celebrate.'

'Congratulations.'

'Thanks.'

'I'll make you something and then put you to bed.'

She jerked, her eyes widening and her cheeks flushing, which at least gave her some colour. 'No,' she said hotly. 'Absolutely not.'

At the thought evidently going through her mind

Marcus let out a sigh of exasperation and dragged a hand through his hair. 'Oh, for heaven's sake, Celia.'

Her eyes flashed. 'I *don't* need a nurse.'

'You need food.'

'I need to be left alone.'

'Well, that's too bad because I'm not going anywhere.' Two could play the obstinacy game, and with the state she was in she didn't stand a chance of winning. How on earth could he leave her when she obviously wasn't well at all? Dan would have his balls on a plate.

'I hate you seeing me like this,' she said.

He hated seeing her like this too. He'd always thought of her as so strong and resilient, and to see her a mere shadow of herself was twisting something in his chest. 'I've no doubt you do, but you might as well get used to it.'

'Well, you can't make me something to eat,' she said, clearly sensing that this battle was one she wasn't going to win and, to his relief, giving in. 'There's nothing in the fridge apart from bread. I don't cook, remember.'

'Then we'll get something in.'

'Not sure I feel like eating.'

Ignoring that, Marcus spied the pile of takeaway menus on the immaculately gleaming counter, snatched up the one on the top and hauled out his phone. Tonight, it seemed, they'd be having pizza. Not quite the gourmet spread Lily had probably planned, but good enough.

'What else is wrong besides the headache?' he asked, tapping the number into his phone.

'Nothing, really.'

He shot her a look of warning. 'Celia.'

'OK, sometimes I ache.'

'Ache where?'

'All over.'

'And?'

She bit her lip and frowned. 'I might have been having a few heart palpitations as well.'

Marcus froze, then blanched, his thumb hovering over the dial button. Migraines? Aches? Heart palpitations? What the hell was wrong with her? 'A few?'

She shrugged. 'More than a few.'

'Anything else?'

'No, that's about it, I think.'

Well, it was quite enough, he thought grimly, deleting the number and scrolling through his list of contacts. Sod the pizza. Sod tucking her up in bed and keeping an eye on her till morning. She was going to see a doctor. Now.

'I need a taxi,' he said the second his call was answered, and then reeled off her address.

'I thought you were calling for food,' she said, looking a bit bewildered.

'Change of plan.' Then into the phone, 'No. Half an hour's too long. Make it ten minutes and I'll double the fare.' And with that he hung up.

'Where are you going?' she asked.

'*We* are going to A and E.'

She stared at him in surprise and then gave a weak laugh. 'I'm sure I don't need to go to A and E, Marcus. I'll just take some more aspirin and go back to bed. You're overreacting.'

He looked at her steadily. 'Heart palpitations, Celia?'

'Stress,' she said firmly, dismissively, and he wanted

to shake her. 'Which will undoubtedly diminish now that the deal's gone through.'

'What if it isn't just stress?'

'What else would it be?'

'I don't know,' he said, struggling to keep a lid on his temper because she just didn't seem to be taking this seriously and it was threatening to make him lose it. 'How about burnout? How about a breakdown? How about a bloody heart attack?'

She recoiled. Went as white as the walls of her pristine flat, and he bit back an instinctive apology because he was glad he'd shocked her. She *should* be concerned.

'Fine,' she said, coolly rallying and pulling her shoulders back. 'You win. I'll go and get dressed, then, shall I?'

By the time Celia's name was called four hours later and she went off to see the doctor Marcus was practically climbing walls.

She'd been quiet while they'd been waiting. Monosyllabic in her answers to his occasional question about how she was feeling, but that was hardly surprising since he must have put the fear of God into her with talk of burnout, breakdown and heart attacks. Not to mention the way he'd practically bullied her into coming, even though he'd had no choice because, God, he'd never met a more stubborn woman.

But she hadn't commented on his methods or his motivation, which was actually something of a relief because he wasn't sure he could explain the reason for the sky-high level of concern that had gripped him when he'd laid eyes on her earlier. He could tell himself as much as he liked that it was Lily, or Dan, or his conscience, but he had the vague suspicion it was something else. Something he didn't want to investigate too closely.

Instead she'd just sat there, calmly flicking through leaflets and then absorbing herself in her e-reader. She'd drunk the coffees he'd bought, and worked her way through half a sandwich, an apple and a chocolate bar that he'd picked up from the canteen. She'd even had a nap, stretching across four of the uncomfortable plastic chairs and point-blank refusing the offer of his lap as a pillow.

In short, she couldn't have been more composed.

He, on the other hand, had been going increasingly nuts. When not occupied with the job of going for food and drink, he'd spent practically all of the past four hours pacing, shoving his hands through his hair in frustration and wishing he could just barge in and insist she be seen then and there. But this was a Saturday night in London, and a woman with a headache and the odd palpitation—as she'd insisted on describing herself when asked about her symptoms—came pretty low down on the list when it came to emergencies.

He didn't like hospitals; the smells, the lighting, the sounds made him shudder. He'd spent quite enough time in them when his father had been ill. He didn't like the memories they stirred up much either. Memories of his mother's grief following his father's death and the way she'd shut him out. The way he hadn't understood that and so had reciprocated by shutting her—and everyone else—out.

As an only child with an emotionally absent mother he'd been alone with his grief, and, unable to handle it, he'd gone off the rails, partying too hard, drinking too

much and sleeping with too many girls. He hadn't noticed that his mother wasn't coping either. She hadn't
displayed any sign that she wasn't and he hadn't realised she'd been caught in the claws of deep depres-
sion until the day he learned she'd locked herself in the
garage with the engine of his father's car running and
had had to identify her body in yet another hospital.

But where else could he have taken Celia at this time
on a Saturday night? It was the only option he'd had
because maybe she was right and he was overreacting
but the symptoms she had worried him, and if it came
to it he was not going to have another woman's death
on his conscience.

Given that they'd been waiting so long, the fact that
Celia emerged a mere fifteen minutes after she went
in was unexpected. He didn't know if the speed of
her appointment was a good thing or a bad one. He
scoured her face but her expression gave nothing away.
She didn't look happy. Or sad. She just looked blank.

As she went and sat down, Marcus strode over to
her, his heart pounding and his blood draining to his
feet as something like dread began to sweep through
him. God, if there was something really wrong with
her he didn't know what the hell he'd do.

'What is it?' he asked.

She looked up at him. Blinked as if whatever the
doctor had told her hadn't sunk in yet, and he got the
impression that she wasn't really looking at him. That
she was miles away.

'Celia? Tell me. What is it?'

She opened her mouth. Closed it. Frowned. 'Stress,
mainly,' she said finally.

Marcus sank into the chair next to her, almost sagging with relief. Not a breakdown. Not burnout. Not a heart attack. 'Thank God for that,' he said roughly.

'I wouldn't go thanking God just yet.'

'Why not?'

'Because it's not just stress.'

'Then what else is it?'

'I'm pregnant.'

Celia watched as the news she'd barely registered herself hit Marcus' brain. Watched him reel as she was still reeling. Watched the shock cross his face and thought that it couldn't be anywhere near as great as the shock she was feeling. The shock that had made her throw up in the doctor's wastepaper basket, not that she'd be sharing that delightful detail with him.

'Pregnant?' he echoed faintly.

She nodded. 'Six weeks, they think.'

'Mine?'

'Couldn't be anyone else's.'

Marcus swore brutally and shoved his hands through his hair.

'I know,' she muttered.

Except she didn't really know anything about anything that had happened in the past six or so hours. She didn't know why when Marcus had rung her buzzer she'd wanted him to leave, not because she'd thought she was fine, but because she hadn't wanted him to see her in such a state. She didn't know why she'd secretly been so pleased that he'd refused to take her hints and go. Why she was glad he'd insisted on her coming to A and E. Why she was grateful for his support now.

She was a modern, intelligent, self-sufficient woman. She shouldn't need looking after. She shouldn't like it. It didn't make any sense. But then nothing about her behaviour around Marcus made much sense. Her reaction to him after a month of not seeing him certainly didn't. He ought to have no effect on her at all, because she was so over him and what they'd done, yet he'd mentioned tucking her up in bed—platonically, obviously—and she'd nearly gone up in flames. He'd suggested she rest her head in his lap and she'd practically scooted over to a row of seats on the other side of the waiting room.

Despite the composed front she'd put on she'd been almost unbearably tense. And not just because of the effect Marcus had on her. Deep down the way she'd been feeling for the past couple of weeks had terrified her. Not that what she'd found out once she'd been called to see the doctor had dispelled any of the tension.

She'd gone in there imagining that maybe she'd be told to ease up on work. Perhaps be prescribed the beta blockers that most of her colleagues seemed to be on.

The appointment had started normally enough. The doctor had taken a note of her symptoms. He'd asked her about work and then her menstrual cycle. When she hadn't been able to tell him the date of her last period he'd asked her whether she'd had sex recently.

And then it turned a bit chilling. The questions began to head in one horrible direction, terminating with her peeing on a white plastic stick and two blue lines appearing.

What had come after that was a bit of a blur. All she'd been able to hear was a sort of rushing in her ears through which the doctor's warning about the dangers of stress and the instruction to make an appointment with her GP had only very dimly filtered. Then she'd stumbled out on legs that felt weak and wobbly and wholly unfit for purpose, and collapsed into the nearest chair.

'What the hell happened?'

At the sound of Marcus' voice, shock and horror evident in every word, Celia snapped to and blinked. 'Condoms are only ninety-eight per cent safe,' she said, recalling the statistic she'd read in one of the leaflets she'd flicked through earlier and what the doctor had reiterated. 'Seems like we're one of the unlucky two per cent.'

'How?'

'I don't know. Maybe it had expired. Maybe it wasn't on properly. Maybe it broke. Who knows?'

As they lapsed into silence she could hear the plasticky tick of the clock on the wall, the hum of a busy hospital A and E department and the distant chatter of staff, but the sounds of the cogs and wheels of her brain were fast taking over and her head was beginning to ache more than it had at any point today.

'So what the hell do we do now?' he said, still sounding a bit stunned.

'I have absolutely no idea.' And now, with all the adrenaline draining away and events catching up with her, she suddenly felt very, very tired. 'And you know what, Marcus?' she said, getting to her feet and hauling the strap of her handbag over her shoulder. 'It's late, I'm shattered and I don't think I can deal with this right now.'

He glanced up at her, frowned as he scanned her face, and then stood. 'I'll take you home.'

'I'd appreciate that,' she said with a weak smile. And then, just in case he got it into his head that he'd be staying and fussing over her when she wanted nothing more than to sleep and then process the news and figure out what she wanted to do about it in her own time, added, 'But then, if you don't mind, I'd like to be alone.'

Marcus did mind. Very much. Still. Even though he'd got home a couple of hours ago and Celia probably hadn't given him a moment's thought the second he'd driven away.

He hadn't wanted to leave her. He'd wanted to stay the night. He'd wanted to put her to bed and then keep an eye on her to make sure she was all right because she'd had quite a shock and in her fragile state he wasn't sure how she'd cope with it.

But she'd thanked him for dropping her off, told him she'd call when she was ready to talk and said a very firm goodnight. And now he was at home, sitting in his study, staring out into the garden and working his way through the bottle of whisky that had been gathering dust unopened at the back of a cupboard in the kitchen.

Thinking.

Remembering.

Wondering.

And, the more he thought about that afternoon, going into such mental detail that he could recall every move they'd made, finally realising what had probably happened.

Celia had been wrong in only two of her answers to his stunned enquiry into how she'd got pregnant. The condom hadn't expired. And he had enough experience to be able to put it on properly, however desperate he was.

But he *had* ripped at the packet with his teeth.

He could see it now. His body shaking. His hands trembling as he fumbled for the condom and he bit at it, his teeth very likely nipping a hole in the latex…

He swore again and shoved his hands through his hair. How the hell had he made such a schoolboy error? He'd *never* been so heavy-handed. So damn careless. What was it about Celia that had made him lose his mind so completely that for the first time in his life he'd screwed up? And how the hell hadn't he noticed something was amiss afterwards?

Her pregnancy was his fault, he thought grimly, re-filling the glass for perhaps the sixth time although he'd stopped counting at three. Entirely his fault. She'd just had her life turned upside down because of him and his complete and utter loss of control and there was no one to blame but him.

Which meant that what happened next wasn't up to him. Back in the hospital he'd asked what the hell they did now, but there was no 'they' about this. It was up to her. Wholly up to her.

How he did or didn't feel about fatherhood—and he couldn't allow himself to think about it—was irrelevant. He didn't have the right to form an opinion about it either way. Whatever course of action she chose she was the one who'd have to physically go through it. He'd put her in a position he was pretty sure she'd never expected to find herself in, so all he could do was accept whatever choice she made and offer his support.

The best thing he could do *now,* he thought, screwing the lid on the bottle and taking it and his glass through to the kitchen—the only thing he could do, in fact, if he didn't want to drive himself insane with speculation and impatience—would be to put it from his mind until she was ready to talk.

CHAPTER EIGHT

PREGNANT.

Hmm.

The following morning, after what had—strangely enough, given the events of the past twelve hours—been the best night's sleep she'd had in weeks, Celia sat at the little square table in her kitchen and stared at the pile of pregnancy tests she'd bought just in case the one last night had been as faulty as the condom they'd used.

As proven by the half a dozen pairs of blue lines dancing in front of her eyes it hadn't, and so now she was going to have to face facts.

Heaven only knew how, but overnight she'd managed to block it out. Most probably she'd been in too great a state of shock, too overwhelmed by the enormity of the news and too knackered to process it. This morning, however, she felt refreshed. A bit calmer, at least with regards to her health. Her headache had gone, and the pain and palpitations were dwindling, as if discovering the reason for them—coupled with the sheer relief she hadn't been suffering any of the things that Marcus had suggested—had alleviated them.

Not that she was feeling all that calm about the fact

that she was pregnant. No. That was making her insides churn, the coffee she'd drunk earlier and the toast and marmalade she'd just rustled up rolling around in her stomach and from time to time threatening to reappear.

What a bloody mess.

The emotional side of her was livid at the situation. At bad luck, statistics that left room for failure, and most of all with herself for not being stronger willed in that damn vegetable garden.

The rational side of her thought there was little point in being angry or trying to apportion the blame. What was done was done and she just had to deal with it. She had to put all that to one side and figure out what the hell she was going to do about it, which meant that she now had to face options she'd never expected to have. Had never wanted to have.

She could keep it. Or she could not keep it.

What a choice.

A tiny piece of her wished she didn't have to make it. That the law, society, religion or even her own moral stance on the subject dictated what she had to do and the decision would be out of her hands.

But she squashed that piece of her because she was lucky to live somewhere where she had the choice. The same somewhere that gave her the opportunity to have a career, independence, freedom of thought and speech and deed.

If she gave her options the kind of logical consideration she gave everything—with the exception of that one crazy afternoon of hot sex with Marcus bloody Black—she'd come to the right decision. She trusted in her ability to do that. She was intelligent, confident and had a whole world of information at her fingertips.

She'd research. Weigh up the pros and cons and search the depths of her heart and soul, if necessary. And then she'd make up her mind, and know that whatever she chose it would be the right thing to do.

For her, at least.

What Marcus' opinion on the subject would be she had no idea. But while he was many things he wasn't a fool and she had no doubt that he'd make up his mind about how he'd like to proceed, just as she would. If their wishes coincided, great. If they didn't… Well, she'd cross that bridge if and when they came to it.

Ever since Celia had rung at the crack of dawn this Monday morning, Marcus had been pacing, his nerves as frayed as the carpet he was wearing to death. The past twenty-four hours hadn't been easy for him, although he was under no illusion that they'd been anywhere near as tough as Celia's.

After knocking his monster hangover on the head and updating Lily on Celia's state—omitting the news of her pregnancy, naturally—he'd gone to the gym, where first he'd ploughed up and down the pool for a good couple of hours and after that had run for miles on the treadmill. When he'd got home he'd tried to work. Then he'd eyed the piles of paperwork on his desk and thought about filing. Ten minutes later he'd made an omelette and stuck a film on.

But no matter how hard he'd tried to distract himself he'd still spent every single agonisingly slow second of the day battling the desire to ring her. She'd said she'd wanted to be left alone and he had to respect that, but it had been hard. So when she'd called this morning he'd nearly fallen to his knees in gratitude because he didn't think he would have been able to hold out much longer.

Wasn't sure how much he—or his carpet—could, because by his reckoning an hour and a half went way beyond the 'about an hour' she'd told him she'd be.

Just as he was shooting a quick frustrated glance at the clock on the mantelpiece and wondering if he shouldn't call her, the peal of the doorbell burst through the house and he stopped mid-pace, whipped round and strode to the front door. He opened it, drew it back and at the sight of her felt a great wave of relief rock through him.

She looked *so* much better than she had on Saturday night. Her complexion was pink instead of grey, her eyes bright instead of dull, and even though she was still way too thin, of course, she seemed to have her energy back.

And totally unexpectedly, the overwhelming urge to pull her into his arms and kiss the life out of her slammed into him.

He curled his fingers around the edge of the door to stop himself from reaching for her and concentrated on keeping his feet planted on the floor instead of moving towards her, because taking her into his arms and kissing her was so inappropriate given the circumstances it filled him with self-disgust.

'Good morning,' she said, smiling faintly, with any luck completely unaware of what was going through his head.

'Hi,' he said, his voice so hoarse it sounded as if he hadn't used it for months. He cleared his throat, flashed her a quick smile of his own and then stepped back. 'Come in.'

'Thanks.'

She walked past him, looking up and around, at the pictures on the walls, at the furniture in the hall. Even though he'd been intending to take her straight into the kitchen and offer her a drink, when she veered into the sitting room he let her because something deep inside him, something he wasn't keen on analysing too closely, wanted her to like what she saw.

He thrust his hands into the pockets of his jeans, watched as she peered at photos, ran her gaze over his bookshelves and took in the furnishings, and he had to bite back the urge to ask her what she thought because he was pretty sure that she wasn't here to discuss his interior design.

'You have a nice house, Marcus,' she said, once they'd made it into the kitchen and he'd handed her the glass of water she'd requested when he'd offered her something to drink.

'You sound surprised,' he said, the gratification that she liked it overriding the irritation that despite everything she still harboured some of the old impressions she'd had of him.

'I am a bit, I guess. It's big but somehow it feels cosy. Lived in.' She lifted the glass and took a sip. 'It's unexpected.'

'Why, what did you expect?'

She shrugged and shot him a smile. 'I don't know, really. Something more along the lines of a shag pad, I suppose.'

'You haven't seen the bedroom.'

The minute the words left his mouth he wished he could scoop them up and stuff them back in because that had sounded an awful lot like flirting, and what the hell he thought he was doing flirting with Celia, *now,* he had no idea.

She snapped her gaze to his, her eyes widening and her breath catching. 'No,' she said softly. 'I haven't.'

Marcus ignored the temptation to suggest that she go with him and check it out, and told himself to get a grip. He had to pull himself together. He really did. Before he made even more of a fool of himself.

'So how are you feeling?' he asked, folding his arms, leaning back against the granite counter and deciding that whatever it was that was affecting his ability to think straight it might be safer if he stuck to the likely reason she was here.

'Better after a couple of good nights' sleep,' she said dryly, 'but strange.'

'Strange' he could understand. He was feeling very strange indeed. A bit baffled by the way she was affecting him given the situation they were in. On edge and horribly awkward, which was a new one when it came to the things he felt around her. A new one for him generally, come to think of it. 'How's the headache?'

'Gone.'

'The palpitations?'

'Receding.'

Thank goodness for that. 'Nausea?'

'No.'

He ran his gaze over her figure, taking in the summery dress that hung off her a bit too loosely, and frowned. 'Are you eating?'

She nodded. 'I am.'

'Properly?'

'Properly. I went to the supermarket this morning and everything. Scout's honour.'

Good. 'So no work today, then?' he said, remembering it was Monday.

'I took the day off.'

'That must be a first.'

'The first in two years.' She shot him a quick wry smile. 'Stuff on my mind, you know?'

He did. On his mind too, actually, and frankly he'd had enough of skirting around the issue with small talk and edginess. 'So I imagine you're here to talk about the pregnancy.'

'I haven't been able to think about anything else for the last twenty-four hours.'

'No, well, it's kind of all-consuming, isn't it?'

'What's your take on it?'

He didn't have one. At least not until he knew what hers was. 'I'd rather hear yours.'

She tilted her head and looked at him steadily, a frown appearing on her forehead. 'Have you actually thought at all about what you think we should do?'

'Of course I have,' he said, because he *had* thought about it. Sort of. Not that he'd really come to a conclusion one way or another. What would have been the point of that when, as it wasn't his decision to make, any opinion he had would only be irrelevant?

'Because you do realise that the only way we can work through this is if we're honest.'

'I do.' And he would be honest, because he wanted what she wanted. 'Want to sit down?'

'Sure.'

She pulled out the nearest chair and sat down and he walked round the table to take a seat opposite her.

'OK. Right. Well. Here goes.' She put her glass on the table, leaned forwards to rest her elbows on the table and took a deep breath. 'As you can probably imagine *I've* given it a *lot* of thought and the way I see it we have three options. One, I keep it. Two, I have it and give it up for adoption. Or three, I have an abortion.'

Even though he could feel his heartbeat speeding up Marcus didn't move a muscle. 'Go on.'

'As far as I'm concerned option number two isn't viable. I have no moral grounds for going through the whole nine months of pregnancy only to give the baby away at the end.'

'So that leaves options one and three.'

She nodded. 'It does.'

'And which have you decided on?'

'Option number three.'

There. It was done.

Celia held her breath as she waited for Marcus' reaction to the conclusion she'd spent so many heart-wrenching hours coming to. So many thoughts going round and round in her head. So many scenarios playing out over and over again. So much turmoil churning around inside her.

She hadn't come to the decision easily. She'd never given anything more consideration. She'd applied logic, practicality and emotion, looking at it from every angle she could think of. And then she'd looked at it from what she thought might be Marcus' angle, even though she was becoming increasingly aware that he may have angles and depths she'd never considered before.

Given what she knew for certain of him, though, she'd assumed that he'd be on board with her decision. That he wouldn't want the disruption to his life any more than she did.

But right now his face was so totally unreadable she couldn't tell what he was thinking and it was disconcerting to say the least.

'I see,' he said, his voice devoid of any emotion whatsoever. 'You want an abortion.'

'I wouldn't exactly say I *want* one, but I think it would be for the best.'

'Right.'

There was still nothing in his expression to let her know what he thought, and she felt a flutter of alarm. What if she'd been wrong in her assumption he'd think the same? What if he wasn't on board with this? What if he wanted the baby while she didn't? What would happen then?

'Look, Marcus,' she said, bracing herself for the possibility of having to negotiate or compromise or who knew what, 'while I don't rule out having children at some point in the future, the timing of this one couldn't be worse. My career is very important to me. I travel a lot. I work horrendous hours. I'm up for partnership, and after everything I've worked for I can't jeopardise that. This pregnancy was an accident and I—'

'You don't have to justify your decision, Celia,' he cut in, thankfully putting an end to her rambling, which was in danger of becoming faintly hysterical.

'Don't I?'

'No. Because I happen to agree with you.'

She blinked. Sat back. A little bit stunned and a whole lot relieved. 'You do? Really?'

He nodded. Once. 'Really.' He leaned forwards and

looked at her, his gaze intense and unwavering. 'You wanted to know my take on it? Well, this is my take on it. I don't want a child either. It's not something I've ever wanted. While the timing is neither here nor there for me I think we're both well aware I'm hardly father material. We're not in a relationship. And when it comes down to it I'm not sure we really even like each other.'

Oh. That took her aback, although she didn't really know why, because he was right. She might still be fiercely and annoyingly attracted to him but did that constitute like? She didn't think so.

'So what kind of people would we be bringing a child into that situation?' he continued.

'My thoughts exactly,' she murmured, and wondered if he'd somehow been able to read her mind because so many of his arguments were hers.

'We'd both end up miserable and God only knows what effect that would have on a child.'

'Not a good one, and I should know.'

'So that's it, then,' he said briskly. 'Decision made.'

Thank goodness for that. Celia blew out a breath she hadn't realised she'd been holding because this conversation had gone a lot more smoothly than she'd dared to hope. 'Are you sure?'

'I'm as sure as you are.'

And she was one hundred per cent sure. She'd employed every resource she had and had thought about it for so long and hard that how could she be anything but? 'I'm sure,' she said firmly, then she sat back, every single one of her muscles sagging in relief. 'You know, for a moment there I was really worried you'd want it,' she said with a faint smile.

'And have to curb my lifestyle?' he said dryly.

'Well, quite,' she said, her smile faltering for a second as it struck her that, while much of his behaviour recently had surprised her, some things were still the same. Such as his love of chasing after anything in a skirt. Or bikini, if those press reports of his antics over the past month, complete with photos, were anything to go by.

But she pushed aside whatever it was that was needling her—disapproval, most probably—because what did she care what he got up to, and instead focused on the tiny arrow of guilt that was suddenly stabbing at her conscience. 'Are we being terribly selfish?' she said, suspecting they were, but if they were at least they were in it together.

Marcus shook his head. 'I'd say we're being sensible. Realistic. Responsible.'

'That sounds more palatable.'

'It's true. You know it is.'

He was right. She did. 'I know.'

'So what happens next?' he asked after a moment.

'I'm going to take the rest of this week off.'

'Can you do that at such short notice?'

She shrugged, for the first time in her career not giving a toss what her boss would think. 'They'll just have to live with it. I nearly killed myself pushing that deal through. They can spare me for a week.'

'Are you serious?'

'Deadly.'

He shot her a quick grin that flipped her stomach. 'I'm staggered.'

'I know,' she said dryly, reminding herself that her stomach had no business flipping since he'd clearly moved on to pastures new. 'A temporary shift to my work-life balance. Who'd have thought? But seeing as how I've made an appointment to see my GP this afternoon—and presumably there'll be others—it makes sense. Having my boss wonder what's wrong with me is not something I'd want to encourage.'

'Want me to come along?'

She shook her head. 'I should be fine this afternoon,' she said and then, trying not to think too much about why she wanted or needed his support, added, 'But maybe you could come with me to the clinic or wherever I have to go.'

'Of course.'

'I'll call you with dates.'

Celia got to her feet and picked up her bag, and as Marcus walked her to the door she found herself wondering if he really was as on board with this as he claimed. There was something about his lack of emotion, the way he'd agreed with her so swiftly, that didn't feel quite right. She'd have thought he'd question her thought process a bit more, and the fact that he hadn't made her faintly uneasy.

He opened the door and she stopped. Turned to him and, dismissing the little voice inside her head questioning why she'd want to challenge him when his agreement suited her so well, said, 'Marcus?'

'What?'

'Do you really think we're doing the right thing?'

The look he gave her was firm and resolute and wiped away all her doubts, even before he nodded and said, 'Absolutely.'

CHAPTER NINE

BUT MARCUS KNEW that he'd lied. Unwittingly perhaps, but he'd lied nonetheless, because he didn't think they were doing the right thing at all.

Sitting with Celia in his kitchen and talking it through, he'd been convinced that going along with whatever she wanted was the only course of action he had any right to take.

But the conversation had clearly opened some kind of cupboard in his head into which he'd stuffed everything he'd told himself to block out because she'd left and within minutes his head had filled with everything he'd not allowed himself to think about.

As a result, thoughts had been ricocheting round his brain for the past three days, messy and jumbled, but all pointing to the conclusion that he thought they were making a mistake.

He couldn't explain it. He shouldn't want a child. His current lifestyle—which he worked hard at and enjoyed—wasn't conducive to one. His arguments for terminating the pregnancy had been extremely valid, and God knew all the reasons Celia had put forward were ones he could understand.

Then there was the indisputable fact that he didn't

want to be tied to anyone, least of all someone who had a problem with the way he lived—and what greater tie was there than a child?

And finally there was the deep-rooted fear that history would repeat itself and he wouldn't make it past his child's seventeenth birthday, and dread of the possible fallout from that.

Yet all he had to do was see a mental image of him holding his child in his arms and something inside him melted. When the mental image of Celia holding his child in her arms came to him, he melted even more. And as he wasn't someone who melted, ever, the feeling was both bewildering and alarming.

Rationally he knew that if she had the baby his life—and hers—would become horribly complicated and messy and fraught with tension. There'd be logistics to sort out, all kinds of obstacles to negotiate and endless arguments over decisions that would have to be made.

But none of that seemed to be of much importance.

Instead, whenever he thought about having an actual child he was assailed by memories of his own childhood. The love and attention his parents had lavished on him. The days out. The walks, the trips to the zoo, the beach. The holidays. The happy little unit they'd been before he'd hit adolescence and become a normal moody teenager.

Logically he was aware there must have been tough times and his childhood couldn't have been hearts and flowers every second, but all his memory chose to focus on were the happy ones.

Logic also told him that his and Celia's situation was about as far from the situation into which he'd been born as it was possible to get, but that didn't seem to matter. He wanted to be the kind of father to his child that his father had been to him. He wanted to be the kind of father who lived to see his child grow up. He wanted to be a father full stop. As they emerged from the clinic where they'd just had an appointment with the doctor to whom Celia's GP had referred her the feeling he had that what they were doing was dreadfully wrong was even stronger.

The sight of all those children's drawings papering the walls of the waiting room—which seemed so insensitive it had to be deliberate, as if testing the strength of the decision made by the people who'd wait there— had practically torn his heart out.

When they'd gone into the appointment itself and the ultrasound had shown a heartbeat, all he'd been able to think through the fog in his head was that that tiny little fetus was his child. *His child.* A weird kind of force had slammed into him, something that was instinctive, primal and surely had a lot to do with evolution, making his entire body shake with the strength of it.

And when the doctor had explained the procedure she recommended, his stomach had curdled and his chest had felt as if it had a band around it, squeezing tighter and tighter until he felt as though he could barely breathe. By the time she was through he'd just wanted to drag Celia the hell out of there.

Not that Celia had seemed in any way as affected by the appointment. She'd sat there, a bit pale, yes, but calm and composed, asking questions in a cool voice that suggested she was still as sure as she'd ever been and wasn't suffering anywhere near the kind of mental turmoil he was.

But what could he do about it?

He'd told her he was fine with the decision she'd made. He'd convinced himself it was the right thing to do, and he still stood by that. With his head, at least, which knew that he had to be fair and not put her in an even more difficult position.

His heart, however, was wondering if he could let her go through with it without at least telling her how he felt. If he could live with himself if he didn't at least mention it.

With the battle still raging in his head, he held the door to the street open for Celia and then followed her out. He spied a pub across the road and thought that never had he seen a place more welcome.

'I don't know about you,' he said, shoving his hands through his hair as if that might wipe the past half an hour from his memory, 'but after that I could do with a drink. What do you say?'

When she didn't answer, he stopped. Turned. To see her standing on the pavement looking pale, drawn and miserable.

'Are you all right?' he asked, which had to be the dumbest question of the century because she obviously wasn't all right at all.

'Not really.' Her voice was rough. Cracked. Filled with despair.

'What's wrong?'

Her eyes welled up, her chin began to tremble and she clamped her hand to her mouth. 'Oh, *God,*' she mumbled, and it sounded as if the words were being wrenched from somewhere deep inside her.

'What is it?' he asked, his heart hammering with alarm and who knew what else.

'I'm so sorry, Marcus,' she said wretchedly, 'but I don't think I can go through with it.'

And then, just as he was identifying that something else as hope, relief and a crazy kind of elation, and just as he was thinking that however complicated things were going to be he'd do his damnedest to make sure they'd be all right, she burst into tears.

Celia barely noticed Marcus taking her arm and making for the garden that filled the middle of the square. She was too busy crying like the baby that up until she'd seen the ultrasound she'd been so convinced she didn't want and making a complete mess of the handkerchief he'd thrust in her hand with a muffled curse.

He sat her down on a bench, wrapped a warm, solid arm around her shoulders and pulled her into him, murmuring that everything would be all right, and that just made her burst into a fresh bout of weeping.

What was she doing? she wondered desperately as she collapsed against him and sobs racked her body. Why was she crying? She never cried. Not even when she'd graduated top of her year and her father hadn't bothered to turn up to the ceremony had she shed a tear.

Maybe it was the stress of everything that had happened lately. The exhaustion of working so hard. The terror that she was falling apart and the relief to learn she wasn't. The shock of finding out she was pregnant. Being utterly convinced she wanted to have an abortion and then being knocked sideways by the thundering sensation that she didn't. Or maybe it was just her hormones going mental.

Whatever it was she couldn't seem to stop it. Tears leaked from her eyes, drenching the front of his shirt, her throat was sore and her muscles ached, and while she completely lost it Marcus just sat there calmly holding her, supporting her, comforting her in a way she'd never have expected.

Why wasn't he running a mile? Surely tears weren't his thing. Why hadn't he bundled her in a taxi and sent her home? She must be mortifying him. She was certainly mortifying herself. She'd thought that the night of Lily's dinner party when he'd come over to her flat, clapped eyes on her and his jaw had dropped in absolute horror was about as low as she could get, but this sank even lower. Her eyes would be puffy, her nose red and her skin blotchy, but that was nothing compared to the fact that by breaking down like this she was being so pathetic, so weak, acting so out of character.

And while the thought of falling apart in front of any man was distressing enough, to do so in Marcus' arms was enough to crush her completely.

Yet he didn't seem at all fazed by either her dramatic declaration on the pavement outside the clinic or her subsequent watery collapse. He was coping magnificently.

Surprisingly magnificently actually.

Although maybe it wasn't all that surprising, because now she thought about it he'd taken everything that had happened over the past week or so totally in his stride. He'd dealt with it all far better than she'd have imagined. Far better than she had, she thought, realising with relief that *finally* she seemed to be running out of tears.

As the sobs subsided and the tears dried up, she

sniffed. Hiccuped. Then drew in a ragged breath. 'Sorry,' she said, her mouth muffled by his chest.

'You have nothing to be sorry for.' His words rumbled beneath her ear, the vibrations making her shiver.

Fighting the odd urge to snuggle closer, she unclenched her fingers from his shirt and drew back, wincing when she saw the black mascara smudges all over him. 'I do. I've ruined your shirt.'

He removed his arm from her shoulders and gave her a faint smile. 'I have others.'

His gaze roamed over her face and she went warm beneath his scrutiny. Squirmed a bit because the man was used to being surrounded by women who were gorgeous and heaven only knew what she looked like. A wreck most probably. But she could hardly whip out her mirror to check and rectify the damage. Not when presumably there was an important conversation about to be had. Like—

'Did you mean what you said back there?' he asked quietly, and she suddenly felt as if she were sitting on thorns.

Yup, like that.

She pushed her hair back and swallowed in an effort to alleviate the ache in her throat that might have been left over from her crying jag or might be down to the doubts now hammering through her. 'About not wanting to go through with it?' she asked, mainly to give her a moment to compose herself.

'Yes.'

His eyes were dark, his face once again unreadable, but there was an air of tension about him that told her it mattered. Well, of course it did. She'd probably just turned his life upside down, very possibly on the basis of a mere wobble.

She swallowed, her heart thumping as she tried to unravel the mess in her head. 'Maybe,' she said, rubbing her temples. 'I don't know.'

She wasn't lying. She didn't know, because she couldn't work it out. What on earth had happened back there? She'd been so sure she had it all figured out. That the course of action she'd started on was the right one.

Logically she thought that still. But emotionally... well, emotionally, she was all over the place, and had been pretty much ever since they'd turned up at the clinic.

She'd sat in that doctor's office, listening to what she'd said as if hearing the words through a wall of soup, and weirdly and worryingly her resolve had begun to weaken. And then the doctor had done an ultrasound and it had drained away completely.

How could everything she'd spent so long analysing be thrown on its head by one tiny little pulse fluttering at a hundred and sixty beats a minute? It didn't make any sense.

'I mean, it was fine when I thought it was just a bundle of cells or something,' she said, aware that Marcus was waiting for her to explain. 'But seeing the heartbeat...' She tailed off because how could she ever even *begin* to describe the feelings that had pummelled through her, and, in any case, why would he even want her to try?

'I know,' he said gruffly.

'And before that, all those pictures...'

'I understand.'

'It set something off inside me. Something instinctive.' She shrugged as if it were nothing but a minor blip, forced a smile to her face and shoved aside her doubts. 'But don't worry, I'm sure it'll pass.'

It had to, didn't it? Because she couldn't change her mind. She'd told him that she thought abortion was for the best and he'd agreed. He'd been quite firm about that. How selfish of her would it be to back out now and land him with the kind of commitment that lasted a lifetime, the kind he clearly didn't want?

He frowned. 'You really think so?'

Her throat went tight but she nodded. 'Of course. I mean, what the hell was I thinking? I can't have a baby.'

'Why not?'

Huh?

She stared at him, faintly taken aback. Had he forgotten the conversation they'd had only three days ago? 'We talked about this, remember?'

'We talked about why not having a baby was a good idea. We didn't discuss option number one at all.'

'No, well, we didn't need to. We were in agreement.'

'I have a feeling we still are.'

She blinked, a bit baffled by that. 'What?'

He looked at her intently, his eyes glinting, his jaw set with a determination she'd never seen before. 'Tell me why you think you can't have it.'

'Because I love my job. I want the partnership. I deserve it. It's what I've been working towards.' Hadn't they been through this already?

'Plenty of other women have children and a demanding job, don't they?'

'Of course they do.'

'So why not you?'

'It's not that simple, Marcus,' she said, wondering

how he'd forgotten about all the other reasons they'd come up with for why having this baby would be a bad idea.

'Isn't it?'

Exasperation slid through her. What was he trying to do here? Did he *want* her to change her mind? That didn't make any sense at all. 'You know it isn't.'

'OK, well, let's look at it hypothetically.'

'Hypothetically?'

He nodded. 'We didn't discuss it before, but I think we should now.'

'Isn't it a bit late?'

He shook his head. 'Now's the perfect time,' he said. 'So, hypothetically, if you'd decided to go with option one, what would you have planned to do when the baby was born?'

Worryingly and interestingly enough, she didn't even have to think about it all that hard. 'I'd have gone back to work,' she said, her heart beating fast and her head swimming for a second at what that might mean. 'Possibly hired a nanny. Maybe roped in my dad. He's been banging on about grandchildren long enough, and he's about to retire so presumably he'd have been prepared to step up to the plate. And Mum would have helped too, I'm sure. Hypothetically speaking, of course,' she added hastily, because it was a scenario she could now envisage all too clearly but one that could never happen because Marcus didn't want it to.

He stretched his legs out in front of him and crossed them at the ankles, staring straight ahead. 'And where would I have figured in all this?'

'You wouldn't have figured at all. Unless you'd

wanted to. Which you wouldn't have because you don't even want a baby.'

'Don't I?'

Her heart squeezed but she ignored it. 'No.'

'Assume I do. For the hypothesis.'

Why was he doing this? she wondered, feeling uncharacteristically flustered. Was he making sure she'd thought through everything before going ahead? Or was it something else?

'OK, fine,' she said, her brain too frazzled to be able to work it through, 'but I don't see it would make any difference, because how could you help?'

'I could look after the baby when you go back to work.'

She stared at him in surprise. 'You?'

'Why not? My time is my own at the moment so it would make perfect sense.'

'What about your projects?'

'I can work on them from home.'

'You'd do that?'

'Yes.'

She didn't quite know what to make of that. 'Have you ever changed a nappy?'

He arched an eyebrow. 'Have you?'

'Well, no,' she conceded. 'But what about when the baby's six weeks old or something and has been crying non-stop all night and you realise just what you've taken on? Would you still want to stick around then?' And if he didn't, what would that mean for her career?

'Of course. Once I start something I don't give up.'

Except when it came to relationships, she thought, but before she could say anything, he added, 'And there's no way I'd give up on my child.'

'But wouldn't you mind?'

'What about?'

'About what other people might think if you stayed at home looking after a baby while I went back to work, for a start.'

'I don't give a crap what other people think.'

Which was admirable, but now it struck her that somewhere along the line this conversation had become less theoretical and more real so she steeled herself and said, 'But what does any of this matter? It's all totally irrelevant. Hypothetical.'

'Right.' He drew his legs back, sat bolt upright and swivelled so he was facing her, his jaw tight and his eyes practically burning into hers. 'But what if it wasn't?'

Her heart skipped a beat and her breath caught. 'I don't understand.'

'What if I said I'd changed my mind too?'

'I haven't changed—' She stopped. Stared at him. 'What?'

'You heard.'

'*Have* you changed your mind?'

He nodded. 'I have.'

'You want this baby?'

'I do.'

She reeled. 'But how? Why? You said you weren't fatherhood material and never would be.'

'I know I did.'

'So what happened?'

'Nothing happened. I just wasn't being entirely honest when I agreed with you that we should go for option number three.'

'Why on earth not?'

'Guilt, mainly.'

She stared at him. 'Guilt?'

'It's my fault you're pregnant.'

Her heart stumbled for a second. 'That's very noble of you, Marcus,' she said with small smile, 'but it does take two to tango. And we were careful. No one's to blame. It's just one of those things life likes to throw at you to really screw up your plans.'

'No, it really is. I opened the condom packet with my teeth. I think I might have ripped it.'

It was a possibility, she supposed, but, 'You don't know that you did.'

'Do you have a better explanation?'

'It could have been anything.'

'Doesn't matter,' he said resolutely. 'My condom, my application, my fault.'

For a moment she didn't know what to say. 'That's mad,' she managed eventually. 'None of this is anyone's fault.'

He shrugged. 'I should have been more careful. It's no excuse, but I wasn't thinking all that straight at the time.'

'No. Well, who was?' said Celia, going warm at the memory.

'Anyway, because of the guilt I decided that I'd go along with whatever you decided.'

With some difficulty she dragged herself back from the memory of that afternoon. 'So you lied?' she asked, frowning.

'Not exactly,' he said with a shrug. 'I simply didn't allow myself to think about what I wanted in case you wanted something different.'

Nothing simple about that, she thought, as she

waded through it all. 'So given that,' she said, only about eighty per cent certain she got what he meant because the realisation that had she not said anything he'd have let her go through with it despite wanting the opposite was too much to handle right now, 'how do I know that your change of heart now doesn't simply reflect mine?'

Not much point in denying that she had had a change of heart any more, was there? Not when just the thought of holding her child made her heart practically burst from her chest.

'Because I've been having doubts for days.'

'So you think we should have this baby.'

'Yes.'

'But we don't like each other,' she said, knowing she was grasping at straws but trying to buy some time to absorb the enormity of where the conversation was heading.

His eyes glittered. Darkened. 'Don't we?'

Celia shivered at the heat that flared in his eyes but ignored it because the situation was complicated enough without adding chemistry into the mix.

'We live miles apart.'

'So move in with me.'

She gaped at him. On what level would that be a good idea? 'No.'

'Then how about into the house next door to me?'

'What?'

'I own it. I rent it out, but I can give the tenants notice and you can move in. Rent-free.'

'No way.'

'All right. Pay the rent. I don't mind. But it would be convenient, don't you think?'

'You've given this some thought.'

'None at all,' he said with a wry smile. 'I'm doing this very much on the hoof. But we have resources. Lots of them. The obstacles aren't insurmountable.'

He was formidable, she thought with a shiver. Determined and assertive and just a little bit overwhelming. Which was odd because a couple of months ago these weren't words she'd have used to describe him, although presumably he wouldn't have created a business worth millions if he hadn't been.

The combination was also very attractive, and she wished she could go back to thinking him laid-back, shallow and debauched because somehow those characteristics seemed a whole lot safer than the ones she'd seen in recent days.

With not a small amount of formidable determination of her own she pushed aside the realisation that she found him way more attractive now than she ever had before and concentrated on the conversation.

'I have a place of my own,' she pointed out, telling herself that just because what he suggested made frighteningly good sense it didn't mean she was ready to abandon her highly valued independence just yet.

'You have a pristine flat up four flights of stairs and there isn't a lift. Think about it.'

She did, and at the vision of herself struggling up them with a pushchair could see his point, not that she was going to admit it because the speed with which things were going if she did she could well find herself moved in to his house next door by the end of the week. 'How did you get to be so practical?'

'I always have been. You just haven't noticed.'

Seemed she hadn't noticed quite a bit. 'You're not

going to suggest we get married or anything, are you?' she said, with the arch of an eyebrow and the hint of a grin.

He froze, a look of horror flashing across his face. 'Do you want me to?'

'*God,* no,' said Celia with a shudder, although part of her wondered what he'd have done if she'd said yes. 'My parents only married because my mother was pregnant with Dan and look what happened there. And despite the mess they made of things, and the effect it could have had on us, Dan and I have turned out pretty much OK, I think.'

The tension eased from his body and he shot her a quick smile. 'You turned out more than OK.'

'Nevertheless,' she said, going warm and knowing that annoyingly it had little to do with the heat of the midday sun, 'if we have this child you do know it would tie us together for ever, don't you?'

'Only in one respect. We'd still be free to pursue our own interests.'

No need to ask what those interests would be, she thought a bit waspishly as those photos of scantily clad Sardinians flashed into her head and the heat inside her faded. 'It would seriously cramp your style.' Not to mention hers, because, even though she didn't have much of one at the moment, at some point in the future she'd like to meet someone who didn't think of marriage as a fate worse than death.

'That's my problem to worry about.' He shifted on the bench, and as she caught a trace of his scent she tried not to inhale deeply.

'With the issue my parents have family parties would be a nightmare.'

'But manageable.'

'Do you have an answer for everything?'

'Not everything.'

'But most things.'

He gave her the glimmer of a smile. 'Do you have any other arguments to put forward?'

'No,' she said a little dazedly as she thought about it. 'I appear to have run out.'

'And?'

She tilted her head and stared at him, noting the dark intensity of his eyes, the set of his jaw, and wondering about both. 'You really want this, don't you?'

'Yes.'

'Why?'

'For the same reasons you do.'

Hmm. She doubted that, but she was hardly going to probe further. If she did then she'd have to go into *her* reasons, which she suspected went a lot deeper than the effect of a wall of paintings and an ultrasound.

But whatever his reasons, and however surreal today had been, however they were going to figure it all out, she knew what she wanted beyond the shadow of a doubt. And so, with her heart hammering, she took a deep breath and said, 'Then I guess we're going to be parents.'

CHAPTER TEN

'YOU'RE PREGNANT?'

At the volume of her brother's voice and the sudden hush that fell over the tapas bar where she, her brother and her sister-in-law were having supper and a catch-up for the first time since the happy couple had been back in London Celia winced. 'Not sure they heard you in the kitchen, Dan,' she muttered. 'Would you mind keeping it down a bit?'

'Yes, I bloody well would,' he said hotly. 'We've been here for over an hour, and you didn't think to mention it?'

She put down her fork, arched an eyebrow and shot him a look. 'And interrupt the fascinating and lengthy tales of your adventures on honeymoon?'

'You did go on a bit, Dan,' murmured Zoe, picking up her glass of wine and taking a sip.

Celia grinned. 'To tell you the truth, I loved hearing about what you got up to,' she said. 'Especially the bit where you got chased by a herd of angry alpacas. That's definitely one to bring out at your diamond wedding anniversary. And anyway, I'm mentioning it now.'

Dan frowned. 'How pregnant are you?'

'Twelve weeks, give or take a day or two.' She'd had

the scan yesterday and when she'd seen those tiny little hands and feet and then been told that everything was progressing as it should had felt a mixture of relief, excitement and terror.

Marcus had been there too, the first time she'd seen him since they'd reversed their decision about the abortion. He'd sat next to her, asking questions and squeezing her hand and for a split second she'd felt this deep, *deep* longing that they were together. For each other, not just the baby. Which didn't make any sense whatsoever because they hadn't seen each other for four weeks and for all she knew he'd bedded half of London in that time. And while she knew that it was undoubtedly down to hormones, all in all it had been a rather peculiar, faintly unsettling quarter of an hour.

'Congratulations,' said Zoe, beaming.

'Thank you.'

Dan shot his wife a look. 'Why don't you sound as surprised as I am by this?' he asked suspiciously. 'Did you know? Two months in and do we already have secrets?'

Zoe shook her head and patted him on the arm. 'Calm down, Dan. Of course I didn't know. But when a woman declines alcohol and avoids the prawns it doesn't take a genius to work it out.' Then she shot him a wicked smile. 'And you might as well get used to the secrets thing because I have loads. You might even like some of them.'

His gaze locked onto his wife's and something flickered in his eyes that Celia didn't even want to try and analyse. 'Right,' he murmured, softening for a second before snapping his gaze back to her and glaring.

'You can stop looking and sounding all outraged,'

said Celia, refusing to rise. 'This is the twenty-first century, you know. Women do get pregnant by accident and out of wedlock.'

'I know,' said her brother, shoving his hands through his hair and frowning. 'I'm just a bit stunned, that's all. I'd never have thought you…' He tailed off. Looked a bit bemused. Then rubbed a hand over his face as acceptance settled in. 'Do Mum and Dad know?'

'Not yet. I'll tell them soon.'

'Who's the father?'

Celia didn't see the point of not telling them. If Marcus was intending to be as hands-on as he claimed they'd find out soon enough anyway. 'Marcus.'

Dan nearly fell off his chair. '*My* Marcus?'

'If you want to put it like that.' Although to be honest she didn't think he was anyone's. Nor, in all likelihood, would he ever be, given his track record, his comments on the subject and the look of horror that had filled his face when she'd jokingly asked if he was going to suggest they got married.

'I thought you couldn't stand each other,' said Dan, while Zoe merely smiled knowingly and helped herself to the last of the prawns.

Celia lowered her gaze and studied her non-alcoholic cocktail. 'Yes, well, things change,' she said, ignoring the sudden and unexpected urge to ask her brother if Marcus' aversion to commitment was simply down to an enjoyment of variety, because why would she need to know that?

And actually, things had changed quite a bit, she thought, turning it over in her mind as she twiddled her straw. Primarily her opinion of him. How she could ever have thought him shallow and pointless and ir-

responsible she had no idea. He might go out with—
and probably sleep with—a lot of women but he was
none of those things, and she'd been stupid and arrogant in her presumption that she had the measure of
him all these years.

There was clearly a lot to learn about the father of
her child. A lot of assumptions she had to ditch. So
maybe she could do a lot worse than spend the next six
months trying to figure out who Marcus really was,
because if she was being honest he was turning out to
be more fascinating than she'd ever have imagined.

'Since when?' asked Dan, slicing through her
thoughts and making her head snap up.

'Since your wedding,' she said, and to her irritation
she felt a blush storm into her cheeks.

Zoe flashed Dan a smug grin. 'Told you,' she said.

'So much for not ending the drought,' Dan muttered.

Celia snapped her gaze to him. 'What?'

'Before you, Marcus hadn't slept with anyone for
six months.'

Blush forgotten, her jaw dropped as yet another assumption exploded into bits. 'Six months?'

'Exactly. We talked about it at the wedding. He had
an ex who turned into a bit of a stalker. I told him
that as you were the only single woman there and you
weren't exactly each other's flavour of the month I
didn't think that'd be changing. Seems I was wrong.'

'You were,' she murmured, intrigued and a bit distracted by the stalkery ex.

'I take it you're keeping it?' said Zoe.

'I am,' said Celia, dragging her thoughts back on
track and deciding that there was no need to go into
detail about the roundabout way they'd made that par-

ticular decision. Dan had only just got over his shock at finding out she was pregnant.

'And how the hell's that going to work out?' he asked.

She took a sip of water and thought about all the very practical—if faintly overwhelming—suggestions Marcus had made sitting on that bench in the square outside the clinic. 'I'm not entirely sure at the moment. We've tossed around a few ideas, but I guess we have six or so months to figure it out.'

And to figure out other things. Such as the truth behind his wicked reputation. Such as why he wanted to keep the baby. Such as whether she and Marcus had anything in common other than chemistry.

Her brother frowned. 'Have you considered the fact that Marcus has about as much stickability as an old Post-it note?'

'I have,' she said with a brief nod. Mainly in the moments of doubt she had when she wondered what the hell they were doing, if maybe a couple of years down the line she wasn't going to be left literally holding the baby. But then she'd recall what he'd said about never giving up once he'd started something, the steadfast determination etched into every inch of his face and the burn of his eyes, and her doubts eased somewhat.

'And he might be my best friend,' said Dan darkly, 'but *Marcus* and *responsibility* aren't words I'd put in the same sentence.'

'Oh, I don't know,' said Celia, unexpectedly finding herself bristling a bit on his behalf. 'I think you'd be surprised.'

Dan looked at her, his eyebrows shooting up. 'Would I?'

'I think he actually has quite a strong sense of re-sponsibility,' she said, a bit taken aback by the strength of her desire to set the record straight. 'I mean, look at the way he made sure all his staff were taken care of when he sold his business,' she said, remembering something she'd read in the press weeks ago. 'Look at the plans he has now. Business mentoring? And that apprenticeship scheme thing for kids who've slipped through the system? He said it was his way of giving something back, and if that isn't a sign of recognising one's responsibilities I don't know what is.'

And then look at the way he'd taken care of her when she hadn't been well. The way he was stepping up to the plate now. All in all, she thought he was a remarkably responsible individual, even if Dan and Zoe couldn't see it.

Realising her heart was beating rather too fast and that she was feeling a bit fired up, she took a couple of deep calming breaths and gradually became aware that Dan and Zoe were staring at her.

'What?' she said, swinging her gaze between them as her pulse slowed and her indignation faded.

'Interesting,' said Zoe, regarding her thoughtfully.

'It is interesting,' she said firmly. 'Very. And I'm sure he'll make a success of it all.'

'I don't mean his plans,' said Zoe. 'Although those do sound good. I was referring to your defence of him.'

'I'm not defending him,' said Celia. 'I'm simply being honest.'

Zoe picked up a menu and smiled knowingly. 'If that's what you want to call it,' she said in an annoy-ingly conciliatory fashion. 'Now, who's having pud-ding?'

* * *

Two hours later, lying in the bath, enveloped in orange-blossom-scented bubbles and surrounded by a dozen flickering bergamot-scented candles, Celia dropped her head back and closed her eyes and pondered that disconcertingly knowing smile of her sister-in-law's.

What Zoe thought she knew Celia had no idea. She *was* being honest when she'd said all that stuff about Marcus being more responsible than everyone gave him credit for. And yes, maybe a teensy bit defensive, but so what? It didn't mean anything. She was just setting the record straight, and anyway, she was sure that if he ever learned that she'd leapt to his defence like that he'd split his sides laughing at her.

Zoe was too smug by half, thinking that she had the measure of their relationship. She didn't have a clue, apart, possibly, from identifying the chemistry, which now didn't matter all that much when there were so many other far more important life-changing decisions to be made.

Marcus might have alluded to the fact that they were still attracted to each other when they'd been sitting on the bench in that park, and, heaven only knew, he was in her thoughts a lot, sometimes all laid-back and smiling that lethal, lazy smile, sometimes all dark and intense, either way refusing to budge and making her pulse throb and her body tingle, but that didn't mean they were going to act on it, did it?

She, for one, had absolutely no intention of doing so. She had her child to think of and a relationship to build with its father, and sex complicating that and messing with her head was the last thing she needed.

How hard could it be to keep the attraction in hand

anyway? It wasn't as if she were completely at the mercy of her hormones or anything. She was far too mature and sensible for that. It was simply a question of willpower, and that she had in abundance. So she'd easily be able to handle her attraction to him. She probably wouldn't even see that much of him over the next few months, apart from the occasions she intended they got together to work on that relationship. They were both busy, after all, and he had 'interests'…

Actually, she thought, not particularly wanting to contemplate Marcus and his 'interests', bearing that in mind, maybe she'd better get in touch with him to suggest fixing up the first 'getting to know you' session, because who knew how long it might be before they found a date they were both free?

Figuring out how he was going to adapt his lifestyle to incorporate looking after a child wasn't giving Marcus nearly as much trouble as figuring out what he was going to do about Celia.

The former wasn't a problem at all. Ever since the afternoon of Dan and Zoe's wedding, despite the concerted effort he'd made to move on, the thought of sex with anyone other than her was so off-putting he hadn't even bothered trying.

At first he'd found his lack of interest in anyone else infuriating, not to mention frustrating. Then he'd made himself relax because what could he do about it? He could hardly force himself to take things further, could he? Anyway, it was bound to be nothing more than a hiccup.

But if it was, then he was still hiccuping. And weirdly, not minding all that much. To his surprise he wasn't missing the thrill of the chase, the dating or even the sex. He'd been getting more than enough kicks from the work he'd been throwing himself into. The apprentice scheme he was setting up was an idea he'd been toying with for a year or two now, and it was great to be able to finally get it started. And while un-profitable—at least in financial terms—it meant so much that it felt good to be getting stuck in. Very good.

With a puritanism the Victorians would have been proud of he was working hard and sleeping alone, and he'd never felt more virtuous.

His thoughts about Celia, however, weren't virtu-ous at all. They were wicked and filthy and sometimes came to him at the most inappropriate of times. Such as during the scan she'd had a couple of days ago. She'd hopped onto the bed, and, with a wriggle that was sexier than it ought to be, had lifted her top. It had been the least erotic of occasions, yet at the expanse of taut, tanned stomach she'd revealed he'd found himself tuning out the voice of the obstetrician and wondering whether anyone would mind if he leaned over and ran his hands and mouth across her skin.

She was in his head all the time. And not just with the smiles she occasionally shot him. He found her fascinating. The contradictions that characterised her were intriguing. She was an intoxicating combination of strength and vulnerability, pride and self-depreca-tion, confidence and bewilderment.

Not that anyone got to see the softer side of her. He was willing to bet everything he had that he was the only person who knew about her craving for her fa-ther's approval, the only person ever to see her in the state she'd been in the night they'd dashed to A and E. The only person to hold her as she cried her heart out.

But even though he was now sufficiently not in denial to know that he still wanted her—and quite desperately—that didn't mean he was going to do anything about it. He couldn't, could he? His relationships, however long they lasted, always ended, and he'd never seen the point in keeping in touch.

If he and Celia had sex again, whether once, twice or a hundred times, when that side to their relationship burned out—as it inevitably would when he felt he needed to move on—it would make things unbearably awkward between them. Decisions they'd have to make would be clouded by things that were totally unrelated.

So they'd both be far better off ignoring the chemistry and concentrating on what was important here, namely the child.

Thank God she'd turned down his offer of his house next door. Heaven only knew what he'd been thinking when he'd suggested that. He might have been just throwing things out there but if she'd actually taken him up on the offer she'd have been living a mere stone's throw away instead of five miles, and his resolve to disregard the attraction that arced between them would have sorely been put to the test. Simply being in her vicinity did that as it was. A half-hour hospital appointment had been bad enough. Twenty-four-seven might just about do him in.

At least there was no reason to see her for a while, he thought, abandoning the Sunday papers for a moment, and reaching for his phone, which had just begun to ring. He'd use the time to shore up his defences and build up an immunity to her, so that when he next came across her he'd be rock solid, utterly immutable and ruthlessly focused.

Unlike now.

Feeling as dizzy and winded as if someone had thumped him in the jaw and then followed up with a punch to the gut, Marcus scowled and glared at the name on the screen.

For a split second he was tempted to ignore the call, let it go to voicemail and get back to her once those barriers were in place and he was immune. But that smacked of weakness and he had *some* pride, so he braced himself and hit the button. How disturbing could a phone call be anyway?

'Celia,' he said, pleased and relieved to note that he sounded cool and casual and not at all bothered by the fact that she'd rung.

'Hi,' she said, and, even though he could just about ignore the wave of heat that swept through him at the sound of her voice, there wasn't anything he could do about the goosebumps breaking out all over his skin.

He set his jaw, shifted his chair so he was sitting in a shaft of lovely warm sunlight and told himself that the sooner he made a start on building those defences, the better. 'How are you?'

'Fine, fine. You?'

Exhibiting worrying displays of a complete loss of control, but nothing he couldn't handle. 'Couldn't be better.'

'I'm so glad.'

She sounded glad. She sounded all warm and soft and seductive and he wondered what she was doing at half past ten o'clock on a Sunday morning. Where she was. What she was wearing… 'So what can I do to—I mean, for, you?' he said, his voice just as warm and soft and seductive, which *so* wasn't the plan.

'I'm ringing to see if you'd like to come over for supper some time.'

Mentally giving himself a slap and pulling himself together, he echoed, 'Supper?'

'That's right.'

'Why?'

'Well, I've been thinking,' she said, and he thought that it was a good thing that at least one of them was. 'You're the father of my child and it occurred to me that if we're going to do this together, it would make sense to discuss values. Opinions we might have about parenthood. And other stuff.'

What other stuff? Sex other stuff? His head swam for a second and his pulse spiked and then he calmed down because, no, not sex other stuff, clearly. He was the only one having trouble with that at the moment. 'I see.'

'I also thought that it would be a good idea to get to know each other a bit better and learn to communicate without the sarcasm. Food seemed like a good idea. So what do you think?'

Marcus thought that was a fine idea. Maybe in a few months' time, say around January, when he'd have had the chance to build up those defences.

'Makes sense,' he said, carefully vague.

'Great,' she said brightly. 'So what about tonight?'

Marcus nearly dropped the phone. 'Tonight?'

'If you're available.'

He was. He was available a lot of nights these days. Not that that was the point. 'What's the hurry?' he said, trying to maintain the cool and calm tone he'd been foolishly quick to congratulate himself on only a couple of minutes ago. 'We have months.'

'I know. But it's going to fly by and I'm busy every night for the next week or so. So, are you free?'

Breaking out in a sweat, he shifted his chair out of the sunlight. 'No,' he said abruptly. 'And I won't be for a while.'

There was a moment's silence and he inwardly cursed because he could have turned her down a little more tactfully.

'Oh,' she said flatly. 'Right. Well. When you do have a moment free in your busy schedule let me know.'

Despite the flatness of her tone, he could hear the disappointment in her words, and as guilt swept through him his conscience suddenly started prodding at him. All she was suggesting was supper. Surely he could manage that. He always had before. Where was this idea that Celia somehow posed a threat to him coming from anyway? It was ridiculous. *He* was ridiculous.

'Wait,' he said, hearing a rustling sound and guessing she was about to hang up.

The rustling stopped. 'What?'

He sighed and shoved a hand through his hair. 'Look, let me see what I can do.'

'Really?'

He closed his eyes, pinched the bridge of his nose and reminded himself that it was only supper. 'Really,' he said. 'What I had planned shouldn't be too difficult to get out of.' Which was true seeing as the only thing he had in his schedule was a night in front of the TV with his laptop.

'Won't she mind?'

At the hint of waspishness in her voice, Marcus found himself opening his eyes and smiling faintly. 'She won't mind at all.'

'One of these days you're going to come up against someone who does.'

As the memory of his ex flashed into his head he shuddered, his smile vanishing. 'Not in my plans.' He sat back and idly flicked through one of the colour supplements. 'And anyway, what was that you were saying about learning to communicate without the sarcasm?'

There was another pause. 'Fair enough,' she muttered eventually. 'Sorry. Old habit.'

'If it's too tricky to resist, I'm more than happy to join in. I might even find myself having to make some kind of comment about the fact that you're willing to sacrifice a night's work for supper with me.'

She huffed, all contrition gone. 'You've made your point, Marcus.'

'Have I?'

'For the moment.'

'Until the next time you forget.'

'Until then,' she conceded after a moment.

'So, shall we say seven?' he said, thinking that that gave him enough time to throw up at least a few barriers.

'Sounds perfect,' she said.

'Although maybe it would be better if you came over here.'

'Why?'

'You don't cook and I've seen the state of your fridge.'

She hummed. 'Another point well made.'

'See you later, Celia.'

'I'm looking forward to it.'

As they hung up and the prospect of having Celia in his house, a mere floor away from his bed, sank in Marcus thought that she might be looking forward to tonight, but he wasn't. At all.

CHAPTER ELEVEN

'SOMETHING SMELLS GOOD,' said Celia, inhaling deeply as she stepped into Marcus' house just past seven and thinking that she wasn't just talking about the delicious aroma wafting from the kitchen.

Not that how heavenly he smelled or how gorgeous he looked was of any interest, of course. No. Tonight was purely about finding out what made him tick. Revealing a bit about how she ticked. Laying the foundations for a solid, long-term, *platonic* relationship. If she focused on that, she should be all right and wouldn't make any more mistakes about which things smelled or looked good.

'Roast beef,' he said, standing back as she brushed past him, his breath hissing softly through his teeth.

'With everything else?' she asked, wondering about that hiss and what it meant. If it meant what she thought it meant then he was finding the attraction that still sizzled between them as disruptive as she was. And if that *was* the case, then she could only hope that he'd come to the same conclusion as she had and had decided to ignore it, because if he had other ideas, such as wanting to explore it, then who knew what might happen? Her willpower was strong, but would it be strong enough to resist him if he suddenly grabbed her right now and kissed her?

'Naturally.'

She glanced at his mouth and her own watered. At the sound of supper, obviously, not at the thought of kissing him. 'Great,' she said with a bit of a strained smile.

'Go through to the kitchen. You know the way.'

Technically she did, so she walked down the hall and made for the kitchen. Metaphorically, however, she was floundering, not really knowing quite in which direction to head.

What on earth was wrong with her? She never normally had this much trouble with her self-control. She'd read about the brain sometimes going AWOL during pregnancy but it hadn't occurred that it would ever happen to her. The possibility that it had was unsettling. And it meant she had to be extra specially careful when she was around him.

He indicated that she should sit down, so she did. She ran her gaze over the table, laid for two—no candles, thank goodness—and then she turned it to the chef, who was busying himself with supper.

After switching the oven off, Marcus opened it, took the meat out and stuck a cloche over it, and then deftly dealt with a saucepan that was bubbling over.

His back view really was magnificent, she thought idly, her mouth watering at the aroma as she put her handbag on the chair next to hers and slowly let her gaze drift over him. In a purely objective fashion, of course, because objective appreciation of her host was allowed. It was good manners, in fact. Practically an obligation.

Whatever it was, she ogled the broad shoulders that tapered down to a slim waist that she envied now that her own was thickening, great bottom and long muscled legs, and let out a soft sigh of admiration.

Why was getting it on with him a bad idea again...?

'Drink?' he asked, turning around and making her jump. She went bright red, as if she'd been caught doing—and thinking—something she shouldn't have been. Which she had.

Wishing she could down a double gin and tonic for the sake of her nerves, Celia asked him for a tonic and to hold the gin, and once she'd quenched her suddenly rampant thirst decided it might be wise to do a little less of the ogling and a little more of the small talk.

'When did you become such a good cook?' she asked, putting her glass down and watching him lift a lid and peer into a cloud of steam.

'When I realised it was either that or starve. Then I discovered I liked it. I find it relaxing.'

'The ability to feed is a much sought-after quality in a man, I'd have thought.' In any man she ever ended up with, that was for certain, if he didn't want to go hungry.

'Not sure it's my most sought-after quality,' he said, shooting her a lethal grin over his shoulder.

Celia went warm, and half-heartedly tried to convince herself that it was merely down to the heat the oven was throwing out. 'No, well, I imagine not.'

He turned, leaned against the counter and shot her a quizzical look. 'Do you really not cook at all?'

'Toast and eggs I can do. Beyond that, not a lot. I usually grab something from the canteen at work and eat at my desk.'

'Even now?'

His gaze slid down her body, stopping at her abdomen, and she blushed. The oven again, undoubtedly. 'Even now.'

'It's really not that hard.'

She thought of her spotless kitchen and the devastation she would likely bring with a set of beaters or a food processor, and shuddered. 'I'll take your word for it.

'You should try it.'

Celia muttered sceptically beneath her breath and decided to move from her non-existent skills to his very much in-existence ones. 'Do you cook for your dates?'

'Sometimes.'

'I guess you'll have to pull out all the stops for the one you blew out this evening.'

He grinned and she ignored the jealousy stabbing at her chest. 'Four courses at the very least.'

'Hmm.'

'If there really had been a date.'

Her heart skipped a beat and just like that the jealousy vanished. Which would have worried her had she had the time or the inclination to analyse it, which she didn't. She was too giddy with relief. Disproportionately giddy, actually, which was something else that probably needed analysis. 'There wasn't?'

'Nope.'

She stared at him as she computed this. 'So why let me think there was?'

His grin deepened and a wicked glint appeared in his eyes. 'I couldn't resist. You're so determined to think the worst of me.'

She frowned and slowly rotated her tumbler between fingers. 'I don't think the worst of you at all.'

His eyebrows rose. 'No?'

She shook her head. 'No.'

'Wow, when did *that* happen?'

'I think it's been happening gradually. And then, of course, I heard about the drought.'

Now it was Marcus' turn to frown. 'The what?' he said, his smile fading.

'Your six-month period of abstinence.'

'How the hell did you hear about that?'

'Dan.'

His mouth twisted. 'Of course.'

'No wonder you were so desperate when I basically ordered you to ravish me amongst the runner beans.'

His dark eyes glittered and she shivered at the desire suddenly flaring in their depths. 'That had nothing to do with the drought and everything to do with you.'

She swallowed and sought a way to stop her body responding. 'I imagine you've been making up for lost time.'

'Why would you imagine that?'

'I've seen the photos.'

'Photos of what?'

'You and countless women.'

'Where?'

'In the press.'

'Right.'

He fell silent and she bristled with indignation. 'Is that all you have to say?'

'In these photos were me and these women naked and horizontal?'

'No, of course not.'

'Well, then.'

Well, then, what? Maybe she'd got the wrong end of the stick from the photos but that didn't mean Marcus hadn't been shagging his way round London like a thirsty man looking for a drink. After all, he hadn't been naked and horizontal with her, had he? Yet they'd still managed to have a pretty great time.

'I hope you're not going to say that I'm the only person you've had sex with in the last nine months,' she said, aiming for withering incredulity but, what with the unfathomable feeling of hope bubbling through her, failing dismally.

'That's exactly what I'm saying.'

'Really?'

'I've hardly been out recently, let alone swinging from the chandeliers.'

She sat back and stared at him. 'So why *did* you tell me you were busy tonight?'

His eyes were on hers. Steady, dark and intense. 'Because you *are* the only person I've had sex with in the last nine months,' he said, 'and I'm finding wanting a repeat of it increasingly on my mind.'

'Oh,' she said faintly.

'Quite.'

'That's the last thing either of us needs.'

'I know. Doesn't mean I don't still think it.'

As did she. All the time, if she was being brutally honest. But they'd just have to live with that. They weren't animals. They were rational, sensible people who knew what was good for them, and what wasn't. Still… 'Maybe we should keep off the subject of sex tonight.' It wasn't as if they didn't have plenty of other things to talk about. It should be a doddle.

'Good idea.'

Her stomach growled and his mouth hitched up into a small smile. 'And eat.'

'Even better.'

Keeping off the subject of sex was fine. Keeping from thinking about it was an entirely different matter. Ever since Celia had walked through the door Marcus had been aware of every move she made, no matter how tiny. All his senses felt heightened and it seemed to him that his body was trying to tune itself into hers or something. Whatever was going on it was odd. Frustrating. Deeply disturbing.

It didn't help that she kept groaning in ecstasy at the food he'd cooked. Every time she did, all he could think of was his bed upstairs and her on it. That was, when he wasn't mentally sweeping aside everything on the table and feasting on her down here instead.

As his body tightened uncomfortably Marcus thought that whatever Celia hoped to achieve by tonight, they wouldn't be doing it again, because this wasn't just 'supper', this was torture.

'This is delicious,' she said with a wide, warm smile that only strengthened his resolve to keep his distance once the nightmare of this evening was over.

'Thank you. Like I said, it's not hard.'

She put her fork down and took a sip of tonic water. 'So what have you been up to since I saw you last?'

'Work.' Driving himself insane.

'Is that all?' She arched an eyebrow and grinned. 'Careful, Marcus, you might turn into me.'

'To compensate I also spent a couple of days climbing in the Peak District.' In the hope that the physical exertion might result in mental exhaustion, and he'd be able to go five minutes without thinking about her. Not that it had worked.

Her eyes widened. 'I heard Dan took it up a while ago, but I didn't know you climbed too.'

'There's a lot you don't know about me.'

'And that's what tonight's all about.'

It was, and he could do a lot worse than focusing on that rather than the way her hair shone and her eyes sparkled. Because conversation was easy enough, wasn't it? And with any luck it would make the time fly. 'What about you?'

She shrugged and gave him a self-deprecating grin. 'Work, mainly.'

He returned the grin. 'Goes without saying.'

'But I also had supper with Dan and Zoe last night.'

'How was their trip?'

'It sounded fantastic.'

'Did you tell them about the pregnancy?'

She nodded. 'I did.'

'How did Dan take it?'

'Oh, fine,' she said nonchalantly. 'Eventually.'

Marcus went still, the hand holding his fork freezing midway to his mouth. 'Eventually?'

'For a moment I think he wanted to punch your lights out, but, realising it's not really any of his business, he got over it quickly enough.'

He frowned and put down the fork. Hmm. He should have guessed that while Dan would be fine with him dating Celia, he might not be so fine about the fact that his best mate had knocked up his sister.

But as that was a conversation he wasn't particularly looking forward to and didn't need to worry about tonight he put it from his mind. 'Do your parents know yet?'

'I rang them today.'

'And what did they say?' he asked, and braced himself for the news that her father, like son, had taken it badly and was bearing down on him even as they sat there.

'My mother was beside herself with excitement, and offered her full support and help.'

'And your father?'

Celia's smile turned wry. 'Ah, yes, well, after declaring himself delighted you'd taken him up on his suggestion, he said something about one out of three being a start. Not exactly being a new man, though, he wasn't quite so forthcoming with an offer of support and help. But he seemed pleased enough.'

'One out of three?'

'The baby. Marriage and a proper home being the other two.'

'Do they mind about you not being married?' he asked, thinking it best to avoid the subject of homes if he didn't want to have to discuss and retract the offer he'd made her in a moment of giddy recklessness.

'Surprisingly not,' she said, and then paused as if a thought had crossed her mind. 'Although I imagine that neither of them have much faith in the institution after what they went through so maybe it's not all that surprising.'

'They've never remarried, have they?'

Celia shook her head. 'No. I think my mother's too scarred by the experience and my father's having too much fun leching after twenty-five-year-olds.'

'Did the divorce scar you?'

She started as if startled by the question. 'Me? Oh. Well. Not really. I mean, I was fourteen when they finally split and it was pretty horrendous but things had been awful for years. Dad had been having affairs practically since the ink was dry on the marriage certificate although I don't think Mum found out until a few years later. But I've nothing against marriage as a concept, and I'd quite like to do it one day. Although with things the way they are,' she said, indicating her abdomen with a wave of her hand, 'I can't see myself doing anything about that for a while.'

'No,' he muttered, a stab of guilt prodding him in the stomach as he collected up the plates and cleared the table.

'So what's put you off marriage?'

Marcus picked up a dish in the middle of which sat a chocolate tart, then sat down and used the business of cutting it into slices and sliding one onto the side plate she was holding up to think about just how open he wanted to be. The answer to which was, not a lot. 'What makes you think I'm against marriage?' he hedged.

She put her plate down and grinned. 'The look of horror that you had when I brought it up.'

'Right.'

'So?'

He shrugged and decided there wasn't any harm in telling her. It wasn't as if he had a problem with it or anything. It was just the way things were. 'I'm not against marriage in general,' he said, serving himself a slice. 'Just for me.'

'Why?'

'I've seen the damage that love can do. I am the damage. Or at least, I was.'

She nodded thoughtfully, presumably remembering the shocking stories about him that he knew Dan had regaled her with. 'So you steer clear of love too?' she said, taking a mouthful of tart and groaning softly in appreciation.

'Yes,' he muttered, giving his head a quick shake to dispel the faint feeling of dizziness. 'Although it's never been an issue because I've never been in love. But if I ever am I'll resist it with every bone in my body because in my experience love is messy and tragic and who needs that kind of hassle?'

'And that's where we differ,' she said, smiling wistfully and scooping up another bit of tart. 'Because I've never been in love either but from what I've seen it's lovely and so I'd like to experience it some day.'

Suddenly losing his appetite for pudding, Marcus sat back and ignored whatever it was that shot through him at the thought of her with someone else, because that she would be eventually was inevitable. 'I'm sorry,' he said gruffly.

'For what?'

'Putting you in this position.'

'Oh, it's fine,' she said airily. 'Now I'm beginning to come to terms with the reality of a baby I've mentally rearranged a few things.'

'Love and marriage being amongst them.'

'I'm not sure there's a lot you can do about love, but marriage was only a very vague goal anyway.' She grinned. 'So you don't need to worry—I won't be hassling you on that front. Unlike some, I imagine.'

Marcus frowned. 'What are you talking about?'

'I heard you have a stalker ex.'

Oh. 'Dan again?'

'Yup. And I have to say I'm completely agog. So come on, spill.'

'You want details?'

She arched an eyebrow. 'Of course I do. Think of it as part of the "getting to know you" thing.'

'OK,' he said, figuring he had no real reason not to tell her. 'I met her at a party and we went out for two months.'

'A whole two months?' she said dryly. 'A record, surely.'

Marcus shot her a look.

'Sorry,' she added, not sounding sorry at all.

'She wanted more. I didn't. We stopped seeing each other.'

'You dumped her?'

He shifted on his chair but he couldn't get comfortable. The memory of Noelle the Nutcase giving him hives probably. 'Yes.'

'And then?'

'She wouldn't accept it.'

'So what did she do?'

'Kept calling, texting, emailing. She turned up here once or twice, and at the office a bit more.'

Celia grimaced. 'How mortifying.'

'It wasn't the most pleasant of experiences,' he said, which had to be the understatement of the century. 'When she broke in here, arranged herself on the bed and waited for me to get home, I had to take it to the police.'

'And then what happened?'

'She was issued with an order to stay away both physically and electronically.'

'Has she stuck to it?'

'Thankfully.'

She hmmed. 'I can see why you'd be wary of getting involved after something like that.'

'Quite.'

She regarded him thoughtfully for a while and then leaned forwards. 'So tell me, Marcus, given your abhorrence of commitment, why do you want this baby so much?'

Where that had suddenly sprung from he didn't know, but the question didn't come as a huge surprise. 'It's hard to explain.'

She winced. 'I know the feeling.'

'Not just the ultrasound and those pictures for you, then?'

She shook her head. 'No. Although that afternoon was the key that unlocked everything, if that makes sense.'

'More than you probably realise.'

She put down her spoon and fork together on her spotlessly clean plate and bit her lip. 'For me I think it was a combination of things, really. My friends marrying and starting families. And then that thing my dad said about my age. It got into my head sort of insidiously and then stayed there, niggling away. I mean, I know I still have time, but after we made the decision to go for the abortion, I kept thinking what if this is my only chance? What if I got rid of this baby and I never got pregnant again? Would I regret it? And if I did, would I be able to live with the regret?' She shrugged and smiled, although there wasn't any humour in it. 'Silly, huh?'

'Not at all.'

'So what was it for you? Don't tell me you were envious of your friends settling down and having kids.'

'No.'

'And age wouldn't be an issue, so what was it?'

'Some stuff going back a while.'

'What kind of stuff?'

While he'd been absolutely fine with talking about love and marriage, this was veering into territory that would make him sound like a sentimental sap. 'Just stuff,' he muttered, hoping she'd leave it but knowing she wouldn't.

Celia tilted her head and looked at him. 'Come on, Marcus, I told you my reasons. You can tell me yours. Come to think of it,' she added contemplatively, 'you already know a lot more about me than I do about you, and didn't you once say you were all for equality?'

He had, and, after what she'd just told him, maybe he owed her the truth in return. Besides, if he carried on protesting she'd read more into his reluctance than there was to be read.

'Fair enough,' he said, sighing and running a hand along his jaw as he wondered where to start. 'Becoming a father isn't something I'd ever have chosen to do,' he said finally. 'But presented with the possibility, it opened a box for me too. Mainly to do with my father and our relationship.'

'Which was good, right?'

'Very good. I kept thinking about my childhood—which I remember as being improbably idyllic—and was filled with the overwhelming need to recreate it.

I guess I'd like to have that father-child bond again, albeit from a different angle.'

'What if it's a girl?'

'Doesn't matter.'

'And the sacrifices you'll have to make?'

'Those don't seem to matter either. My lifestyle's already changed for one reason or another and I find I don't mind at all. You know, maybe I've been waiting for something like this to happen.'

Her eyebrows shot up. 'An accidental pregnancy?'

'Not exactly, but something that makes me evaluate my life.' Which was something he'd been doing quite a bit of actually. Recently the thing Dan had said about Marcus turning into Jim Forrester had been gnawing away at him. Did he really want to be fifty and chasing every woman he could? No, he didn't, so maybe once things had settled down he'd look at embarking on a proper relationship. One that might cure him of his inconvenient and impossible attraction to Celia.

'Do you miss him?'

Marcus shrugged and twirled the stem of his wine glass, watching the dark red wine swirl around. 'It's not too bad any more.'

'But you did for a while?'

'Like a missing limb.'

'And that's why you went off the rails.'

He nodded. 'Mainly.'

'And what about your mother? Do you miss her?'

Something inside him chilled a little and he abandoned his glass to pick up the knife and point it at the tart. 'More pudding?'

Celia shook her head. 'No, thanks. It was delicious, though.'

'Coffee?'

'No, thanks,' she said again, only this time with a tiny frown.

'Tea?'

'Nothing, thank you. Except an answer. That would be nice.'

It wouldn't be nice at all, he thought darkly, clearing the table and refusing her offer of help. Which, with hindsight, was probably a mistake because instead of being busy with dishes, she had time to wonder.

'Why are you avoiding the question, Marcus?' she asked, and he could feel her eyes on him.

'Because it's a tricky one to answer,' he muttered.

'Why?'

With a deep sigh, Marcus abandoned the crockery and turned to lean against the counter. 'Following my father's death neither of us were very good at dealing with our grief,' he said, folding his arms across his chest as if that might somehow suppress the memories. 'I went wild. She withdrew into herself. Ultimately she'd loved him so much she couldn't live without him. Literally.'

She nodded, her eyes filling with sympathy, compassion and pity, and he couldn't work out whether it pissed him off or made him grateful. 'I heard. I'm sorry.'

He shrugged. 'Nothing to be sorry about. She just couldn't go on without him, that was all.'

'She must have been in a very bad way.'

'She was. She was deeply depressed, even though I don't think she realised it. I certainly didn't.'

'No, well, how could you have?'

The guilt struck him square in the chest and his jaw

tightened. 'If I'd been less hell-bent on self-destruction I might have.'

'She'd have found a way whatever you'd done.'

'If I'd at least tried she might have thought I was worth sticking around for.'

For a moment there was absolute silence and Marcus wished he could take back the words because he'd said too much. Way too much.

'I'm sure that wasn't it,' she said softly.

'It was,' he said bluntly. 'She left a note. Basically saying that she loved me and that she realised she'd be leaving me behind but that it wasn't enough to stop her.'

Celia looked stricken and a dozen different emotions flickered across her face. 'Oh, God,' she murmured.

He arched an eyebrow. 'You did ask.'

'I know I did.'

'Regretting it?'

'Not for a second.'

He gave her a dry smile. 'Hardly the best of gene pools, is it?'

'Oh, I don't know,' she said, running her gaze over him and, whether she knew it or not, making him forget that horrible couple of years and return his focus to her.

He watched her eyes darken, heard her breath catch, and desire hit him like a blow to the chest. His hands itched. His mouth went dry and he was a second away from hauling her up from the chair and into his arms when she blinked, snapping the connection and making him recoil.

'So how did you get from hurtling off the rails to where you are now?' she said a little hoarsely, sounding as shaken as he was.

Marcus gathered his wits and thanked God Celia

had had the sense to pull them back from the edge. 'Just after my mother died and I was spinning really out of control, a friend of my father's basically took me in hand. He put me to work in one of his companies, a brokerage. It turned out I had an affinity for stock picking and I moved up until I set up my own business. The rest you know.'

'Didn't any of your own friends try to help?'

'Dan did a bit. But we were eighteen, nineteen. I was determined to raise as much hell as I could and I was very good at it. There was nothing he could have done.'

'Is that why you're setting up this scheme to help people like you once were?'

'Yes.'

'Paying it forward.'

'In a small way.'

'And what about the business mentoring and the angel investing?'

'I had no idea you were listening so closely.'

'I was listening.'

'Right,' he said, wondering why the thought of her listening would make his heart beat this hard and this fast. 'Well, that's because I enjoy taking risks and making money.'

Celia gave him a smile that was hot and wicked and threatened to blow his noble intentions to keep his hands off her to smithereens. 'I'm glad to hear you're not all good.'

There was a crackling silence, and as they looked at each other, with heat and tension filling the space between them, all Marcus could think about was how much he wanted her. How much he always had. To hell with what was right or wrong. Screw the consequences. He wanted her, and she wanted him, and he, for one, was going to go mad if they didn't do something about it.

'Are you?' he said softly, taking a step towards her and seeing her eyes widen with alarm.

She stood up, nearly knocking her chair over in her haste, and grabbed her bag. 'Of course,' she said way too brightly, edging back and keeping the distance. 'Just think of your reputation.'

He was having trouble thinking about anything but her and what he wanted them to do together. 'I know it comes fifteen years too late,' he said, keeping his eyes on hers, 'but I'm sorry about making up the bet.'

'Fine,' she said quickly. 'And I'm sorry about what I said about using you.'

'Were you? Using me, I mean?'

'No.'

'So why did you say you were?'

'I was confused. Overwhelmed.'

'By what?'

'By you and the effect you have on me,' she said breathlessly.

His pulse spiked and a bolt of desire thumped him again. 'And what effect is that?'

'You know perfectly well.'

'It's entirely mutual, you know.'

She swallowed hard and took a breath, as if struggling for control. 'It's also utterly irrelevant.'

'Remind me why,' he murmured because for the life of him he couldn't remember.

'Sex would only make a complicated situation even more complicated.'

'Would it?'

'And the awkwardness when it fizzles out would be hideous.'

There was that, he thought with the one brain cell that was still functioning, but this tension, frustration, was pretty hideous too. 'Nevertheless, I have a suggestion.'

A tiny flicker of alarm leapt in her eyes. 'I don't want to hear it.'

'You don't know what it is yet.'

'It's something along the lines of getting it out of our systems so we can move on, isn't it?'

He gave her the glimmer of a smile. 'The idea has merit, don't you think?'

'It's insane.'

'We could try it and see. It worked before, didn't it?'

'I should go,' she said, shaking her head as if to clear it.

'Should you?'

She nodded hard. 'Definitely.'

'This isn't going to go away, Celia, even if you do.'

'No, but if we're sensible, it'll be manageable.'

Sensible? Manageable? 'How?'

'We ignore it.'

'Not sure that's an option.'

'No…' she agreed a little desperately. 'OK, then, how about from now on we stick to meeting up in public?'

CHAPTER TWELVE

OVER THE COURSE of the next few weeks that was what they did.

They met in restaurants, bars and various parks. Despite having known each other for nearly twenty years, so much of that time had been clouded with animosity that they'd never really talked.

Now, though, they did nothing but.

They discovered that, while they disagreed about many things, about the big things, the important things, they were more or less on the same wavelength. They also found they had plenty in common. An interest in obscure French cinema. A deep dislike of cats. A love of chilli and being terrible patients, amongst many other things.

And, of course, the still-scorching chemistry.

That hadn't gone away, thought Celia, blotting her lipstick and trying not to think about the evening she and Marcus had had fish and chips and he'd reached out to rub away a blob of ketchup at the corner of her mouth.

If anything it was getting worse, because mature and sensible and not at the mercy of her hormones? Who the hell had she been kidding? Her hormones were going so mental that she couldn't believe that at one point she'd seriously thought that ignoring what was going on between her and Marcus was an option.

It had taken all her strength to walk away that night she'd gone for supper at his house. She'd been so very tempted to simply fall into his arms and yield to the need that had been clawing away at her, especially when he'd so clearly been up for it. But some sixth sense had warned her against it, and thank *God* she'd got out of there before she'd given in to temptation.

Their conversation that night had been unsettling. Not the subject matter—although that had revealed more about him than she ever could have imagined—but the way she'd responded to it.

When he'd asked what her family thought about the pregnancy it had occurred to her that he didn't have anyone to tell, and her heart had wrenched. When he'd told her he had no intention of falling in love or ever marrying because of his experience, it had wrenched a little more. And when he'd been talking about his mother's suicide and the note she'd left, well, that had just about torn her apart because it clearly affected him, making him think that somehow he wasn't good enough when he was. He so was.

It had been disconcerting, because Marcus wasn't supposed to tug at her heartstrings. He wasn't supposed to have as much depth as he did, although quite why he wasn't when he'd been through such a tough time she didn't have a clue.

She wasn't supposed to like him so much either, but there was another anomaly, because she did. A lot. He made her laugh. Entertained her. Challenged her and made her think and question and argue. So much so that the days they were meeting up she woke up on a high and then spent the rest of the day fizzing with excitement and counting down the hours until she could leave to go and see him. Sometimes she even left work early, which, given that she was meant to be doing everything she could to win the partnership, was madness.

She ought to be wary of seeing him, not excited. Because every time they met up the occasions were underscored with such a strong current of tension that she'd started to think that perhaps they *should* have gone to bed that night. Perhaps Marcus had been right and it *would* have got things out of their system. Maybe the fact that they hadn't was what was making the idea of it so compelling.

Frankly, it was hard to see how sex would have made things any worse because the tension between them was sky-high. Every date that wasn't a date was filled with fleeting touches. Laden looks. Conversation that tailed off. Sizzling, thundering silences and a hundred electrically charged moments before they said an awkward goodbye and each headed home separately.

Not that it ended there, for her at least. Marcus was in her head pretty much constantly. Her dreams were full of him, and during the day she frequently found herself storing tiny things away to tell him later.

She didn't know how he was dealing with it all, but for all her fine words about sense and manageability her resistance was rapidly weakening. She couldn't remember why sex with him had seemed like such a bad idea. She'd been thinking it might be a very good idea indeed for a while now. Now she was thinking that tonight, finally, she'd like to do something about it.

It might be reckless and it might be rash, but she'd had enough of the excoriating frustration and the agonising tension. She'd had enough of the sleepless nights and the feverish dreams that assailed her when she did eventually manage to drop off. It wasn't doing her nervous system any good at all and, heaven knew, she didn't want her palpitations to reappear.

So today she had a plan. This afternoon she'd find out whether she'd got the partnership, then later she and Marcus were going out for dinner at a three-Michelin-starred restaurant. And whether they were celebrating or commiserating, one thing was for certain: they were going to end the night together, in bed and having fabulous, hot, sweaty sex.

Tonight Marcus was going to end this 'getting to know you' crap.

He stood at the basin in his bathroom, leaned forwards and wiped away enough condensation from the mirror to be able to see his reflection, which was actually pretty grim. No surprise there, he thought darkly as he picked up a can and squirted a ball of foam into his hand. He'd been feeling grim for days. Tense and grumpy and frustrated as hell.

With hindsight, agreeing to her plan to get to know each other had been nuts. Going along with it had been even more insane. Where the hell had the intention to make that night she'd come for supper a one-off gone? When she'd suggested they stick to meeting up in public and he'd said fine without a moment's consideration, what on earth had he been thinking?

Shaking his head in disbelief and wondering when

exactly he'd lost his mind, Marcus began lathering up his face.

As if simply meeting up in public was the way to handle the scorching attraction that sizzled between them. Hah. They might not be able to act on their feelings in public but that didn't make them go away, did it? No. It was simply making them worse. For him, at least.

He had no idea how Celia was dealing with it but he was handling it badly, because over the past three weeks or so that they'd been seeing each other he'd been finding it increasingly hard to resist her.

At first it had been fine. Well, not exactly fine, but he'd told himself that he could keep his impulses under control, and he'd more or less succeeded knowing it was a bad idea and, more importantly, why. Lately, though, they met up and it was all he could do not to grab her arm, hail a taxi and take her home. He was in a permanent state of confusion and arousal, and it was driving him crazy.

Picking up his razor, Marcus tilted his head and cut a swathe through the white cream and winced as he nicked his jaw. Dammit, he *had* to put a stop to these meetings. They'd been an indulgence he could ill afford and it was time to end them.

Anyway, the whole idea behind them in the first place had been to get to know each other and by now they knew plenty. Too much, in fact. Celia had told him things he didn't want or need to know. Things that had him wondering how on earth he could ever have thought her an uptight, judgemental pain in the arse. Things that had him thinking that, on the contrary, what with her sharp wit and her spot-on insight, her warmth and her self-deprecation, she might be rather wonderful.

In return he'd found himself telling her things he'd never told anyone. Big things. Small things. Either way, a lot of things. He'd given her so many little pieces of himself over the past three weeks, in fact, that she nearly had the whole.

As much as he might have wanted to prevent it she'd got under his skin. And he could tell himself all he liked that it was merely down to the fact that he hadn't had the chance to build up those all-important defences, but that didn't eradicate the feeling that even if his defences had been the height of Everest she'd simply have bulldozed them down.

He didn't know what it meant. Wasn't sure he wanted to know.

What he wanted, he thought, finishing up and wiping his face clean, what he *needed,* was space. A bit of distance and time to get some perspective and figure out what was going on here. And then, if necessary, put a stop to it.

So after tonight that would be that. He'd tell her he needed a break, and tomorrow he'd make plans to go away.

If he still lived by the principles he'd had at eighteen—and right now he wished he did—he'd have cancelled this evening. But he knew how important this partnership deal was for her and how hard she'd worked for it. And he knew that despite her apparent confidence that it was in the bag, that she'd worked so hard it had to be hers, she was nervous about the outcome.

So they'd go for dinner as planned and he'd order a bottle of champagne just in case she wanted half a glass whatever the result, he'd be as charming as she was expecting him to be, and after that, as he'd done so many times before, he'd bid her goodnight and put her in a taxi.

And then tomorrow, in a bid to get that distance, he'd be off.

Celia stood on the pavement outside the restaurant from which she and Marcus had just emerged, her body buzzing and her pulse racing. Not with delight about getting the partnership, which, if she was being honest, didn't come anywhere near the thrill of being out and celebrating it with him, but with the thought of what, hopefully, was coming next. Which was, with any luck, her.

Dinner had been sublime. The heavenly array of food, the seductive lighting and incredibly romantic atmosphere and above all, Marcus, who'd gone out of his way to make tonight special.

He'd ordered her a bottle of champagne and then asked for it not to be opened so she could keep it and drink it when she was back on the hard stuff. He'd told her to have whatever she wanted or everything, if that took her fancy. He'd asked her all about her meeting this afternoon, and had seemed more enthusiastic about the fact that she'd got the partnership than she was.

And now… Well, now, come hell or high water, she was going to take him home with her.

He wanted her; she knew he did. Even if they hadn't spent the past three weeks communicating it with everything other than words, every now and then this evening she'd looked up to find him watching her, his eyes blazing with hunger and desire before the shutters snapped down and he made some comment designed to make her laugh and forget about what she'd seen.

But she couldn't forget. Nor did she want to because she'd hungered for him for so long and she couldn't stand the frustration any longer. She didn't think he could either.

'Thank you for a lovely evening, Marcus,' she said, her voice husky with the desire that she couldn't be bothered to hide any more.

He glanced at her, his jaw tight and a faint scowl on his face as he shrugged on his jacket. 'No problem.'

'And thank you for supper.'

'Least I could do,' he said, adjusting the collar and then tugging at the cuffs of his shirt beneath his jacket.

And, OK, so his mood seemed to be worsening with every second they stood on the pavement, which wasn't particularly encouraging, but what the hell? He could always say no. She'd been thinking about this for what felt like for ever and she had to give it her best shot because she'd never forgive herself if she didn't.

'Marcus,' she said, her heart thundering and her mouth dry as she inched towards him.

'What?' he said, thrusting his hands in the pockets of his trousers and looking down at her unsmilingly in the darkness.

She stepped closer and fought the temptation to sway slightly as her body responded to the magnetism he exuded, and then took a deep breath. 'Will you come home with me?'

Marcus wanted nothing more than to go home with her. And nothing less.

Tonight had been agony. Celia had sparkled from

the moment she'd sat down at the table where he'd been waiting for her, and he'd known practically right then and there that he was doomed. That it was going to take every drop of his control to put her in a taxi alone at the end of the night.

But he'd got through it. And had thought he'd succeeded.

But dammit, he should have known that Celia would suggest something like this. He'd seen the desire in her eyes all evening, not banked as his was, but alive and burning and so very tempting.

He should have realised that excitement and the high of success would spill over into recklessness. He should have been prepared. Even better he should have cancelled in the first place, he thought grimly, mentally cursing every principle he possessed.

But as he hadn't, right now he just had to be stronger, more resolute and more ruthless than he'd ever been before. For both their sakes.

'Stop it, Celia,' he said, his voice as rough as sandpaper with the effort of holding onto his control and not grabbing the next taxi that passed, bundling her in and clambering in after her.

'Why?'

'You know why.'

She tilted her head and her hair rippled, gleaming in the light of the street lamp, and he fought back the urge to reach out and wrap a chunk of it round his fingers. 'I thought I did,' she said softly, 'but now I'm not so sure.'

Then he'd make her sure. 'It would screw everything up.'

'Isn't everything pretty much screwed up anyway?'

His jaw tightened. 'And you want to make it worse?'

'I want to make it better.'

No. *He* was going to make it better. 'I'm going away.'

She stared at him, wide-eyed and momentarily speechless. 'Where to?'

'I don't know. Anywhere.'

Her eyes filled with understanding. 'I see. When?'

He'd have gone now if he had a plan, which he didn't because right now he wanted her so badly he could barely *think*. Which was bad. Really bad. 'Tomorrow.'

'Then we still have tonight.'

'We'd be mad to even consider it.'

'You want it as much as I do.'

Of course he did. He was as hard as rock and had been since for ever, but even though his self-control was stretched more than it had ever been it was still holding firm. 'So what?'

'This has been brewing for weeks.'

'I know.'

'What's the point of resisting it any more?'

'There are a billion points.' Although he was damned if he could remember any of them.

'I'm tired of it, Marcus. And I know you are too.'

'I've never stayed on friendly terms with any of my exes,' he muttered, and then wondered what the hell that had to do with anything, because he wasn't seriously considering this, was he? God. No. He couldn't be...

'Nor have I,' she said. 'But one night does not an ex make.'

'What does it make?' he said, his head swimming as much with confusion as desire.

'I don't know. Heaven?'

Heaven sounded good. So good… 'And then?'

'Who knows?' she said with a small smile that just about undid him. 'But what if you were right?'

'About what?' he said, his voice sounding as if it came from a million miles away.

'Maybe we *should* try and get it out of our systems.'

'No,' he said, but the denial was weak. 'You're not thinking straight.'

'Actually, I've never been thinking straighter. Avoiding it doesn't seem to be working, does it? So what other choice do we have but to confront it? Because it's not going to go away.'

'It has to.'

'What if it doesn't?'

If it didn't they'd have a lifetime of it, tearing them up inside.

At the thought of that Marcus went dizzy, his heart hammering and his stomach churning. A lifetime of this? How would he stand it?

Especially when he didn't even have to.

Collapsing under so much pressure, so much need, Marcus felt what was left of his self-control disintegrate. He'd clung on for as long as he could and he knew it was the worst idea in the world to take Celia up on her suggestion but he was only a man. He had his limits like everyone else and she was pushing him way past his.

He'd tried to resist, so hard, he had for months, but the pleading in her voice, the hunger in her eyes, the sense she was making when it was everything he wanted had chipped his resolve right away. He was a man at the end of his tether, and, really, she was right. What was one night?

'Whatever happens after,' she said, stepping closer, putting her hands on his chest and splaying her fingers, her proximity scrambling his head even more and making him feel quite weak, 'I know what I want, Marcus, and I know what I'm doing.'

'Do you?' he grated as the last of his resistance shattered and he gave in, body and soul. 'Really? Because I don't have a *clue* what I'm doing.'

And with that, he pulled her into his arms, one round her waist and the other at the back of her head, and crashed his mouth down on hers.

Her hands slid up his chest, burning a trail he could feel right down to his toes. She wound them round his neck and locked them there as she pressed against him.

She moaned and he pulled her tighter and it was as if someone had thrown a match on a tinderbox. Heat surged between them. Fire ran through his veins. His heart thundered and desire surged through his blood, thick and drugging and nearly making him forget where they were.

But not quite.

He pulled back, breathing harshly, and she whimpered.

'Don't stop,' she mumbled, pulling his head down and kissing him again.

'We have to,' he said, somehow finding the strength of will to unwind her arms from around his neck and peel himself away.

'No,' she protested. 'Why? Surely you're not going to turn all scrupulous on me *now*.'

'God, no,' he said, thinking he was too far beyond the point of return to come up with all the reasons they shouldn't be doing this.

'Then why?'

'Because for one thing,' he said, taking her arm and scouring the street, 'if we don't we'll be arrested for indecency, and for another we need to find a taxi.'

CHAPTER THIRTEEN

THE JOURNEY TO Celia's flat passed by in a bit of a blur, although not because they were going particularly fast.

In fact, after that first frantic kiss on the pavement during which she'd nearly gone up in flames with longing and relief because his strength of will was such a powerful force that for a moment she'd doubted her ability to break it, she and Marcus were now going achingly slowly.

The minute he'd slammed the door behind them and the driver had pulled away from the kerb, he'd slid an arm around her shoulders and pulled her to him. She'd leaned into him and lifted her hand to the back of his neck, and their mouths had met and they stayed like that, necking like teenagers as they crossed London, sharing long, slow, drugging kisses that blew her mind and obliterated her control.

At one point, she tried to straddle him, desperate for the feel and the friction of his hardness against the place where she needed it most. She didn't get very far, though. She'd just slid her leg over his and Marcus had just clamped his hand to her thigh to help her climb onto his lap, when a not so discreet cough from the taxi driver had them stopping in their tracks and sticking to kissing.

She was so dizzy with desire and desperation, so out of her mind with need, she barely noticed the taxi coming to a stop outside her building. When Marcus peeled away, her brain was too frazzled to be able to work out why until her head cleared enough to see that he'd got out and was thrusting a couple of notes through the window and muttering something about there being no need for change.

How she managed to get her key in the lock when her hands were so shaky she didn't know. And as for climbing all the stairs to her flat, well, since her limbs had turned to water she must have floated. Either that or Marcus had somehow carried her up as they carried on kissing.

But eventually, still entwined but now grappling at clothing, they made it through her front door, and she slapped at the light switch before they stumbled into her sitting room and tumbled down onto the sofa.

Marcus landed first. Celia followed, straddling him the way she'd wanted to in the taxi. She shed her jacket and her shirt while he shrugged off his and then his hands were around her back unhooking her bra.

Shivering, although not with cold, she put her hands on his chest, *finally* finding out what he felt like, and he inhaled sharply, tensing beneath her touch. She splayed her fingers, slid her hands over the sprinkling of coarse hair, the hot skin over tight muscle and then the thundering of his heart and she thought it couldn't be hammering nearly as hard or as fast as hers.

Especially not when he moved his hands down round her waist and up to cup her breasts. Heavier, thanks to the pregnancy, and…oh, Lord, *super*sensitive. He brushed his thumbs over her nipples and as sparks showered through her she groaned and arched her back in an instinctive attempt to increase the pressure.

In response Marcus nudged her back and then bent his head, and as he closed his mouth over her breast, his tongue flicking back and forth, Celia yelped and nearly came right then and there.

She'd never known anything like it, she thought dazedly, staggered at the sensations coursing through her. She'd had sex. Good sex. And not just with him. But this… This was something else. She felt as if every nerve ending were tingling. As if every muscle were tightening and every cell were bracing itself for heaven.

Was it just her hormones or was it him?

Did she care?

Not really. All she cared about was doing this. Right now.

She thrust her fingers in his hair and brought his head up. Captured his mouth with hers and ground herself against him as he was grinding himself against her.

Enough. She couldn't take it any more.

And clearly neither could Marcus because he was lifting her onto her knees and shoving his jeans and shorts down. A second later he was running his hands up her stockinged thighs, brushing over the nubs of her suspender belt and groaning, and pushing her skirt up and ripping first one side of her knickers and then the other.

'You have something against knickers?' she mumbled against his mouth.

He choked out a laugh. 'Only yours.'

'They were expensive.'

'I'll buy you more.'

And then he slid a couple of fingers inside her and she couldn't remember what they'd been talking about. All she could do was bite her lip to stop herself from crying out, and try to cling onto some kind of control.

'God, you feel good,' he muttered.

'So do you,' she moaned. 'I need you, Marcus. Inside me. Now.'

It must have been the sob that accompanied the 'now' that told him of her desperation because within a second he'd slipped his fingers out of her, took himself in one hand and held her hip with the other, and whether she thrust down or he thrust up, she didn't know. All she knew was that just when she couldn't bear it any longer he was lodged deep inside her, filling her and stretching her and she was losing her mind with the pleasure spearing through her.

'Don't you think this was the best idea ever?' she panted as he began to move and she with him.

'Not able to think,' he muttered, one hand clutching at her hip and the other clamped to the back of her neck.

And then nor was she because he was slowly pulling out of her and then driving into her over and over again, and she could feel the tangle of feeling swelling inside her, her head spinning faster and faster until she erupted, crying out his name as she came and then again when, a second later, he exploded deep inside her.

She collapsed against him, stars flashing behind her eyelids and her body weak and trembling, the rasp of his breathing the only thing she could hear.

'So,' she said dazedly once she'd got her breath back

and her heart rate had subsided. 'Would you say it's out of your system now?'

Marcus laughed raggedly and shook his head before resting his forehead against hers. 'Celia, sweetheart, it's not even looking for the exit.'

Giddy with relief she grinned and shifted and murmured against his mouth, 'Then how about this time we *finally* get naked and find a bed?'

Celia sat on her window seat in her bedroom, stared out into the moonlit darkness as she listened to Marcus' deep breathing from where he lay sprawled across her bed, and thought that she might as well face it. She was head over heels in love with the man.

She didn't know how or when it had happened, only that at some point over the past two months or, more likely, fifteen years, it had, and that now she was aware of the fact it was hard to imagine not being in love with him.

When she thought about the criteria she'd always considered important in a man, he fitted. In almost every way. He was strong, loyal and supportive. Hardworking, driven and ambitious. He had a strong sense of moral responsibility, played to his strengths and accepted his weaknesses. In short, he was amazing.

How had she not seen it before?

Smiling gently, still slightly stunned by the realisation she was nuts about him when only a short while ago she'd loathed him, Celia hugged her knees to her chest and grimaced when her tummy got in the way. So she stretched her legs out instead and crossed them at the ankles and thought about the way he made her feel. Apart from the sex, which was mind-blowing as well as eye-opening, he made her feel as if she could do anything, be anyone. He was the first person she wanted to turn to, whether with successes or failures. The first person she'd go to if she was ill, doubtful or needed a different take on something. The only person she wanted to love, live with and have a family with.

And the best, truly amazing, thing was, she was pretty sure Marcus was in love with her too. She'd felt it in his touch tonight when they'd made it to her bed. She'd seen it in his eyes. Heard it in his words. He'd explored her so thoroughly, so tenderly, lingering over the slight rise of her abdomen, almost as if he'd been worshipping her.

She was equally sure, however, that he wouldn't want to be in love with her, and that when he realised he was he'd reject it with everything he had. But that was fine. She wasn't planning on going anywhere for a while, even if he was. He was worth it so she'd wait. And not just for him to wake up and take her into his arms once again.

But, as he was still dead to the world, in the wake of the earth-shattering realisation that she was mad about him, maybe now would be a good opportunity to take stock of her life to date. To think about what she *really* wanted for the future. For herself and her child. She needed to consider her responsibilities and work out her priorities. She needed to figure out why she hadn't been more excited about getting the partnership as she'd always envisaged.

And, frankly, it was about time.

Rolling onto his back, still half asleep, Marcus thought that if the night he'd just had was a dream he didn't plan on waking up any time soon. It had been astounding, and, he suspected dozily, not just because it had been a while since he'd had sex.

Celia had been voracious, he recalled, the images flickering through his head making him smile. And demanding. On the way to her bedroom she'd told him what she wanted him to do to her, blushing fiercely and muttering something about pregnancy hormones. He didn't know about the validity of that, but nor did he particularly care because whatever it was that was driving her desire to almost insatiable levels it had seriously turned him on. They'd combined hot and fast with slow and sensuous, his fantasies with hers, and it had been everything Marcus had imagined.

And everything, he suspected, he'd feared.

Searching for her with his hand and hoping to roll her beneath him before the doubts and fears took hold, when he came up with nothing he cracked open an eyelid. To see she was sitting on the window seat, wrapped in a dressing gown, her legs crossed as she looked out of the window, a thoughtful expression on her face.

He levered himself up onto his elbows and rubbed the sleep from his eyes. 'How long have you been sitting there?' he asked, blinking and noting that the sky beyond was no longer the deep black of night, but the teal-blue of imminent dawn.

'A while,' she said, giving him a smile that made warmth unfurl in the pit of his stomach and his body stir.

'What are you doing?'

'Thinking.'

'About what?'

She gave a little shrug. 'Just things.'

'What kind of things?'

'You really want to know?'

'I do.' He shouldn't, but as things he wanted to think about even less were threatening to invade his head he did.

She swung her legs off the window seat, stood and walked over to the bed. 'OK,' she said, sitting on the mattress and crossing her legs Buddha style. 'Well, first, I'm going to turn down the partnership.'

That did the trick, he thought wryly, shock pushing those creeping thoughts back as he stared at her. 'You're what?'

'I'm turning down the partnership.'

He opened his mouth. Then closed it. 'Why?' he said eventually. 'I thought it was everything you've ever wanted.'

'So did I. But I now realise it isn't.'

'Since when?'

'Probably since the moment they told me and instead of feeling fireworks going off inside me what I felt was more like a damp squib.'

He shoved his hands through his hair and gave his head a quick shake because this wasn't small. This was huge. Worryingly huge. 'Are you sure?'

'I'm sure,' she said with a firm nod. 'I've been so focused on getting it, working so hard and making so many sacrifices, and now I can't help thinking, for what? So I can work even longer hours, more weekends? And end up with burnout, having a breakdown or worse? I don't want to do that. Not any more. It's not fair.'

She rubbed a hand over her stomach and he wondered if she realised she was doing it.

'More to the point,' she continued, 'I don't need to.'

He frowned. 'What do you mean?'

'Most of my entire adult life has been driven by one thing. Getting my father's approval. And the partnership was tied up with that because I really thought that he'd be proud of me. But I rang him this afternoon to tell him and all he did was bang on about some woman he'd met on the Internet. Whatever I do I doubt I'll ever have his approval and I doubt he'll ever be proud of me. He's just not the type.'

Marcus felt his entire body shudder with the strength of the protective instinct that streaked through him and he suddenly burned with the desire to drive to her father's house right now and shake him until he realised what an amazing daughter he had.

'And you know what?' she added, almost as if she was talking to herself. 'I'm actually fine with that. I don't need his approval. I'm good enough without it. More than good enough. And what's so great about him anyway? He might be a first-class lawyer, but as a human being, as a man, he's pretty pathetic.'

He wanted to cheer and then wrap her in a massive hug, but, a bit baffled by that, instead he said, 'So what are you going to do if you don't take the partnership?'

'Resign, definitely. Maybe move firms, if I can find one with a child-friendly policy. Maybe switch to a different kind of law. Maybe work from home a bit. I'm not entirely sure, but I do know that I don't want to rush back to work the second I give birth. I want to spend some time getting to know my child. I mean, I'll probably go mad after a few months, but at the beginning, at least, I think the time is precious.' She stopped and frowned at him, even as she smiled. 'What?'

'Nothing,' he said, trying to untangle all the emotions rushing through him. 'I'm just a bit taken aback, that's all.' Or try stunned. Confused. Deeply, *deeply* disturbed.

'Not half as taken aback as I am,' she said dryly. 'You were right about my work-life balance all along, Marcus. I do need to change it. I also ought to learn how to cook. And I'd like to take you up on your offer of the house next door, if it still stands, because you were right about this place as well. I mean, the stairs, the neighbours, all this white immaculateness… Hardly compatible with a messy, crying baby.'

He didn't know what to say to that. How could he retract the offer of his house now? When she'd obviously put a lot of thought into these decisions. These life-changing decisions.

Made because of him. Made possibly because of the night they'd just spent together. Damn, now—too late—he remembered why sex with her was a bad idea. It was never going to be just sex. It was potentially life-changing and he didn't want lives changed. Not hers, especially not his.

'There are a couple of other things you ought to know, Marcus.'

'What?' he muttered, feeling a cold sweat break out all over his skin because one night of spectacular sex and she was turning into someone he wasn't sure he could handle.

'Firstly, I'm in love with you.'

He froze, went numb for a moment before his entire body filled with dread, dragging him down. 'And secondly?' he said, sounding as if he were deep under water. Which maybe he was, because he certainly felt as if he were drowning, because he knew what was coming next.

'Secondly, I think you might be in love with me too.'

The room tilted, spun, and if he hadn't already been lying down he'd have crashed to the floor. He felt sick. Weak. His brain imploding with the effort of denying it.

'I'm sorry, Celia,' he said, his head a mess and his throat tight and the word *escape* flashing in his brain in great big neon letters, 'but I can't do this.'

'Can't do what?' she said calmly.

'This.' He waved a hand between the two of them, struggling to keep a lid on the panic. 'I'm not in love with you.'

She nodded. 'OK, look, Marcus, I get that this has all probably come as a bit of a shock to you, and I know how the idea of being in love terrifies you, so if you need to leave, that's fine. If you need some time to figure out how you feel and what you want that's also fine. I can wait. Not for ever,' she said with a soft smile that he didn't understand at all because he couldn't think of a situation that less required a smile, 'but I can wait.'

CHAPTER FOURTEEN

'So what's going on, Marcus? First you knock up my sister and then you abandon her? On what planet is that OK?'

At Dan's words—spoken so casually, so conversationally and a mere couple of metres to the right of him—Marcus froze. For the briefest of seconds his concentration shook and his foot slipped. His shoulders wrenched and the muscles in his arms screamed and he had to grit his teeth against the sudden shocking pain. Cursing his so-called friend with what little breath he had, he strengthened his grip on the crimps and jammed his foot back into position.

Trust Dan to wait until they were halfway up a wall and thirty feet off the ground before launching his attack. They'd met up around half an hour ago, and at any point since then he could have brought it up, but no, as the owner of one of London's most successful advertising agencies, Dan was all about maximum impact.

'I wouldn't put it quite like that,' Marcus muttered, although that was exactly what he'd done.

'Then how would you put it?' said Dan, swinging his arm up and latching onto a sloper.

Marcus braced himself and hitched himself up a

foot and absolutely refused to wince as his shoulder protested. 'I needed a bit of time and space to figure some stuff out.'

'What could take a month?' Dan asked through gritted teeth. 'I only took a fortnight.'

Well, now, wasn't that the question of the century? thought Marcus, stopping for a moment to catch his breath. Why was it taking so long to work out? As Dan had said, it had been four long, agonising weeks, and he was still no closer to unravelling the mess inside his head than he had been when he'd walked out of— no, *fled,* would be a better description for the way he'd left—Celia's flat.

'Just stuff,' he muttered.

'Ah,' said Dan knowingly, grabbing his water bottle, unscrewing the lid and taking a glug. 'Stuff. Gotcha.'

They stayed there like that for a moment, breathing hard and rehydrating as Marcus tried to figure out what it was Dan thought he knew, until he couldn't bear the thundering silence any longer. 'Anyway, Celia was the one who suggested I take a break,' he said, as if that made what he was doing all fine.

'I doubt she meant quite this long.'

Marcus did too. And that simply added guilt and shame to the chaos in his head. 'Have you seen her?' he asked.

Dan leaned back into his harness and wiped his brow. 'Yup.'

'How is she?'

'Getting big. Looks a bit tired but other than that, fine.'

'Good.'

'She resigned, you know.'

'She mentioned she was going to.'

'And she's started house-hunting.'

Marcus winced, but Dan carried on regardless. 'You know, I knew she was making a mistake thinking you'd stick around,' he said.

Marcus stared at him and nearly dropped his water bottle. What the hell? He *was* sticking around. Of course he was. He was just trying to figure out how. And coming up with a blank because how was he supposed to keep himself safe if he saw her all the time?

'She said you'd decided to face up to your responsibilities and was actually quite strident in her defence of you. But I had my doubts.'

Marcus felt his chest tighten. She'd defended him? When was the last time anyone had defended him? Been on his side the way she was?

'And actually I don't blame you,' Dan continued, 'because being tied to Celia for the rest of your life? That's not something I'd wish on anyone, least of all my best mate.'

OK, that was enough. 'What the hell are you talking about?' he snapped.

'I know I'm her brother, but that doesn't make me blind to her faults. I love her to pieces but she can be difficult. She's stubborn and uncompromising and as tough as nails.'

'She's not any of that,' said Marcus grimly, feeling his heart begin to thump and his head pound.

'No?'

'No,' he said even more grimly.

'Then what is she?'

Fabulous. That was what she was. Brave, loyal,

clever, brilliant and gorgeous. The mother of his child and the woman he was head over heels in love with.

As the truth of it broke free from the shackles he'd bound it with, his head swam, his vision blurred, his muscles weakened, without intending to he let go of the wall.

Down he fell. Down, down, down. Jerking to a juddering halt a metre from the ground. Every bone in his body jarred. Every muscle screamed. But his head was clearer than it had been for weeks.

He'd spent the past month trying to work out how to resist falling in love with Celia but what was the point when it had already happened? He might have been in free fall only a moment ago, but his heart had been in free fall for weeks, month, years probably.

He was nuts about her. Well, of course he was, because how could he not be? She was the most amazing woman he'd ever met and the time he'd spent with her had been the best, most stimulating, fun time of his life.

She was the only woman he wanted to commit to, and not just because she was having his baby. The only woman he could ever imagine living with, loving, till death did them part, which would hopefully be later rather than sooner. They were having a child together, going to be a family, if he hadn't totally screwed things up.

It wasn't the fact that Celia had told him she loved him that had put the fear of God into him. No. That made him feel as if he were on top of the world, as if he were the strongest, bravest, best man in the world.

It was the fact that she'd suggested that he was in love with her. He hadn't wanted it to be true because he'd always thought of love as dangerous. Treacherous. Life destroying and very much not for him.

But maybe it didn't have to be like that. Maybe it could be as lovely as Celia had said. She'd scared the life out of him when she'd told him that he was in love with her, but really what was there to be scared of? Dan seemed to be doing all right.

Maybe when it came down to it, there came a time when you had to stop wallowing in the past and get on with things. Like life. And maybe that time was now.

'Are you all right?' said Dan, who'd abseiled down the wall and was looking shocked and a bit pale.

'Never felt better,' said Marcus, now burning with the need to sort out the utter balls-up he'd made of things.

'Are you sure? No whiplash? Torn muscles?'

The only muscle tearing was his heart, because when he thought of what Celia must be going through because of his thick-headed selfishness it made him physically *hurt*.

'I'm fine.'

'You scared the life out of me.'

'Sorry.'

'That's all right. Anyway it's only fair since I probably scared the life out of you.'

Ah, thought Marcus as it all became clear. His friend, with all his talk of love and marriage happening to him one day, all that nonsense about Celia being tough and difficult and uncompromising prodding him into accepting the truth, was more perceptive than he'd ever given him credit for.

'Thanks, Dan,' he said, lowering himself to the floor and unbuckling his harness.

'No problem,' said Dan with a broad grin. 'First Kit, now you. What can I say? It's a gift. In fact I ought to start charging.'

'Then send me the bill. Right now, though, I need to go.'

When she'd told Marcus she'd wait, Celia had assumed he'd need maybe a week to realise he was in love with her and come to terms with it. A fortnight at the most. But here she was a month after he'd walked out on her and she still hadn't heard a word.

She'd started off so patient, so calm and confident, absolutely certain that she'd done the right thing in putting the 'love' thing out there for him to confront, but as the days had dragged by and he still hadn't come to find her her calm had shattered, her confidence had crumbled and she'd slowly fallen apart inside.

The past week had been agony. She'd thought love sounded lovely, but it wasn't. It hurt like hell. She only had to think of him and she physically ached. Something would happen, something she'd do, and she'd want to tell him. The first time she'd felt the baby kick, the job offer she'd received, the stupid mobile she'd bought for a nursery that she didn't yet have... She'd picked up the phone. And then had to put it down again, her heart wrenching and her eyes stinging.

And while outwardly she put on a good front, catching up with friends, keeping doctor's appointments and house-hunting, her heart had broken piece by tiny piece. Until now there was practically nothing left of it.

Nothing left of anything really, she thought miserably. She was all out of anger at his obstinacy. All out of frustration. And all out of hope.

She'd been so stupid. So naive. Had she really thought she'd be able to defeat his strength of will? Had she really been so arrogant as to presume she knew what he was feeling?

If only she hadn't resigned. Then at least she'd be working, keeping so busy that she wouldn't have time to think about him. But she had, and as a result she'd thought about little else, wondering what he was doing, who he was with, and driving herself mad by going over that last conversation and beating herself up with regret over pushing him too hard too soon, wishing so much she hadn't done it.

But she couldn't change any of it. All she could do was learn to live with it and hope that by Kit and Lily's wedding next weekend she'd have built up enough strength to handle seeing him.

It wasn't as if she'd be able to drink herself into oblivion to get through it, was it? So maybe she'd take a date. If she could find one who didn't mind her five-months-pregnant belly. Maybe she'd hire someone instead. Someone witty and gorgeous and who'd pretend to be utterly devoted to her. Someone who'd show Marcus that she wasn't missing him. Wasn't thinking about him. Wasn't—

The buzzer buzzed and Celia jumped. She cast a quick glance at the clock and frowned. She was going out with friends tonight in an effort to perk herself up, but the taxi she'd ordered was an hour early. Damn. Maybe she'd given the wrong time. A couple of months ago she'd never have made such a mistake but now it felt as if she was making them all the time.

Whatever had gone wrong, she wasn't anywhere near ready. She was still in her dressing gown, make-up free and her hair was still wet. She wasn't going anywhere for a while, so with a sigh she walked over to the intercom and lifted the handset.

'I'm sorry,' she said, 'there's been a bit of a mix-up. Could you come back in an hour?'

'No mix-up,' said the voice at the other end, a voice that made her breath catch, shivers run up and down her spine, goosebumps break out all over her skin and her heart lurch. 'And as I can't wait an hour, or even another minute really, if you wouldn't mind, I'd like to come up.'

Celia's heart began to thump as her head swam and emotions like joy, relief, love and hope began to surge through her. Oh, God, this was what she'd been waiting for for so, *so* long. He was here. At last. And in all the scenarios she'd envisaged she was looking immaculate and composed instead of a washed-out wreck, but it didn't matter. He was here, and that was all that counted.

Unless, of course, he was here to tell her that she'd been wrong, she thought, her heart suddenly plummeting and all those lovely feelings vanishing. That while he'd always be there for the baby he'd never be able to be there for her. That he didn't love her and never would. Because of what happened with his parents. Because he was as stubborn as a mule, because… Well, because of just about anything, really.

Ordering herself to get a grip before she got hysterical, Celia pulled herself together. Whatever the reason he was here she wanted to know, and the only way she was going to do that was by letting him in. So, reminding herself that she'd be wise to keep her emotions in check and her face blank, even if it killed her, she took a deep breath and pressed the buzzer.

Marcus pushed open the downstairs door and felt a wave of relief sweep over him. He was in. That was a start. Now for the hard bit.

He jogged up the stairs, his heart beating hard and fast, which had nothing to do with the energy needed to climb four flights of stairs and everything to do with the woman at the top of them.

Who was standing there, looking neither ecstatic nor horrified to see him, merely inscrutable. And so utterly, gorgeously magnificent he couldn't believe he'd taken so long to realise just how much he loved her.

'Marcus,' she said coolly.

'Hello, Celia,' he said, not fazed by the coolness one little bit because what with the idiotic, selfish way he'd been behaving he hadn't expected anything less.

'What are you doing here?'

'I've come to see you.'

'Clearly,' she said witheringly. 'However, I'm about to go out.'

'Not for another hour.'

She frowned. 'OK, fine. What do you want?'

'How have you been?'

'Me?' she said, looking a little surprised at the change of conversational direction. 'Oh, absolutely fine.'

'And the baby?'

'Fine too.'

'What have you been up to?'

'Well, I resigned.'

'I heard.'

'So I've been relaxing.'

'About time.'

'And learning to cook.'

He grinned. 'How's that going?'

'Messy. I'm a long way off roast beef with all the trimmings, but I'm getting there.'

'I can't wait to try it.'

She arched an eyebrow as if to suggest there wasn't a hope in hell of that, and if it hadn't been for the desire in her eyes, the faint blush that stained her cheeks and the way she was tightening the belt on her dressing gown he'd be worrying that he was too late. That he'd lost her and she'd already moved on.

'I've been offered a job that I think I might take.'

God, he was *so* proud of her. 'Congratulations.'

'Thank you. I've also put an offer in on a house.'

Marcus went still. Well, hell, *that* wasn't happening. 'Withdraw it,' he said.

Her eyebrows shot up. 'What? No. It's in a great location, has loads of space and a lovely garden.'

'So does mine.'

'Huh?'

'Move in with me and let's be a proper family. I love you, Celia. So much. I'm sorry it's taken me such a long time to figure it out, but I adore you. Everything about you. You're amazing and I'm so, *so* proud of you. Our child is the luckiest child in the world to have you as its mother. I should have told you all this that night, but I was spooked, as you knew I would be. Running away was a knee-jerk reaction but I stayed away out of fear, obstinacy, stupidity, and I'm so sorry.'

He stopped, breathing hard, his heart thumping and his blood racing as he watched her, standing there staring at him speechless, as if it was all too much to take in. And suddenly he thought, Oh, to hell with it. The most efficient way to show her how he felt and to find out how she felt was to simply march over to her and kiss her.

As Marcus' arms came round her and his mouth descended, his eyes blazing with everything he'd just told her he felt for her, Celia melted.

It had been so hard maintaining a cool, stony-faced facade when all she wanted to do was hurl herself at him and beg him to love her. She'd so nearly cracked when she'd mentioned the sensible but soulless house she'd found. And then he'd said what he'd said and she was still reeling, still hardly able to believe it.

Was it really true? Did she really not have to be miserable any more? Could she really let herself believe it?

His kiss told her it was, she didn't and she could, and she nearly passed out at the happiness coursing through her, filling every corner of her and making her heart beat madly.

'I love you, Celia,' he murmured raggedly against her mouth. 'We have so much to look forward to. I've spent so long looking backwards it's clouded my judgement. For far too long. But not any more. Will you marry me?'

She went dizzy, practically about to burst with happiness. And then she winced and took in a quick, sharp breath.

'What?' he said, drawing back and looking down at her in concern. 'Too much? I knew it would be too much. Or is it too soon? OK, we can wait. If that's what you want. I'd marry you right now if I could, but I can understand if you have doubts. I mean, *I* know I'm a sure bet but of course you'd have concerns. Especially when I've been such an idiot—'

'No, it's not that,' she said, her heart almost bursting as he stumbled over his words.

'Then what is it?'

'The baby kicked.' She took his hand, and put it on her bump. 'Here. Feel.'

'God. That's incredible.'

'*You're* incredible,' she said softly. 'I don't have any concerns about you, Marcus. I have no doubts. Because I love you too. You're my best man and you always will be, and of course I'll marry you.'

'Seriously?'

'Seriously.'

He looked down at her. 'Who'd have thought?' he said almost in wonder.

'Who'd have thought?' she echoed softly.

For a moment he looked at her, his eyes shimmering with love and hope and a tiny glint of wickedness. 'So this thing you're meant to be going out to tonight…' he said, tugging on the belt of her dressing gown and pulling her towards him.

Her breath hitched and desire began to surge through her. 'Easily cancellable.'

'Anything else in the diary for the next few months?' he murmured.

'Nothing important.'

'Good,' he said, smiling and lowering his head, 'because we're going to be a while.'

* * * * *

JUST CAN'T GET ENOUGH
ROMANCE
Looking for more?

Harlequin has everything from contemporary, passionate and heartwarming to suspenseful and inspirational stories.

Whatever your mood,
we have a romance just for you!

Connect with us to find your next great read,
special offers and more.

Facebook.com/HarlequinBooks
Twitter.com/HarlequinBooks
HarlequinBlog.com
Harlequin.com/Newsletters

⬧HARLEQUIN®

A *Romance* FOR EVERY MOOD™

www.Harlequin.com

"I gather you want to talk."

Nik spun back to her with the liquid grace of movement
that always caught her eye, and frowned at her, black brows
drawing down, wide sensual mouth twisting in dismissal.
"No. I don't want to talk," he told her abruptly before he
tossed back the finger of whiskey he had poured neat and set
down the empty glass again.

"Then *why?*" she began in confusion.

Months ago she would have shot accusations at him,
demanded answers, and would have thoroughly upset herself
and him by resurrecting the past that consumed her, but that
time was gone, she acknowledged painfully, well aware that
any reference to more personal issues would only send him
out the door faster. Nik had always avoided the personal,
the private, the deeper, messier stuff that other people got
swamped by. From the minute things went wrong in their
marriage she had been on her own.

Nik scrutinised her lovely face, willing himself to find fault, urging himself to discover some imperfection that would switch his body back to safe neutral mode again. Nor could he think of anything that could quench the desire holding him rigid, unquestionably not the tantalising awareness that Betsy, all five foot nothing of her and in spite of her lack of experience before their marriage, was absolutely incredible in bed.

"*Se thelo*…I want you," he heard himself admit before he was even aware that the words were on his tongue.

So Nik, *so* explosively unpredictable, Betsy reasoned abstractedly, colour rushing into her cheeks as a hot wave of awareness engulfed her. Jewel-bright eyes assailed hers in an almost physical collision, and something low and intimate in her body twisted hard. Her legs turned so weak she wasn't convinced they were still there to hold her up, but she was held in stasis by the intensity of his narrowed green gaze.

"And you want me," he told her thickly.

* * *

Read
CHRISTAKIS'S REBELLIOUS WIFE
by Lynne Graham
in July 2014!

HPEXP0614-1

ALISON DeLAINE

**brings you the thrilling tale of a hellion on the run...
and a gentleman determined to possess her.**

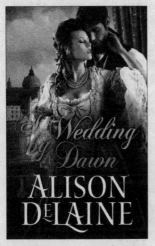

Lady India Sinclair will stop at nothing to live life on her own terms—even stealing a ship and fleeing to the Mediterranean. At last on her own, free to do as she pleases, she is determined to chart her own course. There's only one problem….

Nicholas Warre has made a deal. To save his endangered estate, he will find Lady India, marry her and bring her back to England at the behest of her father. And with thousands at stake, he doesn't much care what the lady thinks of the idea. But as the two engage in a contest of wills, the heat between them becomes undeniable…and the wedding they each dread may lead to a love they can't live without.

Available wherever books are sold!

Be sure to connect with us at:

Harlequin.com/Newsletters
Facebook.com/HarlequinBooks
Twitter.com/HarlequinBooks

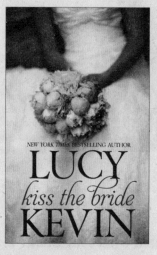